THE FALLING DETECTIVE

Christoffer Carlsson was born in 1986. The author of several previous novels, he has a PhD in criminology, and is a university lecturer in the subject. *The Falling Detective* is the sequel to *The Invisible Man from Salem*, and is the second volume in the Leo Junker series.

To Mela, always

THE FALLING DETECTIVE

Christoffer Carlsson

Translated by Michael Gallagher

Scribe Publications
18–20 Edward St, Brunswick, Victoria 3056, Australia
2 John St, Clerkenwell, London, WC1N 2ES, United Kingdom

Originally published in Swedish as *Den Fallande Detektiven* by Piratförlagets 2014
First published in English by Scribe 2016, by agreement with Pontas Literary & Film Agency

Copyright © Christoffer Carlsson 2014
Translation copyright © Michael Gallagher 2016

Typeset in Dante by the publishers
Printed and bound in the UK by CPI Group (UK) Ltd, Croydon CR0 4YY

Scribe Publications is committed to the sustainable use of natural resources and the use of paper products made responsibly from those resources.

9781925321210 (Australian edition)
9781925228397 (UK edition)
9781925307399 (e-book)

CiP records for this title are available from the British Library and the National Library of Australia.

scribepublications.com.au
scribepublications.co.uk

Willard: They told me that you had gone totally insane,
and that your methods were unsound.
Kurtz: Are my methods unsound?
Willard: I don't see any method at all, sir.

Apocalypse Now

It was the winter of the raging storm.

A scientist died, a Dictaphone passed from one hand to another across Stockholm, and it caused trouble wherever it turned up. A demonstration spiralled out of control, and a pair who had once been friends met at the swings where they had played as children.

At the bottom of Lake Mälaren lay a mobile phone, which had nothing to do with what happened, other than that it had been thrown into the water by the perpetrator. In a hospital bed, a man lay dying, and his last words were *sweetest sisters* and *Esther.* Whatever that meant. That wouldn't emerge until it was too late. And all the time the clock was ticking down towards the zero hour, the twenty-first of December.

It was a strange and complicated story, everyone agreed afterwards. But was it really that strange? Perhaps it was actually pretty straightforward, banal even, because that was also the winter when one man betrayed another, and that was probably the beginning of the end.

What happened, as far as we know, was something like this.

I

WHO COMES AROUND
ON A SPECIAL NIGHT?

Only one thing is certain: this town is scared. It has shown its true colours now, I'm sure of it. You can hear it in the city's pulse if you get close enough and dare to put your ear to it, if you really listen to it beating. It is tense and nervous, unpredictable — a light bulb that has started flickering, soon to be extinguished for good, but no one is paying attention. No one can see it.

Instead, a lone church bell rings. It's midnight, and the snow is falling gently and slowly. The cold streetlamps make the flakes glitter silver and become translucent. You can hear pulsating, heavy bass from a nearby club, and someone singing *Oh, I wish it could be Christmas every day,* and the screech of brakes a bit further away. The driver blasts his horn.

And in the distance: sirens. It's that kind of night.

One of the alleys off Döbelnsgatan is narrow and cramped. If you stretch out your arms, you can almost touch the worn brickwork on both sides, it's that narrow. And dark. The facades in the centre of town are high, and it's been a long time since the sun reached the crumbling tarmac below.

The little alleyway opens out into a large courtyard. Plastic bins full of refuse line the walls. A thin layer of snow has settled on their lids. When you look up, you can see a patch of sky, framed by the walls of the buildings.

A woman in light-blue overalls is carefully unfurling a large, white awning over part of the courtyard. Under the canopy is a man lying on his back. He's wearing an unbuttoned, thick overcoat, a knitted scarf, dark-grey jeans, and black boots. Four bright, white floodlights illuminate the scene. At his side is a worn-out Fjällräven rucksack, open. Possessions spill from its mouth — a book, a card wallet, a pair of thick socks, a bunch of keys, some cash. He'd been wearing gloves, but had taken them off. They're sticking out from the pockets of his overcoat.

The man is between thirty and forty years old, dark-haired, and well groomed with a short hairstyle, a few days' stubble, and square facial features. His eyes are closed, so you can't tell what colour they are, and that might be just as well, for now.

I wait a little way away from the tent with my hands in my pockets, and stamp my feet; it might look as though I'm impatient, but in fact I'm just cold. High above, in one of the windows overlooking the courtyard, a red Christmas star glows brightly. It's the size of a car tyre, and behind it a face is just visible. A boy.

'Has he been there long?'

The woman in the blue overalls, Victoria Mauritzon, is crouched on the ground, about to open her bag. She turns around.

'Who?'

I want to keep my hands warm, so I leave them in my pockets, and nod towards the window.

'The boy.'

Mauritzon follows my stare.

'Oh, right.' She squints into the falling snow. 'I don't know.'

She returns to the task at hand. She picks up a camera, adjusts the lens, and proceeds to take sixty-eight photographs of the deceased and the world around him.

Silent blue lights strike the walls of the building, and in the distance the blue-and-white incident-tape is flapping in the wind.

Some passers-by have stopped and are carefully observing the scene, hoping to see something. Every now and then there is the flash of a mobile-phone camera.

Mauritzon has put the camera back in its bag and carefully inserted a digital thermometer into his ear.

'It's quite fresh,' she says.

'How fresh?'

'An hour, maybe not even that. I'm less confident than I would normally be. This method just gives a very rough indication, but I haven't got the other one with me.'

'How did he die?'

'No idea.' She removes the thermometer, and makes a note of the reading on the form. 'But dead he most certainly is.'

I enter the tent carefully and crouch down next to the rucksack. Mauritzon hands me a pair of latex gloves, and, reluctantly, I take my hands out of my pockets. The gloves make my skin paler; make my fingers look even bonier than they really are.

Warmth spreads along my spine. Nausea is building inside me, and then cold sweats. I hope Mauritzon doesn't notice.

'He looks smart,' she says, glancing at the body. 'Not exactly the kind of person you'd expect to find in a yard.'

'Maybe he was meeting someone.'

I pick up the wallet. It's small, black, and made of leather. Various cards stick out from the little compartments: a credit card, an ID-card, some sort of key card, and a white one, with a curly blue motif and UNIVERSITY OF STOCKHOLM written in the same blue. I pull out the ID-card, and swallow twice to control the nausea.

'Thomas Markus Heber.' I compare the picture with his face. 'It looks like him. Born 1978.'

I make a note of his national ID Number, and I have the strange feeling that I have stolen something from the deceased. Then I put the card back in the wallet and turn to the other items that have spilled out of the rucksack. The bunch of keys reveals nothing more than the fact that the victim didn't own a car. There are three keys: one to his home, one that isn't immediately identifiable but in all probability is to his workplace, and a bicycle key. The thick socks are dry, but have been worn; the smell is like putting your nose in a shoe.

The book is *The Chalk Circle Man,* by Fred Vargas. The dust jacket is a little bit worn, and halfway through the book one of the pages is dog-eared. I open it at that page, and my eyes focus on the sentence at the top.

Can't think of anything to think.

I wonder about the meaning of the sentence before closing the book, putting it back and standing up. It's my twelfth day back on duty; the second on nights.

The question is what the fuck I am doing here.

The Violent Crime Unit responsible for the city centre and Norrmalm gets called the Snakepit by other police. Intoxicated people hitting, kicking, stabbing, and shooting each other; junkies and pushers getting found in cellars with holes in their necks; women beating men to death, and men beating women to death; consignments of drugs and weapons changing hands; riots, demos, wild chases, and torched cars. That's the Snakepit. But now this: a well-dressed middle-aged man dies in a backyard. No one is safe.

Officially, I was out in the cold until the New Year. Before then, active duty was unthinkable, mainly because of what had happened at the end of the summer. It might have been a conversation with the psychologist that changed all that.

My psychologist is the sort who values his clients in monetary terms, and I had long since ceased to be a lucrative investment. The hour-long sessions consisted of me alternating between floods of tears and sitting in despondent silence, smoking cigarettes, despite that not being allowed. The psychologist, for the most part, looked bored, admired his own tanned face in the mirror behind my back, and ran his fingers through his neatly combed hair.

'How are you getting on with the Serax?' he asked.

'Good. I'm trying to cut down.'

His eyes lit up.

'Good, Leo.' He wrote something on his piece of paper. 'Good, that is good. A huge step forward.'

Not long afterwards, the psychologist declared that I no longer needed his help. I went through a ludicrously simple check-up a few days later, and the person examining me saw no reason why I shouldn't return to serving the law.

That might have been because I didn't say anything about the nightmares, nor did I mention the sporadic hallucinations. Nothing about the occasional strange impulse to hurl a glass at the wall, smash up a chair, punch someone in the face. For some reason, nobody asked, and even if they had, I wouldn't have told the truth. If there's one thing I've learnt, it's that in the police, it isn't that hard to lie your way out of trouble.

Internal Affairs was out of the question, bearing in mind what had happened, but I should have at least been allowed to start with some desk job somewhere, maybe on the burglary or sex-crime unit. Somewhere in the deepest recesses of the bureaucracy, where I couldn't really do any harm.

But no.

I was doomed to the Snakepit again, where I'd once been trained by Levin. The National Police Authority has been throwing money at the area, and that might be why I'm here. Those extra resources, as far as we can tell, don't help much. The drone of the big city makes people mad, they say, and maddest of all are those at the source of the drone, the heart of the city. Anyone who has ever earned their crust in the Snakepit can tell you that.

I take off the latex gloves. The boy is still standing up there, half hidden by the big, glowing star. He's six, maybe seven years old, no more, with large eyes and dark, curly hair. I lift my hand in a friendly gesture, and am surprised when the boy, expressionless, does the same.

'Someone should talk to him.'

'Who?' says Mauritzon.

'The boy.'

'I'm sure they'll get around to him eventually.'

Mauritzon is right. It's late, most of the windows overlooking the yard are in darkness, but, one by one, lights come on as people are woken by my colleagues, who've started the door-to-door. I take a Serax from the inside coat pocket, the first one since the start of the shift. It's small and round, like the 'o' on a keyboard.

Seeing it, holding it, makes my mouth water, and I feel the sweats subsiding. I can almost feel it, the sensation of slowly being wrapped in cotton wool and the world reverting to its correct proportions. I hold the tablet in my hand before discreetly returning it to my pocket, and instantly regret not having put it in my mouth.

'Where's his phone?' I ask, and notice that my voice is unnaturally thick.

'The deceased's? No idea. Maybe he's lying on it. I need to roll him over, I'd like to see his back.'

She waves over two uniformed constables. They're ten years younger than me, and shivering, maybe because of the cold. She gives them latex gloves, and they help to carefully turn the body over so that Mauritzon can study the back and the backs of the legs.

The ground under Thomas Heber's body is browny-red. The blood has melted the snow and turned it into a purple-brown slush.

'Strange that there isn't more blood,' I say.

'It's the cold,' Mauritzon mumbles, and investigates the back of the wet coat. 'It makes bodily functions shut down more quickly.' She frowns. 'We've got something here.'

A marked gash in the back, close to the heart.

'A knife?'

'Looks like it.' She turns to the two uniformed officers. 'Can we put him back, carefully?'

'And get Gabriel Birck down here,' I say.

'He's not on duty, is he?' one of the officers asks.

'No, not officially.'

'Well, can't it wait till tomorrow then?'

I look up from Thomas Heber's body to the officer standing there. My nausea has returned, and my pulse is increasing. The fear creeps up on me, creatures emerging from the earth and trying to get to me.

'What do you think?' I manage. 'We need to get someone to run the show.'

The officer turns to his colleague.

'You do it,' he says.

'He asked you to do it.'

'Just do it,' I hiss, and I feel the walls around us closing in, about to tumble down, about to fall and crush me.

The constables head off, sighing. Mauritzon returns to her examination. In the nearby club, someone's singing *Oh what a laugh it would have been if Daddy had seen Mummy kissing Santa Claus that night,* and Mauritzon is humming along to the melody.

Maybe it's the club and the thought of alcohol that makes the sweats flare up again and flood through me, squeezing out through my pores and making me short of breath. I walk hurriedly away from the crime scene, down the alleyway and out on to Döbelnsgatan, and I don't know how noticeable it is, but it feels as though I'm stumbling. I collapse, and I'm gasping for air. I can't breathe.

Everything goes black, and somewhere between the body and the edge of the cordoned-off area I lean against the wall. The bricks are cold and hard, but the wall is the only thing keeping me upright. Then my stomach turns inside out. I bend double. The remains of a half-digested hotdog, bread, and coffee form a foul-smelling mix that splashes onto the snow.

My muscles give in and I fall to my knees, feel the cold seep through my jeans and up my thighs, but it's a numb feeling, lost in the sweat, the shivering, the hoarse, rasping noise from my throat, and the absolute conviction that this is how my life is going to end.

'Looks like murder gets to the old hands, too,' I hear one of the uniformed officers say in the distance.

The photographers' camera flashes fire off. Everything is a thick fog. I keep my eyes open, but they are filled with tears from the throwing up. Everything is murky. My throat is burning, my stomach wracked with cramps.

With one hand against the brick wall and the other fumbling in the inside pocket of my coat, I haul myself up. It's not the first time this has happened. When did I last have one? Must have been a day or two ago. Is that really all it is? I'm still falling, deeper into myself.

It isn't the city that's scared, not Stockholm that is the flickering light bulb, about to give up. It's me.

The door is cold and heavy, with the name THYRELL emblazoned on the letterbox. I raise a shaky index finger towards the doorbell before I decide to knock instead. There's something unpredictable about children that makes me nervous.

I am dizzy, but the Serax has started working, and its haze is slowly enveloping me. My legs are still weak, but the cold sweats have evaporated, leaving my skin bristling. As soon as my knuckles make contact with the door, I can hear movement from inside, as though someone is waiting for me. The lock turns with a click, and the door swings gently open.

Behind it is a thin little boy, with sunken eyes and skin so pale that it seems to be translucent at first.

'I'm ill,' he says.

'It's alright. It's no problem.'

'Pneumonia,' the boy explains slowly, as though the word demanded great exertion.

'What's your name?'

'John. Yours?'

'John. That's a good name. My name is Leo, and I'm a policeman. Are your mum and dad home?'

'Dad's away.'

Somewhere behind him, a door opens, and out comes a woman about my age, who's obviously just woken up. Her nightie is adorned with a faded Bob Dylan print.

'Did you open the door, John?' She asks and puts her hands on his shoulders. 'What's this about?'

'Something …' I hesitate. 'I'm a police officer. Something has happened down in the yard, and I think John might have seen it. I would like to talk to him.'

'Can I see your badge?'

I show it to her.

'Do you have to talk to him right now?'

'Yes. If that's okay?'

John purses his lips as though weighing up the pros and cons of letting a strange man into his home. Eventually he moves out of the way.

'You have to take your shoes off,' he says.

'Of course. How old are you, John?'

'He is six,' the woman says.

She introduces herself as Amanda. Her hand is warm. The little hall is short and narrow, leading into a larger living room, passing a kitchen and the half-open door to the parents' bedroom on the way. I stand by the large Christmas star glowing on the windowsill, clear and red.

'What has he seen?' she asks.

'When you saw me down there, John, when we waved to each other — you were here, weren't you, standing by this window?'

'Yes.'

'What is it that he's seen?'

Amanda walks over and looks down to the yard below, gasps, and puts her hand to her mouth.

'Oh my God.'

She asks John if he's okay, if he can really talk to me.

'Yes, I can.'

'Okay, I'll just …' She composes herself. 'I'll put the kettle on, I think. Would you like some tea, John?'

He shrugs. She walks away, unsteady.

I put my hands on my thighs and crouch down to see the world down there, as he must have seen it. Even from here you get a good view of the yard, where Mauritzon is in the process of carefully removing the dead man's shoes.

More people are now moving around close to the body — and judging by Mauritzon's body language, this has done nothing for her mood.

'You smell,' the boy says.

'Do I?'

'You smell of sick.'

'It's my coat. We policemen meet a lot of people who are sick, and you don't always manage to get out of the way in time.'

'But your eyes?' The boy squints, suspicious. 'They're red.'

'I haven't slept for a long time.'

John contemplates the truth of this statement before apparently letting it go.

'Someone is lying down, down there.'

'Yes.' I straighten up again. 'Yes, that's right.'

'He's dead, isn't he?'

'Yes.'

I look for something to sit on, and find a large leather armchair next to a low glass table. I perch on one of the wide armrests, and at that moment John coughs — a violent, hoarse cough. His lungs gurgle like a blocked drain, and he grimaces with pain, and goes red in the face.

Amanda seems to have forgotten why she went out to the kitchen, or else she changed her mind on the way. She returns with a glass of water, puts it on the table, and sits on the sofa, pulling a blanket over her legs.

'I would like to be present.'

'Oh, naturally.' I look over at the window. 'You saw me down there, John. That's right, isn't it?'

16

'Yes.'

'How long were you standing there?'

The boy folds his arms.

'A while. Not that long.'

'Can you tell me what you saw when you came to the window? What was happening down there?'

'Nothing.'

'There was no one there?'

He shakes his head.

'But then someone came.'

'When?'

John coughs again, but not as violently this time.

'You're asking me to tell the time, but I haven't learnt that yet.'

'That's right. I'm asking about time.' I hesitate. 'Don't worry about it. Who came into the backyard?'

'A guy. The one who's lying there now.'

'How do you know it was him?'

'Because that's what I think.'

I stifle a tut. Kids.

'Was he alone?'

'Yes.'

'Then what happened?' I ask.

'I don't really know. I had to go to the toilet, and when I came back he was lying where he is now.'

'Was he still alone?'

'No. Someone was standing next to him, looking in his bag.'

'Can you describe what he looked like?'

John pauses.

'Black clothes.'

'Was he tall or short?'

John looks me up and down.

'About the same as you.'

'What colour was his hair? Could you see?'

'No, he had a hat.'

'Did he have a hat you can pull down over your face?'

This question makes the boy laugh — a deep, clucking laugh, a pleasant sound that gives me a feeling of wellbeing. The laugh gives way to a cough, and John's face goes red again.

'Drink some water, love,' Amanda says.

I hold up the glass towards him. He takes a gulp. He grimaces, as though it hurts.

'No,' he says. 'You don't have hats like that.'

'When you came back, there was somebody next to the guy down there, looking in his rucksack. Is that right?'

'Yes.'

'Did he find anything?'

'I didn't see what it was.'

'But he found something?'

'Yes. Then he went.'

'Which way did he go?' I point out through the window, and get the boy to follow my finger with his eyes. 'That way, or this way?'

'The first one.'

Back towards town.

'And then,' the boy continued, 'the other one disappeared, too.'

'The other one? The guy lying down there?'

'No. The one who was hiding.'

'Was there another person there, hiding?' I raise my hand and stick my thumb out. 'First there was the guy who's lying down there ...'

The boy nods. I extend my index finger.

'Then there was the one standing by the rucksack.'

John nods, again. I stretch out my middle finger.

'And then there was one more.'

'Yes.' John looks pleased with himself, as though he's just completed the none-too-straightforward task of getting an adult to understand something. 'Exactly.'

'Was it a boy or a girl, this last one?'

'I don't know.'

'What about their hair — was it long or short?'

'I didn't see.'

'Where was this person hiding?'

'Behind one of the green bins. When the one who was looking in the rucksack had gone, the other one came out and then disappeared.'

'How did this person move? Slowly or quickly?'

'Quite quickly.'

'Nimbly? I mean …' I say to the boy, who obviously doesn't understand, 'did he seem clumsy? Was he walking straight or wonky — did he trip up or fall over?'

John shakes his head.

'He just walked.'

'So maybe it was a guy after all?'

'No, I don't know. You're the one saying "he".'

The boy is right, and I don't say any more. I head over to the window instead. The floodlights illuminating the body are blinding. Mauritzon is giving him something resembling a pedicure.

'Were you alone the whole time?'

'Yes.'

'You never got up?' I ask Amanda.

'No.' She looks as though I've insulted her.

'That's not what I meant.' She doesn't say anything, and I turn to the boy. 'That's good, John. Thanks for your help. You've told me some important things that might help us.'

'He's dead,' the boy says again. 'The one lying down there.'

'That's right. That much we can be sure of.'

The Christmas star causes the backdrop to melt away, makes the snow falling outside a blurred, dark-grey sludge.

'Are you going now?' the boy asks.

'I think so.'

'Happy Saint Lucia, then.' His gaze falls away, towards the hall. 'Don't forget your shoes.'

Down by the body, a lot has changed, yet nothing has changed. He's no longer wearing shoes, and someone has taken off his overcoat. From a distance, the body is scarcely visible, obscured by everyone moving around it. Outside, far away near the edge of the cordoned-off area, what could be an undercover police car is waiting. In fact, it belongs to *Aftonbladet* or *Expressen*. The constables are nowhere to be seen. They might be composing themselves after calling Gabriel Birck. It's even colder now, at least it feels like it, but changes like these are neither here nor there, because the dead man is just as dead, the snow is falling as relentlessly as before, and some nights that sort of thing is all that matters.

'Who made the emergency call?' I ask, holding my phone in my hand.

I don't trust my memory anymore, and I need to summarise the conversation with the boy, but I don't have anything to write on, apart from my phone. One of the uniformed constables is holding a notebook in one hand and a half-eaten ham-and-cheese roll in the other. His name is Fredrik Marström, a young officer from Norrland with shoulders like a weightlifter.

'Oh yes,' he says, and flips back two leaves. 'It was an anonymous call made from a mobile. The individual's voice sounded strange, as though he or she was disguising it. But we don't know. I've ordered a copy of the recording, which is being sent to you. The duty officer tried to get their name, but then they hung up, apparently. Fortunately they decided to send someone down anyway.

'And that was you?'

'Me and Hall,' Markström says, taking another bite of the roll. Åsa Hall is from Gothenburg, and is essentially the complete opposite of Fredrik Markström: chatty, small in stature, and cheerful.

'Who came after you?'

'Larsson and Leifby.'

'Larsson and Leifby?'

'That's right.'

'What the hell were they doing in town?'

Markström takes another bite.

'No idea. They said they were in the area.'

Larsson and Leifby are beat officers out in Huddinge, and they're the type that almost never get to represent the force on information days and at recruitment events. One is scared of heights, the other of guns — burdens that are troublesome, to put it mildly, for police officers to carry. Not only that, but they like a sensational story as much as the tabloid hacks do.

When Markström and Hall arrived at the scene, they did everything by the book. Larsson and Leifby were charged with talking to possible witnesses. Neither is anywhere to be seen, and I wonder if that's a good thing or a bad thing.

I head over to the big bins that line the walls of the yard. They smell sour. I kneel down in front of them, once again feeling the cold from the ground surge through my jeans and up my thighs, only this time my senses are slightly dulled and the cold is blunter, more bearable.

Behind one of the containers, the thin dusting of snow is not intact. Someone has been standing there, taking a few steps back and forth. The shoeprints are indistinct. Boots, but well-worn — the sort you wear if you can't afford to buy new ones every year.

'Victoria,' I say quietly, causing Mauritzon to look up from the body. 'I think someone has been standing here.'

She makes a note in the notebook she keeps in the breast pocket of her overalls.

I walk out onto the street and down the road, go past the cordon, and smoke a cigarette. The music from the club is pulsating, this time an old tune that's been remixed, so that you can dance to it. I remember the melody from being a teenager, and for a second I wish I was fifteen years younger, that I was still in education, that the future felt a little more unwritten.

In the inside pocket of my coat, my phone vibrates. It's a text from Sam.

are you asleep?

no I'm on duty

having a good night?

I consider my answer, take a drag.

it's alright I end up writing. *murder in vasastan,* I go on, but then change my mind, delete it, and write *how about you?*

i miss you, comes the reply, making me wish that I was somewhere else right now.

tomorrow?

yes, tomorrow's good for me.

I wonder what it means. Sam almost always cancels or postpones when we're supposed to meet up.

A well-dressed man with equally well-kept hair and with his unbuttoned overcoat flapping behind him walks through the snow towards me. He raises his hand and looks at the cigarette between my fingers, with a disdain that becomes desire as he gets closer.

'Happy Saint Lucia,' I say.

'Can I have the end?' he asks.

I give Gabriel Birck the half-smoked cigarette, and he sucks the life out of it.

'I didn't know you smoked.'

'There's a lot you don't know. Who's in charge here?'

'You.'

'Me? We need a commissioner. Where's Morelius?'

'On leave.'

Birck rolls his eyes.

'Well, get Calander down here then. He's not on leave, and I know that for sure, because I saw him by the hotdog stand on St Eriksplan a few hours ago, and he looked very much ready for action.'

'He's busy with the axe man on Tegnérsgatan.'

'Fuck. What about Bäckström? He's better than nothing.'

I shake my head.

'On secondment with the National Crime Squad.'

'Fucking hell. Poor NCS.'

Birck stubs out the last embers against the wall of the building and moves as if to leave, but then stops, sniffing the air.

'Have you been sick?'

'No.'

'You smell of vomit.'

'I haven't been sick.'

'In that case, someone's been sick on you.'

'Not today.'

This tickles Birck, and he laughs. He pulls a pair of gloves from the pockets of his coat.

'Where is he?'

'In the yard at the back.'

'We've got one witness,' I say, and look up at the window where the Christmas star is still glowing. 'John Thyrell. He has, in all probability, seen the perpetrator.'

'How do you know that?'

'I've spoken to him.'

'And what did he say?'

'Well, quite a lot, I think, but …'

'What?'

'According to his mum, he's six years old.'

'Six years old?' Birck grimaces. 'Great.'

He crouches beside Thomas Heber's still, lifeless face. The card holder is lying in its spot by the rucksack, and he picks it up and pulls out the ID-card.

'A good-looking bloke.'

'They die too, you know,' says Mauritzon.

Birck puts the card back in the card holder and puts it back on the ground, gets up and looks around, taking a couple of minutes to orientate himself at the crime scene.

'Heber comes here,' I say. 'He stands here. Maybe there's already someone else here, behind one of the bins. There probably is. Another person arrives, the one who puts the knife into Heber. Considering the wound is in his back, he probably comes from behind. Heber drops, and then the perpetrator roots around in his rucksack, finds what he's looking for — we should probably assume — and then leaves the scene, probably with Heber's mobile phone on him, since we haven't found one here. He's heading for the city centre. After that, the person behind the bins also leaves, according to the witness. Maybe it's him, the one behind the bin, who makes the call to the police. The question is, what was he doing here? Either he's got something to do with it, or else it's a coincidence. Maybe some homeless bloke or a junkie.'

'Your witness is a six-year-old boy,' says Birck.

'But his account tallies with how it looks behind the bins. Someone has been standing there.'

'Let's hope there are other witnesses.' He looks around. 'It could have been a robbery. But why leave the cash, in that case? It must have been something else.'

'Yes. The question is what. The phone, maybe?

'But would Heber have had it in the rucksack? How many people keep their phone there?'

Markström approaches us with his notebook in one hand and coffee in a plastic cup in the other. I wonder if I have ever seen Markström without food or drink in his hands. I doubt it, but then again haven't known him that long.

'Thomas Markus Heber,' he says, then slurps some coffee. 'Born seventy-eight. Single, no children. Living at Vanadisvägen 5, less than a kilometre from here. Convicted of assault eleven years ago, 2002, and a breach of the peace the year before that.

'Assault and breaching the peace,' Birck says, turning to me. 'You'll take that?'

'Yes.' I look up at the window again. 'I suppose I will.'

John has disappeared, probably forced into bed by his mother. I wonder if this has affected the boy, whether this evening will stay with him. I hope not. 'Tomorrow.'

'I'll do his apartment,' says Birck.

'Have you got a key?'

Birck points quizzically at the key ring lying on the ground. I hesitate.

'Do you want company?'

'No. But you can't always get what you want.'

Those who don't know that there's something wrong with the door never notice, despite Christian having used a big fucking hammer. That was all he could think of at the time, the only thing he took with him. The door handle is hanging loose, and the door won't close completely, but that's all. In the dark it's hardly noticeable.

He's standing on the road, in full view. The lights in the building are off, apart from an advent wreath in one of the windows a couple of storeys up. It's just after half-past nine in the evening. Less than an hour until Thomas Heber dies.

He's stuffed the plastic bag with the knife in inside his coat, and he can feel it against his body, moving in time with his strides. He leaves Kungsholmen in a hurry, on foot. He throws the hammer into a builder's skip near St Eriksplan. No one sees him. No one sees anything anymore.

Christian and Michael spent half their lives without each other; half, together. There's a symmetry to this that tells you something, isn't there?

They were fifteen, fifteen years ago. They were at a party in Hagsätra, in one of the tower blocks by the centre. It was March, and no other month can drag on forever the way March sometimes does. Everything was grey.

They knew of each other, but had never talked, just seen each other in the square and at the recreation ground a few times.

Christian went out on the balcony for a smoke, and there he was. They started talking. There was something weird between them, at least that's the way he felt, but at first he couldn't put his finger on what.

Then he realised that they were both wearing T-shirts with SKREWDRIVER on them. They both noticed at the same time, looking down at each other's chests. They laughed. Christian's was white. He had got it from his brother, Anton. Michael had a black one.

'Do you like Skrewdriver?'

'I've only heard the first album, nothing else,' Christian replied. 'I got that and the T-shirt from my brother. But I do like that album.'

'Same here. I like *All Skrewed Up*, but not the others. You know they became Nazis later, right?'

'What?'

'Neo-Nazis.'

Christian was stumped. The T-shirt print changed, became threatening. He wondered if Anton knew, if that was why he'd given him the T-shirt. To wind him up. So that Christian would get beaten up.

'No, I had no idea.'

'Fucked up,' said Michael. 'That a band start out as punks, then do a whatsit, what's it called?'

'U-turn.'

'That's right. Fucked up, isn't it?'

'Yes.'

On the other side of the glass, inside the flat, someone fell off the sofa's armrest. They turned around and peered into the room.

'That's Petter,' Christian said. 'He's in my class. He always gets too drunk.'

Inside the flat, Nirvana were singing about finding their friends.

That's how it started.

'Do you live in Hagsätra?' Michael asked.

Christian nodded, and shuddered from the cold.

'On Åmmebergsgatan, over by the recreation ground. You too?'

'Glanshammarsgatan.' He pointed between the tower blocks, where candles were lit in the small windows. 'Can you see the lower block between those two high ones?'

Christian strained to focus, and adjusted his glasses. He smoked only occasionally, and when he combined it with beer, it was like he got twice as drunk.

'Yes,' he said.

'The second window from the top, second from the right. That's my room.'

The lights were off.

Christian had severe acne and was extremely short-sighted, so he wore glasses so thick they made his eyes look like drawing pins. There was a big guy at school, called Patrick, who used to shout, 'Hello, zit, how's it going?' at him so that the girls would laugh. Christian tried to shrug it off. He was a sporting talent, good at basketball and floorball and table-tennis. That's how he made friends, even if he did suspect that they talked about him behind his back.

His new friend was just like him, he would soon realise. They were similar in that sense, apart from the fact that his new friend had neither acne nor glasses.

'I need another fucking beer,' said Michael.

'Me too.'

They dropped the cigarette butts from the balcony, watching them as they twirled away into the darkness. Then they opened the balcony door and went in. The warmth and humidity inside the flat made Christian's glasses fog up. When Michael saw the white screens hiding Christian's eyes, he burst out laughing.

'It can't be easy to make a good first impression looking like that.'

It wasn't. Christian remembers it now. Under different circumstances, he'd probably have laughed at it. It must have looked funny.

Between the tower blocks, strong feelings built up, and most of the time there was nowhere to get rid of them, so you carried them around. You carried them in the corridors at school, kept out of the way of those you were scared of, and got drawn to those you hoped might be a bit like yourself. You carried them when your best friend's locker got prised open and someone had drawn a swastika on the inside of the door. You carried them when you had your first kiss, eleven years old at a disco in the clubhouse at Hagsätra's recreation ground. Her name was Sara, and she had the smoothest skin Christian's fingers had ever come across. They were together for a month. Despite being only twelve, Sara had started wearing a bra, and the day before they split up she'd let him touch her breasts. He wondered if that was why, that she didn't want to be with him because he'd been too forward.

You carried those feelings when you were fourteen and fell in love for the first time, and her name was Pernilla and she wrote *they can laugh if they want to, sneer at us — we're moving forward, they're standing still* on a note that she sneaked into his locker through the little gap in the door. It was with her he had had sex for the first time, at a party not unlike the one he wore his Skrewdriver T-shirt to a year or so later.

They were there when you saw three immigrants hitting a Swede in the gut, two holding, one hitting, behind the gym hall, and you carried them when you saw four Swedes beating an immigrant the following day, behind the kiosk owned by one of the Swedes' dads.

You carried them the first time you met someone at a party and he had the same T-shirt as you, and you soon realised that he was going to be your protector and executioner.

There's no catalyst, no single event that starts things rolling. No answer to the question *Why?* There are only events followed by events, and if you go back far enough, everything becomes an ethereal web of them. And that might be, Christian thinks to himself, how we end up becoming the people we are.

As instructed, he avoids the tube and its CCTV, and makes his way out to the university by bus instead. He makes a few detours, changes several times so as not to arrive too early. At each bus stop, he's freezing cold. The buses come coughing out of the darkness, and none of their drivers are Swedish. He passes The Vasa Real School, where someone has written JEWISH SWINE, followed by the number 1488. He wonders who held the pen. Snow has started falling. By Odenplan, a Saint Lucia procession made up of students winds past him, laughing and stinking of alcohol.

Stockholm University's large sheet-metal complex towers over him as he steps off the last bus into the darkness. He is waiting in the shadows by one of the corners of the complex, Christian can sense it as he gets closer. And, sure enough, there he is, eyes fixed on one of the windows above — the only one with the lights on.

'Any joy?'

'Yes.'

'You don't sound sure.'

'I'm not.'

'Give it here.'

Christian pulls down the zip on his coat, and gets out the plastic bag. Michael takes it from him.

'What were you goi—'

'Get out of here. We'll get to that later.'

'But I …'

'No. Not this time. See you tomorrow.'

Michael looks up at the window again. The lights are still on. A second's hesitation gets stretched and becomes unnaturally long. Thoughts are washing through Christian like a strong current.

'Alright,' he says, and turns to leave. The snow crunches under

31

his feet. In front of him, the Statoil signage shines large and orange. Traffic swishes past, but it is strangely quiet. It's an evening where old feelings come back.

They were fifteen years old, fifteen years ago. *We're moving forward, they're standing still.*

Christian turns his head one last time, looking for the window with the light on, but doesn't see it. The lights are off, and, by the corner of the complex, Michael isn't there anymore.

There's a lot of things said about Gabriel Birck, and most of them are contradictory, like splinters of evidence pointing towards different stories, different fates.

Some say he has no sense of smell, yet others say he can smell a person's saliva. That he's gay, but that he once dated a woman from the Hamilton clan. The same person claims that Birck changed his surname when he did National Service and that he actually comes from a wealthy aristocratic family. Others say he comes from a poor background — that he grew up on the estates with a loner alcoholic father who beat him every weekend. That he once married an Estonian woman to save her from a trafficking league. That he was approached by the Security Service while he was still training, but that he'd never been tricked into joining them. Others are convinced that he does in fact have a murky past in that very organisation.

And so it goes on, and nobody knows for sure. I believe about half of what is said, but which half changes from day to day, depending on what sort of mood Gabriel Birck is in. I think he lives a fairly solitary life, that Birck is a loner. We have that in common, and that's why we can work together.

By some kind of unspoken agreement, we decide to walk to Vanadisvägen 5. We become silhouettes as we move through the night in the capital. As we leave the crime scene, Birck stops dead.

'Hmmm,' he says. 'Look at that.'

The contents of my stomach that I expelled less than an hour ago are already covered by a layer of ice crystals.

'Is it yours?'

We're inside the cordon. They're going to do tests on it. There's no point in lying.

'Yes.'

'Are you ill?'

'I don't know, but I was nauseous. It might have been the body.'

Birck leans forward and studies the vomitus more closely. I find this very embarrassing, as though he's seen me naked.

'What do you eat anyway?' he says.

Almost nothing — that's part of the problem with the Serax come-downs. My appetite disappears completely, and I'm constantly weak, with quivering hands.

'What everyone else eats,' I say. 'Can we go now?'

'You really should change your eating habits.'

We've turned off the wide Sveavagen, and we're now outside Vanadisvägen 5. It's just before two. It is now the thirteenth of December.

'Are you going to St Göran's now, on Lucia?' he asks.

'No.'

'But you're going at Christmas?'

'Just for a short visit, maybe. Nothing more.'

'How often do you go? How often do you see him?'

'As often as I need to.'

'Here.' He holds out a packet of Stimorol. 'For my sake,' he adds.

I take a piece of chewing gum. Birck puts his gloves on, and takes the key from the plastic bag and slides it into the lock of the main entrance. The door is lighter than you'd think, and if it does creak or scrape, the sound is drowned out by the noise of the city.

'Fifth floor.' Birck reads the list of residents. 'Second from the top. No, you can keep it,' he says when he spots the chewing-gum packet in my hand. 'You need it more than I do.'

Outside the door — light brown with HEBER above the letterbox — I take my boots off, and Birck steps carefully out of his black shoes. The lock looks untouched; there's no sign of anyone having tried to force their way in.

'Shall we ring the bell?' I ask.

'What for? He's dead, you know.'

'There might be someone else in there. A friend or a girlfriend. Or boyfriend.'

'Didn't you see his shoes? A man who wears shoes like that is definitely not gay.'

'You know what I mean.'

Birck looks for a doorbell, finds it, and then pushes it. There's no sound from inside. I place my knuckles against the door instead, and knock three times, hard. When nothing happens, Birck puts the key in and opens the door.

The place where Thomas Heber lived the last few years of his life is a little one-bedroom flat with high ceilings. It's sparsely furnished, with three fully laden bookshelves along one wall of the first room, next to some kind of reading chair whose only companion in the flat is a floor lamp peering over its shoulder. Otherwise, the room is empty, apart from a pile of packing boxes against the opposite wall, the traces of a man who lived his real life outside his home.

'How long had he lived here?' Birck asked.

'According to Markström's background check, two years.'

'Looks more like two weeks. I would've had a nervous breakdown if my home looked like this after two years.'

'Will you do the bedroom?'

Birck walks off without saying anything. I walk over to the bookcase and tilt my head to one side, reading the titles of well-thumbed books about sociology and philosophy. In one corner of the bookcase there's a collection of books that really stick out, like *The Activists Handbook, Manual for Militant Political Siege,* and *The Occupy Movement: an instruction for practice.* I pull one out. It's been read in great detail — the pages are marked and annotated with the illegible handwriting of an academic. In another corner of the bookcase are several copies of the same book, his own PhD thesis in sociology, *Studies in the Sociology of Social Movements: stigma, status, and society.*

I take a couple of steps back. Nothing grabs my attention. That's annoying. I head for the kitchen instead. It's narrow, with units along both sides, and then opens up into a small square space with a smaller but equally square wooden table and four chairs. The windowsills are empty, with no plants or lamps, and each window is framed by a light-blue curtain. On one windowsill is a little saucer, empty and clean.

'Did he smoke?'

'Not as far as I know,' Birck's voice comes back.

I open the fridge. Inside are two bottles of Czech lager, a jar of Taco sauce, some butter, and a sad little piece of cheese with less than a day to go before its sell-by date.

I go into the bedroom, where Birck is kneeling in front of the wardrobe and pulling out a pair of shoes. He investigates the laces, and then the soles and the inside of the shoes, before putting them back.

'Nothing?' I ask.

Birck shakes his head.

The bed is unmade. I put my nose to the bed sheets and smell them. They haven't been washed in a long time. A desk is next to the bedroom's only window, and I flip carefully through the papers lying on it — an invoice for December's rent, a wage slip from the Stockholm University, and a mobile-phone bill. I pick up the bill and find the number, get my phone out, dial the number, and put the phone to my ear. A cold, robotic voice tells me that the person I have called is unavailable.

'Switched off or no coverage.'

'Wasn't expecting anything else,' says Birck.

Under the phone bill is a scrunched-up piece of paper. I carefully pick it up between two fingers and unfold it.

'What's that?' Birck asks.

'A receipt. Heber bought a coffee at Café Cairo on the eleventh of December. Looks like he paid by card. That's it.'

'Cairo. That's near us, isn't it?'

'Mitisgatan,' I read. 'Yes, it's near the bunker.'

'Put it back.' Birck stares at my hand, which is heading for my coat pocket. 'It has to be here when the technicians arrive.'

'Shall I scrunch it up for them, too?'

Birck rolls his eyes. I leave the receipt on the desk, and we go through the bathroom and the closet together, but the flat says very little about its owner. Next to nothing, in fact.

'Do you reckon he was on his way home?' I ask. 'That he'd stopped off on Döbelnsgatan to see someone he'd arranged to meet there.'

'I don't reckon anything,' Birck says, his eyes glued to the floor in the hall.

'Everyone always thinks something.'

'I reckon that whatever has happened, we're not going to find the answer here.' Then he stops, and crouches down. 'Is this yours? This shoeprint?'

'How could it be mine? We took our shoes off out there. I thought you were a good cop. Anyway, what footprint? I can't see anything.'

'I think you need to be right over here, crouching down where I am.'

I take two steps forward, crouch down, and it appears. The print is a bit bigger than mine, and from a heavier boot. There are two, three, four more in the hall. The pattern is smeared, as though someone has hastily tried to hide them.

'Have we ruined them?'

'I don't think so. We walked along the wall.'

'It's not the same person,' I say. 'The one who was hiding behind the bins on Döbelnsgatan, and whoever's been here. Not the same tread.'

'How did we miss this on the way in?' says Birck. Then he stands up, and takes two steps towards the door. He laughs. 'Bugger me.'

Light and shade often play games with your eyes. In Heber's

hallway the ceiling light makes the shadows scatter and the light reflect off the floor. It's probably a coincidence but when you stand by the door, you can't see the prints unless you know they're there.

Birck pulls out his phone and takes a picture of the prints.

'They're not dry,' he says. 'We'll have to get Mauritzon to check them out.'

'How the hell did they get in?' I say. 'The door was untouched.'

'Must've had a key. Like we did. Maybe it was Heber himself. I don't fucking know,' Birck adds when he sees my confused expression.

Clues like these, just like the stuff found by the body, mean nothing in isolation, without the story that ties them all together. They are like road signs without symbols or letters.

Somewhere halfway between Vanadisvägen 5 and the scene of the crime on Döbelsgatan, two cars collide head-on at a junction. A violent confrontation ensues. We stop and observe it from a distance.

'You do realise,' Birck says, 'that if word gets out that you're trying to come off Serax, but that your withdrawal symptoms are so bad that you're throwing up, you'll be pulled off duty again?'

'I'm clean. Ask my psychologist.'

Birck sniggers. From a nearby bar, a child's voice sings *I believe in Santa, and he's coming to my house.*

'How long did you believe in Santa for?' I ask.

'We didn't have Santa. You?'

'Long enough that it made me sad when I found out he wasn't real.'

'You're breaking my heart,' says Birck.

A stream of loud, drunk men and women walk past us. They're laughing.

'How on earth did you not have Santa?' I ask.

Morning. Another St Lucia procession sloshes through the sludge on the other side of the road, led by a woman about my age. The children are wearing long tunics and red Santa suits, holding battery-powered candles. Cones, hoods, and glitter adorn their heads. None of them seem particularly enthusiastic. Stockholm is still swathed in darkness, but the city woke up a long time ago, if it had even been asleep. Out on Hantverkargatan, the exhaust fumes from the heavy traffic rise into the hazy glow of the streetlamps.

The floor of the building that is home to the City and Norrmalm Violent Crime Unit is quiet, apart from a photocopier in a room a little way away spitting out paper, and a radio playing St Lucia songs. A waist-high plastic Christmas tree fills one corner. It's covered with gold and silver handcuffs, red and blue truncheons, candy-striped pistols, and wooden policemen which are supposed to have been hand-painted by the previous, now retired, chief constable Skacke. At the top is a perfectly normal Christmas star.

My office comprises a desk with a computer on it, a desk chair, and a rickety old wooden chair for any visitors. Behind that is a row of empty bookcases. All the furniture came with the room, and several days passed before I even noticed the cigarette-burn marks on the surface of the desk.

A little square window in one of the walls gives a view of a little square piece of the world — of the snow, which has started falling again. That's it.

On my desk is a pile of paper that Birck has printed out, consisting of the preliminary investigations into Thomas Heber's two convictions, and the first reports from Döbelnsgatan. Nine or ten hours have passed, and the victim's family have been informed and interviewed. Circumstances meant that this had to be done by telephone, and now the transcripts are lying in front of me, signed by Birck. The last report is recorded at 5.27 am, and it's details like that which make me wonder if Birck ever actually sleeps.

Witness accounts have started to emerge and to be processed, but so far nothing significant has surfaced. A prosecutor, Ralph Olausson, has been assigned to the case, and will lead the preliminary investigations. I've never heard of him, but a note on my desks instructs me to contact him as soon as possible. I wonder who wrote it.

Thomas Heber's parents were devastated by the news of the death of their only son, and Frederika Johannesson, who was apparently the dead man's most recent girlfriend, took it almost as hard. In terms of the investigation itself, none of them had anything relevant to tell Birck. The parents described their son as likeable and popular, but had great difficulty in telling Birck who his close friends were. He worked as a sociology lecturer at Stockholm University and, according to the mother, he had twice won prizes for his work. He'd split with the girlfriend more than two years before, when he was finishing his thesis, and apparently it had been the work that had caused the split. It had torn them apart. Frederika Johannesson had no idea whether Heber had had any romantic involvement since then, but she assumed he had. Who that may have been with, she had no idea.

I put the reports away, go out of the room and past the Christmas tree, over to the coffee machine, and push out a black cup. As I wait for it to fill, several sleepy colleagues file past with snow on

41

their shoulders, pale cheeks, and bloodshot eyes. They avoid eye contact, and say nothing. It's been like this since I got back on duty. To them, I'm just the rookie from Internal Affairs, the idiot who lacks team spirit and who put a bullet in a colleague's neck. The old lag who, since that day, has been unable to hold a firearm without being crippled by panic.

I want a Serax, but I don't take one. I wonder when the anxiety and the fear of weapons will subside. The psychologist insisted that it was important for me to give it time, but he was never any more specific than that. I should have asked him before he got rid of me.

Back in my room, I turn to the preliminary investigation into Heber's breach of the peace in November 2001, and the assault in December 2002. Attached to the reports are the subsequent court verdicts.

On the thirteenth of November 2001, neo-Nazis gathered in central Stockholm to commemorate the anniversary of the death of King Karl XII. The number of skinheads who came to pay tribute to the old king was greater than it had been for many years. Counter-demonstrations were organised by groups on the far left, and one was led by Thomas Heber, a young sociology student considered at the time to be a leading figure in AFA, the Anti-Fascist Action network. AFA had not applied for a permit for their demonstration, and their protest against the neo-Nazis was broken up by police, who also made sure that the youths were hit with pretty hefty fines.

The following year, in December 2002, demonstrations took place in Salem in honour of another Swede, Daniel Wretström, who was seen as another victim of anti-Swedish violence and immigrants' hatred of Swedes. By then I had moved away from Salem, and so never attended the annual demonstrations, but my parents sometimes talk about them. It's an event that makes the residents of the town steel themselves, as they would before a violent storm. Windows are boarded up, cars parked in their garages, and if possible, people spend the day and night somewhere else entirely.

Every year, Salem becomes a battlefield. During the 2002 demonstration, the third since the murder of seventeen-year-old Wretström, Thomas Heber assaulted a man. He hit a neo-Nazi with an empty bottle, which, unfortunately, broke. Was this down to an existing crack, which Heber could not possibly have known about, or was the strike so powerful that the bottle shattered? The prosecution claimed the latter. The question was considered at great length and in great technical detail during the investigation and, indeed, the trial. In spite of this, the answer could not be established beyond doubt, and Heber was given a two-year suspended sentence and community service.

The sins of youth?

Perhaps.

I stand up and walk over to the window. Outside, the Stockholm morning is lighter now. Need to talk to someone. Need to keep moving.

It happened during one of the first meetings at St Göran's, and I've been tangled up in it ever since. I should have known that I was always supposed to end up in this struggle, a struggle that seems more and more likely to be in vain.

'You haven't thought about quitting?' Grim asked.

'What do you mean?'

'Those things.'

Grim pointed at the little tube in my hand. I made no attempt to hide it from him.

'Yes, I've thought about it.'

'Does Sam know you're taking them?'

'No.'

'What would happen if she found out?'

'I don't know.' That was true. I didn't know how she would react. 'But I don't think she'd like it.'

'Hmm,' said Grim.

'What does that mean?'

'Well, you want to get back on duty, don't you?'

'Yes.'

Grim leaned forward.

'Why is it so important to you? Getting back on duty, I mean.'

'I ... I've got nothing else to do. I don't know how to do anything else. And I need something to do.'

44

'Haven't you got Sam?'

'No.'

'I thought you were together.'

'We're not.'

He nodded.

'Considering your background, they're not going to have you back as long as you're taking them. Or rather,' he corrected himself and flashed a grimacing smile I remembered from when we were friends, 'as long as they *think* you're taking them.'

'I don't know if I can stop.'

'Have you tried?'

'No.'

'Aren't you going to try?'

'I'd need to do it myself. If I get help from outside, people in the building are going to notice. And, as you said, with my background, I'm not going to stay around for long. I can't risk it.'

'Do it yourself then. Try cutting down. If you do succeed, you'll feel liberated.'

I stared at him.

'The only reason we're talking about this is because you think it's going to fuck my life up even more, and that's the only kind of injury you can inflict from in here.'

'You don't understand a fucking thing.' Grim raised his arms and rattled the handcuffs around his wrists. 'If I could,' he went on, 'I would hit you so hard in the face right now.'

The vast, green university campus is beautiful, even in December, but the large South Building still feels like the kind of place where you'd park the mentally ill for secure storage. It stretches up nine stories, in bleached-out light blue, with small windows. I arrive at the same time as a thousand students, who all seem to be dreaming of better days. A few are talking, but the vast majority are walking in silence, staring at the ground, holding plastic cups of coffee and carrying heavy rucksacks. Posters for a leftist demonstration cover the walls, and someone has defaced them with the words LEFTY PIGS, RED BASTARDS, COMMIE WHORES. The graffiti has in turn been crossed out with a thick black pen, by someone who had has also taken the time to leave their own message: DIE NAZI PIGS.

The Sociology Department is at the top of the South Building. I buy my own cup of coffee on the way, mainly to give my hands something to do. Up in the department it's quiet; it feels more like a prison than anything else. The head of the department, Marika Franzén, is sitting in her office a little way down the corridor, in the only room with the door ajar.

'Leo Junker,' I say. 'Stockholm Police.'

She spins around in her chair, clearly surprised.

'Sorry,' I say, 'I didn't mean to …'

'No, don't worry.' I see her eyes scanning me, from my boots up to my unkempt hair, and then she gets to her feet and shakes my hand. 'Come in.'

From the desktop speakers I can hear a choir singing Lucia songs. Marika Franzén is short, with dark hair. She has a narrow face, large glasses, and a little, round button-nose. It's a funny look.

'I need to ask you a few questions. It's about Thomas Heber. I'm assuming that you have heard?'

'Yes,' she says, turning down the volume, before deciding to turn the sound off altogether. Her brown eyes reveal that she is shaken, but she is otherwise composed. 'I have heard. It's awful. I can't quite believe it. Please, sit down.'

One corner of the room is dominated by a three-piece-suite, and I ease myself into one of the armchairs. A pile of papers is lying on the table, and next to that is a bottle of brandy, and two glasses, one of which has traces of lipstick on it.

Marika follows my gaze, and puts the bottle and the glasses into a cupboard. She blushes.

'I had a drink with a colleague last night — we had a late meeting.'

'What time was the meeting?'

'We started at five, and it went on till eight.'

Marika sits down opposite me, on the edge of the sofa, as though prepared for me to spill my coffee and ruin her armchair at any moment.

'Was Thomas still around?'

'He was here then. His door was open, and I saw him as I was leaving.'

'Do you know what time he left?'

'Well, I did ask if he was going home, as it was getting on. But he'd arranged to meet someone at half-past ten, so he was going to stay till then.'

'Half-past ten,' I say, pulling a notebook from my inside pocket. 'Do you know who he was going to meet?'

'No, but he was doing fieldwork at the time, so I just assumed that it was one of his interview subjects.'

'Fieldwork?'

'That's what we usually say — gathering information, empirical data — we call it fieldwork. It's part of the research process.'

'What was he researching?'

'Social movements.'

'And what does that mean?'

She crosses her legs.

'Social movements is a rather fluid notion, but generally we're talking about groups, like networks or organisations, and their collective actions. The focus is on the group rather than the individual members.'

'Like AFA, for example?'

'Exactly. Like AFA.'

For a second, her gaze seems clear and sharp. Then suddenly her eyes glaze over, becoming almost murky, and she lifts her hand up to her mouth and grimaces. She sniffles, straining to concentrate on the facts. It might be a coping strategy.

'Social movements are generally concerned with protesting against the status quo, so it's a sensitive subject in many ways.'

'So it's about political groups?'

'Not necessarily. It can be about other things — of course, that depends on how you define political. In Thomas's case, it was about the anarchist networks, groups like AFA or Revolutionary Front on one side, and the nationalist movement, like Swedish Resistance, on the other.'

'Left- and right-wing extremists, in other words?'

'If you want to use those terms, yes. Thomas got funding from The Swedish Research Council to study how the members of various social movements interact with one another, above all members of those social movements that are diametrically opposed to one another. Those who are in effect struggling against each other.'

The page in my notebook is empty. I write *social movements, far r, far l*, AFA, then a question mark. My phone rings in my inside pocket. I divert the call without looking at it, and hope it wasn't Sam.

'I'm wondering about his choice of subject matter.'

'You mean why he chose social movements?'

'Why he was looking at the far left and far right. Why them?'

She shrugs.

'It's no secret that he himself has … had a history in the anarchist movement. We tend to choose research subjects that are close to home, one way or another, and he was no exception.'

'So you know about his past, with AFA?'

'Of course. I'm also aware of the assault and breach-of-the-peace convictions. I'm reminded a couple of times a year, in those emails we get sent.'

'What emails?'

'They come from Nazis, racists, and all sorts of internet trolls.'

A little bubble of clarity has gathered somewhere immediately behind my eyes. I wonder if it is visible to others.

'Tell me more about the emails.'

'You know,' Marika says, gesticulating, 'it's nothing unusual. Sociologists are sometimes rather vulnerable, particularly if the research concerns a subject that is politically contentious at that moment. Lots of people have been sent similar emails, and we always act, report it to the police and everything. Since Utøya and Breivik — well, actually, since 2010, when the Sweden Democrats made it into parliament — we've had a lot more from extremist groups, left and right.'

'When were these ones sent?'

'I think the most recent ones were early autumn, but we've received them before. Of course, it's very serious, but there isn't an awful lot we can do about it, besides sending them to the security department, who in turn come to you.'

'And you said that they come from Nazis, racists and …' I look down at my notebook, searching for the word. 'Internet trolls.'

'In Thomas's case. As far as I'm aware. The sender was never identified.'

'Breach of the peace to sociologist,' I mumble. 'Had his political convictions changed over time?'

'He was very left-wing, but I don't think he believed in direct action anymore. I think he got older — it was as simple as that.'

'Older?'

'Getting older is quite enough to change people. But he wanted to understand everything he'd seen during his time as a member.'

'Was he still a member?'

'I can't answer that. I don't know, but I wouldn't have thought so.' Marika looks terrified, as though a gruesome face had suddenly appeared above my right shoulder. 'Was he really murdered?'

'Yes.'

'And you don't know who did it?'

'No, not yet. I'm trying to understand,' I continue, slowly, 'the period leading up to his death. Was there anything different about him?'

She pauses for a second, her eyes gliding across the spines of the books on the shelf.

'Not that I can think of, no.'

'What did he do yesterday daytime?'

'Thomas always got here about nine,' she says. 'Like most of us up here do. Thomas came in at nine yesterday, too. I was here before him, and I was standing in the kitchen when he arrived. After that, he sat in his room. I think he was transcribing interviews. He was still sitting there when I left, and he said he was staying until that meeting at half-past ten.'

'And you don't know who he was going to meet?' I say, one more time.

'No, that's right, I've no idea. Oh yes, one more thing. At some point during the day, just after lunch, I think, he went for a walk with Kele, Kele Valdez. They often do that, go for a stroll round the campus.'

'What sort of a person was Thomas?' Did he have any friends, relatives that he would talk about, anything like that?'

'Thomas was … a loner. He did have a girlfriend when he started, I remember that, then they split, and after a year or so he started seeing someone, but that didn't last either. His closest friends were his colleagues. Kele Valdez in particular. I don't think he's been informed yet.' She hesitates. 'Could y—?'

'I'll do it,' I say, and make a note on the pad. 'I need to talk to him anyway.'

Everybody is missed by someone. Grim used to say so, when one of our friends from Salem had disappeared and nobody seemed to notice. When someone dies there's always someone who lies awake at night, always someone who walks the streets where the deceased once walked, someone who'll go through their wardrobe to avoid letting go. I wonder who that person is this time.

Outside Marika Franzén's window, the snow has stopped falling. The world seems strangely quiet, as it often does from a distance.

Valdez hasn't turned up yet, so I do Heber's office first. It's only half the size of Franzén's, yet it's home to roughly as many objects and as much furniture as his apartment. The only things missing are a camping stove and a toilet. If he'd had access to those, he could easily have lived here. One wall is lined with bookcases. Along the opposite wall, a little sofa is squeezed in next to the wide desk. There's a cushion and a plaid blanket on the sofa. The desk is covered with piles of paper and books, a computer and keyboard, an Eighties telephone, and a printer.

On the hook on the back of the door hangs a black tongue of a tie, a blazer, and, over that, a badminton racket in its case. I carefully check the blazer pockets. They're empty.

A framed diploma hangs above the desk, declaring that Thomas M Heber has been awarded the Faculty of Social Science's prize for the best thesis of the year. Next to it is a similar certificate declaring him 'Young Sociologist of the Year', this time awarded by the European Society of Sociology. It was for his article, 'Notes on the Relations between "Insiders" and "Outsiders" in Social Movements', published in the British Journal of Sociology.

A rising star, already shining brightly. Now dead.

I slump into the desk chair and fumble with the mouse, in the hope that Heber's computer might be on. It isn't, and, once I've turned it on, the password screen stands between me and access to its contents. I stare at it for a second before I pick up the phone and dial the extension for the IT department, which is scrawled on a note next to the phone.

'I need your National Identity number,' the technician says in a monotone voice when he returns to the receiver.

'My ID number?'

'I need to be able to check that you are actually a policeman.'

'How do you know I'm not going to give you someone else's number?'

The IT guy sighs, as though he has this conversation every day.

'Just give it to me.'

Heber's desktop is full of folders and documents, and I click through them in no particular order. All I find is drafts of articles, saved copies of other people's publications and minutes, agendas and decisions ahead of meetings — the kind of information that can make a policeman glad he's not an academic.

One of the folders, marked only with an 'F', leads to another marked FIELD, which contains lots of documents. One comprises a list that starts at 1580 and finishes at 1602. Alongside most of the numbers are abbreviations — AFA, RF, FF, P, SM, RAF-S, RAF-V — as well as several others. They're his interview subjects, I guess, and perhaps the initials of the groups they belong to. The next document is called LOG, and when I open it I feel a shiver down my spine.

This is Thomas Heber's diary, more or less. The first entry is just over two years ago. He had just started the research project that would occupy him until his death. The document is fifty-four pages long, and ends on the twelfth of December, yesterday, with the words:

12/12
Meeting 1599, to talk. Might tell them what I've heard. I don't know. We're meeting at our usual spot at 2230. I'm nervous and unsettled, hesitant. Haven't got much done today.

I click back to the list of interviewees and find a 1599, with the abbreviation RAF-S. I imagine how Heber arrived early to their agreed meeting and how 1599, when he or she came into the yard, plunged his knife into the sociologist's back. But it doesn't quite make sense — something in the sequence of events doesn't add up. Like wearing a jumper inside out, it works, but it's not right.

The interviewee, 1599, is the first to arrive, and waits for Heber behind the green bin. Heber slips into the alleyway and looks around, searching for his contact. Then, from out of the shadows of the capital's streets, a third silhouette appears and sticks the knife into Heber.

Has 1599 lured Heber into a trap? Perhaps. How much time passes between Heber going up the alley and the assailant following him? Is it a second, or a minute? Do Heber and 1599 get the chance to say anything to each other? Maybe, but probably not. Why does 1599 ring the police, if indeed it was 1599 who made that call? Why is Heber nervous and unsettled, and what is it that he's heard? Who has been in Heber's apartment and left shoeprints there? Was that before or after the murder?

My questions are becoming more and more like knots. As soon as I get close to an answer to one of them, it turns out I've made too many assumptions, and I have to go back and start again. I need to talk to Birck — he's more analytical than I am.

I print off two copies of the list and then two copies of the long, diary-like document. While the printer on Heber's desk spits out sheets of paper, I read the list of numbers and abbreviations, and circle '1599'.

Just before 10.00 a.m., the man arriving to open up at Café Cairo notices that something weird has happened.

His name is Oscar Svedenhag, and he heads in the back way, through the courtyard, and unlocks the empty premises, lights the soft lighting, and weaves his way through the tables and chairs over to the counter. He dumps his rucksack, puts the keys down on the side, and starts whistling. He starts preparing the coffee machine, and checks that they have all the produce they will need for the day.

There are a few minutes left till opening when Oscar notices: there's a slight hum in the café. The door out onto the street, through which customers come and go, is not closed. The door handle is hanging limp, as though someone has broken it.

As if that wasn't enough, something else isn't right here, behind the counter. But what? Then he realises. There's something amiss with the black-matte handles of his set of knives sticking out from the little wooden block in the corner — one of the knives is gone.

On top of that, the float is missing from the till.

There are lots of ways to react to this, one of which would be to call the police. He doesn't do that. He does, however, stop whistling.

Kele Valdez is sitting in his room, hunched over his desk, his face hidden behind black curls, reading a text very carefully. Valdez is wearing a black jacket, black shirt, and black jeans, as though the feast of St Lucia also included a funeral. It might be just as well.

'Knock knock,' I say, feeling every inch the unpleasant surprise as Valdez lifts his stare from the page.

'Good morning,' he says, taking off his dark-rimmed glasses. 'How can I help you?'

'I'm from the police.'

'The police?' Keles eyebrows rise slightly, causing his forehead to crumple. 'What's this about?'

He takes the news of his colleague's death as you might expect. During our conversation, Kele's voice is mechanical and empty, the sound of a person in shock. That's the voice with which he confirms that they took a walk together yesterday.

'How did he seem, on your walk?'

'I don't know, there was something a bit ... he seemed nervous, a bit snappy. Do you know what I mean?'

'Maybe,' I say. 'How?'

'He was a bit short, as though he had his mind on other things, I suppose. I don't know what it was about — I just assumed it was something to do with work.'

'But you didn't ask?'

'No. No, I didn't ask. Should I have?' he adds, as though hoping I could relieve him of a burden.

That's something that police seldom do.

'No,' I say, 'I don't think so. Would you consider that there was any threat to Thomas's safety?'

'There was,' Kele says. 'But not something that I would consider serious. There were threats made against him, especially since the Utøya massacre. Thomas's thesis was pretty new when it happened, and extremist movements got a fair amount of coverage after that. Thomas was interviewed, and participated in debates and so on. That made him a public figure, and, I suppose, dangerous. The far right recognised him from his time with AFA, if you were aware of that.'

'I am aware of that. But nothing I've heard would suggest it could go as far as murder or manslaughter.'

'No, that's true. But you asked about threats to his safety, which certainly existed.'

'Do you think that these groups are potent enough to do something like this?'

'You mean on the far right?'

'Yes, exactly.'

Kele has shifted in his chair. His legs are still crossed, but his arms are now wrapped around his torso, as though he were freezing, or trying to protect himself. His voice is steady, but his eyes are shifty and glazed.

'No, I can't imagine that they are. But I'm not the right person to ask.'

'I was wondering,' I say as I pull out the printout of Heber's LOG document. 'I found this on his computer.' I hold it out, towards Kele, who takes it from me. 'I haven't read all of it, but there's a note at the end that I'd like you to have a look at. I'm not sure what it means.'

Kele reads the first page before looking up.

'I don't think you should be reading this. Have you got permission to go through his computer?'

'When someone dies the way Heber died, we do get the warrants we need, sooner or later. And I think this might be important.'

'These are his fieldwork notes. It's like a researcher's diary. You have no right to be going through this, breaking confidentiality and everything. I need to at least see a formal request.'

'I can get back to you with one of those. But until then, there's this one thing I've been wondering about, on the last page.'

Kele flips reluctantly through the document and reads the last entry.

'1599 must be an interview subject,' he says, stroking the paper tenderly, carefully.

'I wonder if you know anything about this bit,' I say, showing him. 'What it is that he's heard? It doesn't feel like an ordinary entry,' I add. 'If you read the others, this one sticks out. It feels more personal.'

'I have no idea what it means.' He puts the document to one side and looks devastated. 'I don't want to read this — it's far too personal. Have you got any more copies?'

'No,' I lie.

Happy lucia

The text arrives, and I read it as the lift carries me up to the floor to where the violent crime unit is based. Grim.

I didn't know they'd given you a phone, I reply.

A new text arrives straightaway, as though Grim were sitting, phone in hand, waiting for it to beep. Which is probably exactly what he's doing. The activities put on for the sectioned patients at St Göran's are pretty limited.

they haven't, he writes. *I stole it*

For some reason, this makes me titter, standing there alone in the lift. Then I call the psychiatric ward at Sankt Göran's and tell them that someone ought to check what the occupant of room 22 has managed to acquire.

'And,' I add, 'make sure he doesn't find out it was me who tipped you off.'

Birck, Olausson, and Mauritzon are sitting in one of the numerous meeting rooms. Mauritzon is holding the handle of her coffee cup in one hand, a task that appears to be the only thing keeping her awake.

'I've got two grandchildren,' she says. 'Five and two. When my daughter can't cope, they come to me. They arrived this morning, just as I was getting ready for bed. I've hardly slept.'

'You poor thing,' says Olausson, his eyes half-closed.

Prosecutor Ralph Olausson is a lanky man. His nose makes a quiet whistling sound as he breathes, and his suit needs pressing. A rough scar high on his chest becomes visible as he loosens his tie and unbuttons his collar.

'Where are the others?' I ask.

'What others?'

'You mean this is it? This is a tenth of what we need.'

'This is it, for now,' is Olausson's only comment.

'But you'll sort out some more bodies, right? We can't run a murder investigation with three people.'

'That's where we are right now.' Olausson studies his hands, as though they were more interesting than this business. 'Okay, let's get started, shall we?'

We spend half an hour going over Thomas Heber's death. The other witness statements appear to corroborate little John Thyrell's version of events. Heber arrives, then another person, presumably the assailant, who then leaves and is followed by a third, who emerges from behind the bin. No one knows when the third person got there, because nobody saw anything. A taxi-driver stops to pick up a fare on the other side of Döbelnsgatan and notices two people emerge from the alley, one at a time. The timing puts this just after the murder has taken place. In one of the apartments overlooking Döbelnsgatan, a sixty-seven-year-old insomniac who is watering her pot plants sees the same sequence of events. Neither she nor the taxi-driver is able to give a more detailed description than young Thyrell's.

'A six-year-old,' says Birck. 'Our best witness is a six-year-old boy.'

'But the sequence of events is nonetheless pretty clear,' says Olausson.

'Er,' I say. 'There are still plenty of questions to be answered.'

'I know, I know,' Olausson mumbles, pulling out his phone without looking at me. 'But I'm sure they'll sort themselves out eventually.'

'Eventually? As in?'

Olausson glances up, and blinks once.

'As in when you lot get on with the job.'

'To do that we're going to need people,' says Birck.

'We'll see what we can do.'

Olausson smiles weakly, and that's that.

'I reckon that whoever was behind the bins wasn't standing there for more than a few minutes,' Mauritzon says, perhaps to keep herself awake. 'That's what the prints in the snow would indicate. There were just a few. And it could be a woman. Not that many men wear size-38 shoes.'

'I might know who it is,' I say, and give a brief account of my visit to the university, and tell them about the anonymous emails Heber had received, the research he was working on, how he had seemed recently, the field notes and 1599, the person he was on the way to meet when he died. 'He also wrote that he had heard something, that he wasn't sure whether to mention it to 1599. I've got no idea what it was, but I did get the distinct impression that it was something important. I didn't have time to read the whole thing, and I wasn't allowed to take the notes with me.'

'So you left them there,' Birck says, without looking up from his notebook.

'Yes.'

'You didn't take any copies?'

'No.'

Olausson is absent-mindedly staring at something through the window, his eyes still only half-open. His mobile is lying next to the case-file on the table in front of him.

Mauritzon asks to see the file, and he nudges it towards her.

'We found this as well,' she says, 'a hundred metres from the body, on Döbelnsgatan.'

She pulls out one of the photographs in the file and pushes it across the table to Olausson, who picks it up inquisitively.

'Vomit,' he states flatly.

'Yes, we've done some tests, but we're waiting for the results.'

'I'm afraid that might be mine,' I say.

'Yours?' Mauritzon's eyes flash between me and the picture. 'Okay.'

'I'd had something that had gone off. The combination of that and Heber's body, perhaps, made me nauseous.'

'Right,' says Olausson.

'I'm sorry. I should have mentioned it.'

'How long have you been back on duty?'

'Why do you ask?'

'Just wondering.'

'Thirteen days.'

'I see.'

'You see? What do you mean by that?'

'Nothing. As I said, I was just wondering.'

He smiles and lets go of the photo. I wonder how he got that scar under his shirt. I wonder if he's married or lives alone, whether he's taping this meeting, I also wonder how good Olausson might be at identifying a liar.

'In that case, it's no use in the investigation,' Mauritzon says, stuffing the photo in her pocket and pushing the open case-file back towards Olausson.

Birck is avoiding eye contact with me, and in turn I'm trying not to look at Olausson. It all goes round in circles, and I suspect Olausson knows. The thought makes me shiver, and my palms get clammy.

'The shoe-print in Heber's apartment,' I change the subject and turn to Mauritzon.

'We're working on the apartment. We're expecting them to be done at some point today, but … I don't expect to get much out of it, other than the shoe-print, of course. What we can safely say is that it wasn't the same person who was standing behind the bins on Döbelnsgatan, and it wasn't Heber either. Whoever it was that was in Heber's apartment has size-44 shoes.'

'The assailant could have been wearing shoes that were too big,' Olausson says.

'Yes, that's true,' Mauritzon replies, tapping the tabletop with her finger. I wonder if it's something she does when she's annoyed. 'But how often does that happen?' she goes on. 'And anyway, the shoe-prints are no use to us, unless we have something to compare them to.'

'What about his phone?' I ask.

'Still missing,' Birck says, flipping through his notes. 'The last signal from his phone was picked up by a mast close to the university about half-an-hour, maybe forty-five minutes, before he died, but they couldn't say who he'd been talking to. We'll get the lists as soon as possible, but it's going to be a while — late this afternoon at the earliest. Right now, the phone's probably switched off. Or lying at the bottom of Lake Mälaren.'

'We need to find this ... what was it,' Olausson says slowly, 'did you say 1579?'

'1599.'

'That's right, 1599. It could be the assailant.'

'I don't think it is.'

'Why not?'

'Doesn't add up.'

'It might be down to the way he was stabbed,' says Mauritzon. 'If he was waiting for 1599 and that person wasn't there when he got there, he's hardly likely to have been standing waiting with his back to the alleyway. How many people wait for someone with their back turned to the direction they're expecting them to come from? If, on the other hand, 1599 had arrived and was somewhere in the courtyard, he'd have no reason to stand there like that.'

Olausson's mobile beeps. A name is briefly visible on the screen: a 'g', and something else that no one manages to read.

'Sounds logical,' he says. 'We'll work on that assumption. And we'll find out what Heber had heard. Well,' he corrects himself as he stands up, 'you will. I've got other things to be getting on with.'

Olausson closes the file that was lying open in front of him, and leaves the meeting room with the file in one hand and his mobile in the other, pressed firmly to his ear.

'He didn't even look in it.' Mauritzon says, shocked. 'The file. I spent hours on those notes.'

Birck, who's been unusually quiet during the meeting, turns from Mauritzon to me, then to the empty chair that seems to be recovering from Olausson's abrupt exit.

'Fucking idiot,' he says.

I stand up.

'And where are you off to?'

64

'I'm going to do some reading.'

'The copies that you didn't make?'

'Something like that.'

Birck glances at Mauritzon, who looks to be only a lullaby away from deep sleep.

'Something's not right here,' he mumbles.

Two coffees later, I'm sitting in my room with Heber's field notes. As I read, I try to piece together something more than an outline of Heber, but the dead sociologist remains a shadow for me. To begin with, his notes are tentative and cautious, and most of them concern leads for the field work. Heber lists and discusses concepts I've never come across.

He starts the fieldwork in January, going via contacts he made during his time in the anarchist movement. He doesn't give any more detail than that.

The first interviewee is, for some reason, referred to as 1580, the second as 1581, the third as 1582, and so on and so on. He conducts the interviews quite intensively, sometimes several subjects per day. He himself writes that he doesn't really have a direction in mind. Later, in March, 1599 appears in the notes for the first time:

13/3
After our interview at Cairo I ask 1598 if he knows of anyone else I ought to talk to. He suggests a member of RAF. He doesn't give me any contact details, says there aren't any, but that if I ask around I should get hold of the person. I'll get started on it — hopefully this is 1599 — as soon as I've marked the students' exam papers.

Contact details that don't exist. 1599 must be a specific person, so it shouldn't be impossible to track him or her down using their network of contacts. Then again, that's not always the problem — it's all about asking the right people. That's harder than it sounds. A couple of days later, Heber succeeds:

16/3

I've been in touch with 1599. Finding her took a while, these last few days I've basically done nothing but look for her. 1599 has no fixed abode, no job, nothing. There's something liberating about that that appeals to me. I wonder if she might be hiding from someone, but I doubt it. I think she just likes living like that. 1599 agreed to take part in the study, we're going to meet tomorrow.

So it's a woman. There's no entry for the following day. Heber doesn't mention their meeting until the eighteenth, and then only in a short note:

18/3

Interviewed 1599 yesterday. It ended up being late, but very rewarding. It gave me a few new ideas, as well as confirming what the other interviewees said. We'll have to meet again — I think 1599 has more to say.

After that, she's not mentioned in the notes for quite some time — six months, in fact. At least not explicitly. In spite of this, the notes seem to have a different tone after their meeting. Heber is more focused, more driven. He concentrates on his research, but other things get a passing mention. He concludes one entry by writing that he is going to 'stop thinking about the research project for today' and go out and eat with his colleagues. He attends meetings, goes to debates, and gives talks to students, politicians, and activists. These activities give him new ideas that he can use in his work, yet he sometimes seems frustrated that others are unable to let go of his past as readily as he did himself:

Twelve years since the Gothenburg riots. I gave a lecture for Stockholm City Council, about what we might be able to learn from them. None of the questions were about my research, all of them were about my time with AFA It's nearly always the way with students, politicians, and bureaucrats. Fucking AFA. Will I ever get away from it? I wonder if it matters, whether I should take it into account when I'm working. I wonder what my interviewees would say about it. What would 1599 say?

I can picture Heber now, standing there, gazing out onto a busy street somewhere, with hazy sunshine behind him. Maybe Birger Jarlsgatan or Vasagatan, where the buildings are all edifices of glass and steel. It is summer, it's warm, and the cars are relentlessly swishing past him, one at a time. When he turns to face the sun, his face is finally there, no longer a silhouette but a person. Everybody is missed by someone.

It's November before she gets mentioned again:

25/11

There is a lot that I ought to be writing down here so that I don't forget any of it, but there's a lot of things that I don't want to be written down. Then again it's not good that I don't have any of it anywhere other than in my head.

She got in touch with me, 1599. I've been keeping my distance (wonder if she noticed) so that it won't carry on. It's so risky. I don't know, there's something about 1599 that I find fascinating. She asked why I hadn't been in touch, as I'd promised, and I didn't have a decent answer so I just apologised.

'We need to meet up,' she said.

'Okay,' I said, 'Why's that?'

'You'll see,' she said.

Then she hung up.

The subsequent entries do not reveal whatever it was that 1599 wanted to tell Heber. I flip through several entries to make sure. She turns up again a week or so later, and is referred to obliquely:

5/12

I'm torn by what 1599 told me. Can I even trust her? My gut feeling says I can, but I'm not sure. If it's true, this is insane. She says I should talk to H. I'm going to try and get hold of him.

I've almost finished reading, but up until Heber makes that last entry, just before his meeting with 1599, she is mentioned only a few times:

7/12

1599. Maybe I should go to the police, even though that breaks every ethical guideline in the book. I've tried to contact H without success.

That same day, however, something happens that puzzles Heber almost as much as it puzzles me:

7/12 (later)

Something strange happened during my interview after lunch, with 1601. He wouldn't let me record the interview, so I made notes. Halfway through the interview he asked me if I had heard the rumour. No, I said, I haven't. I knew about what 1599 had said, but this was about something else. Our conversation went more or less like this (I don't have my interview notes with me, so I'm not completely sure):

Me: 'You mean that someone would go after —?'
1601: 'Yes.'
Me: 'Why?'
1601: 'Isn't hate enough? The feeling of having been betrayed?

How many reasons do you want?'

Me: 'Well, okay. But it still seems incredibly drastic.'

1601: 'I suppose you're entitled to your opinion.'

Me: 'Can you stop it happening?'

1601: 'I wouldn't dare. I can't say any more about it, because no one knows where or when. I've already said too much. I've already … if anybody finds out …'

Me: 'No one is going to find out.'

1601: (Long silence) 'I know someone who will.'

Me: 'Who?'

Then he gave me the name. I am going to contact him as soon as possible, but I daren't call or email him. I doubt he would even answer if he knew it was me.

Two days later, he writes another entry. It might be about the same thing, and the same person, but Heber's notes are vague:

9/12

Spoke to him, tried to persuade him to agree to an interview so that we can talk. He refused. I don't know what to do.

10/12

1599 tells me one thing, 1601 another. I don't know which one is right. Maybe they both are? There's no time for further investigations, and I don't know whether I should go to the police anyway. If I do I'll be breaking my word to 1599. I can't. I still haven't got hold of H.

11/12

I managed to get hold of H in the end, at Cairo. I just went and sat myself in a corner with a coffee and waited, hoping that he might turn up. I was in two minds, unsure what I was about to say and how much I was going to tell him. This is too big to carry alone, the consequences are too serious. I don't which of the scenarios is the right one, and I don't know how much anyone else knows.

After about an hour he showed up and I took him to one side and asked if he knew about it. On the subject of — I didn't tell him who was going to do it (I didn't dare to, out of ethical considerations), just what the target was. I wanted to see his reaction.

I could tell that he'd heard about what 1599 told me, but the fact that I knew caught him off guard. That was obvious. He refused to say any more. I asked if he could check the facts, and get back to me. I was worried, and ashamed for having broken 1601's confidentiality. I had promised not to tell anyone.

H didn't answer my question. He left Cairo.

12/12
Will meet 1599, to talk. Might tell them what I've heard. I don't know. We're meeting at our usual spot at 2230. I'm nervous and unsettled, hesitant. Haven't got much done today.

I find the list of interviewees and look up 1601. The other column contains abbreviations about the organisations the subjects belong to, yet 1601 has no code. He's not the only one. I stare at the list, trying to decipher it, to work out whether it is significant. It might be. Who or what is hidden by '—'? And who is H? A regular at Café Cairo, but not one of his interviewees. In that case, he would have had a number. Could H be an initial?

There's a knock at the door, two sharp taps. Birck. He opens the door and strides in without waiting for a response, and I grab a ring-binder from the shelf behind me, place it on top of the notes, and pretend to be looking for something.

'Busy?' says Birck.

'On my way out, actually.'

'Which is why you're checking ...' Birck cocks his head to read the folder's spine. *'Recovering Evidence from Micro Computers. Renewed and revised.1980.'*

'I was feeling nostalgic.'

'Were you even born then?'

Birck pulls out a chair and sits down, his broad shoulders slumped underneath his dark jacket.

'Olausson,' he says eventually, gazing at something invisible somewhere above my desk. 'We need to talk about him.'

'Okay.'

'After the meeting, I went for a dump and the walls are pretty thin, for better or worse — mostly worse, I suppose. Anyway, I heard someone in the next cubicle, someone who was on the phone but left the taps running at the same time.'

'Okay.'

'I couldn't hear that much of what was being said, but I think I managed to pick up the end: "I just came from a meeting with them, one of them shouldn't be a problem, Bark, or whatever his name is. It's the other one I'm not sure about. But I think he's got an Achilles heel." Then he put the phone down and turned off the taps.'

'Bark,' I repeat, and notice an involuntary smirk tugging at my mouth. 'Better than Birck.'

Birck doesn't seem particularly amused.

'"Shouldn't be a problem"?' I go on. 'Is that what he said?'

'That's what he said. But he doesn't seem so sure about you. And he thinks you've got a weak spot. You don't have to be terribly creative to work out what that might be.'

'But I'm clean. Everything's fine.'

'No, you're not.'

'I am.'

Birck sighs.

'We're his detectives,' I say, changing the subject. 'How can we be a problem? And why aren't we getting more people?'

'Fuck knows. Maybe he's already been told that either the Regional or National Crime Squad are going to take over, and he doesn't want to pull people off other cases. Or it might be that there simply aren't enough cops.'

Birck runs his hand through his hair and yawns silently, blinking a few times.

'I thought you'd know,' he says. 'But keep your eyes peeled. Something about Olausson just doesn't add up. Something about Heber's death doesn't add up either.' He stands up from the chair and gives it an angry glare, as though it had somehow insulted him. 'Christ, that's an uncomfortable chair. If you find anything about 1599 in there,' he continues, nodding at *Recovering Evidence from Micro Computers*, 'then give me a call.'

I close the folder.

'I think I'm going to go to Cairo. You know, the receipt we found yesterday, from the café? That place is also named in those papers I didn't take copies of.'

'Good.'

I hesitate, contemplating the possible ramifications of appearing in the doorway at Café Cairo accompanied by a great wolf of a policeman.

'Are you coming?'

'Busy,' says Birck, waving his mobile phone. 'Heber's autopsy.'

'Well, come when you're free.'

'Don't do anything stupid at Cairo.'

True to form, that's precisely what I'm about to do.

Mitisgatan is a narrow ribbon, just one block long and lined with old five-storey buildings that look strangely squashed compared to their neighbours. Under a troubled sky, I nip over the pedestrian crossing, my hands in my pockets, shaking from the cold.

At street-level is a dark-green steel door. It is so mute and lifeless that it must surely be the door to a storeroom, yet above it hangs a little sign: CAIRO.

I push down on the door handle and let the heavy door swing open. It groans like an old man woken from slumber. It could be mistaken for just another café, but that's before you realise where you've ended up, and once you do, you're gone, whoosh, you've been sucked into another world.

Café Cairo is a hangout for anarchist sub-cultures with a weakness for all things extra-parliamentary. The premises are large, with wooden walls and wooden flooring. The walls are painted black and red, and the roof is adorned with old banners and placards from earlier demos, like relics or trophies. One wall is decorated with a large, framed print of a photograph showing a masked demonstrator throwing paving stones at a wall of police on Kungsportsavenyn in Gothenburg.

People are sitting in twos and threes, evenly spread throughout the café, sitting at small tables, and when I open the door they turn their heads towards me, young men and women with serious expressions. A news bulletin is being broadcast on the radio. Now I notice that the door handle is hanging loosely — it's broken.

I don't belong here, and you can tell that by looking at me. I look like a man who has plenty of money but not enough time to wash his clothes. I'm a police officer, and at Cairo they can smell a cop a mile off. I don't share their faith in the ideology they're fighting for. I am not concerned about what the state might be capable of doing in the name of capitalism, I don't hate the fur industry or the patriarchy. I don't do resistance. I don't do anything. I'm not one of them, and therefore I'm nobody.

A guy about my age is standing behind the counter. He's as wide as a doorway, and his rectangular ribcage stretches the fabric of the shirt he's wearing. He has dark, close-cropped hair, and on the right-hand side of his chest a white badge sits proudly with the letters RAF written in red and black. His hands are holding a baking tray full of brownies.

'We don't serve coppers,' he says. He has grey eyes and some sort of eczema on his chin, like a red, open wound, glistening. He puts the brownies on the worktop. 'Go to Klara's on Hantverkargatan.'

'Is it that obvious?'

'That you're a cop? Yep. It's about the door, right?'

'The door?' I say, confused.

'Someone broke in last night. It was open when I got here.'

'You've had a break-in? Did you report it?'

'No.'

'So how would I know about it?'

'There's always some prick who rings the police whenever it's anything to do with us, doesn't matter what. I assumed you'd heard about it.'

'No,' I reply. 'No, this isn't about the door. This is about Thomas Heber.' Pause for effect. 'You know about that? That he's dead?'

'We heard this morning.'

75

'Do you know how he died?'

'As I said, we heard this morning.'

'Who's we?'

He shrugs.

'What's your name?' I change tack.

'What's your name?'

'Leo Junker.'

I put my hand out. The man hesitantly stretches out his own hand, angular and hard like a piece of timber.

'Oscar,' he says. 'Oscar Svedenhag.'

'I just want to ask a few questions.' I can feel how nobody's looking, but everybody's watching. 'Could we go somewhere else?'

'This is fine,' Oscar says as he notices that the coffee pot is empty. 'Hang on a minute.' He disappears through an opening in the wall and returns with a new pot, full and hot.

'Do you want some?'

'I'm fine, thanks. Your badge.' I stare at the little, round plastic badge sitting on his chest. 'RAF.' I pronounce each letter, unsure of how it should be read. 'As in Royal Air Force, or like the beginning of *raf*ter?'

'R-A-F' Oscar says frostily. 'As in Radical Anti-Fascism.'

'And what exactly is Radical Anti-Fascism?'

'A group.'

'Like AFA?'

This makes him laugh — a patronising, weary laugh.

'If you like.'

'And what does RAF-V stand for?'

'That doesn't concern you.'

'I think it does.'

Oscar gestures silently towards a group behind me who are watching carefully. He turns to me again.

'Don't raise your voice. I can't be arsed with any trouble here.'

I lay my forearms on the counter, smell the aroma of fresh

coffee, strong and bitter, and I contemplate buying a cup after all.

'I think we have a witness to Thomas's murder. A woman who might be involved in RAF.'

'There are over one hundred active RAF members in and around Stockholm,' Oscar says. 'About thirty of them are women. You're going to have to be more specific.'

There's something odd about him — something about his eyes.

'You knew him well. You and Thomas. You knew each other.'

Oscar tilts his head slightly to one side, as though weighing up the possible implications of his answer.

'Not well. I knew who he was.'

'I don't really believe that.'

'I don't give a shit. Get out of here now. People are going to start wondering what the hell you're playing at.'

'Either we do this here,' I say, 'or we take a stroll down to the bunker. It's your call.'

He smiles, turning his back to me again, and moves the baking tray out of the way as he cleans the worktop. In the corner of the surface is a collection of knives in a wooden knife-block.

'Is that block normally full?'

'Why do you ask?'

'I'm the inquisitive type, you know.'

He stalls, well aware of what the answer could mean.

'Yes, it is normally full. I don't know where it is.'

I can't make out the blades. It could be one of them, the missing one, the one somebody stuck in Heber's back. I try to get a look at Oscar's shoes. They could be a size 44.

'Ultimatums don't tend to be very effective here, especially not if they come from a disgusting cop.'

'Disgusting. That's a new one.'

'You like your job, right?'

'I've got nothing against it,' I say, truthfully.

'You can tell.'

'What do you mean?'

'Looks like you like interrogating people. It's your thing.'

'I don't like it when people go round stabbing each other. I think it's more that that's my "thing".'

Oscar stands up, and that's when it happens. I've seen it before, how people change as the realisation hits them. He drops his cloth. The big man seems struck with deep grief.

'If you answer my questions, I will leave you alone.'

Oscar bites his lip, stretching the skin over his chin and causing the glossy, red eczema to change shape.

'How much detail do I need to give you?'

'As much detail as you can.'

His heavy shoulders slide forwards, and his posture slumps.

'We got to know each other in Gothenburg, during the riots. Almost thirteen years ago now. We belonged to different factions within the same network and we stayed at the same guy's place down there.'

After Gothenburg they were close, until a couple of years ago. There was no particular reason why they started drifting apart. They were getting older. Thomas disappeared into academia, while Oscar was still active in AFA and working part-time at Cairo. A few years ago he left AFA and went over to RAF instead.

'He was doing some research when he died.' I say. 'Were you one of his interview subjects?'

'Yes, I was,' Oscar says. 'One of the people who gave him access to new people to interview. He'd been away from politics for quite a while, at least in terms of direct action. Thomas didn't know the new people, and they didn't know him either.'

'Had you ever helped him before?'

'No, up till then he'd managed without me, he said.' Oscar takes a mug from the cupboard behind him and pours some coffee. The mug is white, with the words I'D TRADE MY BOYFRIEND FOR TRUE DEMOCRACY printed in black capitals. 'But not this time.

So I pulled a few strings for him.'

'Do you know anything about who the others were? The others who were helping him?' I clarify.

'I asked, of course. But no, when it came to that sort of thing, he wouldn't give anything away. He said that it applied to me as well, that I would be protected by confidentiality, too. That I'd just be a number.'

'What number?'

'Eh?'

'What number were you?'

'1584.' He takes a swig from his mug, peering over my shoulder again. 'Academics, eh? Secretive lot. Worse than AFA.'

'I've been wondering,' I say, scratching my cheek. 'I've been wondering about his family life.'

'What about it?'

'Well, we ... He doesn't seem to have had one. Men his age, our age, they're usually at least thinking about settling down with someone. Do you know whether he was in a relationship with anyone?'

'No, no idea.'

'Did he often come here?'

'Often wouldn't be the right word. Sometimes.'

'I have a receipt that puts him here a few days ago. The eleventh. I think he met someone here, possibly someone with a first name or surname beginning with H. Were you working that day?'

'No, I was on my way home from a demo in Jönköping that evening.'

'Could you check who was working then?'

'We don't have lists like that — I'd need to ring round to find out. I won't be doing that.'

'Do you know of anyone who would have been here then? Someone who's here now?'

'If you want to know, you'd better ask them. But I would advise you to choose your words carefully.'

I turn towards the patrons, who have gone back to their conversations. A handful are sitting and reading alone, including a man whose head is too big and whose hands look small and hard. He's wearing a light-grey leather jacket with a RAF badge on the chest.

'Good book?' I ask.

'What the fuck do you want?'

'To talk.'

'No thanks.'

'That wasn't a request.'

The man still hasn't looked up.

I lose patience.

'Right. Fancy a nice walk back to the bunker with me?'

Everything goes very quiet. Behind me, Oscar lets out a heavy sigh. On the street outside, a car pulls up. The little man puts the book to one side and stands up. His eyes are like a bird's — round and jerky, bulbous.

'Who the fuck do you think you are?'

He's a full head shorter than me. That doesn't matter, because behind him another four or five, maybe more, are getting up from their seats, surrounding me, looking at me the way you look at an insect before you swat it. The short man takes a step towards me, and plants a sharp punch in my guts. I feel the air leave my lungs as I fall to my knees, hissing.

I can hear them laughing above my head.

I struggle to stand up. It takes an embarrassingly long time, but in the end I manage it. From the corner of my eye, I notice someone standing up from their table and leaving Cairo — a woman.

I look down, still gasping for air after the blow. Mind-blowingly stupid, this.

The men are so close that their chests are touching my arms, their shoes are touching mine. None of them seem particularly angry, but several seem interested in what might happen next.

'Your turn,' the short guy says to one of them.

Then something happens. The door to Cairo swings open again, and Gabriel Birck steps in, with his hands in the pockets of his trench coat and an inquisitive look on his face — a policeman in a far-too-expensive suit and with a profile so sharp it wouldn't look out of place on a coin. When he spots the crowd and my head just visible between their shoulders, he walks over and takes his hands out of his pockets.

'Is everything okay?'

'Not great,' I wheeze.

'I recommend that you leave the premises,' Oscar says from behind the counter.

'That sounds reasonable,' says Birck.

I turn around, and my eyes meet Oscar's.

'Ring me,' I say, but I can't say whether or not he responds, because before I know it I'm out on the street again.

'I told you,' Birck hisses, as we head for the car. 'Don't do anything stupid.'

'I know.' I'm massaging my stomach. It feels empty and sore after the little man's punch. 'Sorry.'

'This is precisely why I said no, when you asked if I was happy working with you. You're too unpredictable.'

'Sorry,' I say again.

'Fuck you. Have you got a cigarette?'

Embarrassed, I pull one out of my pack. We get into Birck's black Citroën. It has a unique smell: a mixture of leather, aftershave, and winter.

'You should report that punch,' he says. 'Assaulting a police officer. That little leftie would get spanked.'

I shake my head.

'We might need to contact them again. If we make a complaint, that'll become impossible — they'll hate us even more. Did you see anyone leaving at about the same time as you came in?'

'A woman,' Birck says. 'Why?'

'Did you get a good look at her?'

'Not really.'

'I think that she might be our witness, 1599.'

'What makes you think that?'

'A feeling.'

'Feelings? Completely useless in this line of work.'

I wonder if Birck might be right. Maybe.

'He called me disgusting.'

'Who?'

'The guy who told us to leave.'

'Disgusting,' Birck says thoughtfully. 'Aren't we all?'

The autopsy on Thomas Heber confirms that he died from somebody putting a knife in him and then twisting it a quarter-turn. The blade was pretty big, somewhere between twelve and fifteen centimetres, and partly serrated. The knife tore several major arteries close to the heart, the medical names of which Birck doesn't remember.

The gist of what the autopsy told us was less complicated. It happened quickly. The assailant knew what he was doing, and Heber was unlikely to have remained conscious for more than a few seconds — half a minute at most. After just a minute or two, medics would not have been able to save his life.

Heber had drunk coffee a few hours before his death, and his intestines were in the process of digesting the remnants of a sandwich he'd grabbed along with the coffee.

'Who conducted the autopsy?'

'Khan, thank God.' says Birck. 'That's why I didn't feel like I had to go down there, that a call was enough. If there was anything significant there, Khan would have found it.'

Nothing else was found on Heber's body — no usable skin particles from the assailant, no textile fibres, nothing. A few fibres had been found on Heber's coat, at shoulder height, but they had been destroyed by the elements, Mauritzon explained once Birck had read her report. They might possibly have come from a glove, but even the type of garment was unknown.

'Destroyed by the elements,' I say. 'The weather, in other words.'

'That's right.'

'Which shoulder?'

'Eh?'

'Which shoulder did they find the fibres on?'

'Left.'

'So,' I say. 'The assailant comes from behind, puts his left hand on Heber's shoulder to get some extra force when he stabs him.'

'Maybe,' says Birck. 'I guess so.'

Birck parks his car in the garage back at HQ. He turns off the engine and undoes his seatbelt, but stays in his seat.

'I've been researching Heber on the internet. Aside from the Nazi sites, which have profiles about him, there's surprisingly little out there.'

'What did it say in the profiles?'

'Nothing we didn't already know. AFA, conviction for assault, sociologist and academic, et cetera. I could try and establish who wrote those posts, but I doubt it would work. It's probably a waste of time.'

'Yes, more than likely.'

A fluorescent lamp flickers, and the ceiling in the garage hangs low. I wonder if we'd make it out if the pillars collapsed and the ceiling fell in. I've been having a lot of thoughts like this recently. I haven't mentioned it to anyone.

'Something's just not right,' I say.

'Is that a feeling you've got?'

'Yes.'

Birck goes quiet, in what becomes a long silence.

'Me too,' he says eventually, and opens his door.

A man wearing a black suit, a white shirt, and a thin, black tie is standing outside my office. His blond hair is neatly slicked back.

From a distance he looks quite dapper, but up close I notice the creases in his suit and the flecks of grey in his hair. He dyes it, perhaps trying not to seem so pale, but his latest attempt has only been a partial success. He holds himself like a man who was on his way somewhere before forgetting his destination. As he spots me, he smiles weakly and pulls his hand from his trouser pocket.

'Leo Junker, isn't it?'

'That's correct.' I shake his hand. It is dry and cool. 'And you are?'

'Paul Goffman.'

'Goffman,' I repeat. 'Rings a bell.'

'Have you got a minute?'

'Do you work in the building?'

'You could say that.' He glances at the closed door to my room. 'Can we talk in your office? This won't take long.'

'I'm actually pretty busy. And what do you mean you could say that?'

'I can explain. I'm here to help you.'

'Help me? What do you mean?'

'Exactly that.' His eyes flit between me and the key in the door. 'It's about Thomas Heber.'

Ah. Our reinforcements.

Goffman's stare is clear, and his eyes are such a pale blue that they look almost white, like ice in strong sunlight. This doesn't feel good at all.

Goffman surveys the room, wall by wall, as though he were looking for some detail that might tell him more about its occupant. The only problem is that, aside from a coffee cup and an empty fag-packet, the room is completely devoid of 'details'.

'I've been back thirteen days,' I say, for some reason feeling the need to explain myself.

'I know.' Goffman replies enigmatically, placing his hand on the little wooden chair. 'May I?'

'Of course.'

The man sits down carefully, as if unsure whether it would take his weight.

'Thomas Heber,' I say, and sit down in my own chair.

'Yes, Heber,' says Goffman, shifting in his seat as though he's just been reminded of the purpose of his visit. 'I would respectfully ask that you let us deal with Heber.'

'Us?'

'Yes?' Goffman looks puzzled. 'Us.'

'Who's "us"?'

'Didn't I say?'

'No. Are you from National Crime Unit?'

'Sorry,' Goffman says, laughing, and shaking his head. 'I thought I'd said. I'm wrecked, haven't slept in ages. I'm from The Bureau and we ...'

'SEPO.'

I attempt to conceal my surprise at the fact that he's with the Security Police. To no avail. Goffman is by no means as confused as he likes to appear.

'That's correct.'

They no longer sit in the same building, having recently moved to their own premises, tucked away in Solna. And he says The Bureau, not SEPO, so he's been there for ages.

'I understand.'

'I thought you would. And we do need to take over.'

'You need to take over.'

'That's right.'

'Need?'

Goffman is like a chess player, reading the board, trying to decipher the logic of his opponent's moves. At least that's what he would like to think.

'That's right,' he says, again.

'Okay.' I rest my forearms on the edge of my desk, and there's

a sharp pain in my abdomen, possibly from the punch at Cairo.
'Why? Why do you need to?'

'Those details are not something I am at liberty to discuss with you, as I'm sure you understand.'

'Have you cleared this higher up?'

'That is, of course, a given.'

'How high up? Does Olausson know?'

'He understands full well what is going on, and has stepped aside. We'll be putting in one of our own to lead the investigations.'

I stare at the empty cigarette packet, pick it up, and scrunch it in my fist before throwing it into the bin. 'You ought to be dealing with Birck, he's the one leading the inves—'

'I'll be talking to Gabriel, too.'

I hate being cut off. I glare at him, but I don't think he even notices, let alone cares.

'What is it about Heber that makes this your case?'

'Well,' Goffman says, laughing again, showing his clean, even teeth, crossing his legs, and waving his index finger. 'You're a canny one. I am not permitted to discuss this with you.'

'No details,' I say, and I'm struck by a sudden urge to smack him in the face. 'You said you can't discuss details. If you're going to take over, I want to know why — that's not a detail.'

'True,' Goffman says. 'I'm sorry, but this chair is incredibly uncomfortable.'

'I think that might be the point.'

'Of course. Must be. Do you mind if I stand?'

'No.'

Goffman stands up and is unnaturally tall, standing there in his crumpled suit, running his hand through his hair, studying the rickety heap of a chair he has just vacated.

'If you want to make someone feel uncomfortable, you make them wear clothes with no pockets. It must be the same idea.'

'What do you mean?'

'People reveal more about themselves when they're uncomfortable?' He waves his hand, dismissively. 'Anyway. Heber has a past in extreme-leftist groups. You know that as well as I do. Then he straightens himself out, becomes some kind of pseudo-academic at the university, and what does he research? Social movements on the far left. Himself, basically. And now someone puts a knife in his back. Do you think that's a coincidence?'

'I think,' I reply, 'that you are very polite and that you'd like me to believe that I know as much as you do, when in fact you know far more than you're letting on.'

Again, Goffman looks perplexed.

'And what might that be?'

'Well, the real reason for you taking over the case, for a start. What you've given me is just an excuse. We've dealt with cases like this before.'

'Ah-ah-ah,' Goffman says, raising his index finger again. His fingers are long and bony, like you'd expect an accomplished pickpocket or a magician to have. 'Details.'

'If you're taking the case off us, I want to know why.'

'You said,' Goffman says, this time putting his index finger back in his pocket, along with the rest of his hand. He paces back and forth in the room, as though the situation has made him restless. 'I, however, have neither the desire nor any need to answer that. Besides, you're taking the wrong approach entirely. You talk about "us" and "you", but that distinction is not valid. We're all working for the same ends.'

'You're the one who started talking about "us" and "you", not me.'

He stops dead. Then he shrugs.

'You don't have any say in the matter,' he says, in a voice that sounds almost mournful but which might very well be elusive, mocking.

'I want to see the papers, at least.'

'You may see the papers. I wouldn't be here if I didn't have them, but I don't have them with me right now.'

'Shame,' I say.

'Give me the case file. Time might be running out.'

'It's not here, Birck's got it.'

'Hmm,' says Goffman. 'Send it by courier.' He opens the door. 'Thank you for your time. Happy Lucia.'

'Who is it?'

Goffman stops in his tracks.

'I beg your pardon?'

'Who is at risk?'

'I'm sorry, I don't follow?'

'Someone is at risk, a threat linked to Heber's death. That much I do understand. And that's why you're taking over. I want to know who it is.'

The index finger again.

'Details.'

He blinks, smiles, and disappears.

I look at the wooden chair. A while passes, maybe a minute, maybe much longer, and then I stand up, walk round the desk, and slump onto it.

Goffman was right. It's seriously uncomfortable. I sit there, staring at my own empty chair on the other side of the desk.

Can't think of anything to think.

'I, erm …' says a voice at the door, I turn my head. Birck is standing outside. 'What are you doing?' He comes into the room, closing the door behind him. 'Why aren't you sitting in your own chair?'

'I … don't know.'

Birck sits down in my chair. I try to picture the inside of my own head. Just a fog — no actual thoughts worthy of the name.

'What the hell are you doing, sitting there?' he mumbles, and starts messing with the levers underneath the seat, adjusting the backrest.

'It took me an hour to get that right.'

'And yet you're sitting there like a little old man.'

My phone buzzes: it's a message from Sam.

would it be okay if we met up tomorrow instead?

I close my eyes. Friday or Saturday, makes no difference to me, but I wonder why she wants to put it off this time?

yes I reply. *if you really want to?*

yes

good

Birck clears his throat, leans back in my chair, and puts his feet up on the desk.

'We no longer have a case,' I say, looking up from my phone.

'What?'

During the time it takes for me to tell Birck about Goffman's visit, Birck's shock gradually subsides until he is just sitting there, perfectly still, with a blank expression on his face. At one point he starts looking for something in the inside pocket of his jacket — perhaps cigarettes, maybe a comb — but for the most part he just sits there, staring at his shoes.

'Didn't see that coming,' is his only comment.

'Are you being sarcastic?'

'I think so. Did he have the paperwork?'

'No, but it does exist.'

'Are you sure?'

'Yes.'

Birck takes his feet off the desk, stands up, and runs his hand through his hair.

'Well, blow me down.'

'Goffman didn't tell me the real reason why they were taking over, that much I'm sure of. What he told me was just a hackneyed excuse.'

'There are hundreds of potential reasons, and I'd say less than half of them are legit. But it must surely have something to do with his leftist background?'

'Of course,' I say. 'That's what he said. But fuck knows.'

'They're taking everything we've got, then?'

'Everything in the case file.'

'So,' Birck says in a hushed voice, 'have we got anything that isn't in it?'

'Maybe,' I say, glancing involuntarily at the folder on my desk, and Thomas Heber's field notes, sticking out from underneath it.

'I thought as much.'

'He mentions someone,' I say, 'in his notes.'

'1599? We know.'

'No, someone else. On the seventh of December he interviews someone he calls 1601, who tells him something. I don't know whether they were talking about people, but I guess we have to assume that they were. It could also be groups, organisations or anything, really. Then 1601 names someone else, apparently the one who's "going to do it". Whatever "it" is. I lift the file and pass the printout to Birck. 'Read it yourself.'

Birck takes it from me and flips through to the page in question. He reads it with a frown:

7/12 (later)

Something strange happened during my interview after lunch, with 1601. He wouldn't let me record the interview, so I made notes. Halfway through the interview he asked me if I had heard the rumour. No, I said, I haven't. I knew about what 1599 had said, but this was about something else. Our conversation went more or less like this (I don't have my interview notes with me, so I'm not completely sure):

Me: 'You mean that someone would go after —?'

1601: 'Yes.'

Me: 'Why?'

1601: 'Isn't hate enough? The feeling of having been betrayed? How many reasons do you want?!

Me: 'Well, okay. But it still seems incredibly drastic.'

1601: 'I suppose you're entitled to your opinion.'

Me: 'Can you stop it happening?'

1601: 'I wouldn't dare. I can't say any more about it, because no one knows where or when. I've already said too much. I've already … if anybody finds out …'

Me: 'No one is going to.'

1601: (Long silence) 'I know who is going to.'

Me: 'Who?'

Then he gave me the name. I am going to contact him as soon as possible, but I daren't call or email him. I doubt he would even answer if he knew it was me.

'Hmm,' is the extent of Birck's reaction.

'Further down you'll see the entry from the ninth. Heber tries to contact whoever 1601 was talking about, I think. But the guy refuses to agree to an interview.'

'You can't say for certain that that's who he's talking about,' says Birck. 'Heber doesn't say any more than that he's spoken to him and tried to get him to do an interview, and that he refuses.'

'I know. But he could be talking about the same person.'

'In that case, it should be someone Heber knows,' Birck says, his eyes still glued to the printout. 'They must at least know of each other. Or Heber should know, or at least guess, that this person doesn't want to speak to him. Or someone like him. Here,' he says, putting his finger on the page to show me. '"I doubt he would even answer if he knew it was me."'

'Exactly.'

Birck tidies the printout into a pile and puts it on the desk.

'No, hold on. Look at the last entry again.'

Birck picks it up again and flips to the last page.

'"Meeting 1599, to talk,"' Birck reads aloud. '"Might tell them what I've heard. I don't know. We're meeting at our usual spot at 2230. I'm nervous and unsettled, hesitant. Haven't got much done today." Can I put it down now?'

'The thing is, did he ever speak to 1599 about what he'd heard? In that case, she knows. Yes, you can put it down now.'

'That's true,' Birck says. 'But it might not have anything at all to do with what happened to Heber later on.'

'I know. But maybe.'

'If you know all this, why are you telling me?'

I sigh, and shake my head. Nothing happens. Everything's quiet. My fingers are twitching. I want a Serax. When did I last have one — was it just before I went to Café Cairo? No longer than that?

Birck gets out of the chair and walks over towards the door.

'How do you make contact without using a phone or email?' I ask. He turns around.

'I don't know. Carrier-pigeon? Telegram? Smoke signals?'

II

A TOWN FULL OF
HEROES AND VILLAINS

Christian is sitting watching telly at his friend's house out in Enskede. One of the party leaders is giving his opinion about some insignificant issue. They've muted the TV to avoid having to listen to that bollocks. Sometimes that's the only thing to do.

He reads the words, one at a time, on the big banner hanging on the wall above the screen. Christian thinks about the knife — how it felt, resting there inside his coat.

'Wanna beer?' Michael shouts from the kitchen.

'No whisky?'

'Oh yeah.'

Michael emerges with a couple of fingers of scotch in two round tumblers.

'Jesus, look at the state of you,' he says, and hands one to Christian.

'I didn't sleep very well.' Christian looks up. 'I bet you did?'

'Yes, why?'

'Well, considering ...'

'I didn't do it for the hell of it. I had to. You know that.'

'Yeah. But ... didn't you feel anything?'

Michael takes a swig, with a determined expression on his face.

'If you weren't the one asking, that question would make me fucking furious.' He puts the glass down. 'What the fuck do you think? Course I fucking did. But some things ...' He hesitates. 'I learnt that inside. Some things just have to be done. And this was necessary. Everything could have been fucked otherwise.'

Christian wants to stand up and walk out, but he can't. So he sits there.

They got to know each other at parties. That's how it worked back then; maybe it still is. Every time they met, Michael had a new phone — always a Nokia. Christian didn't have one but, before long, Michael gave him one of his.

'You can have that,' Michael said. 'It's got Snake. But if you break my record, you're in deep shit.'

It took Christian a week to break the record. He didn't mention it. He swapped his glasses for contacts and took Accutane for his acne, three a day. Six months later, his skin was clear and smooth, and since that day he hasn't had so much as a pimple.

Christian didn't know much about his new friend. He worked out that he wasn't from Stockholm, because when he'd had a few, a completely different accent would spout from his lips. It was warmer, more rolling, and fuller than his normal voice.

'Where the hell are you from anyway?' Christian asked, laughing.

'Borlänge.'

'And where the fuck is that?'

'In Dalarna.'

'That's in Norrland, isn't it?'

'Dalarna is in the middle of Sweden. Norrland starts about five hundred kilometres north of Dalarna.'

'Well, how did you end up here, then?'

'Mum got divorced and met a new bloke who lived here. I must have been six or seven when we moved down.'

'Did you want to move?'

Michael shrugged, smiling.

'When you're little, I suppose you don't want things to change. But it wasn't too bad.'

Michael's mother and her new partner both worked in insurance. They were the kind of family who could afford to own their own home.

Christian himself was born in Stockholm, growing up first in Bredäng and later Hagsätra. His mum worked behind the till in one of the shops by the square, and his dad … well, only his dad really knew what had happened to him, and Christian would probably have given him a smack if he'd ever had the good fortune to bump into him. He'd left when Christian was ten, and they never heard from him again. His mum just said that he was living somewhere on the west coast, with some woman, but apart from that they never talked about him.

That might have been the precursor to Christian falling out with his new friend for the first time. Afterwards it was difficult to say what it had been about.

Every time he thought about his dad, even now, years later, Christian recalled that betrayal: how he'd woken up one morning and discovered that there were only three people in the apartment. How his dad's big Fjällräven rucksack, the one he used to take on their motoring holidays down in Skåne, was missing. Christian's mother was lying awake in bed, crying. It was a Tuesday — he even remembered that. Anton was in his room, and when Christian asked why dad wasn't home, he looked uninterested.

'Dunno. Don't care either.'

Anton and his dad had never seen eye to eye. They were too much alike — at least that's what Mum put it down to, maybe because that was easiest.

'What happens if he never comes back?' Christian asked.

'I think he'll be back,' Anton said, matter-of-factly. 'Now, get out of my room.'

'But come on, would it have been better if they'd stuck it

out and been unhappy and argued and fought?' his new friend wondered.

It was now early evening, and they were sitting on a bench close to Hagsätra's recreation ground. Autumn had arrived, and the grass on the pitch in front of them was covered with frozen dew. Lone runners ran round and round, coldly illuminated by the strong floodlights, their breath chugging ahead of them like thin white smoke.

Sometimes, late in the evening, Christian would run there himself. He'd been doing it for years — couldn't even remember when he'd started. Had he been eleven? Maybe twelve? Down here it felt like the vault-roof of the sky above was further away, and that running lap after lap had some kind of purifying effect.

'They could have sorted it out,' Christian said. 'If he'd had the bollocks to stay and fight for it, then they wou—'

'You don't know that.'

'Yes, I do know that. They'd had problems before, but they'd always sorted it out.'

They were fifteen, and both believed that they understood everything. In fact, they understood nothing.

Later, Christian looked for his wallet in the pockets of his jeans, but couldn't find it. They had shared a bottle of spirits that Michael had got cheaply, out in Salem, and at first Christian thought he'd got too drunk and lost it somewhere. He did his best to look for it in the darkness, but it wasn't there.

'Weird, eh?' he slurred. 'I was fucking sure I had it with me.'

'You must have left it at home,' Michael slurred back, taking a swig from the bottle. 'I haven't seen it since we came out.'

They were both tipsy, and Christian was starting to enjoy the sensation of tilting over. Focusing took a while. Michael climbed down from the bench to go for a piss behind one of the dugouts. He swayed, reeled over to one side, and hit the ground. He laughed, and so did Christian.

The fall had caused something to glide out of Michael's jacket pocket: a wallet. Christian noticed it from the corner of his eye, squinting as Michael tried to get to his feet.

'What the fuck ...' Christian began as he leant forward to pick it up.

He opened it. It was his.

'What is this?'

'Your wallet.'

'You said you hadn't ...' The three hundred-kronor notes were missing. 'Where's the money?'

'I don't know.'

'You nicked my fucking wallet!'

Michael managed to stand up and laughed, dismissively.

'I was going to give it back to you later, when you'd got properly paranoid.'

Something about his tone of voice made Christian not believe him.

'Are you a fucking benefits-scrounger, or what? Who the fuck does a thing like that? Give me my fucking money!'

The next minute, Christian was lying on his back next to the bench. His cheek was throbbing, and his jaw ached like hell.

'What the fuck?' Christian hissed as he struggled to get to his feet.

He leaned against the bench for support, and once he was standing up he grabbed Michael's jumper and jumped on his friend, pushing him over and then clenching his right fist.

It must all have been over in seconds, but it felt much longer: they found themselves on the ground below the bench, hitting each other in the face, kneeing each other wherever they could reach. Christian managed to bust his friend's eyebrow, and his own nose was clicking. One of his teeth was loose.

'Who the hell nicks their mate's wallet?' Christian spluttered.

'Who the fuck calls someone a benefits-scrounger? Look at

them at school, you can tell who's on benefits and who isn't. Don't compare me to them.'

'I didn't.'

'Shut up.'

Later they went to A&E and explained how they'd been attacked by a couple of immigrants. They'd worked that out themselves, that that would be the easiest solution. They got stitches and bandages, and somewhere along the line a police report was filed, but nothing ever came of it, which wasn't really surprising.

As they left the hospital, Michael thrust his hand out in the darkness, without a word. In it were three hundred-kronor notes.

'When will the others be coming?' Christian asks now.

'In about an hour. First we'll have the meeting, map out our strategy, and then we pep each other up.' His mobile phone buzzes. 'Jonathan's already on his way,' he says, his eyes fixed on the screen.

Jonathan. The poor sod got trapped with an amphetamine habit last summer, and they've been exploiting him ever since. And he's got no idea. Or maybe he does suspect something.

The television news-anchor is staring into the camera. Beside her is a picture of the leader of the Sweden Democrats.

'Fuck this,' Michael says. 'Turn that shit off.'

'Don't you want to hear it?'

'I don't want to hear anything to do with that bastard.'

Christian picks up the remote. The screen goes black.

Stockholm. From above, it looks like a patchwork of water and greenery, with the odd cluster of high-rises, suburban detached houses, and other buildings dotted about. People have long since forgotten that the only thing saving them from extinction is that Mother Nature hasn't decided to brush them from her shoulders. Lifetimes have passed since she last showed her true force, and, considering how humans behave, that is somewhat surprising.

'Don't you think?' the taxi-driver concludes.

I'm sitting in a car that is moving through the streets of Kungsholmen, about a kilometre from the yard in Vasastan where someone pushed a knife into Thomas Heber. It is late afternoon. Darkness has fallen. On the radio, someone is singing *If you've got no place to go, let it snow, let it snow, let it snow*. St Göran's is rising in front of us.

'Eh?'

The taxi-driver sighs audibly.

'Never mind.'

The car stops on the turning circle. I pay in cash, and step out into the cold. I think I tell the taxi-driver to have a good evening. He waits for the door to close, and then drives off without saying a word. I stand there, my eyes following the red tail-lights as I smoke a cigarette.

Another car arrives. It heads into the car park, turns into a space before the lights, and then the engine turn off, and it stays there. I drop the cigarette onto the ground. It fizzes in the snow.

The visiting rooms are sparse and cool, very quiet. At St Göran's, they've decided that it's best this way. The place is a storage unit for those unfortunate souls who, one way or another, have stared into the abyss. They've seen the abyss staring back and blinking before it tried to consume them.

A renowned physicist is resident here after having attempted to kill his wife. It was covered in the media, the story of him discovering how, while he was spending his nights in a lab underneath the Technical University, she was being entertained by his closest colleague. They had been professional rivals, with diverging theories on why something was the way it was. One night, he came home early to discover his wife and his colleague in the same bed. Exhausted and sleep-deprived, he attempted to kill them both, but was unsuccessful.

Others sitting here fell into psychoses from which they have never emerged, yet all of them made sure to commit a couple of grievous crimes before disintegrating altogether. All are heavily medicated. Surprisingly few had troubled childhoods. Surprisingly, many had no baggage whatsoever.

I could have ended up here — if things had got a little bit worse, if everything had spun out a little bit more. A whisper in the dark might have tipped me over the edge. That might still be all it would take.

'It's been a while,' says Johanna, the nurse who leads me to the visiting room.

'I know. Must do better.'

'I never said that. You shouldn't ask too much of yourself. John will be here shortly. I'll be outside if you need me.'

'Thanks.'

She walks out, leaving the door open.

The first time I came, they wouldn't let me keep my shoes on when I met him. I had to take my belt off, and put it in a plastic tray along with my keys, my phone, and a lighter. After that, they searched me. It was for my own safety, as well as the safety of patients and staff, since there had recently been a spate of attempted escapes. Apparently the renowned physicist had convinced one of the other patients that his family had come to take him to the gas chamber. If you take that sort of thing seriously, which is probably easily done in here, it makes for a pretty good reason to flee.

Every now and then you hear them, the noises which reveal that all is not quite as it should be — the monotonous banging on walls, mantra-like mumbling, the occasional outburst. Most of the time, you hear the most telling sound of all.

Silence. As though the world has been heavily anaesthetised.

The sound of clinking chains comes through the open door. Grim is led in by a warder I recognise: Slog. He's an ogre with a shaved head, freckled skin, and a red goatee. Slog spent a couple of years of his increasingly distant misspent youth on Stockholm's football-hooligan scene, and he was eventually convicted of involuntary manslaughter. He went through one of the Prison Service's rehabilitation programmes, and before long he managed to use his contacts to get himself employed as a warder. The nickname dates from back then. He later applied for and got a job at St Göran's, his success probably due in no small part to his physical stature.

'Leo Junker,' he says. 'I haven't seen you in ages. Good to see you.'

'Same to you.'

We shake hands. It feels good, Slog has a reassuring handshake. He helps Grim into the chair. This takes a while. Grim's hands are bound, and from his wrists a long chain runs to his ankles. No one moves quickly in that get-up. It's by no means standard issue for St Göran's, but Grim is considered so dangerous that it is deemed necessary. He avoids looking at Slog, instead staring at an invisible spot on the floor, between his feet.

'We'll be outside,' Slog says.

'I know.'

I manage to smile weakly at him, and then wait until he has left the room and closed the door behind him before I turn to Grim.

The time in St Göran's has changed the man who was once my friend. The short hair is longer, but unkempt and uneven. The warders tell me that he sometimes rips out tufts of it in his sleep. His medication has caused him to put on weight, making his face seem unnaturally swollen. It has also made him colour-blind, a rare but evidently possible side effect. He might, of course, be lying. Nobody knows. When it comes to John Grimberg, no one can ever really be sure of anything.

When our eyes finally meet, his are hollow and grey, reflecting nothing more than the tabletop that separates us.

'Hello,' he says.

'Hello.'

'You got them to take my phone again.'

'It wasn't your phone, though, was it?'

Grim shrugs and looks away again.

'You wanted to see me,' I say. 'Well, here I am.'

'How's Sam?'

'Is that what you wanted to know?'

'Did you say hello from me, last time?'

'No.'

'Why not?'

'I forgot all about it.'

'Are you lying now?' Grim says, grinning.

When he smiles, he's seventeen again, and I start trembling inside.

I can't remember how many times I've been to see him. Every time I meet him, it's as though I've entered a bubble where space and time are slightly distorted, twisted. Sometimes I'm convinced that I've been there for at least an hour, when in actual fact it has been just a few minutes. Other times, I think I've just got there, and then when I get out I realise I've spent over two hours with him.

Grim doesn't really get up to anything, at least nothing that could be considered leisure. The patients at St Göran's are subject to strict treatment regimes, are heavily medicated, and those who have been sectioned are treated like the prisoners they really are. Not only that, but Grim is in 'special measures', and his visitors are vetted.

At first, Grim would ask me to visit, not the other way round. According to the staff, he doesn't get any visitors, aside from the occasional police officer who wants to quiz him about some crime that, for one reason or another, they believe he has some knowledge of. Grim has no family, no real friends. The ones he does have are the kind of people who might disrupt his treatment if he were to meet them. A month or so ago, a man called 'Jack' managed to talk his way in. He had once been a policeman, which probably explains how he did it. He turned his back on the law, and the force, many years ago, and now does assignments for whoever pays most. What he wanted with Grim is still not clear, but whatever it was must have involved a pay-off of some kind. Since that incident, the staff are even more careful, even more controlling, in terms of who gets to see him.

Despite all this, Grim still manages to get hold of mobile phones and cigarettes. If you can do that, you can also get hold of other stuff. Like weapons.

Grim might actually be insane. Either way, being locked up here twenty-four hours a day can't be good for him. Grim isn't a sociable person, never has been, but the isolated world of St Göran's could grind anyone down. Sometimes, when we're sitting opposite each other, I realise that I'm quietly suffering with him.

It might well have been this that made me agree to meet him, after a long period of reflection. I agreed on one condition — that

Grim would stick to the truth. I realised that he would demand the same from me.

'If you lie to me, I won't come back,' I said.

'If you lie to me, I don't want to see you,' Grim replied.

When I don't respond, Grims says, 'She's not with that fucking body-piercer anymore.'

'No, that's right.'

'Well, you can thank me for that.'

'I'm not going to thank you for anything.'

'Okay.' Grim shrugs. 'I heard about the murder on Döbelnsgatan.'

'Oh, did you?'

'How's that going?'

'No idea.'

Grim raises one of his thin eyebrows.

'That bad, eh?'

'It's no longer our case. SEPO took it off us.'

'Ahh,' Grim says, sticking his bottom lip out, 'Poor little Leo, did big, bad SEPO come along and pinch the exciting murder case?' He grimaces and puts his hands to his eyes. The chains clink, accompanying his pretend crying. 'Boo-hoo.'

Then he starts laughing.

I pick my phone up. I've been sitting here for two minutes. That's all.

'Fucking cops,' Grim says, looking serious again.

These sudden mood swings are another side effect of the medication, the staff at St Göran's tell me. But they don't know Grim like I do, and I'm not so sure. He's always been unpredictable. I read the most recent text he sent, the one I got earlier.

stop getting them to take the phones off me, can you come over?

'It didn't take long for you to sort out a new phone,' I say. Grim doesn't reply. I've suspected this for a while — he's got someone on the inside, someone he's managed to manipulate enough that they are prepared to smuggle in phones for him.

'What else do you have access to?'

'What do you mean?'

'You know what I mean.'

Grim smiles, feigning ignorance.

'Are you and Levin still not on good terms?' he asks.

'Me and Levin?'

'Yeah.'

'I think he's avoiding me.'

Grim stares at his palms, as though looking for instructions on what he should do next.

A little over six months ago, I hit rock bottom. To call it anything else would be skirting around it. I had shot dead a colleague on Gotland, in Visby harbour.

That's bad. I know.

His name was Markus, Markus Waltersson. That day still haunts me, and not only in my dreams. Sometimes I glimpse his face — a face in the crowd at a market or in an underground station.

The whole thing is now referred to as the Gotland affair and it became common knowledge, so I assume that providing the exact details won't be necessary. I was working at the department of Internal Affairs, and was then posted to Gotland on Superintendent Charles Levin's instructions. A consignment of weapons was due to change hands. IA were there, since the police operation relied heavily on informers, but something went wrong. Shooting broke out, I hit a colleague in the neck, and I was then suspended. That summer flew past in a haze of cigarettes, prescription drugs, and strong alcohol. They asked if I wanted to meet the family. I said no. I think he had a sister.

Then something happened. A woman was found dead in my apartment block; she had been shot. The person ultimately responsible was John Grimberg. Or Grim, as people called him. He had once been my closest friend.

Everything could be traced back to what had happened when I was sixteen. I was responsible for Grim's sister Julia's death. At least, that's how Grim saw it.

Julia's death started a chain of events that shattered the already dysfunctional Grimberg family and swept Grim to the edges of society, to its dark underbelly. He slowly managed to drag himself up, becoming someone else. He decided to go back to the beginning, where everything had started to go wrong. And that's where I came in.

I was going to lose something, just as Grim once had. I was going to lose Sam.

There is some kind of absurd logic to this that stayed with me for a long time afterwards; it might even still be there. At least part of the logic. It's possible that he used Sam to draw me in. Nobody really knows, perhaps not even Grim himself.

Exactly what happened on Gotland was never established, besides the fact that I had been stationed there by Levin as a fall guy if something went wrong. Levin had, in turn, been forced to do that by someone else, someone higher up. Secrets from his past were to be exposed if he didn't do as they said. What it was that would have come to light, I still don't know. Levin refuses to discuss it.

Grim knows all this. He has asked me, and I have answered. No lies.

'How does that feel?' Grim asks. 'That he's avoiding you?'

I put my phone away and notice the grey desktop, the distance between us growing.

'I don't know how it feels. Your turn. Why am I here?'

Grim's eyes dart around the room. He's now leaning forwards, with his back arched and his forearms resting on the edge of the table. Plit's bearded face is occasionally visible through the little round window in the door.

In two hours' time I'm meeting Sam, and I want to get home in time to have a shower and, with luck, if I've got time, a shave as well. I'm already hungry. Not only that, but someone is wandering around out there knowing that they've killed a sociologist, and if that isn't bad enough, I'm technically powerless to do anything about it. SEPO are now the only ones who can, and the thought of that is driving me up the wall. People have gone mad over less.

'I'm bored,' he says. 'I wanted a visit.'

Grim was always good at steering his body language and the signals he sent out — he could even use it to send whoever he was talking to barking up the wrong tree. It was a vital skill in the business he was in. But now something has happened. He'd been addicted to heroin a while back, but had then replaced it with a prescription substitute, which he bought on the black market. He can't do methadone any more, because it would clash with the drugs the hospital has put him on. That might be it. Grim is more open, more vulnerable.

I feel vibrations in my coat pocket. I take the phone out, and read the message, which is from Birck.

ME 737 was outside my place yesterday, and by the off-licence on klarabergsgatan just now as I came out. if you see it, it's SEPO.

ME 737. A number plate.

'Is that Sam?'

Grim smiles weakly. You can see his little dimples when he does that. They've always been there, and seeing them again makes my stomach tighten — a feeling that is almost like missing him.

'No. A colleague.'

A car had arrived at St Göran's just as I got out of the taxi. The car was then parked, its engine was switched off, and yet nobody got out. Is that what happened? It can't be the same car, but maybe they use several.

My eyes meet Grim's. Suddenly, he seems very old, a boy who has aged too fast and is now worn out.

'Why do you keep coming?'

'What do you mean?'

'What I said. Why do you come when I ask you to?'

It's a question I've been asked before. Not by Grim but by others — by Birck, Sam, even Mauritzon, who somehow knows about my visits and feels entitled to ask me about them. Everyone asks, puzzled and unsure, and I usually give them whatever answer is most true at that particular point in time. I need to find out what happened to the friend I once shared everything with, and the only way I can do so is to keep talking to Grim. Or, I feel guilty about what happened, and I go there as a kind of penance. The most far-fetched answer is the one I usually give my colleagues: Grim has committed dozens of crimes that he has never admitted to. I am trying, if possible, to get enough information out of him to solve those cases, perhaps even enough for a conviction.

None of my answers are lies, but nor are any of them completely true. What keeps me going back, time after time, is the same old thing, the intimate bond that exists between us. That connection

— despite me feeling more cautious, tenser in here than anywhere else — is what makes the visitors' room the one place where I can be myself. Nothing exists, apart from me and Grim and the chains around his wrists. Sometimes we sit in silence for hours, as though we need to be close to each other to survive — Grim in here, me out there. Other times, some nights, I find myself longing to be here. And I am ashamed of that.

That is an answer I've never given to anybody, and I never will, especially not to Grim. If he knew that he still had that kind of power over me, anything could happen.

'I've got nothing better to do,' I say. 'I have to do something, don't I?'

'That's not true.'

'But it's not a lie, either.'

Grim nods slowly.

'No Serax?'

'Eh?'

'You always take a Serax when you're here.'

'No I don't.'

'You do,' Grim says. 'But not today. Why not?'

'I'm trying to cut down.'

'How's that working out?'

'It's working,' I say, not sounding as convincing as I would have liked.

'And people think you've come off them? I mean, you're back on duty.'

'Something like that.'

'But you haven't.'

'No.'

It's just possible, for a second, to mistake his reaction for concern.

'If they find out …'

'I know.'

Grim's lips tighten to a narrow line, and he opens his mouth, hesitates, and then thinks better of it.

'Be careful,' he says.

'What do you mean?'

'If you get thrown out of the force, you're not just going to hole up in your flat. You'll end up in here.'

'Isn't that what you're after?'

Grim sighs, shaking his head.

'You know he was here, right?'

'Who?'

'Levin. I saw him in the corridor, on my way to lunch. He was with one of the other patients. I don't think I was supposed to see him. Well, no, I know I wasn't supposed to see him. He was very discreet. But he must have seen that I'd seen him ... you get me?'

'Yes. He's here, and you happened to see him. But how do you know he saw you?'

'Later on, I was sent out to one of the visiting rooms, and there he was.'

'Okay? And?'

'He wanted to talk to me — I think the phrase is "damage limitation". He wanted me to keep quiet. I got a phone for my trouble.' He smiles. 'But I have no obligations to anyone, other than you.'

'Who was he with?'

'A woman. Did you know about this, that he visits someone here?'

'No,' I say. 'I didn't.'

I wonder if it's true. Grim shrugs.

'I thought you might like to know.'

'Do you regret it?' I ask. 'What you did?'

His eyes flicker.

'To you?'

'Yes.'

I've wanted to ask this since I started coming to see him, after the verdict in October, when Grim was sent here. I did ask him the first time, but I didn't get an answer, just a snigger. Now it's different. The medicines have had an effect, and time has passed, although it's not even two months ago. That combination can have a strange effect on a person.

'No, I don't.'

That comes as a relief, oddly enough. If he had regretted it, it would be as though it had all been for nothing. Grim's posture has changed now, gone from an exhausted slump to a tense, spiky position, as though he's waiting for a chance to throw himself across the table and attack me.

'The fact that you're here,' I say. 'The fact that it was me who put you here. That it was me who made you fail. Has that made you hate me even more?'

'I never said I'd failed.'

'I can't see how sitting here,' I say, stretching my hands out, 'could be considered success.'

Grim doesn't answer. He just stares at me, perhaps to stump me. He takes every chance he gets to throw me off balance.

The problem is that it works. I do my best not to show him that I'm scared. Instead I ask him the real question, the one I still haven't got an answer to and that grinds at my temples on those sleepless nights.

'What were you trying to do?'

Grim doesn't answer, maybe because he doesn't want to reveal that, but maybe because he doesn't know what to say.

'Considering what you did to us, we deserve to know.'

'What I did?' Grim laughs, derisively. 'Considering what *I* did?'

'I have to go,' I say, standing up from my chair, drained. I realise that I have lost once again. 'Unless there is something else, I'll be off.'

'Are you meeting Sam?'

'Yes.'

'Are you going to tell her about this?'

I find myself standing over him, with my hands on the back of my chair.

'Yes.'

'You're not lying now?'

'No.' I move slowly towards the door. 'We'll be in touch.'

'Yes. I've got your number, of course.'

Grim laughs, and, for some reason, the corner of my mouth tugs upwards, and soon I'm laughing too, audibly. But no one could mistake that sound for happiness.

In reception, I take a Serax without thinking about it, just as I get a call from a number I don't recognise.

'This is Kele Valdez,' says a man's deep voice. 'From the University. I'm in Thomas's room at work.' He clears his throat. 'I'm sorry, it's …'

'Isn't that room cordoned off?'

'They were here doing the investigation yesterday, and this morning. They said they were finished, so I checked with Marika, Marika Frantzén, who you met, and then came in. I wanted to sit here and see … if I could find anything, something to help me understand. It's just mad, that he's gone.'

'And have you? Found anything?'

'No, and I do apologise for calling on a Saturday, but I was wondering about Thomas's Dictaphone.'

'His Dictaphone?'

'I should have mentioned it yesterday, but it didn't occur to me, because … well, I thought it was in here somewhere, but it isn't. So he must have had it with him. It's important that you don't listen to the interviews, or, if you have to listen to them, keep them secure.'

'I don't remember anything about a Dictaphone,' I say, picturing Mauritzon's hand-written note about the contents of Heber's rucksack. 'Can you describe it?'

'A small, dark-blue Olympus one, a few years old.'

'I'll get back to you.'

I head for the exit, and the sliding doors hiss open. The cold bites at my cheeks, and I button my coat, scouring the car park to see whether the car that arrived just after me is still there. I've forgotten where it was. A taxi is waiting on the turning circle, and I get in and slump into the back seat, which smells expensive and clean. The driver is a dark-skinned man with a photo stuck to his dashboard. The photo shows three children in a country that isn't Sweden, where the floor might be an earth-coloured rug. Or earth.

'Mäster Anders, on Pipersgatan,' I say, and pull my phone out again, to disturb Birck first, who sounds tired and irritated, and then Mauritzon.

Neither of them have any memory of a dark-blue Dictaphone. I contemplate ringing Olausson, but don't. Instead, I call Valdez, who is still sitting in his dead colleague's office.

'What did he keep on this Dictaphone?'

'His interviews.'

'And are they, er, meant to be stored like that?'

'No, not really. They're kept in a safe, here in the department. But … you suspect Thomas was on his way to do an interview when he died. A follow-up interview? At least, that's what it looked like in his last note, the one you showed me.'

'That's right.'

Valdez must be sitting completely still; there's no background noise whatsoever. I push the phone harder to my ear. Someone on the pavement throws a beer can into the road, causing the taxi-driver to swerve and to swear loudly.

'When you're doing this kind of interview, sometimes you want to remind yourself what happened in previous meetings — what's been said in earlier conversations with the same person. There can be long periods between interviews, so you want to avoid asking the same questions twice, that sort of thing. Thomas, I, and several others usually transfer earlier recordings and listen again, to refresh the memory. So the earlier interviews with this ... what was it ...'

'1599.'

'That's it. They were probably on the Dictaphone.'

Sam. There's something about her — something indefinable, huge. It's as though the molecular structure of the air changes as she walks into the restaurant. She has one hand, the one that now only has four fingers, in the pocket of her jacket, while the other one sways in time with her footsteps. Her nails are unpainted, and her skin is pale. When she finds me, sitting hunched at a table far from the entrance, half-hidden behind a thick pillar, she smiles, and it's that smile Sam gives people if she's not sure whether she knows them.

I brush aside thoughts of the dead sociologist, his missing Dictaphone, and 1599 — the case that is no longer ours — and straighten up. Outside Mäster Anders, darkness has fallen over Pipersgatan, and you can just hear the music coming from the speakers at low volume, someone singing *Sometimes I feel very sad*, again and again.

'Hi,' she says. 'I'm sorry I'm late.'

'You're not.'

'I know,' Sam says with a giggle, one hand winding her scarf from around her neck. 'Why do you say that? "Sorry I'm late," when you're not even late?'

'Because you've kept someone waiting?'

'Yes,' she says. 'It might be that. Sorry to have kept you waiting.'

'It's fine. You had no way of knowing I was going to be early.'

'No, exactly.'

Jesus. We're talking about nothing, and even that is excruciating. It's been like this since that day, in late summer, when Grim stood between us and nearly killed us both. It pulled Sam away from Ricky, her partner at the time, but it didn't bring her closer to me. She's lonely now, and you can tell. Her eyes are jumpy and quick, as though she's forgotten how to behave when out among people. Her eyes are green, but cloudy. The clarity they once had is gone, and their spark is missing.

At first she was just happy to be alive. Then she moved on, and blamed me for everything. She can't work as a tattooist anymore. Every time she looked at her hand, she was reminded of what I'd done to her, even though it was actually Grim who did it. I used to be the one ringing her, when I was high and alone and couldn't help telling her that I still missed her, still needed her. Recently, it's been Sam: the phone rings in the darkness, and it's her on the other end, sometimes screaming and crying, but mostly just silent. She was on medication in the beginning — strong drugs, the kind I wish I could get my hands on. After a while she stopped. She didn't want to be dependent on them just to function, she said. She's not that kind of person. She is, on the other hand, seeing a therapist, and she'll probably need to do that for some time to come.

I wonder if she knows that I can't cope without Serax. Maybe. I wonder what she'd say if I told her I'd thrown up at a crime scene the day before yesterday.

I drink from my glass, and Sam takes off her coat. Her other hand glides out of her pocket, and from the corner of my eye I spot the gap where her index finger used to be. But I don't look, more for my sake than hers.

'How are things?' she asks as she sits down. As she does so, a faint whiff of her perfume brushes past me, a scent that makes me remember the way things used to be.

'Good,' I answer, realising that I have nothing else to say. 'How about you?'

'Good,' she says, opening the menu with one hand and continues, without looking up, 'Have you met him today?'

'Who?'

'You know who I mean.'

'Ah-ha. No.'

'Does he still contact you?'

'Every day, pretty much. He always manages to get a message to me. He even sends texts — he's got hold of a phone.'

'Did you answer?'

'No,' I say, opening my own menu. 'I rang St Göran's, and got them to take the phone off him.'

This makes Sam laugh, a genuine laugh that reaches her eyes, making the skin around them crease lightly.

'Good,' she says.

Neither of us want it to be like last time, for it to end the way it did then. We're finding a way to make it work, but it's still very fragile. Whenever we're in each other's company, I'm only ever a sentence, perhaps just a word, away from losing her. At least that's how it feels. For the likes of us, the past is dangerous.

I want to touch her hand.

We order. Both of us drink water. Me because I mustn't mix with alcohol with Serax, and Sam because she's stopped drinking. On the road outside, between the dark outlines of buildings, a car passes, and its headlights illuminate an estate car parked outside the restaurant. Inside is a figure, sitting there in the darkness. That's as much as I can process before the first car passes by and the stationary one is in darkness once more. Well, that and the fact that the driver's face is looking at us, staring straight at me and Sam, as we're sitting there at our window table by the big pillar. It could be the car that pulled up at St Göran's.

'Leo?'

'Yes?'

'What is it?'

'Nothing.' I think I shake my head at this point, as though that might make the lie more convincing. 'I was thinking about something.'

'What were you thinking about?'

'That I've missed this.'

'Me too.'

She smiles, and looks away. When the food arrives and we're about to start eating, she fumbles with her knife, perhaps because of the finger that's no longer there. The knife falls to the floor.

'I'll get it,' I say.

'Don't worry,' Sam says as she bends down. 'I'm getting used to it.'

A car drives past the window, and this time I manage to read the letters on the parked car's number plate. WHO. Then the car is returned to darkness, the driver just a silhouette. It could be Goffman.

'Have you been to Salem recently?' she asks.

'Not for a while. I haven't had time.'

'Mm hmm,' Sam says, her mouth full of food.

'And,' I go on, 'I just can't face it. Partly because of what happened in the summer. It's as though ... everything comes flooding back. But partly ... it's tough seeing Dad.'

'He's not getting better?'

'If you've got Alzheimer's, you don't get better.' I drink some more water, and wish it was something stronger. 'So, no.'

'Shit.'

'My brother is there a lot. He probably can't really face it either, but he does it for my mum's sake. Micke always was mummy's boy. He was the oldest. I was my dad's instead. I think that might be why I'm finding it tougher, seeing him like that. Now he can't even remember how to change the batteries in a remote control.'

'But he,' Sam says, hesitantly. 'He does recognise you?'

'For now, yes. Most of the time. Sometimes, especially when

he's tired, he'll get me mixed up with Micke. But, then again, he always has.' I laugh.

Sam grasps her glass tightly and takes a swig.

'Are you still in touch with, what's his name, Ricky?'

'No.' Sam puts her glass down. 'No, not at all.'

'Do you miss him?'

She shakes her head.

'Not like I missed you.' Then, as though realising she's just revealed something significant, she says she needs to go to the loo, and stands up. 'Won't be a minute.'

Once she's gone, I pop a Serax out of the blister pack and spin it between my fingertips. It's comforting. After a few rotations, I put it back in my pocket. Outside the window, the car is still there. When it is lit up once again by a passing vehicle, this time a lorry, I manage to read the whole number plate: WHO 327. I eat another mouthful, drink some water, and I write the registration number in my phone and then send it to Birck.

I adjust myself in the chair. It's not easy to act normally when you know you're being watched.

where's the car right now? Birck sends back.

outside mäster anders, SEPO?

yes

you sure?

yes

Questions buzz around my head. If it's one of their bureaucratic pseudo-agents sitting in that car, it becomes, on one level at least, more understandable that they had us under surveillance even while Birck and I were still on the case. They are paranoid little sods, as everyone — including the general public — well knows. But now City have handed the case over, they should be happy with that. Is there a microphone, some kind of bugging device, close by? Have they been listening to my chat with Sam? I try to recall Goffman's movements in my office, strain to picture his hands and what they

124

might have got up to. Did he plant something when he was there? My coat? I pat down my coat, which is hanging in the back of my chair, and search the pockets and under the collar. Nothing. I think.

That's the problem with SEPO. Their paranoia is contagious. I sigh, and my gaze falls on my phone again. Could *that* be …

'Something important?' Sam asks as she eases back into the chair opposite me, making me look up.

I put the phone away.

'No, work, sort of.'

'You were on call the night before last, weren't you?'

'Yes.'

'I read about Döbelnsgatan in the paper.'

'We're not on that case anymore.' My gaze slides back towards the road outside, involuntarily. 'It's elsewhere in the building now.'

'You're doing it again,' she says.

'What?'

'Staring.' She looks at the street outside. 'What is it?'

'I don't know.'

'You know I've forgiven you, don't you? For what happened. You don't need to feel … whatever it is you're feeling. If you are, you don't need to any longer. It's okay. But I need … I just need some time.'

'That's great,' I say, cautiously. 'I understand that you need time.'

'You used to say that you would never make it without me. Is that still true?'

The question catches me off guard.

'Yes.'

'Same here.' She laughs. 'At least we've got that in common,' she says, and something unspeakably heavy and tragic lands between us, and for a long time we are silent.

'Do you really mean that?' I say. 'That you can't make it without me?'

'Yes.'

'Speak soon,' she says once we've left the restaurant.

The snow's started falling again, and the wind is blowing. The last chime rings from a bell tower somewhere. It is ten o'clock, and I can't find the black car. It's disappeared.

'Won't we?' Sam says.

'Eh?'

'Speak soon,' she says.

'Yes, maybe tomorrow?'

'Yes, maybe.' She bites her lip. 'It won't have to be like this forever, you do know that? It's just that now it's …'

'I understand,' I say, which probably isn't true, but me saying so makes her smile, again, and that feels good.

I walk her to the tube, hoping that the car might appear somewhere, but the only thing that comes is yet more snow, and when I slip on an icy patch it's Sam who helps me up, and that feels good, too.

As soon as I've said goodbye to her — a hug, nothing more — the tiredness crashes over me and I just need to get home, get home and get some sleep, I can't remember when I did that last. When something moves from the shadows along the streets of Kungsholmen, I shudder; I realise that I still can't tell what's real, and what's imagined.

Jonathan can't sleep. He's too jumpy; his nerves are too frayed. It might be down to tomorrow's demo. The alcohol won't have helped. Sometimes, when he's had a drink, it's as though his thoughts are spinning noisily round and round his head and he can't get them to stop, or make them quiet. They're not necessarily unpleasant or anxious thoughts, just ordinary everyday ones. He incessantly hops and dances between, from one to another, unable to slow down. Just like being on speed.

This time, though, his stomach churns.

As if that wasn't enough, the kitchen sofa he's lying on is so uncomfortable that the bare floor is beginning to look like a more attractive option. He can hear his leader snoring loudly in the bedroom, and despite that noise being steady and regular, it makes it impossible to sleep. He should have gone home anyway, like Christian, even though it is a long way from Enskede.

The kitchen table is next to the sofa, and the chief's MP3 player is lying on it, complete with little in-ear headphones. You can say what you like about the leader, but he certainly has good taste in music, and Jonathan has always found that listening to music helps you nod off. If nothing else, it should mask the sound of snoring if he plays it loud enough.

He leans on the armrest, pulls the player over and pops the earphones in, and presses 'Play'. The songs have weird titles, no words, just four-digit numbers. Maybe they went wrong when he synched with the computer? He picks one, curious to see which band the top man's been listening to.

But Jonathan doesn't hear music. Instead, he hears voices, a man and a woman, which makes him sit upright in the darkness and squint at the little screen.

Her: 'Hello.'
Him: 'Hello.'
Her: 'Have you got a fag?'
Him: 'No, sorry.'
Her: 'Shit. I'm all out.'
Him: 'We can go and buy some in a bit?'
Her: 'I'm … we shouldn't really be meeting like this.'
Him: 'Why not?'
Her: 'I have … I've been asking around, since we met last time, about what we talked about, and I think that some people think I've been a bit too curious, nosy. At times I've felt like I was being followed. It's not good for your research, what with all the confidentiality and all that, if we're seen together.'

Jonathan hasn't got a clue what they're talking about, but he keeps listening. Then the penny drops, and he realises what he's listening to, and suddenly he goes cold.

It's dark blue, the little player, and pretty worn. The blue has been worn off at the edges. He pulls out his phone and writes a text, just two sentences. He daren't write more.

by the swings at 8am. I've got something you need.

As soon as he's sent it, he leaves the flat. He can't stay — he needs to get out of there.

Hallunda, early Sunday morning. There's an old playground behind the shops. It's definitely seen better days — the fence is covered in graffiti tags, the swings hang wonkily on their chains, and the wooden rocking-horses are rotting away.

Two young men make their way towards the playground from opposite directions. They are surprisingly alike, in their looks and in their clothes. One has darker skin, and the other has a few more scars on his face, but otherwise there's nothing to tell them apart. They're both wearing dark jackets and light jeans, they both have cropped hair, and their movements suggest a reluctance to do whatever it is they're about to do: their hands stuffed deep in their pockets, heads down and eyes on the ground. One is coming from the underground station; the other, from the tall, pale high-rise blocks on Klövervägen.

And, even as an observer, you can almost taste it — the time that's passed since they were children, and everything that's happened along the way.

Hallunda, early morning. They meet. The man who came from the underground seems apprehensive. He keeps his hands in his pockets. It looks like the other guy is the one who's asked to meet. He's leading the conversation. They stand, an arm's length apart, and talk, surrounded by the silence. Before long, they're each sitting on a swing.

One of them pulls his hand from his coat pocket. In it is a small, dark-blue Dictaphone. In spite of the cold, a little bead of sweat has gathered on his narrow top-lip.

Day three. We no longer have an investigation, but the media don't yet seem to have grasped that fact. They're still naming Olausson as the prosecutor, although it's someone else now. Someone has leaked the news that there's only a handful of officers on the case, and an editorial column has expressed the broadsheet journalist's surprise at this information. She blames the decline of the Swedish Police and a reduction in resources, which doesn't make any sense whatsoever, because our resources have been significantly improved over the last ten years.

I keep myself to myself, hiding away in my office. I fill in the minutes of earlier meetings, print out interview transcripts, and write short reports on my movements since the start of the operation. In one note, I refer to the dead man's missing Dictaphone, and speculate that it may be in the hands of his assailant. Then I attach a copy of the fieldwork notes, despite the fact that I don't have permission to access them, and say that that's the only known copy, aside from the one on Heber's computer. It's now their problem. I then formally cease my involvement in the investigation into Thomas Heber's death, and send the lot over to SEPO. I do what's been asked of me. What I'm supposed to do.

There's a good boy.

Olausson's not around, and nor is anyone else. An invisible hand seems to have redirected all incoming emails surrounding Heber's death away from my account and into someone else's. So my inbox is quiet, apart from a message that seems to have evaded the invisible hand. This informs me that Heber's parents are coming to Stockholm today, to say farewell to their son. Chances are it won't mean anything, other than possibly for the parents. Sometimes parents are just that — nothing more.

I call Olausson, and I rack my brain for something to say as I listen to the ringing tone. I don't yet know what it is I want to find out, but something just isn't right. I'm not going to try to dupe him, and not because it would be wrong, but because it would be impossible. He won't be fooled. He's too clever, too reserved, too careful.

As with so much else in a police officer's life, this preparation turns out to be wasted, because Olausson doesn't even answer. A cold, automated voice instructs me to leave a message, and I'm about to, but after the beep it's my turn to speak and I just sit there in silence, staring at the uncomfortable wooden chair on the other side of my desk, unable to say anything. *Can't think of anything to think.*

I hang up. After a few minutes, maybe just one, I ring Oscar at Café Cairo. He doesn't answer either. Primarily to check that my phone is working — a thought that often strikes me when I ring several people and no one answers — I ring Birck. It rings for ages, and when he eventually does answer, he hisses his surname down the phone.

'Am I disturbing you?' I ask.

'What the fuck do you think?'

'What are you doing?'

'I was on call last night.'

'No you weren't.'

'Okay,' Birck says. 'I wasn't. I'm on the fucking job. Ring this afternoon.'

'Who are you fucking?'

Birck hangs up.

Just before lunch, there's a knock on the door. It's Olausson, the almost skeletal prosecutor, who pushes the door handle, breathing through his nose with that characteristic whistling sound.

'I've been trying to call,' I say.

'Handover go well?' He asks loudly, as though he hadn't heard me.

'I think so.'

'Good.'

'You knew all along, didn't you?'

Olausson lets go of the door handle, and takes two steps into the room. He notices the chair, and seems to be considering sitting on it before thinking better of the idea and staying on his feet.

'What do you mean?' he asks as he closes the door and crosses his arms, causing his expensive blazer to creak.

'That they were going to take over the investigation.'

'No, I had no idea about that.'

'Why are you lying?'

'If you're going to accuse me of lying, you can at least have the decency to look at me while you're doing it.'

I look up.

'If you're going to lead murder investigations that you know we're not going to be allowed to hold on to, you could at least be straight about it.'

'But I didn't know.'

'You and Goffman,' I say, 'were at law school together, at Stockholm University. A little more than twenty years later, you're hand-picked to join SEPO by Goffman himself. You stay there until you are thrown out after the failed police operation at the Gothenburg riots in 2001. Nothing, however, points to the two of you still being friends. Now, correct me if I'm wrong, but in fact the handling of this case suggests that on the contrary, you are actually very close.' I tap the papers on the desk. 'I've got my contacts in the building, too.'

Olausson is studying me with an inscrutable expression. It sounds like he's sighing, but I can't tell whether the situation is getting to him or not.

'Is it okay if I sit down?'

'At your own risk, apparently.'

Olausson slumps onto the chair, crossing one leg on top of the other.

'Christ. You wouldn't want to sit here for long.' He scratches the back of his hand, making a raspy sort of noise that is almost pleasant. 'What do you want me to say, Leo?'

'I want to know why the case was taken off us.'

'Because it contained certain threats to national security, which meant it was always going to end up with sepo.'

'National security?'

Olausson laughs out loud.

'Hardly.'

'What is it then?'

'I don't know. Paul and I are friends, not colleagues.'

'So you don't know any more?'

'I know exactly what I just said.'

He pulls a piece of paper from the inside pocket of his blazer and hands it to me.

'That's what I got.'

The paper is a formal request for the Thomas Heber case to be transferred from the City district's Violent Crimes Unit to the security services. I have seen them before. They bear the signature of the Security Police: a definite air of paranoia and secrecy, combined with an absurd form of patriotism. I make a note of the date. It is signed on the thirteenth, at half-past two in the morning, just hours after Heber's death.

As Birck and I were in Heber's apartment, trying our best not to fall out, someone at the security services had already worked out that this was a case for them.

Olausson stretches out his hand, and I fold the letter and give it back to him.

'Why didn't you say something? Why did you even let us start the investigation at all, if they were always going to take over?'

'That,' he says slowly, 'I'm afraid I can't answer, beyond that those were Goffman's orders. That really is as much as I know.'

It is always like this. We do the legwork and the hard graft, and then it's handed to them on a plate. It will look good in their statistics. It's never immediately clear which department has done what during the investigations, and only those keen enough to read the detailed reports ever find out the truth. And no one can be bothered with that. Internal criticism has come from some real heavyweights, who feel that SEPO, despite enormous resources, actually does very little in the way of field work. This is an easy way to keep everyone, including themselves, happy, since they can sit behind their desks and occupy themselves with the sorts of things that are too complicated for anyone beyond their corridors to understand.

I think about asking whether he's aware of the two SEPO cars that have shadowed our every move since the very beginning of the operation. Olausson's facial expression — smug, the look of a boss who has convinced his underlings that he can't be blamed for any of what's happened — persuades me not to bother.

'If anything else to do with this case should show up on your desk,' Olausson says, getting up from the chair, 'which it might well do, considering the delay in handing over and all the rest of it, then get in touch with me and hand it over, and I'll pass it on to Paul.'

'And what happens if I don't?'

'Oh,' Olausson says, 'you might well ask. But that vomit on Döbelnsgatan shouldn't be too difficult to test for certain substances

135

in your blood, or piss. Blood and piss are not hard to get hold of — a routine test would be sufficient. In your case,' he goes on, 'it would be perfectly reasonable for someone to request such a test, considering how recently you returned to duty, and the stress which you have already been exposed to.'

He pulls something from his pocket and drops a photo onto the desk.

The picture is taken from a distance, with a poor-quality digital camera, perhaps a mobile phone. It's the night before Lucia, in Vasastan. Incident tape flaps in the foreground, and a little way away, propped up against a wall, I spot myself, down on my knees and busy puking. My skin is pale pink, the strain of vomiting visible in my cheeks. The first thing that strikes me is how small I look.

The wind is knocked well and truly out of my sails. I hope he can't tell, but I'm sure he can.

'Do you understand me?'

'How did you get hold of this?' I ask.

'Do you understand me?' he repeats.

It's as though the colours in the photo are getting stronger, sharper, right in front of me.

'Yes.'

He opens the door.

'Good.'

Once he's gone, I rip the photo in half. Then I tear the halves in two, and again, into smaller and smaller pieces until they get so small it's difficult to hold them between my fingertips. I cannot stop.

The threat makes me groggy. I make my way out into the corridor, past the Christmas tree to the coffee machine. I wait there as it spits and splutters and prepares to fill my cup.

In the room opposite, a colleague is sitting with a few documents. Next to her, the televised annual Christmas serial plays on a monitor with the sound turned off. A man with a white beard, a paunch, and ruddy cheeks is lying comatose on a kitchen sofa, in a forest cabin. He's either drunk or delirious. This episode seems to alternate between his story and that of three children, two girls and a boy, as they hurry across a snowy landscape. Above the man is a ticking clock that presumably must have some significance.

I'm following the plot to avoid having to think, to deflect the craving for a Serax and something stronger, and to distract myself from the knowledge that the day I'm going to get caught is getting closer and closer. By the end of the episode, the kids have arrived at the cabin and are struggling to wake the man, without success.

The end-credits roll. My cup is ready. I return to my office. The seasonal programming takes me back to my childhood Christmases, the ones that always turn white when you think back but never actually were. I remember the smell of the candles and the Christmas tree, and the sound of Mum, standing in the closet and wrapping presents while my dad would entertain me and

Micke. For a moment, everything just washes over me again, and perhaps it's no coincidence that the phone starts ringing and the word SALEM is blinking on its screen.

'Hi Mum.'

'Er, hi Leo.'

The voice on the other end is deep and clear, serene — a voice I haven't heard for a long, long time.

'Hi, Dad.' I put my cup down. 'How ... how's it going?'

'Good, all good. We've just had breakfast.'

Mum cares for her husband as my dad's mum cared for hers, Arthur Junker, my grandfather, who was struck by the same illness. The fate of a family goes in cycles.

'You sound well,' I say.

'Oh yes, bloody well actually.'

'That's great.'

'What are you doing? I'm not disturbing you?'

'No, don't worry. I'm at work.'

'What would you like for Christmas?'

'I, oh, I don't know.'

My dad is with it, in a way he hasn't been for a very long time. How that could be possible, I have no idea, but the emotion is overwhelming.

'We thought we'd all chip in for a holiday for Micke,' he says now. 'He never gets away from work any more.'

'Okay. Yes, of course. How much should I put in?'

'Two thousand? Maybe three. Is that too much? Your mum and I were thinking we'd put in six, so altogether it would be eight or nine thousand. That's enough for a trip, or if he wants to go further afield he'd just need to put up another thousand or so himself.'

'But that's only enough if he goes on his own. Isn't he going to go with someone?'

'He's been saying how he'd like to travel on his own,' Dad says, determined.

'Okay.'

One day, I've got a dad who no longer knows how to flush a toilet, because he doesn't understand how it works. The next day, I've got a dad who doesn't use loo paper, but wipes himself with his towel instead. On the third day, as though the previous days have been distorted fragments of a dream, he's perfectly able to use a telephone and to do arithmetic.

'What do you think?' he says. 'Can you chip in?'

'Of course,' I say, again. 'Shall I take out some cash?'

'That's more fun than a voucher, don't you think? Cash is king. Isn't that right? Or is that just me being old-fashioned?'

'Saying cash is king isn't old-fashioned,' I reassure him.

Dad laughs.

'Are you coming down soon?'

'I ... yes. I'll try and come over before Christmas, otherwise I'll see you then.'

'Good. Your mum wants a word. Here she comes.'

I hear rustling and crackling before my mum's voice arrives.

'Mum, what was that? He sounds perfectly n—'

'I know, love, I know.'

I notice that I'm holding my breath.

'What does this mean?'

'Not a lot. He's like this sometimes, little bursts.' She lowers her voice. 'It's been ... I think he can tell when he's slipping again. That's why he put me on now, he doesn't want you to hear.'

'Why haven't you mentioned this?'

'You make it sound like a conspiracy. I just didn't want to get your hopes up, do you understand?

'And you wouldn't be,' I say.

'I can tell that you're not telling the truth, you know that.'

We carry on talking, but she soon sounds distracted, perhaps because Dad is nearby, fiddling with the vacuum cleaner. It sounds as though he's decided it's not working and he's going to fix it.

'I'm going to have to give him a hand,' she says. 'But I'll be in touch, about Micke's present?'

'Yep,' I say. 'Speak soon.'

Everything's back to normal.

Sitting up here, I feel so far removed from the world down below, it could go to pieces, and no one within these walls would even notice. I think about the photo I tore up, a photo that I will never so much as name for anyone.

My computer bleeps — it's a feed from the intranet. A demonstration in Rålambshov Park is just getting underway. Far-left activists are protesting against the deportation of asylum-seekers and refugees, whilst the far right are demonstrating against the left-wing demonstration. There's a significant risk of clashes, so the police are there in numbers.

My phone rings again.

'Are you finished?'

'You should probably come to my place,' Birck says.

'Why? And where do you live?'

'Lützengatan 10, fourth floor. I have someone in my hall claiming to be 1599. And I think she's telling the truth.'

Lützengatan is located in an understated upper-class neighbourhood, behind Karlaplan's great plaza. These blocks have the lowest reported crime-rates in the city, but the truth is probably that there's just as much crime here as anywhere else. Everyone knows this, but everyone keeps quiet, because no one wants to lose face.

The street is paved with cobblestones, fanning out in a classic pattern and ending in a neat turning circle. The taxi comes to a stop and I climb out, to the strains of the radio and the accompanying taxi-driver, both singing *Who's got a beard that's long and white? Who comes around on a special night?* in a strained, excitable, never-ending polka.

Further down Lützengatan, at the corner where the little strip of cobbles meets Wittstocksgatan, a dark-coloured Volvo is parked, and silhouettes are visible inside. I light a cigarette and try to decipher the number plate, but the angle at which the car is parked makes this impossible.

Santa's got a beard that's long and white! Santa comes around on a special night!

I get my card back, and the sound of the polka is suffocated as I close the car door. The taxi rolls off. I take a drag, and the cold makes me shudder.

Many people's homes will tell you something about their occupants, but Gabriel Birck's apartment isn't one of them. It is large, with high ceilings, yet somehow it still seems small. Its many doors, cubbyholes, and nooks and crannies make it easy to get lost in. The flat contains very few books, but plenty of films, DVD box-sets, and paintings. None of the furniture is from IKEA, apart from the kitchen. The IKEA sticker is still there, on the inside of the cupboard door I open in search of a cup. The mug is blue, and features the Moderate Party emblem, and yet there are various pamphlets and flyers from a public meeting arranged by Feminist Initiative lying in the hallway. On one wall in the kitchen there's a large photo of Twiggy, androgynous and symmetrical. On a worktop near the window is a pair of small speakers, playing music from Birck's phone at low volume.

Above the sofa are twenty, thirty, maybe more, photos in black frames and varying sizes. They're not arranged in a neat pattern but untidily, in a sort of collage. Some of the images depict children. Most of them feature men and women, and in some cases something unclassifiable in-between. Birck himself is not present in a single picture. These might be photos of his friends and family, but they might just as easily be complete strangers.

And sitting underneath the pictures is a woman. She has her hands in her lap and is constantly interlacing and then separating them, looking at us and then looking at the glass coffee table in front of her, where a dark-blue Dictaphone is lying.

I put the cup in front of her, take the jug, and fill her cup about half full.

'A bit more, please.'

She takes a swig. I sit down in the armchair next to the sofa and wait. Birck is sitting in the other armchair, one leg on top of the other, and with a glass of water in his hand. The water is so cold that condensation has gathered on the glass. He's wearing a white vest, grey tracksuit bottoms with Armani written along the thigh, and, as far as I could tell when he opened the door, no underwear. His hair is wet and tousled, and he smells of shower gel. The woman is short, and her hairstyle reminds me of Twiggy's in the picture in the kitchen, scraped into a strict side-parting. She has big eyes and a small mouth, and freckles that spread from her nose and underneath her eyes. She's wearing black jeans, cherry-red boots, and a thick, knitted jumper, and she doesn't look the type to stick a knife in someone's back, but then you never know these days. She puts the cup down.

'How ...' I say, before changing my mind. 'You are 1599.'

'Yes.'

'What's your name?'

'Lisa Swedberg.'

'With V or W?'

'W.'

'You were at Cairo the day before yesterday, when I was there. You're the one who left.'

'Yes.'

'Why did you leave?'

She doesn't answer straightaway. She drinks a bit more coffee, tapping thoughtfully on the cup. Her nails are short, and painted the same colour as her boots.

'I was scared.'

'What made you scared?'

'It ... everything. I didn't want to see ...'

She doesn't finish her sentence. Birck drinks some water. Watery sunlight shines through the small panes that make up the large window. I feel like another cigarette.

'What are you doing here?' I ask.

'I saw him the day before yesterday, as I was leaving.' She looks from Birck to me, as though she needed to explain herself. 'Gabriel, outside Cairo. I saw the number plate, and checked it with the licensing authority — you can do that on your phone. I got his name and then checked on www.eniro.se. There aren't that many Gabriel Bircks in Stockholm.'

'Impressive,' Birck says. 'Don't you think?'

'Yes, but I thought that car was registered to both of us?'

'My car is my car,' Birck says.

'But why?' I say and turn to her.

'Why what?'

'Why did you want to trace us?'

'It's … I …' She looks surprised to see the cup next to the Dictaphone, as though she thought she still had it in her hand. She grips the handle again, carefully. 'I really don't know where to start. No one knows I'm here. Everyone's at the demo in Rålambshov Park. That's why I came now, so that no one could follow me.'

'Won't you be missed, at the demo?'

She shakes her head.

'I said I was ill.'

'You knew Thomas,' I say. 'You were one of his subjects.'

'Yes.'

'What does that actually mean?'

'Haven't you worked that out yet?'

'We'd still like to hear it from you.'

She adjusts her fringe with two fingers.

'He asked me about stuff, for his research.'

'How did he get in touch with you?'

'Someone I know, who he'd also interviewed, had apparently given Thomas my name. I can't be reached by phone or email or anything like that, but he asked around and managed to find me.'

'Did you know who he was?'

'I knew of him. He used to be a big player in AFA. AFA doesn't have formal power structures, but I know he was big. That he was important to them, when he was involved.'

'When did you first meet?'

'Some time in March.'

'Where?'

'At a café. Not Cairo, another one. It's on Vanadisvägen, near ...'

She goes quiet.

'Near his home?' Birck fills in.

'Yes.'

'Did he tell you that, that he lived nearby?'

'No. No, he didn't.'

'Well, then, how do you know where he lived?'

'I checked him out. A couple of days later, I went back to his place and slept with him.'

Birck isn't surprised. I am. Maybe that's why 1599, or Lisa Swedberg, is so absent from his notes, despite her apparent importance. It must be an ethical quandary to be sleeping with one of your interview subjects. He might have wanted to make sure that nobody would find out, if the notes were to fall into the wrong hands.

We had the impression that Heber was alone, surprisingly alone. And it seems that he was, yet Lisa's eyes have become slightly moist, bearing out Grim's theory. Everybody is missed by someone.

She blinks deliberately. Out in the kitchen, a warm voice sings, 'It's beginning to look a lot like Christmas, everywhere you go.'

Lisa turns to Birck.

'I thought you said you didn't like Christmas songs?'

'But everyone likes Johnny Mathis, surely?'

'Okay,' I say. 'One thing at a time. You started a relationship with him, then?'

'No, that's the wrong word. At least to describe the beginning. It was more of a … an impulse.'

'But it gradually became a relationship?'

'Yes. By some point in April it had become that, if you can even call what we had a relationship. We kept it quiet because he, Thomas, had to. I understood why, but it was still tough. We pretty much only ever met as his place, apart from when we went to the cinema, or some obscure club that he dared to go to with me.'

She laughs, wistfully. My phone starts vibrating, which makes Lisa go quiet. It's Sam. I reject the call.

'Sorry,' I say. 'Go on.'

'I don't really know what to say. It wasn't exactly a high-intensity relationship, if that's the word we're using — well, actually it was, but it went in waves. Do you know what I mean? When we did see each other, we'd see each other quite a lot. Sometimes straight after an interview. He did several with me — I think five, maybe six

146

altogether. There were a few of his subjects who he used that way, like keys. When he'd thought of something new, or come across new leads in other interviews, he would then come back to me and ask about them. I haven't studied much sociology, but Thomas explained that interview-based research often works that way. To begin with, I thought he was just saying it so that he could see me again. That's how big my ego is. But, gradually, I realised it wasn't that. Well, at least not the only reason.

'Did you notice straightaway, the first time?' Birck asks. 'That he was attracted to you?'

'I noticed … I don't know. Thomas was difficult, or rather he was good. He could make you feel comfortable, safe, and listened to. But then that's what an interviewer should do. I found it difficult, at first, to work out whether he was attracted to me or whether his interest was purely professional. I thought there was something there. And after the second interview I knew I had been right about that.'

'How did you know?'

'You just do. It's just there, between the lines.'

She goes quiet for a moment, before taking up the story again. Neither of us say anything. I wonder whether she's lost it.

'Sometimes a month would go by without any contact, and then he'd get in touch and ask if we could do another interview, that new information had come to light which he needed to talk about, and then we'd meet, and everything would just blow up again, intensive as hell for a couple of weeks, and then it would die down again.'

'How did you feel about that?' Birck says. 'Would you have preferred to have met more regularly?'

'No,' she says. 'That kind of relationship suits me. I don't need much — I prefer my own company. A lot of men are quite simply useless, but a few are good at a couple of things that I like. One is having sex. Another is talking politics. Thomas was good at both.

'Thomas kept it to himself,' Birck says, 'your relationship. Did you?'

'Yes.'

'How long was it going on like this?'

'Until ... well until Thursday, I suppose.'

Birck leans forward, his elbows resting on his thighs.

'Okay. Tell us what happened.'

'That night?'

'Yes.'

'We'd arranged to meet ... a place where we often meet up, or used to. An alley off Döbelnsgatan. A friend of mine lives round the corner, and I sleep over sometimes. That's when we'll meet there, me and Thomas, outside the gate, and then walk back to his place. But this time we'd said we'd meet in the yard.'

'Had you done that before?'

'No.'

'So why did you decide to this time?'

'It just turned out that way.' She hesitates. 'I was scared.'

'What were you afraid of?'

'I stood behind the bins,' she continues, as though she hasn't heard Birck's question. 'They were lined up against one wall. I was waiting for Thomas to come round the corner. I stayed there until I heard footsteps. Then it occurred to me that it might not be Thomas, and I wanted to make sure it was him. I could see his profile, from where I was standing, and I could see that he was looking for me, that he hadn't seen me. He took his gloves off and put them in his pocket, and I started walking over, but at that moment I heard something that scared me, made me back away —scurrying footsteps coming rapidly down the alley. And before I knew what was happening, he collapsed onto the ground. My field of vision, or whatever you call it, was blocked by one of the bins, and I didn't dare move, so all I could see was Thomas's face. He'd fallen on his back, and then someone was rifling through his

148

pockets. I didn't even have time to ... he never even saw me.'

'How do you know this person was going through his pockets?' Birck asks.

'I could see his coat was being pulled and tugged at.'

This detail in Lisa's story makes her go stiff, and then stare fixedly at Birck's table, her lips strained and tight. It's always the unexpected details that hit hardest. I know that better than most.

'Then what happened?'

'I heard the rucksack being picked up, the sound of the zip, and someone rooting around in it.'

'And then?' I ask.

'He or she left. I remember being surprised, because I was sure that whoever it was had seen me, and that I'd be next. But he or she made off. I must have been in shock, because my heart was pounding so hard and so fast. I came out from behind the bins and went to see ... I was really terrified ... I was so shocked. I crouched over him and tried to see if he was still breathing. He wasn't. He might not have been dead yet, but ... sometimes you just know it's too late. This might sound strange, but this feeling just came over me ... I couldn't bear to look at him.'

'What did you do next?' Birck asks.

'I said goodbye, without touching him. I was worried that I might leave some trace on him if I did. I didn't want that. I got out of there as fast as I could, and went and called the police.'

'You dialled 112.'

'Yes.'

'And what did you say to them?'

'Haven't you heard it? Those calls are all recorded, aren't they?'

'We haven't listened to it yet,' says Birck.

We had requested the recording, but it hadn't arrived by the time SEPO took the case from us.

'I said that a person had been stabbed, and gave them the address. That was it.'

'Did you disguise your voice?'

'I did my best — I tried to make it a bit deeper.'

'Why did you do that?'

'I didn't want ... I can't ...'

Lisa studies her hands. They are beautiful, clean, the sort of hands that have never had to work to ensure the survival of their owner.

'The assailant,' I say. 'You didn't see him?'

'No, I couldn't even say if it was a man.'

'It takes a fair bit of strength to push a knife into someone like that.'

'Like, women couldn't do it?'

'Yes, sure,' I say, 'they could. But it's far more unusual. What were they after? In his clothes, his rucksack, what were they looking for?'

'That,' she says.

'The Dictaphone? How do you know?'

'Once you've heard the tape, you'll understand. Even if it's not completely accurate, I ... I don't know anymore. I'm so bloody torn.'

'Tell us,' Birck prompts. 'We're going to listen to it later, but you tell us first.'

'I ... I can't.'

'How did you get hold of it?' I say instead.

'Someone gave it to me.'

'The attacker?'

She doesn't answer. Instead, she reaches over and turns it on. The Dictaphone responds with a gentle beep, and the little screen lights up.

She holds it out, towards Birck.

'I haven't had it very long — I only got hold of it this morning. The files are named after people, or his subject number. So the first interview with me is called 1599. The second is 15992, the third, 15993, and so on.

'One more thing,' Birck says slowly, not taking the Dictaphone. 'You know that we're no longer running the investigation into Thomas's death? That the security police have already taken over?'

'I know that. They've already been on to me.'

'What did you say to them?'

She lowers her outstretched hand, and strokes the Dictaphone with her thumb, as if she were cleaning it.

'I've ... SEPO, they never leave us alone. They're so fucking paranoid, they just see terrorists everywhere they look. Like us. You get blacklisted, just because you're struggling for something that they don't agree with. They're fascists, hardly better than the neo-Nazis. So they didn't get a lot out of me. I want his ... I want Thomas's death to get solved, but I don't trust SEPO at all. They called him a pseudo-scientist and a secret terrorist. See what I mean? He was an award-winning international sociologist, for fuck's sake.'

'Who's we?' I say. 'You said "they never leave *us* alone."'

'Oh, I mean the anarchist movement, everyone who has a copy of *The Coming Insurrection,* or any books like that, really. I've heard that they do checks on anyone who buys it and pays with a card. They can trace it that way. It's crazy. And then, of course, there are parts of the anarchist movement who do use violence in the struggle against fascism. It's a form of self-defence. But then the movement also includes animal-rights activists, syndicalists and feminists, anti-fascists who have never used violence.'

'What was the SEPO officer's name, the one you spoke to?'

'Goffman, something. And there was another one — there were two of them. A woman, called Berg, I think. No, Berger.'

'Who gave you the Dictaphone?' Birck attempts.

'I can't say.'

'Are you protecting someone?'

'The person I got it from hasn't heard any of it, I know that much.'

151

No one knows what to say next. Lisa drinks a bit more coffee.

'Radical Anti-Fascism,' I say slowly. 'What is that?'

'Haven't you got Google on your phone?' she asks.

'I have indeed, but the only thing about it on the internet, as far as I can tell, is a homepage with the logo on it — a front that leads nowhere.'

Lisa leans back on the sofa.

'We're not an organisation, even if that's what the media and the police call us. That makes me mad, because the thing about an organisation is that it has a hierarchical structure, with superiors and their subordinates. We oppose the very idea of hierarchy. Radical anti-fascism is more of a network. We're part of the anarchist movement, struggling against fascism and oppression, above all against white-power movements like Swedish Resistance.'

'And your struggle sometimes gets expressed through criminality,' I say. 'Have I got the right idea?'

'That's what you define it as. We believe that it isn't possible to fight fascism through purely legal means, in a society that has inherent fascist tendencies. It's no different to Rentokill treating insect infestations. We …'

'Okay, okay,' I say.

'This is exactly what I'm talking about,' Lisa says, sharply. 'You don't see anything beyond your little, little cop-world. You don't see the oppression going on out there, day in and day out.'

'What I'd like to know,' Birck says, 'is what the difference is between RAF-W and RAF-B? Are they separate movements?'

'No, one and the same. They're called that after the way movements usually act on demos, in a white bloc and a black bloc. The white bloc are the ones who like to avoid conflict, but who can turn to violence if it becomes necessary. The black bloc are the ones who have a more violent nature, who are always ready for confrontation. I think I'm right in saying that they were SEPO's names, named after an earlier organisation where the less violent members wore white, and the rest didn't. But then gradually it became a more general description of how the groups split into different blocs. RAF-W and RAF-B are not names we use about ourselves, but Thomas used them to categorise his interviewees. For us it's a strange distinction, because everyone in RAF is prepared to use physical force to defend themselves in the struggle against fascism.'

'I've been thinking,' I say, 'how … you said that you'd arranged to meet that evening. That's right, isn't it?'

'Yes. It was nearly always Thomas who contacted me, usually when some new pattern or theory cropped up in his research. It was him this time, too.'

'You said that you were scared,' Birck says. 'Why were you scared?'

'I … I can't …' she replies, and turns her gaze away, and you can almost feel them, those words waiting just on the tip of her tongue, yet something is stopping them.

We should be going at her harder, we should be a bit tougher, but the risk then is that she'll clam up instead.

'In the notes that Thomas wrote about his field work,' I say, 'he described his research and his interviews.'

Her look reminds me of someone who has just found out about their partner's infidelity.

'You didn't know he was making them,' Birck says.

'No.'

'Apparently it's not exactly unusual for researchers to do so, but …'

'Have you read them?'

'Yes,' I say.

'Can I see them? Have you got them here?'

I shake my head.

'When SEPO took over, they got all the material.'

She studies my face for a long time.

'Okay,' she says, as though she's decided that I'm telling the truth. 'Shame. I would've liked to read them. Did he write anything about me?'

'Yes,' Birck says. 'But not your name, and nothing about your relationship. He refers to you as 1599.'

'In them,' I continue, 'towards the end, he mentions that you had told him something. That was late November, I think. He wrote that you had contacted him, because you wanted to meet up.'

Lisa doesn't say anything, but nods faintly.

'A week or so later, he writes again, but this time nothing more than that he feels torn by what you told him. He doesn't write what it was.' I hold my breath. 'What was it you told him?'

'I … it was about … I can't say it, because I don't even know if it's still true.'

'Was it about his own death?' Birck asks. 'Did you know that someone was going to kill him?'

'Oh God no!' she says, in a tone that makes you expect her to get up and leave. 'I had no idea about that … there was no threat to his safety, no, it was nothing like that.'

'There was no threat to his safety,' Birck says, 'but there was a threat against someone else? Is that what you mean?'

She doesn't respond.

'Right then,' I say, calmly. 'You're named in his notes, and it also says that you talked about something. He also names another interviewee, 1601.' I try to read her reaction, but it's difficult. I don't think she recognises that number. 'We believe,' I continue, 'that 1601 gave him information about the same event, but that the information 1601 gave didn't tally with what you told him. Maybe what you'd said wasn't altogether accurate.'

Lisa is observing us with her mouth half-open. It's impossible to tell whether or not she knew about this. She might be surprised to hear it — it might be news to her. Or she might be surprised that we know.

'Okay,' she says, eventually.

'You don't recognise the number, 1601? You never talked about it?'

'No, never.'

'Is there anything … in your social sphere, or whatever you call it,' Birck says. 'Are there rumours about something that's about to happen?'

No answer.

'Okay. I'll take that as a yes. Are there different versions of this rumour? Or is it about two or more different things?'

'I …' She hesitates.

'Explain,' Birck persists.

She shakes her head.

'I can't.'

'Why not?'

'It …'

'It's a person,' I say. 'Who is under threat?'

She nods weakly.

'Who?' I say. 'Who is it? You really should be helping us, Lisa.'

She gives me a sharp stare. My words came out sharper, more accusatory than I intended.

'Why the hell do you think I'm sitting here?'

'I …' I start, but there's a beep, and Lisa pulls out her phone and reads the text message.

'Oh Jesus.' She gets up from the sofa. 'I've got to go.'

'Now? You can't go now.'

'I have to.'

She starts getting her stuff together.

'Please, sit down.' Birck says.

'I can't. Something has happened in Rålambshov Park. One of my friends has been hurt. Listen to that,' she says, looking at the Dictaphone before she hurriedly makes for the door. 'Don't give it to Goffman.'

'How do we find you, if we need to talk to you again?'

She gives an address in Bandhagen as she passes by, without even slowing down. I rush to write it down. She opens the door, and in an instant Lisa Swedberg is gone, and it's as though she's never been here.

During the counter-demonstration, Jonathan ends up near one of the trees. He's wearing a hoodie. That's all he needs to withstand the cold — the adrenalin coursing through his veins combined with amphetamine takes care of the rest.

He's holding a flare in one hand, a knuckleduster in the other. There are so many people, everything's a blur. He chucks the flare towards a nearby cop. It lands close to his shoe, smoking and sparking. The cop's colleague must have noticed it, because the next minute someone attacks Jonathan from the left. An unsheathed truncheon crashes into his forearm, causing him to groan loudly.

Jonathan turns around. For some reason, this cop isn't wearing a helmet. It's lying on the ground between them. The truncheon swings in again. Jonathan defends himself, and the second blow crashes against his shoulder. It feels like something's been dislocated. He takes yet another blow. He swings the knuckleduster in front of him, but it slams into the shield, mute and futile.

Someone comes running over and pushes both palms hard in the cop's back. The shove takes him by surprise, making him lose control. Jonathan steps to one side to avoid the collapsing cop, who slumps to the ground.

Ebi is standing just in front of him. He's wearing the same clothes he had on when they saw each other in Hallunda, but now he's wearing a mask, too. Jonathan recognises his childhood friend's eyes. Ebi rushes over to the policeman and pushes him against the tree, making him drop his truncheon.

'Fascist bastard!' Ebi hisses. 'Fuck off!'

Jonathan should've seen it, the fear in the cop's eyes, how his free hand was heading for his holster. In a flash, the cop is holding it in his hand. Ebi lets go too late. The cop's face is white with panic.

As the shot rings out and Ebi falls to the ground, Jonathan can't do anything. He can't even get down on his knees next to him. He wants to so badly, but it cannot be done. Everything would come out.

The tears that force their way from the corners of his eyes are hidden by his mask.

Christian doesn't see it happen. He's there, a couple of metres away, but he doesn't see it.

The smoke from the flares envelops the missiles, the struggling, the shouting and screaming, which mixes in turn with the sound of his own heartbeat. From the corner of his eye, he sees two policemen, armed with batons and shields, throwing themselves onto one of his friends.

A policeman stands pressed against one of the trees, and somehow his helmet has come off and is lying there on the ground. The policeman is holding his shield so close to his face that his breath condenses on it. Christian recognises Jonathan. There's another man with him.

Christian turns around, and that's when a shot goes off behind his back. Everything stops, and Christian turns his head. The other man is lying on the ground. The body is convulsing wildly. Jonathan is staring down at him.

The man on the ground has only one eye.

This is what they say, but no one knows for sure. A riot-policeman in Rålambshov Park with a twitchy trigger-finger somehow succeeded in shooting one of the demonstrators in the eye. The policeman started panicking when he was surrounded and then attacked by demonstrators. And when people with weapons start to panic, it always ends badly.

Those taking part in the demo were primarily Radical Anti-Fascism and Swedish Resistance. Their flyers are strewn over the snow. There are several casualties, men and women from both camps, with forearms and legs bandaged, and large dressings across cheeks and foreheads. A handful of police appear to have suffered grazing. The grubby snow is flecked with blood, spent fireworks, and the remnants of flares.

It is absolute chaos.

The smoke has dissipated, but the strong smell remains. Rows of ambulances stand waiting, and emergency-services personnel are busy patching up demonstrators, whilst police keep a close eye on them, and the media observe and record the whole scene. Beyond them are rows of terrified members of the public. Lisa Swedberg is in there somewhere.

Birck and I wait on the other side of the park, far enough away to make us spectators.

'You see that?'

'I can see,' says Birck.

Lying there on the dirty snow is a RAF flag — red, white, and black.

'Do you really think he's been shot in the eye?' I say.

'Wherever it was, there's going to be a big fucking fuss. Do you remember Gothenburg 2001?'

'I was twenty-one.'

Birck looks puzzled.

'Yes?'

'It was during my training.'

'Didn't they talk about it?'

'I'm sure they did. But not in front of me.'

Birck turns around.

'And this little tail the whole time.' He raises his hand, waves, and smiles at the dark-blue Volvo parked on the verge. 'They're not even trying to hide it anymore.'

I feel the Dictaphone in my coat pocket, and wonder what is waiting on it.

'They know about us meeting Lisa,' Birck says.

'You mean SEPO know?'

'Yes. We should've told her.'

'We didn't get the chance. We should have pushed her a bit more, though, tried to keep her there.'

'Detain an anti-fascist who hates the police?'

An ambulance is moving through the park, with no sirens but with blue lights on to ease its passage through the mass of people. The crowd parts, reluctantly. A little way away, a flyer is flapping in the wind, and several identical flyers lie scattered around. Birck takes two steps forward, picks one up, and I read it over his shoulder:

Swedish culture is now in a critical condition. Our Nordic region has been invaded by foreign races over the last few decades, just as politicians and the media have frantically encouraged us to be tolerant, to accept racial and cultural integration. Every race and culture has the power to shape its own destiny, and thus the right and the duty to defend itself. We have been forced to accept a devastating occupation, and our corrupt politicians have used all their efforts to make sure that disapproval and resistance are categorised as somehow illegal. Our hands are tied, and the disciples of multiculturalism fight to silence our voices too. Desperate times call for drastic solutions. It is our responsibility to break free, to fight back. We must not fall silent. We must ensure the survival of our people and a future for our Swedish children.

At the top of the little flyer is the message: JOIN THE SWEDISH RESISTANCE — JOIN THE STRUGGLE FOR SWEDEN.

'What do you reckon?' Birck smiles. 'Fancy it?'

He drops the flyer to the ground.

'What she was saying about the night of the murder,' I say, meaning Lisa Swedberg, 'tallies with John Thyrell's witness statement. Not bad, considering he's six years old.'

'Shame there's no suspect. That we know of. Then we would have been able to show John a picture and really put him on the spot.'

'I don't think he saw that much,' I say. 'Not from that distance. What he noticed was someone rooting around in Heber's rucksack. I'm guessing he didn't get a good look at the face. Not only that, it was dark as a coal shed in that yard. It's a wonder he could see anything at all.'

Add to that the fact that this was several days ago, and time makes children's memories even less reliable.

'But still,' Birck says. 'Worth a try.'

'Sure. If SEPO actually had anyone to try it with.'

'They might.'

'Who might that be then?'

'Fuck knows.' Birck looks sullen. 'Fucking mess.'

We hang around the park for a while, and my thoughts drift off. I feel pessimistic and lethargic.

In the throng at the far end of the park, Lisa Swedberg flashes past. She has her hands in her pockets, but it's probably not because of the cold. A tall, thickset man is standing next to her, telling her something. It is Oscar Svedenhag. She seems increasingly resolute, and eventually she turns and walks off, briskly. I observe what's happening, but it doesn't register. I'm somewhere else.

'Oi. Hello …'

'Yes?'

'I asked if we should get going. What's wrong?'

'What do you mean what's wrong?'

'You look wrecked. Is everything okay?'

For a long time, I say nothing. Sirens wail. We head back to the car.

'Olausson threatened me.'

'What?'

'If I stick my nose in to the Heber case, I'll be suspended. He thinks I'm still taking Serax.'

'Fucking hell. But then … you are still taking them.'

'It's other things as well,' I say, to change the subject.

'Such as?'

I manage to get hold of a Serax in my pocket. I grip it between my fingers. I think about Dad, about his voice.

'No, nothing. I think I'm just a bit confused.'

Birck unlocks the car. I let go of the little pill, even though the urge is stronger than it's been all day.

We drive away from Rålambshov Park, and the black Volvo follows us, a couple of car-lengths behind. I pull the Dictaphone from my pocket and hand it to Birck.

Dusk is falling. Somewhere in the swarm around Kungsholm Square, the Volvo loses us, and Birck looks pleased with himself, turning on the radio. A Christmas carol has just been interrupted for an update on the events in Rålambshov Park.

'Did you know it was Sunday today?'

Birck laughs.

'What difference does it make what day it is?'

My phone rings. That bastard phone.

It's Birck. I should answer, but I don't want to and I can't, because Sam's waiting at the door. It's evening, and in the flat next to mine you can hear voices, people talking over each other, roaring and laughing. It makes me think of something approaching happiness.

'I've been trying to get hold of you all day,' she says.

'You've rung twice.'

'Can I come in?'

I move to one side and she goes past me, into the hall. She sweeps a scent in with her, a mixture of Sam and the December evening outside, which makes me think of the days when we shared a home. Apart from that last year, they were good times — perhaps the happiest times of my life.

She has unbuttoned her coat, but her handbag is still on her shoulder.

'Can I stay over?'

'Yes.'

'I don't want to sleep alone.'

'I said yes.'

'But I don't want to if you don't want to. You're always saying yes to things you don't want to do.'

I close the door.

'I want you to stay over,' I say, and I stretch out my arm to take her coat and hang it on a hook, and it feels like she has finally come home.

That is what Sam's scent brings with her into the flat, the smell of hope. But it was a long time ago now, yes darling, an eternity, an eternity that has passed and will never come back. Only fools and children think that everything can be fixed.

you really should listen to this

Birck is talking about the Dictaphone. I wonder what's on there. I'm sitting, phone in hand, with Sam's head on my shoulder. She's asleep. The flickering light around us is coming from the film, where Jane Russell and Marilyn Monroe are somewhere, surrounded by men with well-groomed hairstyles and expensive suits, and Jane Russell sings *bye bye baby, remember you're my baby when they give you the eye.*

tomorrow, I reply. *sam's here*

Birck doesn't send an answer, and I'm glad about that. It took a long time for her to get to sleep, and she's a light sleeper — always has been. Carefully, I put my lips to her hair, and she must notice, because she moves a bit, stretches, and pushes her mouth against mine. It's unexpected, after all this time, and even though she tastes a bit metallic and her lips are dry, it still feels like Sam. Skin remembers.

When I get up to get her a blanket, she holds on to me as though she thinks I might leave her to her dream and not come back.

Three blows to the chest, that's all. Well, not blows: sharper than that, more dangerous. The pain is everywhere. She falls on her back, and her eyes are looking up at the ceiling. Can she move her eyes? Yes, yes she can. She shifts her stare, looking at the table, the man in front of her, then back to the ceiling.

She's surprised at this, that the body gives you so long. That she's functioning. But she can't move. For some reason, her legs hurt.

She doesn't understand what's just happened — the phone that rang, three rings, and the man asking if they could meet up. He had something to tell her, information that would turn out to be important, he claimed. Considering who he was, she was sceptical, but the conversation with the two policemen had left her shaken and afraid. Desperate, almost — that's the word she's looking for. The fact that it takes so long to find that word makes her realise that there isn't long left. An image pops up: someone starting to blow out a candle, the flame about to give up and disappear.

Desperate. That's why she went along with it. That must be why: she was desperately trying to understand what was going on. And now he's here, she understands even less.

The one thing she does know is that she's been tricked. That realisation fills her with rage, that something as banal as getting tricked is going to take her life.

She remembers opening the door to him. He looked at her inscrutably, and as he raised the revolver, she managed to take one, two, maybe even three steps back before the first blow struck her chest. In the corner of her eye, the man is backing away, leaving the flat, disappearing.

A little flash of realisation strikes her: she remembers Ebi Hakimi telling her, as he gave her the Dictaphone.

It is not Antonsson

She wasn't sure he was right. Not even when she saw his anxious expression. Is that why she hadn't told the two policemen? Maybe. Would she have done, if she'd known how it was all going to end? Did she trust them? One of them, she decides. Not the other one. That was also a factor in her keeping quiet, and now it's too late to change her mind.

With that comes insight, and that might be what makes her let go. That makes her understand.

She'd found out that the threat wasn't against Antonsson. That is the truth. That is what has made her dangerous.

That is why she has to die.

The cars they scratched, that winter ages ago — the fun part had hardly started before everything went wrong. They were sitting watching telly at Christian's, images from Gävle telling the story of how the city had been paralysed by the worst snowstorm in history. People were skiing to work, gliding along at the roof-height of the snowed-in cars. Caterpillar trucks brought essential supplies through the snow.

'I wonder if they're bringing beer,' Christian said, and Michael laughed.

The phone rang. Christian's mum answered it, out in the living room. They could hear her voice through the closed door.

'Jesus, I'm bored,' said Michael. 'Shall we ring Oliver?'

Oliver was one of four mobile numbers they had for people who they bought black-market booze from. Oliver was their favourite: always on time, not particularly expensive, and, unlike the others, didn't have nasty knucklehead mates in his car.

'I can't be arsed tonight,' Christian said.

'Me neither, come to think of it.'

There was a knock on the door. Christian turned the sound off on the telly.

'Yes?'

'Phone, for Michael.'

'Who is it?'

She looked over at Michael.

'The police.'

Apparently this cop, a beat officer by the name of Patrik Törn, had first tried to contact Christian's friend by calling his home, but no one answered. Törn had managed to put two and two together and had rung Christian instead, because he suspected that was where he'd be.

It was about a car with scratched paintwork. The owner had filed a complaint. If it hadn't been for one of Christian's classmates cycling past and later informing his dad what had happened, it would probably have stopped there, a complaint that led nowhere.

'Why the hell did you tell them he was here?' Christian hissed afterwards.

'They would've caught up with him sooner or later, and he's done something illegal, so it's only right. I'm just happy it wasn't you they were after.'

'Fuck off.'

His mum looked blank.

'I know who it is,' Christian said a couple of days later. 'The girl that saw you. Her name's Natalie.'

'I wonder whose car it was,' said Michael. 'How many have we scratched now?'

'No idea,' said Christian, despite knowing exactly how many he was guilty of. 'Ten?'

'Good stats, anyway, getting away with nine out of ten.'

Michael was laughing, not seeming to be taking it seriously. Christian didn't know how to react, so he laughed, too. In fact, the total number of cars he'd scratched was no more than four.

Natalie didn't know the name of the one who'd scratched the car, but that wasn't going to stop an industrious man like Patrik Törn. As if that wasn't bad enough, Natalie had also managed to give a partial description of the suspect. He had been wearing a white puffer-jacket, undone, and a dark jumper, possibly black, with Skrewdriver printed on it. The print had been clearly visible in the darkness.

'Shit, man,' said Michael. 'I'm gonna get a stinking great fine.'

But that's not how it turned out. In hindsight, Christian wishes that it had only been a fine.

It all happened quickly, much faster than Christian thought it would. That winter, a few weeks after the complaint, Michael's phone rang. He and Christian were sitting on the bed listening to a new CD, sharing the inlay card between them, examining the photos, following the lyrics. Christian picked up the remote and pointed it at the stereo. The music stopped.

'Hello, yes?' said Michael.

The male voice on the other end was barely audible. It was calm and methodical, and it sounded dangerous. He asked who he was talking to. Christian's friend said his name in a heavy tone that sounded like a confession in itself.

'Right,' said Michael. 'Yes, that's right. But how did you get this number?' The man on the other end carried on talking, and Michael raised his eyebrows higher and higher. 'What ... really? Yes. Thanks. Yes, can do. I'll see you there.'

Michael stared at the phone, as though it had surprised him. He hung up.

'What was that?'

'That ... that was the guy whose car we ... I scratched.'

'Shit.' Christian sat upright on the bed. 'What did he want?'

'He wanted to meet up. If I agree to that, he'll withdraw his complaint.'

Michael picked up the inlay card, and flipped aimlessly between its pages.

'Are you going to do it?'

'If it means I get off a fine, damn right I will.'

'How had he got your number?'

'He said he was good at finding out stuff like that. I don't know what he meant.'

Christian didn't say anything. Alarm bells rang.

It was the twenty-first of December. The shopping precinct in Hagsätra was decorated with green and red rope-lights suspended between the buildings, and on the square four men with guitars sang *Jingle Bells* in broken Swedish. Freezing rain made the ground shiny and slippery. Christian met him by the ticket barriers in the underground station, where they said hello to some people they knew. They went to the same school. Christian didn't say where they were going.

They left Hagsätra and rolled into Rågsved. On the other side of the aisle were four Yugoslavs, or whatever, arguing with each other. It sounded like one big mess. Christian rolled his eyes at Michael, which made him laugh, silently. It felt good.

They swished past Högdalen, before the train slowed and pulled in to Bandhagen.

'Thanks for coming with me.' said Michael.

Christian nodded.

A man leant against a black Volvo. The car gleamed. The man was wearing a black trenchcoat and a light-grey scarf, jeans, and black boots. They noticed each other at the same time. The man walking towards them smiled. Christian noticed how Michael went stiff.

The man pulled his hand from his pocket and offered it to them. He stopped smiling.

Michael put his hand out.

The man was probably ten years older than them, no more. He introduced himself as Jens. Jens Malm. His voice was smooth and pleasant. Then he switched his stare to Christian.

'I'd rather it was just the two of us,' he said to Michael. 'Is that okay?'

'Yeah, of course.' He looked at Christian. 'See you down at the recreation ground in a bit?'

'Okay.'

Christian turned around and walked away. He heard Jens opening the car door behind him.

They were gone for ages that first time, he remembers that. And afterwards it was as though something had changed, but it was impossible to put your finger on what. Christian and Michael met up at the rec, late that evening.

'I should really be home by now,' Michael said, looking at his watch.

'My mum's not bothered.' said Christian.

'Well, mine is.'

'Did it go okay?' he attempted.

'I think so. He just wanted to talk, really.'

'About what?'

Michael laughed.

'He asked me about my Skrewdriver top.'

'What? Seriously?'

'Yes.'

Jens Malm had asked him if he liked the band. Yes, he'd answered, they're dead good.

'After that,' Michael went on, 'he asked me if I knew what they were about, and I said that they had been punks, but that they went on to be Nazis.'

That's right, Jens Malm had said. Michael had got it right, apart from one detail: the correct name was National Socialists. They had gone over to National Socialism after the first album.

'And he wanted to know what I thought about immigrants, about Jews and Muslims, and I said I wasn't really bothered either way. That they might be a bit disruptive sometimes.' He shrugged. 'They are, though, aren't they?'

Christian agreed. They lit a cig each. They looked up at the sky and shivered in the cold.

'He gave me this,' Michael said, pulling out a bit of paper from his pocket. It looked like one of the flyers that was often pinned to the noticeboard at school. 'He said I should think about joining. If I do, he'll withdraw his complaint.'

'I thought he was going to withdraw it if you talked to him?'

'That's what I thought. But he'd changed his mind.'

Michael stubbed out his cigarette.

'What makes you think he won't change his mind again?' said Christian.

'What do you mean?'

'How do you know he's going to withdraw it this time? It feels like you're about to get dragged into something you don't …'

'I asked him that, obviously.'

'And? What did he say?'

'That I could listen to him withdrawing the complaint, on the speakerphone.'

Christian tried to think. He didn't know much about police reports or how the police go about things.

'I think I'm going to do it,' Michael went on. 'He said loads of stuff that sounded spot-on, and I've been looking for something to do. Know what I mean? Everyone else is playing football or music or whatever, and I don't do anything. And neither do you, we don't do anything, me and you. We do this. And if I'm not sure I'm ready to join his group yet, there's another group I can join first, to see what it's like. One that's sort of a bit more open. Not just that …' Michael looked at his watch. 'I've got to get home. I'll see what I decide to do. See you tomorrow?'

'Yes.'

They went their separate ways.

'Are you sure you haven't been to see him? Not yesterday, or Saturday either?'

Early, early morning. That's the first thing Sam says, still lying on the sofa on the other side of the room.

'I'm sure, I haven't.'

'Okay.'

'I was with you on Saturday.'

'But before that?'

'Why are you asking?'

'I want to know.'

'I haven't met him.'

She doesn't believe me, and I don't blame her. After all, I have seen him, but I wonder if she knows, somehow. I can't help being annoyed. No, offended, maybe because this just reminds me so much of how things were at the end, last time round. How we don't share a bed, how the cautious evening reunions become wary, mistrustful mornings after.

'Just like the old days,' Sam says, and laughs, and I don't know how to take it.

'That's just what I was thinking.'

'There are certain things you shouldn't get nostalgic about.' She plays with one of the many rings in her earlobe. 'What would you like for Christmas?'

'You don't need to go buying anything.'

'But I want to.'

I wonder what's waiting on that dark-blue Dictaphone, what it was that Birck was so keen for me to hear.

I haven't really got time for it today. I should be concentrating on a mugging on Torsgatan, where one speed-addled man put a knife to another one's throat. The assailant made off with fifteen hundred crowns in cash, and presumably the victim's stash, because that's nearly always the way. He's still on the loose, but the victim had the poor judgement to contact the police immediately, rather than sobering up a bit first. The result was a drawn-out, confused interrogation at the beginning of last week, before I thanked him for his time and had him put on remand for possession. Since Heber's death I haven't really spent any time on the case.

'I'd like a new coffee machine,' I say. 'The one I've got is on its last legs. I've had it since we … I never bought a new one.'

And then it just comes out, and once it has I can't take it back:

'And you.'

Is that even true? There's something about seeing her, lying on the sofa, the way she's looking at me. I can't work out whether I want to be with her now, or whether I want to wind the clock back and start all over again. They are two very different things, but right now I just can't separate them.

'You've already got me.'

'Have I?'

'If you want me.'

'I don't know if I want you,' I say, 'but I do know that I need you.'

'That might be the nicest thing anyone's ever said to me.'

It's so cold that you can feel the moisture in your nose freezing as you breathe in. And slippery. The ground is shining, covered in ice. There's just over a week to go till Christmas, and three or four days until the Christmas holidays start.

I remember them now, past Christmases, as my footsteps carry me north, across Kungsholmen's streets. Sam's right — there are things you shouldn't get nostalgic about, but this time I just can't help it. I remember early Christmases, at Gran and Grandpa's, Ella and Arthur, my dad's parents. I remember later, when Arthur was gradually eaten away by his Alzheimer's, the years spent at ours in Salem. How Arthur refused to get in the lift, the last few times before his death, because he was convinced that it was actually a death-chamber. Micke and I had to guide him up the stairs, all eight flights.

Every Christmas, Mum and Dad, like so many other mums and dads in Salem, would take out a small loan so they could buy us the things we'd asked for, and would then spend the next quarter paying it off. After those first Christmases, we didn't have Father Christmas anymore. Micke had seen through the fake beard and the red coat that hung in the cupboard throughout the rest of the year, but I still believed in Santa, and my brother mocked me for it.

'Why should we go through all this,' I heard my mum saying, that same Christmas that Santa ceased to exist, 'the stress of shopping, the loan, all of it, and then say that the presents are from

Father Christmas? It's stupid. Is this how we want to raise our kids? He should know that we're the ones who bought it for him, that we're the ones who love him and want to give him this. It's important that he understands.'

'But he's five, Annie. Father Christmas is magical for a child. He represents the fact that miracles happen every day.'

'He doesn't exist though.'

'Not so loud,' Dad hissed. 'He'll work that out, sooner or later. It's not something we need to help along.'

'Yes, it is.'

As happened so often, Mum won, and I, the little fool, was crushed, as though something had been taken away from me. The world had shown its true face.

Today I arrive before Birck, and I wonder how long he was up listening to Lisa Swedberg being interviewed. Probably long enough to oversleep. I call him and, as the phone rings, I click through the emails that have arrived since I was last here.

On the way to the printer to pick up a memo, the thought strikes me again. How did Heber make contact with the man 1601 told him about? By visiting him? Probably not. How do you contact someone without using phones or emails? What was it Birck said — smoke signals? Well, maybe.

The department is quiet this early in the morning, apart from the constant sound that goes on in the absence of people. The buzz of the ventilation system mixes with that of all the computers, a radio that is always on in one of the rooms, and the telly in the lunchroom. The TV is showing the annual Christmas serial, with the three children, the girls and a boy, who have now made it to the fat, bearded man, who's sleeping. One of the girls is shown clambering up on to his big belly and then jumping on it, while the other one pours cold water on his face. Then there's a close-up of one of the man's feet. It is twitching.

I read the memo. It's about the force's pending reorganisation. I chuck it in the waste-paper bin, and watch the telly instead.

The man suddenly sits bolt upright on the sofa, as though someone has just given him an electric shock. The girl on his belly flies off and hits the wall. The man is breathing heavily, and looking around, disorientated. He looks like I feel.

I go back to my office and sink into myself, thinking about Olausson's threat, and working absent-mindedly on the Torsgatan mugging.

Out in the lunchroom, the telly is still on when I go back to get another cup of freshly brewed coffee. It's a repeat from yesterday — a party leader talking to the people. She's the leader of the Centre Party, wearing a spotless suit with an open-necked blouse, and sitting in a dark-red chair. She's talking about traditions and smiling at the camera, as though no one else existed.

'What do you reckon?' I hear Birck's voice behind me. 'Does the sly nationalism appeal? All the party leaders get fifteen minutes each, before Christmas. She's up first.'

'I preferred the Christmas tale,' I say. 'Why don't you answer your phone? How long did you oversleep anyway?'

'I haven't slept at all. I've been here since yesterday, except for a couple of short excursions to a bar and to the hospital.'

Judging by the paleness of his skin and the red rings around his eyes, it's certainly possible that he's telling the truth.

'You should get some sleep.'

'Listen,' he says, filling a black mug with coffee, 'While you were at home snuggling, I was doing my job. Don't tell me what I should be doing.'

'What were you doing at the hospital?'

'Visiting Ebi Hakimi.'

'Who the hell is that?'

'He's the guy our gifted colleague shot in the eye yesterday.' He

179

drinks a big gulp of coffee. 'Fuck,' he hisses. 'Hot.'

'Why did you visit him?'

'I'm pretty sure that he knows why Heber died, maybe even who did it. And what's going to happen next.'

'Eh?'

'Come with me,' he says. 'We'll sit in my car. We've got plenty to talk about.'

'But …'

'What?'

'We're not supposed to be doing this. If we get caught, I'll be fucked. And besides, haven't you been assigned other stuff? I know I have.'

'Yes, I've got other assignments.'

'Shouldn't we get on with them, then?'

'I've finished mine. Haven't you?'

'No.'

'Shame,' says Birck.

I don't say any more, although I should. We take the lift down to the garage and get into Birck's car.

'I've used a setting on the Dictaphone to edit them together.' Birck weighs the little dark-blue player in his hand. 'So we don't waste any more time unnecessarily. I also have the unedited version, in a place that no one other than me knows about or has access to. If you want to listen to them later, I can arrange that.'

He starts the car. I close my eyes, only for a second, but I can feel sleep approaching from a distance.

'I'm tired.'

'Wake up then. Stick with it.'

Birck steers the car out of the garage and up towards the daylight, which meets us, pale and cold.

'Where are we going?'

'No idea. Somewhere where there's water. I like water — it makes it easier to think.'

There are clicking sounds, then a scraping sound with a background of voices, and a doorbell rings. Someone laughs, followed by Thomas Heber's voice:

'Right then,' he says. 'I think it's on now.'

'Think?'

'It's on.'

'I don't want to have to repeat myself.'

'Don't worry. It's on. You do know that you don't have to do this? You can stop whenever you like.'

'I know.'

According to the notes, it's March, and they're in a café. Thomas Heber and Lisa Swedberg are meeting for the first time. They're not far from Heber's home. Her voice sounds wary.

A phone rings close by. The ring tone is the tune from *The Good, The Bad, and The Ugly*. Heber seems calm and collected. He could almost be a radio host, a soothing voice in the night, consonants just barely touched. That's the kind of voice Heber has, a voice that suits his face.

'You haven't been that easy to get hold of,' he says.

'Good. That's the way I like it.'

'Why is that?'

'I had so much grief with the cops a few years back, I got tired of it. This makes it a bit trickier for them.'

'It might also seem a bit more suspicious.'

'Yeah. I guess so. I hadn't given it much thought.'

You can hear the chink of crockery. One of them slurps tea or coffee.

'You used to be in AFA, is that right?' she asks.

'Yes, that's true.'

'Why did you leave?'

Several seconds tick by, with no voices recorded.

'AFA was good fire-fighting politics. We could rush out when somewhere was burning, like when the Sweden Democrats were out demonstrating or marching somewhere. We were effective then. But we couldn't deal with the kind of party that the Sweden Democrats have become today. But,' he adds, 'who knows whether I'm right? Maybe AFA can after all; maybe it's me that's changed. I've got older. It could be as simple as that.'

That makes her laugh out loud.

'How old are you?' she asks.

'Thirty-five. You?'

'I'm twenty-six. But I feel older, for some reason. I always have done.'

'That might tie in to my first question,' Heber says. 'I thought I'd ask how you got involved with the anarchist movement.'

The clip ends.

'This is a load of boring shit and babble about middle-class parents and bourgeois economics, the patriarchy, experience of gender and class oppression, and so on,' Birck says. 'The first interview is actually pretty dull, unless you're a sociologist, I suppose.'

'Weird,' I say.

'What is?'

'Hearing his voice.'

'Ah. Okay. The next clip is very short, at the end of the first interview.'

It's quieter, with fewer customers. A radio has been switched on somewhere, and there's a voice reading the news.

'I need to get going — I'm meeting a mate.'

'By all means,' says Heber.

'Have you got everything you need?'

She's far more relaxed now, sounding more like she's talking to a friend. There's something more there, a desire to make him happy.

'I can't really say here and now,' he replies. 'I really need to listen to the interview first.'

'It's easy talking to you, because you've got the same background. That means I don't have to explain loads of stuff for you, because you already get it.'

'It also means that we, well, that I might miss a lot of things that are actually important. But I'll listen to this and then get back to you. Is there an address or something I can contact you via?'

'Yes.' There's noise in the background, and someone is clicking a lighter. 'Can you turn that off?'

'Of course.'

Rustling. Silence.

'You can hear it, even here. There's definitely something between them,' says Birck.

It's not explicit, but it is there. You can imagine the glances between the words.

'She's already very careful not to let any personal details get recorded, as you will have noticed. She does soften a bit later on, but not completely. I don't even think her name is mentioned during any of the interviews, except once, right at the end. And even then, Heber's the one who says it. But I don't think she knows, at this point, what is going on ...'

Birck goes quiet as he clicks through the Dictaphone to get to the next file.

'What's going on?' I say.

'It's coming. Calm down. This is the follow-up interview that he does a week or so later, at the same café. It's after this one that they go back to his place for a fuck.'

Same place, but something's different. When the doorbell rings during the clip, it sounds distant. They're sitting towards the back of the café. It's late evening. The ten o'clock news is on the radio.

'You know, things have … changed.'

'How do you mean?'

'No, the whole thing. It's got a bit rawer since the Sweden Democrats got into parliament.'

'Why's that?'

'You should know better than me.' There's a short laugh, a clucking sound like a child's. It sounds nice, genuine. 'I guess that … I mean, you can't just have a load of Nazis and racists from out in the sticks sitting in parliament. That's what they are — look at their history, it looks really fucking bad. So since 2010, or rather since they got a new leader in 2005, they've been trying to reinvent themselves, to make themselves more palatable. I saw this slogan, THE PARTY FOR ALL SWEDES, on the internet somewhere. Did you see that?'

'I think so. It sounds familiar.'

'They've toned down what they really stand for, at least on a national level—I don't know what they're like locally. But it's shifted the whole political arena to the right, because all the parliamentary parties, even the left, are affected when a new player comes along. It's just logic.'

'Yes.'

'But it has also meant that the extreme right has become more extreme, because they always need to stand apart from mainstream politics. They believe that the Sweden Democrats are led by a traitor. That he has betrayed Sweden.' She laughs again. 'Can you believe it? How fucked up is that? They are really fucking nasty. They talk about Swedish-ness, the superior race, white culture, stage faked

184

mass-executions of immigrants and homosexuals at their parties, and film them and put them online until they get taken down by some mod. They send them to us, of course, to provoke us. And we stage mass-executions of Nazis, and send the films to them.'

She goes quiet, perhaps to let it sink in.

'We didn't do that ten years ago,' says Heber.

'No, that's what I mean. And it's a good example — they were the ones who started it, but then we, the anarchists, joined in. We're doing exactly what they're doing. As the extreme right gets more extreme, so do we — just in the other direction. RAF had a public meeting two weeks ago, for International Women's Day, and halfway through the meeting they cut the cables to the PA with pliers or some kind of saw, when no one was looking. We don't really find out about their meetings, because they're such a fucking closed group. But for some reason their parties are more open — we got word about one the other week, and went down there. It was in an old barn, near Ösmo, out in the middle of nowhere. It was fucked up, people were wearing uniforms, there were flags and swastikas on the walls, white-power music, and a projector was showing old film of Hitler. Every time a swastika flashed up, they cheered, as though it was a football match and their team had just scored.'

'What did you do?'

'We set fire to the barn.'

He wasn't expecting that. Then the tape records the sound of footsteps and someone coming over to them, a woman with a high-pitched voice.

'Just to let you know, we're closing now.'

'Thanks,' says Heber.

Lisa Swedberg says nothing, and the woman leaves. *All my friends in the loop,* someone on the radio is singing, *making up for teenage crime.*

'What happened to the barn?' Heber asks.

'It burned down. It was in the press the next day.'

185

'Was anyone hurt?'

'No. Unfortunately.'

'I would like to continue the interview, if that's okay with you? Otherwise just say so.'

'Fine by me. Don't you live around here somewhere?'

'How do you know that?'

'That's not really the sort of thing you tell people, as I'm sure you understand?'

I wonder what Heber thinks at this point, and try to imagine his facial expression.

All my friends in the loop, making up for teenage cri—

The clip ends with a crackling sound.

'Well,' I say, 'they go back to his place and have sex now.'

'Yes. No recording, though. Which I think we should be thankful for.' Birck clicks the Dictaphone again. 'They don't seem to have continued the interview that evening, at least not on tape. This was around the twenty-seventh of March — she mentions Women's Day, and that it was two weeks earlier. The next time they meet up for an interview, it's May.'

'The barn that burned down …' I say.

'I checked that out. The organisation she doesn't want to name is Swedish Resistance. The story stands up: there was an arson attack recorded in Ösmo, and our talented local colleagues did their utmost, put everything into finding the suspects — probably because half of them actually sympathise, ideologically, with the idiots at the party. They never managed it, though. The case was closed in June — probably just as well, if you ask me. Listen now. This is when things start happening.'

This time it's quiet, except for a slight hum, perhaps from an open window. Yes, it's spring now, and Vanadisvägen is buzzing away somewhere below them, and they're sitting close to the window, Lisa Swedberg and Thomas Heber. Crockery is chinking.

'Would you like some more?' he asks.

'No, I'm good, thanks.'

A lighter clicks — once, twice, three times. There's the fizzing sound of tobacco being lit. She breathes in the smoke and blows it out again.

'Your flat really is weird,' she says. 'How long have you lived here?'

'A couple of years. In what way is it weird?'

'It feels … uninhabited.'

'I don't spend an awful lot of time here.'

'Your bed works, anyway.'

She might be smiling as she says that — there's a playful tone to her voice. She takes a drag. Heber clears his throat.

'It's been a while since we did an interview,' he says. 'I've spoken to a few others, and I've been thinking that it's interesting, how anarchists like you in RAF, and those in the White Power movement, see each other. I was listening to our previous interview yesterday, and you mentioned setting fire to a barn after they'd sabotaged your public meeting. Can you tell me a bit more about that?'

'How do you mean?'

'Well, what happened next, for a start?'

She giggles.

'This is strange, doing this, when we've already talked so much.'

He laughs. For a moment, he's not a scientist.

'I know,' he says.

She touches him — his arm, or maybe his thigh. Her hand makes a pleasant, rasping noise against the fabric.

'I know it's weird,' he says, obviously uncomfortable, as though he doesn't really know how to deal with the situation. 'But try.'

'It escalated. That's just what happens. We know it; they know it. It's been pretty calm for a while, but it's just a matter of time before something else happens and it gets in the papers again.'

'How did it escalate? In what way?'

'Well, they stole money from us, for one. I think it must have been a couple of days after our last interview. It probably doesn't sound too bad, compared to the barn and everything, and it wasn't a lot — a couple of thousand — but, you know, we have such tight margins. That money could have paid for ten of us to get the train to a demo, or three times as many if we took cars. They really went for the heart of our operation. Of course, on paper, RAF's money doesn't get spent on demos and stuff like that — it wouldn't look good. But organisations like Swedish Resistance and People's Front, they know what we do with our money. And they exploit it. It won't be long before someone ends up getting seriously hurt.'

'I understand.'

'Since then we haven't attempted any counter-attack, mainly because we haven't been able to. It's pretty quiet at the moment — no big demos or anything coming up. But soon. I've heard that the hate is stronger than it has been in a long time. Th—'

A ringtone interrupts her, so loud that it masks the other sounds and makes the Dictaphone's little speaker crackle horribly. The phone must have been lying right next to it.

'Sorry,' her voice says through the racket. 'I need to take this, it's someone I …'

The sentence remains unfinished. The ringing suddenly stops.

'Hello?'

The voice on the other end is surprisingly audible. It's a man.

'Yeah … I don't know,' Lisa Swedberg says. 'Eh? How the fuck did you find that out? You fucking … I'm sick and tired of this now. You can… can we talk about this some other time? No. It's not like that at all. Nothing. I'm putting the phone down now. Don't call again.'

She hangs up.

Only now, when the voice has gone, does it sink in, who it belonged to.

Goffman.

'Goffman,' I say. 'It was him, wasn't it?'

'I think so. The voice doesn't turn up in any of the other clips, so that's all we hear from him. But, yes, it's pretty fucking similar.'

'In that case, what has he got to do with her?'

'Who knows? She did mention that Goffman had been on her case, but surely she meant *after* Heber's murder, as part of the investigation.'

'That's what I thought, too.' I glance at the Dictaphone, as if it were about to reveal everything, at any moment, fit all the pieces of the puzzle where they belong. 'What happens next?'

'Well, it's a while later. It's autumn. It's November before they meet for an interview again.'

We're parked by the water down by Hornsbergs beach on Kungsholmen. It's quiet, almost deserted here. A row of parked cars lines the street. The imposing bulk of Karlberg Palace sits across the water from us. Birck shifts position in his seat. I think he's content, feeling almost peaceful.

He clicks the Dictaphone, next file, PLAY.

And it starts with Heber, alone. He's speaking right into the microphone, as though he were afraid that someone was standing close by and listening in.

'She called this morning,' he says. 'And I thought she seemed scared. I don't know what's going on, or whether something's happened.' Short pause. 'We haven't done an interview since May. I've got a few questions for her, and I was going to call her. But then she got in touch, wanted to know if we could meet up. Something was wrong — she sounded agitated.' There's another deliberate pause. 'I might be imagining it.'

There's a crackle and then silence, and then she's there. She kisses him loudly. The interview starts just like the others, with Heber asking questions and then listening to her long, thorough answers, but there's something between them that wasn't there before. Heber's questions are posed more delicately, and her answers are more ardent — the kind of answers that people give when they're deliberately ignoring whatever is actually occupying their thoughts.

'You sounded different on the phone,' he says. 'There was something you wanted to talk about, wasn't there?'

'No, nothing special.'

'I don't really believe that.'

'Why not?'

'I know what you're like when you're hiding something.'

'Er, no you don't.'

I wish I could see Lisa Swedberg's facial expression. She breathes in and clicks her lighter, but without doing anything else.

'I heard something that … rattled me a bit.'

'What was that?'

No answer.

'Okay,' Heber continues instead. 'Who did you hear it from?'

'Someone I know from RAF.'

'Do I know who this person is?'

'I don't think so.'

'Is it a man or a woman?'

No answer.

'When did he or she tell you about this?' he says.

'This morning. We met in Café Cairo, and then we left together.'

'Do you know this person well?'

'No, but I trust what they tell me.'

'Right. So you think that what you've heard is true?'

'Exactly. That's the thing … that's why I can't just forget about it.'

'I'm going to ask you one more time,' he says. 'Then I'll drop it, because I've no right to demand answers from you. But it feels as though you want to tell me.'

'I do,' she says. 'That's why I rang. I felt that I needed to tell you, but I still don't know if I can.'

'Because?'

'Because I don't know how far your professional confidentiality stretches.'

'A long way,' Heber says, with no obvious effort to convince her. 'If you were to tell me you've committed a serious crime, I still wouldn't be allowed to pass that information on. The only circumstances where I might possibly be entitled to do so — by which I mean the only time I wouldn't be reprimanded by an ethics committee — would be if you were to tell me about a serious crime which will definitely take place. If there was a chance, I could try to prevent the crime. But not even then would I be obliged to do so. It is the researcher's prerogative to determine whether or not they choose to report it, and I would choose not to. So, in effect, my professional confidentiality is absolute.'

'Are you sure you wouldn't tell anyone, even if that was the case? If you knew that a crime was going to be committed?'

'Is that what it's about?'

She doesn't answer.

'I am certain,' Heber says. 'I wouldn't say anything. Not even then.'

'I think,' she says slowly, 'that someone might be about to get hurt. That's it — I don't know who or where.'

'Is this a person on the "other side of the fence", as you call it? Who's going to get hurt?'

'I think so. It's really tense between the groups at the moment. There's a small faction within RAF — well, not even really a faction, just a few people who've got together and started pulling in their own direction.'

'How many of them are there?'

'Roughly ten people, maybe one or two more, or less. Only three of four of them are involved in this, according to my contact.'

She breathes out in the way that people who've just betrayed someone, or something, do. It's taken a toll on her, and Heber's noticed.

'This group,' he says. 'They've started pulling in their own direction.'

The window creaks as someone opens it, and the sound of the city sweeps into the apartment, like a wave. The lighter is being clicked — quick, hard clicks this time. She pulls in smoke, and then lets it out. Heber moves the Dictaphone closer to her.

'They're more extreme; they advocate more violence. They think everyone in RAF should arm themselves. I mean firearms — we've already got baseball bats, and knuckledusters, and stuff like that.'

She takes a drag.

'Do you know whether they've already got guns?'

'I think so. I've not seen them myself, but the person I spoke to said they did.'

'I wonder,' he says, 'whether you think they're prepared to use them? The far right have also been doing loads of this sort of thing, posing with Swedish flags and automatic weapons outside schools in immigrant areas — it's a kind of propaganda. Very few, if any, of those organisations are actually ready to use them. Might the same thing apply to this grouping within RAF?'

'Yes. But I'm certain that at least two or three of these people are capable of using guns. There's something about them, just how brutal they are.'

'You've no idea who it is that's going to get hurt?'

'No. No idea.'

Lisa Swedberg takes several drags on her cigarette. Someone blasts their horn in a car on the street below. That sound is followed by voices, an argument happening at a distance.

'How high up might this person be?' Heber asks. 'Do you know that?'

'No. But I'm guessing it's not someone too high up, nor very low down in the organisation, whichever organisation it is. Too low down is pointless, really. People at the top are impossible, they're too well protected. Where's your ashtray?'

'I don't have one — I usually use a saucer. I can get a new one. Hold on.'

Heber gets up and goes off. A cupboard opens. She smokes more of the cigarette. The tobacco hisses and sizzles. She puts the saucer by the window with a slight clink.

'Personally, I don't give a fuck if some Nazi bastard dies,' she says. 'I've nothing against that, might even enjoy the thought of it. The higher up, the better. Sorry, it's just ... that's how strong my hatred is. On the other hand, it would be an absolute disaster if it actually did happen. You remember in September, when The Party of the Swedes marched through town and people were throwing water-bombs at them? They kicked up a big fuss about that. Their support would increase.'

Heber says nothing for a long time. Nor does she. Something is tapping away, maybe a fingernail on a glass.

'Are you going to try and find out more about this?' he asks. 'About this ... threat?'

'I don't know if I want to.'

'That's not what I asked.'

'Can you turn that thing off?'

'Of course,' he says, but now he's wary. 'But why?'

'Because I want to say that I need to have sex now, and I don't want it to end up on tape.'

This makes Heber laugh.

'I'll cut that bit out,' he says.

The clip ends.

'The next clip is the last one, and it's short,' Birck says. 'But it could be the most important of the lot. If she's actually telling the truth, that is. I think it's some time in early December.'

Birck's phone buzzes. He reads the text.

'Fuck.'

'What is it?'

'We'll do this later. Soon.'

They're outdoors, in central Stockholm. The sound of the city almost tells you how low the sky is hanging, how thick the air is. Cars rumble past. It's daytime, one rush hour or the other, either early morning or late afternoon.

There's the sound of rustling and crackling, and only when a thick rug seems to have been placed over all the sound do you realise that Heber's put the Dictaphone in his coat. The snow crunches under his boots as he moves.

Another set of footsteps emerges from the background hum, growing in intensity, crunching just like Heber's. It's Lisa Swedberg.

'Hi,' she says.

'Hi.'

'Have you got a fag?'

'No, 'fraid not.'

'Shit. I'm all out.'

'We'll go and buy some in a bit, okay?'

'I'm ... we shouldn't really be meeting like this.'

'Why not?'

'I have ... I've been asking around, since we met last time, about what we talked about, and I think that some people think I've been a bit too curious, nosy. At times I've felt like I was being followed.

It's not good for your research, what with all the confidentiality and all that, if we're seen together.'

'Are you thinking about my research?'

'What else would it be?'

'Your own safety, for example.' Heber sounds genuinely worried now. He lowers his voice. 'Have you found out something else?'

'I might have done,' she says.

'But this thing is still on? That they're going to … that something's going to happen?'

'Yes.'

'And when?'

'Don't know.'

'But who? You know who the target is?'

Silence.

'Can you say it? The name?'

A pedestrian crossing switches to green, and the slow ticking is replaced by an intensive rattle. A car beeps.

'Martin Antonsson.'

'The guy who used to be in the Sweden Democrats?'

There's no hint of surprise in Heber's voice, no emotion whatsoever. He sounds very matter-of-fact.

'Yes.'

'Why?'

'I know someone you can talk to who can tell you more about this than I can.'

'And who is that?'

'I really need a cig.'

'Lisa,' Heber says, pleadingly, thereby saying her name for the first time.

'Ebi Hakimi, RAF. Do you know who he is?'

'No.'

'Talk to him.'

'But I …'

195

'This might be the last time we see each other for a while,' she says. 'I'm getting scared. Your place isn't safe anymore.'

There's that crackling, scraping sound again. Heber puts his hand in his pocket. The clip ends. It's the last time we hear his voice.

'Martin Antonsson,' I say.

'The very same.'

I'll be damned. Martin Antonsson is a notorious former member of the Sweden Democrats. He was active in Stockholm City Council, and had an alleged background in Keep Sweden Swedish and similarly alleged connections to the old National Socialist Front. When the Sweden Democrats started polishing their image and becoming socially acceptable, Martin Antonsson was one of those who was pushed out. There was a bit about him in the press then, and his name still turns up when active Sweden Democrats' murkier links are revealed. No one knows what he's up to now, except that he's somewhere on the fringes of the extreme right, causing mayhem.

Martin Antonsson. I'll be damned.

'Why do they want him?'

'No idea,' says Birck. 'It might not even be true. When we spoke to Swedberg yesterday, she told us she was no longer sure it was true. But my guess is that Antonsson is up to something we know nothing about. I did a rather dubious, in operational terms, background check on him — I googled him on my phone because I didn't want it to be registered at HQ, considering, well … you know.

'Considering we're not to stick our noses in?'

'Exactly. But I found nothing, apart from the fact that he's on good terms with Jens Malm, the national leader of Swedish Resistance.'

'He might be supporting them financially,' I say. 'If it's not about ideology, it's about money. That's nearly always the way.'

'I think in this case it might be about both,' Birck replies. 'Antonsson lives in a big house out in Stocksund. I rolled past there this morning, and spotted two unmarked cars in the vicinity, as well as a patrol car outside the entrance. I recognised one of the cars, WHO 327.'

The Security Police — SEPO. So Goffman and his stooges already know about this.

'Ebi Hakimi,' I say instead. 'The guy who was shot in the eye.'

'Oh yes.'

'He's in the field notes,' I say. 'I'm sure of it.'

'As "H",' says Birck. 'I'm pretty convinced myself.'

The cogs are moving. Ebi Hakimi, or 'H' in Heber's notes — it must be him. Lisa Swedberg asks Heber to contact Hakimi, to find out more about the threat to Martin Antonsson. Heber tracks down Hakimi, finds him at Café Cairo, and tells him about Antonsson. Heber can tell that Hakimi knows what he's talking about. Then Heber asks about the other thing, too, whatever or whoever that is, which he's heard about from 1601. Exactly what happens next isn't clear, but Hakimi seems unsettled, and he leaves Cairo in a hurry.

'We need to talk to her again.'

'Well, yes.' Birck doesn't seem convinced. He puts his hand on the steering wheel, and starts drumming with his fingers. 'I think Olausson was right.'

'What do you mean?'

'I'm guessing SEPO have been ahead of us the whole time. They've known more than we have. And this is, as it should be, their case, not ours. We have neither the experience nor the intelligence material necessary to handle the case.'

'You mean we should hand over what we've got?'

'What little we've got, yes. We can hardly get stick for this — Swedberg came to us. I think we should go to them, once we've spoken to Swedberg again. We're not the only ones who want to solve the case, and there are people in much better positions than us to do so. Those who are formally responsible, for example.'

I concede, reluctantly, that Birck's right.

'We need to get Swedberg to talk to SEPO.'

'That's right,' Birck says. 'She obviously already had some contact with Goffman.'

'That's what I don't get. Why she didn't agree to talk to them when they came to her.'

'There might be an explanation,' Birck says, distracted. 'But there is one more thing.'

'Okay?'

'Ebi Hakimi: twenty-two years old, Persian heritage, registered residence out in Husby. His is the only name at that address. Member of Radical Anti-Fascism for the past three years while studying politics, sociology, and economic history at the university. Suspected of criminal damage, civil disobedience, and possessing an offensive weapon, in the form of a knife. This was all on the same charge sheet, from a demonstration in Salem three years ago, almost to the day. And then I've made a little entry here.' Birck waves the Dictaphone. 'When I visited Ebi Hakimi at the hospital this morning. I was down there like a shot as soon as I heard this. Fuck me, what a state he was in. I asked one of the nurses if he'd been conscious at all since they'd brought him in yesterday, but he hadn't been. They operated to remove the bullet, and he was in post-op when I got there, so I just sat there and waited. After two hours, give or take, I got this.'

Birck clicks the file, which starts playing.

There's buzzing in the background, and a monotonous, relentless bleeping from one of the machines. Birck sounds gentle but determined, direct — the kind of voice you'd use if you knew you were only going to get one chance.

'Who killed Thomas Heber?'

'...'

'Who killed Thomas Heber?'

The voice that answers is weak and slurred, wheezing out the vowels. It's almost impossible to make out what he's saying.

'Sweetest sisters.'

'Who's going to die next?' Birck continues, without hesitation or contemplation of the previous answer, as though he were reading out questions that someone else had written.

'Es ... ther.'

'Then he disappeared again,' Birck says.

'Can you play that again?'

'Who killed Thomas Heber?'

'...'

'Who killed Thomas Heber?'

'Sweetest sisters.'

'Who's going to die next?'

'Es ... ther.'

'What's he saying?' I ask. 'Sweetest sisters and Esther? What the hell is that second one?'

'We'll have to make sure SEPO check the names, if indeed they are names. They might not mean anything at all, but we don't have anything else to go on.'

'Well, he doesn't say Antonsson anyway.'

'No, he doesn't, which bothers me a bit, not least because Swedberg expressed some doubt about whether or not it was true. Time will tell, I should think. I spoke to a nurse,' he continues, 'who was furious that I didn't tell them as soon as he seemed to be waking up. Once she had calmed down a bit, I managed to get her to promise to contact me if there was any change in his condition.'

He fiddles with his phone.

'And?' I say.

'I've just been informed that he died two hours ago.'

The water closest to the quayside has frozen. It's snowing; large snowflakes tumble from the sky.

I think about his last words. Sweetest sisters. Esther. I wonder what Heber's last words were. Maybe he said something to a stranger on the way to his rendezvous with Swedberg, perhaps on the underground. Maybe he said no; maybe he gave a beggar some change. Or maybe he didn't say anything.

Maybe there are no last words.

Somewhere along the way, we forgot about each other. 'The People's Home', as the Social Democrats' great project was widely known, became The Home of *The People* — the Swedes. Xenophobia is at record levels. Maybe that's why someone dared to write SWEDEN FOR THE SWEDES on a wall in Bandhagen, and why no one has bothered to wash it off. Whoever's in charge of getting rid of graffiti might agree with the message. No one knows what anyone else believes in anymore, or who anyone actually likes.

The address that Lisa Swedberg had mentioned before disappearing in such a hurry is a four-storey brick-built apartment building. The façade is probably intended to be beige, but against the white snow it just looks yellowish and dirty.

A black Volvo, registration ME 737, is parked outside the address. On its roof, a lone blue light is spinning and flashing. In front of the Volvo is a blue-and-white patrol car with its doors open, like the wings of a bird. The main door to the building is propped open, and through it emerge Dan Larsson and Per Leifby. One is reading something in his notebook, while the other is sucking sugary soft drink through a straw.

'Fuck.'

Not really knowing what he's referring to, I get out of the car and start following him. Birck raises his voice, which makes Larsson look up from his pad.

'She's lying up there,' Larsson says in a coarse, nasal, southern dialect.

'Who.'

'A Swedberg, Lisa,' Larsson reads from his notebook. 'According to her ID she was born ...'

'Is she still alive?'

Leifby releases the straw and looks at us with his mouth half-open.

'I very much doubt it.'

'And what are you doing down here?'

'A man in a suit said he was going to take care of it,' Larsson replies. 'We're going to cordon off.'

'A man in a suit?' Birck repeats.

'Yes?' Leifby sucks on his straw again. It makes a burbling, slurping sound. 'That is correct. He is wearing a suit.'

'And that was sufficient for you to leave the crime scene?'

'It's the Security Police,' Larsson says, wide-eyed.

'Cordon it off,' Birck mutters, and walks past them.

We take our shoes off in the stairwell. The flat is on the second floor and, according to the door, someone by the name of Lundin lives here. The hall is small, and you feel a stabbing sensation at about chest height when you see Lisa Swedberg's dark-red boots in the row of shoes by the door. The stench of the corpse is unmistakable.

'It must have happened yesterday,' I say.

'Shoe prints right the way down the hall,' Birck says as he carefully makes his way towards the threshold of the living room. 'Be careful.'

On the left is a bathroom, then the kitchenette, with unwashed plates and glasses on the worktop. Straight ahead are two more rooms, of equal size. One is a bedroom; the other, the living room, which is dominated by a three-piece suite, a TV, and a dark-brown bookcase. The ceiling is pretty low, and the lino on the floor is discoloured by time and nicotine.

A pillow and a duvet are lying on the sofa. Someone has been sleeping there. On the floor, between the coffee table and the bookcase, Lisa Swedberg is lying on her back. She's wearing a vest-top with no bra, a pair of black, loose-fitting tracksuit bottoms, and thick socks. Her eyes are closed. Her top is stained red by blood, and between her breasts are three bullet holes.

Crouching down beside her is a man I recognise.

'The man with the very uncomfortable chair,' Goffman says, getting to his feet. 'Excuse my being so blunt, but what the hell are you doing here?'

Birck explains the facts behind our presence here. Yet, by the end of it, Goffman appears none the wiser. He turns his head, looking for something, as though he might have forgotten where he put his hat.

'When did the call come in?' Birck asks.

'Fifteen minutes ago. The postman came, and thought it smelt a bit funny in the stairwell. The landlady is a paranoid little witch, so she called the police. Larsson and Leifby decided that they could make the effort, and come and have a look — whatever it was they were doing here. Aren't they based in Huddinge?'

'That's right,' I say. 'So it was Larsson and Leifby who found her?'

'Correct,' Goffman says, as he bends his long, pale fingers, and puts his hands in his trouser pockets.

'Shot,' Birck says. 'Three rounds.'

'It does rather look that way, doesn't it?' Goffman walks a wide arc around the body, and his presence is striking. As he moves around, it's as though the room is moving with him. 'Three hits, anyway. We'll have to check the flat for any misses.' He takes his right hand out of his pocket, forms his fingers around an imaginary pistol. 'One, two, three, in the chest.' His stare drops to the floor.

'I think he must have been standing about here,' he mumbles.

'The shoe-prints stop at the doorway,' says Birck.

'Ah-ha. Of course. And with a revolver, right? No cartridges, as far as I can see.'

'The assailant might have taken them with him,' I say.

'True. But in that case he must have had plenty of time — something that people who've just killed someone don't tend to have.'

'She never had a chance.'

'Dying people rarely do.'

'Someone must have heard something,' I say. 'Someone in the building.'

'Yes,' says Goffman. He pulls his phone from his blazer pocket. 'Maybe they did. The forensic technician is on the way.'

'Get Markström and Hall down here,' says Birck.

'They're City officers, aren't they?'

'They're the best door-knockers I know. And they're on duty.'

Goffman puts the phone to his ear. When someone answers, Goffman introduces himself as David Sandström, Southern Districts Police.

'Fucking hell,' Birck says quietly.

'Did she live here?' I say.

'She did say she was always moving around.' Birck says. 'Before you got there yesterday, when we were chatting. And that she hasn't had a proper home for a couple of years. She stayed here a bit with the girl who lives here, Annelie Lundin. Apparently she's away, gone travelling in the Far East. We'll have to check that, but I'm sure it's right. Then she had a friend on Döbelnsgatan — she used to stay there sometimes. I did a quick search on Swedberg, but didn't find anything. Her parents live in Södertälje. That's where she's from.

'What about her criminal record?'

'Nothing interesting. Little things — vandalism, breach of the peace, that sort of thing. The worst thing I could find was threatening behaviour, against someone from the Party of the Swedes.'

While Birck is talking, Goffman is walking around the flat, muttering to himself, looking for something. Exactly what it is isn't clear, since he doesn't manage to finish any of his sentences.

'Whoever did this,' I say, 'must have been let in. She must have been at home, someone knocked on the door, and she opened it. That means she must have known who he was.'

'Yes,' Birck says. 'Maybe.'

'And that it was someone she trusted. That isn't a very big group of people.'

'No, luckily for us,' Goffman says, standing in the kitchenette, staring into the sink. 'Luckily for us, Radical Anti-Fascism is a small group.'

'Radical Anti-Fascism?' Birck replies. 'How do you know it's them?'

Goffman doesn't answer. I attempt to discern the size of the bullet holes in Lisa Swedberg's chest.

'Shit,' says Birck. 'We were so fucking close. When's that fucking technician going to get here?'

It isn't obvious who he's talking to. I want to put my hand on Birck's shoulder — he looks like he needs it.

'He's coming,' says Goffman. 'Calm down.'

Birck doesn't say anything. Nor do I. There are no last words, and everything is very quiet.

'I wonder why she slept on the sofa,' I say.

'What do you mean?'

'Well, if the girl who lives here, Lundin, is away for a while, why didn't Swedberg sleep in her bed?'

'Maybe she preferred the sofa,' Birck says. 'Who knows.'

'Since we're done here,' says Goffman, who is now standing between us, 'I suggest we take my car.'

'Are we done already?' I ask.

'I've seen everything I need to see. Shall we? Before it gets crowded in here.'

'I've got my own car,' says Birck.

'I know.' Goffman is already halfway down the hall. 'But the music's better in mine.'

'Tragic business, this Heber and Swedberg case,' Goffman says once we're in the car and he's steering us away from Bandhagen. 'So tragic, so very tragic.'

His Volvo is a cool, nippy little car with comfortable seats in the back. You're sitting so low that it feels like you're in a capsule. The world flashes past at eye level. A subtle hint of aftershave hangs in the air. The trim is black and light-grey, and the police radio is switched off. Bob Dylan is singing on the ordinary radio instead, his voice rasping and melancholy.

'Where are we off to?' Birck asks.

'I haven't decided yet.' Goffman stops at a red light. 'The car is a good place to think in. And we need to think. And talk.'

'Is this your own car?' I ask.

'Oh, I wish it were. But no, although I do use it more than anyone else.'

'So it was you then. You've been following us the whole time.'

'That's right.'

Goffman's eyes flit from the road to the rear-view mirror. There is a chink of regret in his eyes, as though he's just admitted doing something he hadn't wanted to do, but it's impossible to tell whether or not it's just a ploy. Everything, including life itself, could be a game to Goffman.

'I'm afraid so,' he adds. 'I'm afraid that's right.'

'Who's in WHO 327?'

'A colleague.'

'What's his name?'

'Her,' Goffman replies, 'name is Iris.'

'Where is she?'

'She's at home, grabbing a couple of hours' sleep, I should think. She's been on duty tonight.'

'Outside Martin Antonsson's house,' I say.

The red light turns amber and then green. Goffman rolls gently into the junction, turns left, and we're heading north, slowly. Through the trees, I catch a glimpse of Globen Arena's distant white dome.

'Yes,' Goffman says. 'Outside Antonsson's.'

'Why?' says Birck.

'Why what?'

'Why have we had you as a tail?'

'Certain people in our department had reason to believe that you hadn't completely handed over the Heber case to us.' He smiles weakly, and the skin around his eyes wrinkles slightly. They are fine wrinkles, revealing a comfortable life, or a tendency to greet adversity with a smile. 'And, once again, unfortunately, it turned out to be true.'

'Yes, about that,' Birck says hesitantly. He takes the little Dictaphone out of his coat pocket, and holds it up alongside Goffman's right cheek. 'I think you should hear what's on this.'

Goffman peers at it.

'I'm afraid I already know what's on there,' he says. 'Interviews with Lisa Swedberg, right?'

Birck withdraws his hand.

'No, no, I didn't mean it like that. I'll take it, gladly,' Goffman says. 'I think that might be for the best, for everyone. Is this the only thing these files are stored on?'

'Yes. But I've edited them, and saved the important parts. Listen to the last file,' says Birck. 'It's not Swedberg and Heber, but it is what I managed to get out of Ebi Hakimi before he died.'

Goffman takes the Dictaphone and puts it in his trouser pocket.

'Ah yes, Ebi,' he says, shaking his head slowly. 'It really is tragic, the whole business.'

At some point since we've been in the car, Goffman has changed the music, from Dylan to The Beach Boys. I try to keep an eye on his hands, but I keep forgetting about it, as though Goffman has perfected the art of diverting attention from them.

'How do you know what was on the Dictaphone?' I say. 'I mean, we're talking about confidential interviews between a researcher and his subject.'

'Confidential,' Goffman says, as if trying it out in his mouth. 'This is where I don't know where to begin.'

'How come your voice is on the Dictaphone? Start there — a telephone call between you and Lisa Swedberg.'

'Yes,' Goffman says, apparently distracted by what seems to be a choice between staying in the right-hand lane or changing to the middle, 'perhaps that is where I should start.'

So Goffman tells us a story, a story which in the end turns out not to be completely true, but maybe it would have been naïve to expect anything else.

It starts one day in February, when Goffman is sitting in his office. He's a man who likes to be on the go, in a car or on foot, and sitting in that same chair in the same old room for too long makes him irritable. That's partly why he reacts so angrily when he gets the message. A note informs him that his duties with the Counter-Subversion Unit have been altered by an unnamed superior. He is now tasked with identifying and collecting intelligence about extremist groups on the Swedish far left.

He's an uncomplicated man with an uncomplicated outlook. He has never been politically engaged, nor felt sympathy for the left or right. He favours simple solutions to complex problems, and what is right or wrong is secondary to what is practical. So he decides to work intensively, to gather sufficient information in as short a time as possible to enable him to claim to have done his bit, and then move on with his life, get on with things in other parts of SEPO's operation that are more productive.

He soon finds himself heading to Cairo, where he and I are both outsiders. He has a good nose, of the kind that can sniff its way to information, and that's what leads him to Lisa Swedberg. He follows her from Cairo one afternoon, and gets hold of her ID-Number.

'You don't want me getting hold of your ID-Number,' Goffman says now. 'Give me that, and anything can happen.'

At the beginning of March, he gets word of Lisa Swedberg's links to a serious crime, the investigation into which was never completed. She was guilty — there was no doubt in his mind, once he'd verified a few basic pieces of information. One morning she wakes up, and he's sitting there, cross-legged on a chair in front of her, his hands joined in the way you do when you appear in front of someone like that.

He tells her what he knows, and how he knows it. Then he 'requests' — that's the word he uses — an exchange of favours. In return for information, she gets Goffman's silence.

'Not regularly,' he says, 'and not anything that could hurt her. That was our agreement, if you can call it an agreement.'

'You blackmailed her,' says Birck. 'You exploited someone who was already pretty much helpless.'

'Yes, true,' Goffman says, 'I suppose we should call things by their proper names.'

Silence. I chew my bottom lip, and think. The Beach Boys are singing about being gone for the summer.

'What was the crime?' I say.

'If there's one thing I have learnt, it is never to speak ill of the dead. A serious crime, but perfectly understandable under the circumstances — let's just leave it at that. She didn't set out to hurt anyone. Where it mattered, she was a good person.'

Unfortunately, trusting people is not a part of Goffman's life, no matter how decent they might seem. That's why he feels compelled to keep her under surveillance, and to keep following her. Later in March — Goffman claims not to remember the exact date, but I'd be surprised if he didn't know not only the date but the exact time as well — he's sitting in a car, rolling along a steady twenty metres behind her, in bright spring sunshine. The sun reflects off the bonnet, causing Goffman's vision to white out for a split second, making Lisa Swedberg disappear, and then suddenly she really has disappeared. She's gone from the street altogether.

Stranger things have happened in Goffman's life, so he parks and walks to the spot where he last saw her, inspects the ground, the nearby side streets, and the shops and cafés. And there she is, sitting in a café.

'With Thomas Heber,' I say.

'That's correct.'

Although, needless to say, Goffman doesn't know who Heber is at this point, he takes a picture of him with his phone. It is Iris who identifies him when she sees the photo a couple of hours later.

They continue with the surveillance, and when she goes home with Thomas Heber a few days later, that's enough to persuade Goffman to do a more thorough background check on Heber.

'I soon found out the same things you know,' he says. 'AFA, the Gothenburg riots, sociology, social movements, blah, blah, blah. It struck me that he might still be the kind of individual our department is interested in.'

Goffman contacts Lisa Swedberg, and she tells the truth, just as Goffman had hoped, except about whether she has any connections to the university. She names various students she knows, people she sympathises or socialises with, but fails to mention Heber. Goffman should really break their agreement at this point and leak what he knows about her past, but — he says, as he taps his nose twice — something makes him stick with it and play along.

'And then bug Heber's apartment,' he adds.

'Of course,' Birck says.

'Of course,' Goffman repeats.

Iris manages to get a youngster from Criminal Intelligence to do it, in exchange for information from SEPO's records, which he wouldn't otherwise have access to. It is the kind of information that will give him a discreet, but nonetheless effective, lift upwards in the organisation's hierarchy.

It's a classic bugging device, speech-activated, and since Heber lives alone but hasn't yet become the sort of person who talks to himself, the recordings are primarily of his conversations with Lisa Swedberg, since she is pretty well his only visitor.

'That was lucky,' Goffman says now, as we glide slowly past Globen. 'It saved us an inordinate amount of work. I'm one of those people who talk to themselves.'

'Yes, I can imagine,' I say.

'Sad really, talking to yourself.' Goffman looks as though he's just realised something disappointing about himself. 'Isn't it?'

'Yep,' says Birck.

Since then, Goffman has known everything about Heber and Swedberg, right down to what they say to each other while having sex. It's strange, he says, knowing how two now-deceased individuals sounded as they came.

'They would have made a lovely couple,' he states. 'Don't you think?'

Neither of us says anything.

'Well, perhaps one can't really say, without ever having seen them together.'

The vast amounts of intelligence they are now gathering on Heber free up resources for other things. When Goffman calls Swedberg to verify a vague tip-off he's received about a threat to a mink farm near Stockholm, he knows that she's sitting face-to-face with the man they're bugging.

'That's when you hear me,' he says, patting the Dictaphone in his trouser pocket, 'when I make my involuntary appearance on this.'

In early December, Goffman confronts Lisa Swedberg with some information that he could only have heard through her conversations with Thomas Heber. It's a slip-up; a moment of carelessness on Goffman's part, and he later feels clumsy, although he is not clumsy by nature. Their agreement states only that Lisa

Swedberg is to tell Goffman the truth, not the other way round, yet something happens to you when you're snooping on someone, hearing all the things that Goffman has heard, so he gives her straight answers.

'Had we been following her? Yes. Had we been bugging her? Yes. Where had we bugged her? In Heber's flat. "Fuck off, you fucking pigs."' Goffman rolls his eyes. 'And so on.'

She doesn't tell Heber, perhaps because she's scared it will end their relationship, or that it might even mean the end of Heber's academic career.

'Actually, she did,' Birck says. 'They met outdoors somewhere, a last meeting. Heber recorded it, even though it wasn't an interview. That's when she told him. She said that his flat wasn't safe.'

This surprises him. He tries to conceal that fact, but doesn't succeed.

'She said that?'

'Yes. It's on the Dictaphone.'

'That could mean all sorts of things.'

The black Volvo rolls over the bridge that links Gullmarsplan and Södermalm, sound-tracked by The Beach Boys at low volume.

The dreamy blue skies and blue sea of the music contrast brutally with reality outside. In Goffman's car, the world feels a bit skewed, like it's leaning slightly and the lines have been erased.

Life carries on as normal in the days leading up to the murder. When the police radio crackles that night, Goffman is sitting in the car outside his apartment in Gärdet, for some inexplicable reason unable to go in. A suspected murder on Döbelnsgatan gets his nose twitching, and he heads down there, peers up the alley, and sees Heber's body lying there. He then goes straight to Vanadisvägen, lets himself in to Heber's flat, using the same key that the young technician had used when he bugged the place, and leaves with the device in his pocket.

... I have watched you on the shore, standing by the ocean's roar ...

214

'I did a poor job,' Goffman says, embarrassed. 'I know I marched straight in without shoe-covers, didn't think first. I was stressed and sleep-deprived. That's one of the reasons we were trying to get the inquiry finished as quickly as possible. I had no choice but to inform Olausson of the complicated nature of the situation straightaway.' He goes quiet while we drive out on to Ringvägen, before adding, 'I'm a practical sort, but I know what the law says about collecting intelligence through listening devices. We would have been in hot water.'

Birck's gaze follows the Christmas decorations in the shop windows. Even the newsstands have put up advent candles and illuminated flashing Father Christmases.

... do you love me? Do you, surfer girl?

'I met Lisa as soon as I could and tried to get her to talk. But she was, as you can imagine, far too preoccupied with anger and grief. I think she blamed us for what happened, even though that is completely illogical, but then those emotions are not guided by reason.'

'She came to us instead,' Birck says.

'I know, we saw.'

'Who killed Thomas Heber?' I say.

'Ah,' says Goffman. 'The sixty-four-thousand-dollar question. We can't answer that yet. What we do know is that a little boy, John Thyrell, almost certainly saw the murderer. We've had him look at a few pictures of faces we know, but rather unsurprisingly, this resulted in nothing more than a waste of taxpayer's money. It was worth a try, my colleagues maintain, but, well, I'm not sure. We also know that one of the knives in the set they have at Café Cairo matches the type of injuries that Heber sustained. We cannot, however, technically tie that knife to his body, because the knife is missing. We can't even put it at the crime scene, since we don't know who used it. We do, however, know that an intruder, or someone wanting to give that impression, broke into

215

Café Cairo that evening. The problem is that one thousand two hundred and fifteen kronor also disappeared from the till that same night.

'An ordinary break-in — they were after the money,' Birck says.

'Or someone on the inside who wanted to make it look that way. That movement is riddled with internal splits, far more so than they would care to admit. Who knows? Someone, of course. Someone always knows. But not us.'

'I was there,' I say. 'At Cairo. They never mentioned the money.'

'Well, I'd say they were trying to avoid attracting any more suspicion. We're already on them fairly hard, for various reasons.'

We turn off onto Hornsgatan, where people are laden down with heavy carrier bags, and have tired but contented, hopeful faces.

'Look at them,' he says. 'Shop, shop, shop. That's all Christmas is about. Anyway, we think it must have been something like this. At the end of November, Lisa gets word of the imminent threat, if that's what we're going to call it. It's probably Ebi Hakimi who tells her, if Heber's notes are to be believed. Swedberg is distraught, anxious, and feels that she needs to talk to someone. She goes to Heber, of course, because the relationship between researcher and subject allows her to reveal it to him without having to worry about potential consequences. The problem is that someone finds out that Heber knows. Who that is, and how they found out, is not known, but in all probability it is someone inside the organisation.'

'The little group within RAF,' I say.

'Yes, let's go with that for now. They suspect that Heber is about to step out of his academic role, become a responsible and upstanding citizen, and go to the police with what he knows. So they silence him. Then comes the next question, which naturally follows from what we already know, and that is: How on earth did Heber know about this? They go through their own lists, and soon realise that it has to be Lisa Swedberg. They decide to act, and,

216

in the hope of avoiding any connection being made between her death and Heber's, they use a firearm this time. They may have known that we had her under surveillance, but that's unlikely. Three people know that; me, Iris, and then one more. It's probably a coincidence.'

'There's one more person who knows about the threat,' I say. '1601. If Heber's notes are to be believed.'

'Yes,' says Goffman, 'If they are to be believed.'

'Do you have reason not to do so?' asks Birck.

'I believe them as much as I believe any scientist. By which I mean, I'm sure that parts of it are true. But he does leave things out. He fails to mention, for example, his relations with Swedberg.'

'Do you know who that is? 1601?'

'No.'

'Would you tell the truth, if you did know?'

'I wouldn't have thought so,' says Goffman.

We're standing at the traffic lights on the approach to the Västerbron Bridge, which stretches out in front of us. I make eye contact with Goffman. His expression is calm, sincere, but I'm still convinced that he's deceiving us.

I've been in this town so long that back in the city I've been taken for lost and gone and unknown for a long, long time ...

'Why Antonsson?' says Birck.

'He is pouring money into far-right groups like Swedish Resistance and People's Front. He's getting older now, must be forty-something? He bought shares in the early Nineties that he had the good fortune to sell at just the right time, before the dotcom bubble burst, so he has been financially secure since then. Anyway, he is now a middle-aged man with far too little time to do anything with the money. Not only that, he is an idealist, one who genuinely loves the White Power movement. We know that, as well as being rather gifted in the field of stocks and shares, he is also a significant player in the distribution of White Power music across northern

Europe. If they managed to get rid of him it would be more than just reducing the cash flow. They would also undermine vital parts of the nationalist movement and the White Power scene, which is all built around music and symbolism. He makes an ingenious political target for left-wing extremists.

… it's all an affair of my life with the heroes and villains …

'Ebi Hakimi,' says Birck. 'It must have been him.'

Goffman raises an eyebrow.

'What must have been him?'

'That she stole the Dictaphone from,' Birck says. 'She claimed she'd been given it, but I don't think that was the case. I think she stole it. It ties him to the crime scene, and to Heber.'

'Yes,' says Goffman. 'That's probably what happened.'

'I never know whether you mean what you're saying or the exact opposite,' I say.

'I do apologise if that's the case.' Goffman watches the traffic light intently. It turns green. 'I can't help that.'

We stop and climb out in front of HQ on Kungsholmen. Three men in heavy overcoats, we could be mistaken for a father and his two sons.

'I am working on the assumption that this is the end of it, for the time being,' Goffman says, with a new, colder expression. 'That we can be done with each other now, that you are going to get on with what you're paid to do, and I'll get on with my duties. And that you'll forward any information you may have to me or Iris.'

'Yes,' I say. 'Alright.'

High above us, so high that it seems to be almost touching the clouds, a large bird sweeps past. No one else seems to notice it. It heads off over the water, with its long wings and gentle movements. I follow it until it disappears. A strange sensation: I'm not really here.

Goffman looks at the car.

'Would you look at that? I forgot to take the blue light off. Typical me, so absent-minded.'

III

LIKE A GHOST

In the days that follow, the temperature in Stockholm drops markedly, from minus fifteen, to minus twenty, to minus twenty-five degrees, causing the homeless, the feral cats, and stray dogs that move in the shadows of the capital to die. As the days pass, rumours of an approaching snowstorm, which the Met Office christens 'Edith', spread through the city. Edith starts in Western Russia and is, strictly speaking, a hurricane. Closest to the eye of the storm, winds of 37 metres per second are recorded, and the hurricane is predicted to peak over Stockholm on the twenty-first of December. Her progress is covered in detail by the websites of the tabloid newspapers. They recount tales of the worst storms in history. They broadcast live. They wait, with bated breath. We all do. Meteorologists, the police, and spokesmen from Fire and Rescue appear on news bulletins, urging people travelling home for Christmas to postpone their journeys until the following Monday, the twenty-third.

As Edith's reputation grows, so does the gathering storm around HQ. Ebi Hakimi's death has caused uproar in the media and the concrete estates around Stockholm. The police, the organisation itself and the bright spark who put a bullet in a demonstrator's eye, come under heavy fire, and accusations of abuse of power fly around. The justice minister cuts short a visit to the UK to deal with the situation, and gets off to a good start by lamenting the death of the protester. Then as everyone expected, she goes on to make everything even worse by calling the demonstrators 'left-wing extremists' and describes the police's actions as 'largely very effective and successful.'

If you're looking for me on the evening of the sixteenth of December, you'll find me on a chair in a flat out in Salem, face to face with my father, within the four walls where I grew up. My mum's gone to a Christmas do with her former colleagues — 'former', since Dad got so bad that he needed full-time care at home.

For people seeing me and my dad for the first time, it probably takes a while for our similarity to become apparent — the slightly crooked nose, the prominent eyebrows, the somewhat lopsided smile, and the way we hold the handle on a teacup when lifting it from the kitchen table.

The TV is showing today's Christmas speech, this time from the leader of the Christian Democrats. He has more of the hedge-fund manager than the politician about him, but he has a friendly voice that puts Dad at ease.

'I think I'm going to go to bed soon,' he says. 'I'm tired, you know. While you've been having fun at school, I've been working all day.'

'Oh, right,' I say.

The clarity that was present in Dad's voice the last time we spoke on the phone is gone, replaced by a thicker fog than any he has been in before. Tonight is the first time he's spoken to me as if I were a child.

'It is fun, isn't it?' Dad says, unsure.

'I almost never had fun at school, Dad. You know that.'

He doesn't answer. His eyes settle on the tea instead, as though he'd forgotten it was there, and he takes a careful sip.

On the telly, the Christian Democrat expounds the value of having your family close at Christmas time, the only time of the year when everyone arrives, from near and far, to gather round the traditional food and the sparkling, hopeful tree. Keeping traditions alive is something we humans do by our very nature, he goes on, and this is more important than ever against a backdrop of huge social change, as illustrated by today's report from The Institute for Social Research.

My eyes move from the screen to the newspaper lying folded on the table.

NEW STUDY SHOWS: CHILDREN OF ETHNIC MINORITIES DISCRIMINATED AGAINST, MONITORED, AND ISOLATED. Children from minority backgrounds are subjected to strict social control by their own families, according to a new report from The Institute for Social Research. The aim is to avoid western-style adolescence. Several anti-racist organisations are extremely critical of the report's working assumptions and its conclusions.

'Did you read this?' I say, and flip the newspaper's front page. He doesn't answer. I don't ask again; I can't be bothered.

We finish our tea. I want to take a Serax, but I resolve not to. I need to try to stop. Before long, my back is warm and sweaty, and my hands are trembling. To distract myself, I help Dad to rinse his toothbrush, and I put some toothpaste on it and give it to him. Dad remembers how to do the brushing, but not the prep work. I imagine a parasite, moving around randomly in Dad's brain, consuming him, replacing his memory with black holes, voids.

I help him to bed, although Mum says he can manage without. Then I carefully press my lips to his forehead, and whisper something, before leaving him and closing the door, and sitting on the chair outside his room where Mum usually sits when he's resting.

It is only then, as I sit there in the hall where Micke and I used to chase each other with our plastic swords and shields, that I start to cry.

Christian is holding himself upright, using the wall next to the stairs for support. Everything is swaying. One minute he's in the stairwell; the next, he's on the sofa.

'How long have you had it?' he asks, attempting to appear normal. 'I mean the sofa? It feels like you've had it for as long as I've known you.'

'I don't know,' Michael says, his eyes fixed on the screen of his mobile phone. 'Fuck's sake.'

'What is it?'

'I got a text from Jens.'

Christian feels a strong sense of foreboding. There aren't many people who scare him. Jens Malm is one of them.

'What does he want?'

'He was asking about Lisa Swedberg.'

'What about her?'

'He wanted to know if I knew who killed her.'

Christian looks up.

'Do you?'

Michael shrugs and smiles. He has a nice smile. It makes his eyes sparkle.

History crashes over him like a wave, and he remembers how it used to be, how he and Michael stuck together when no one else was on their side out in Hagsätra. They were practically children then, yet it still feels so recent: Michael was bored and was wandering around a car park in Salem, moving in between the cars. It was winter. Michael had been a member of the youth movement for less than two months; Christian, a little over one. Michael was convinced he'd ended up in the right crowd; Christian wasn't. Yet.

Christian shaved Michael's head. They did it in Christian's bathroom one night when his mum was out. The thick blond locks disappeared, and coarse stubble took their place. After a few days of deliberation, Christian shaved off his own hair. It felt liberating, almost like becoming a different, cleaner version of himself.

Michael was wearing his black SKREWDRIVER T-shirt under his coat. Christian didn't wear his anymore. He stood smoking a cigarette. A Swedish flag adorned his disposable lighter.

Michael stopped next to one of the cars, a dark-coloured BMW, and spat on it. Then Christian heard the sound of a key scoring into the car's paintwork, relentless and aggressive. He went on and on, from one car to another, until headlights swung across the car park as someone drove in.

He and Christian ran off: he was first, Christian a few steps behind. It was winter, late evening. The moon was out. They were fifteen years old. Christian was turning sixteen in six months, Michael in two.

A few days later, they were back in Salem again, despite the fact that they didn't live there. They'd heard about a new guy who could sort out cheap booze, cheaper than Oliver and all the others in Hagsätra. It was a fair old trip, but it was worth it. They went past the car park on their way there, because Michael wanted to see if the cars were still there.

They were. A couple of shadows were moving in the car park, and then a voice came from the gloom: 'That's him! There's the fucking little whore.'

Time and space, and how they converge. Had they been a minute later, or earlier, their paths might never have crossed. Everything might have been different.

Michael started running, but it wasn't Michael they were after. It was Christian. He didn't get further than the little alley between two of the nearby blocks. That's where they caught up with him, and he can still, years later, feel the force of those blows, the pain of the kicks, the taste of blood in his mouth. One of the kicks snapped something, a rib. The pain made him scream.

They'd got the wrong person, but that didn't matter. He got a kick in the head that turned everything black. His head was shaved, and the ground underneath him was so cold, and he was going to die at fifteen.

That was a long time ago, but he still remembers the way Michael hid in the shadows, invisible to them. Christian didn't blame him, but perhaps he should have.

Michael's wall was decorated with a poster of Charles Manson's face, with the words DO SOMETHING WITCHY TO LET THE WORLD KNOW THAT YOU WERE THERE written across it. He claimed to have been given it, but Christian was pretty sure he'd made it himself.

It was a quarter past three, the twenty-eighth of May. The radio reported a bank robbery that had just taken place in Kisa. Witnesses said that three men had left the scene in a car, heading in the direction of Malexander.

Even though four months had passed since the assault, and breathing was no longer painful, Christian still found walking a struggle. He dreamt about it at night. That's when the fear took root and flourished — the fear, and the absolute conviction.

They weren't members of Jens Malm's movement. This was purely a youth movement, and was somewhat more open, less demanding of its members. It had existed before, but then disbanded, and had recently been re-launched. Jens Malm thought that it would be good for Michael to see how a political organisation was built, from the very beginning. And, if he didn't like it there, Malm had apparently added, he could always talk to him.

But they did like it there, at least to begin with.

Four months since the assault. A lot can happen in four months.

They stood handing out flyers by the square in Kärrtorp. They stood at the entrance to the underground station in Skarpnäck. In Jakobsberg. In Orminge and Gustavsberg, Solna, Danderyd, Gärdet.

They stood all over the place, and they weren't alone. On other squares, in other parts of town, there were others standing there, and then even more. For the first time, something swelled up in Christian's chest: a feeling of strength.

'It doesn't matter whether I know or not,' Michael says now, about Lisa Swedberg's death. 'What matters here is that you don't know.'

'Why am I not supposed to know?'

'What the hell do you think? I don't want you getting in any trouble.'

'I'm already in trouble. I'm the one who stole the knife.'

'The only reason I asked you to do that was because I couldn't be in two places at once. And I don't trust anyone, apart from you.' Michael looks genuinely saddened. 'I didn't want to, but I had no choice. We had no choice. You do understand that, don't you?'

'Course I do,' Christian says, and as he's saying the words he realises they're actually true.

'It was necessary,' Michael says, as if trying to convince himself. 'I still don't get how the fuck she knew about it.'

'Are you sure that she did?'

'If you'd listened to the Dictaphone, you'd know. Not only that, it shows that that fucking Hakimi knew as well.' He laughs out loud. 'Luckily, that cop sorted that out for us anyway. We got out of doing it ourselves.'

All of it, all this death, is spreading inside Christian, like a cancer. He feels nauseous, and wishes he could show it, that he could submit to his body's desire to bend double and throw up.

'It started with Heber,' Michael goes on. 'He said it to Hakimi, who told Swedberg. The question is how the fuck Heber came to know about it.'

'There must be others who've heard us talking about it. That's what happens when you have to deal with things on the hoof.'

'True.' He puts the phone to one side. 'It must be the same bastard who stole the Dictaphone.' His eyes have gone cold, and dark. 'How the hell could we have a leak, with all the entrance tests and checks that we do?'

He gets up, and starts pacing up and down the room. This is what it's been like recently. Michael, unpredictable and paranoid, and Christian, doing his utmost to calm him down. This time, he doesn't succeed. More than anything, he wants to get out of there. Then Christian realises something.

'How did you find out that Heber knew?'

He hadn't asked that question. Once again, he'd just accepted it, because he'd always trusted Michael that much.

'Don't you trust me? Michael asks, as though he can feel Christian's uncertainty.

'Course. This isn't about that.'

Michael is unsure; Christian can see that in his eyes. Then he says, 'Heber called, and wanted to talk to me.'

'And you answered?'

'He rang from a fucking payphone. I didn't recognise the number. I shouldn't have answered it.' Michael stops, over by the window. 'Fuck. Way too many people know, or have heard something, or know someone who's heard something. It's starting to get risky.'

'But did Heber tell you what it was about?' says Christian. 'What he wanted?'

'Yes. He said he knew what we were up to.'

'What did he know? The rumour about Antonsson? How the hell could that have come from us? The only people who know about it are me and you. And Jonathan.'

Michael shakes his head.

'I thought that was what he'd heard about, too, and that Jonathan must have been the leaker. Again. But no, it wasn't about Antonsson. It was about …'

Michael doesn't finish the sentence. He goes quiet instead.

'I think it must have been Jonathan who took the Dictaphone,' Christian says eventually.

'So do I. But I can't prove it — he wasn't the only one who stayed over. And we can't afford to shut him out. He knows too much.'

Christian takes a deep breath, wishing he were somewhere else. 'Should we call this off?' he says.

Six months earlier, it is summer, and Jonathan is turning twenty-two. He's been in for a little over three years, after Christian wooed him at a mutual friend's party in Salem. They've built their movement, Christian says, from the ground up. They are stronger than ever. They are going to change Sweden.

Jonathan cannot resist the temptation, can't say no to the camaraderie and the vision: the interests of the people stand above the interests of the individual. They must be protected. He is tested, goes through initiations, and swears his loyalty. When he looks in the mirror, he stands straighter than he used to, with a look that has more conviction. His life has been instilled with a new purpose.

In June, he gets a phone call from a woman who sympathises with their aims. She wants to give them a present. A Jewish cockroach who took part in the gang-rape of a young woman out in Kista. The Jew, a man from Poland or somewhere, sits in one of the rooms used by the local office of a security company in Kista's shopping centre.

Finally, he has the chance to prove himself. He heads straight for Kista, but on the way he starts having second thoughts. He might be walking into a trap. The sun is shining in his eyes as the underground train glides through Hallonbergen.

He meets the woman. Her name is Iris, and she works with

232

security. She demonstrates that she's on his side by telling him she knows he likes to get high sometimes and giving him a couple of grams of speed.

Jonathan snorts a bit of the speed. His ears pop, and his eyes start running. His airways are burning and wheezing. It's a lovely sensation. She lets him into the room. The Jew is sitting there, captive.

'Fifteen minutes,' she says. 'Don't beat him to death.'

Jonathan smiles. Jonathan is invincible.

The Jew survives, but only just. His hearing will be poor for the rest of his life, and he will need new teeth, might have to lie still in his hospital bed for a few weeks to let the broken bones heal, but he survives.

Jonathan takes a picture with his phone, so that he's got something to show them, but he wipes his hands first. The tiny flash illuminates the dark room.

He steps out of the room. He and Iris are the only ones there.

'Come with me,' she says slowly, and that's when he realises that everything is not as it seems.

A long, long time ago, in Hallunda. Jonathan is in middle school and hasn't started puberty yet. First he gets teased for that, and then, when the bullies realise that you can do a lot worse things than teasing, come the kicks and punches.

The one who helps him — no, protects him — is Ebi Hakimi. Ebi has a strange accent that Jonathan really likes. It's as though Ebi sings when he speaks. He's a warm, gentle person who couldn't possibly set out to hurt anyone. It's not as though he's a pacifist, because that doesn't get you very far in Hallunda. Quite the opposite, in fact. But Ebi is good, and fair. He shares his cigarettes with Jonathan when they go out for sneaky fag-breaks, because Jonathan can't afford his own. He helps Jonathan with homework when Jonathan doesn't get it.

In high school, they drift apart. Jonathan chooses the construction stream, and Ebi chooses social science with communication and leadership studies. They end up in different schools, in different parts of town. They want to stay in touch and at first they do, but before long Ebi makes new friends. So does Jonathan. His friends take him to Totenkopf gigs, and introduce him to people like Christian.

Slowly, Jonathan teaches himself to hate the memory of Ebi's accent. The memory of it is all he has left, since they don't see each other anymore. The accent represents laziness and insouciance. It's not impossible to get rid of your accent. A lot of people do.

And in spite of this, there's the hole. Somewhere within Jonathan, even after he has started socialising with those who are now his brothers and sisters in arms, it's there. The memory of the years spent with Ebi fills him with grief and regret. He doesn't dare to talk about those feelings, not with anyone. That would make him a traitor.

Iris leads Jonathan into a room containing two chairs and a table. On the table is a remote control. There's a man in a suit in there, waiting. He introduces himself as Paul, and has slippery hands. During the conversation, he just stands there, leaning against the wall, observing Jonathan.

Iris explains that the present he's just been given comes with strings attached. She's not asking a lot, she reassures him — just one thing.

'What?' says Jonathan.

'Information. And that you don't show anyone that picture you took. It would look strange.'

'Information about what?'

'A bit about your movement. Things that could be useful for us to know. What you believe, what you think, what you're planning, and so on. That's all. And this is important for us.'

Jonathan gets up from the chair.

'This is illegal. You can't do this.'

'No, no,' says Iris. 'All I did was put the two of you in a room together, with no witnesses. What you got up to in there is nothing to do with me.'

'Fuck off!'

'If you don't agree to this,' Iris says, as though she hasn't heard him, 'we have a problem. So that it doesn't come to this, I've been thinking we ought to be able to reach a compromise that you would be wise to accept. You should get something for your trouble.'

She offers him their complete silence, and money. A lot of money.

'Nothing you say will be traceable to you as an individual,' she says. 'You are anonymous. And I know you need the money.'

She sounds compassionate. This terrifies him.

And as if that wasn't enough, she picks up the remote control lying on the table and points it at the little cube of a monitor behind Jonathan's back. A red light is flashing. She turns it on.

It shows the room that Jonathan was just in — the room where the battered man is still lying.

From now on, he has two phones to keep track of. They are identical, to avoid causing any suspicion. The only way to tell them apart is by the wallpaper. It is a sickening task. Jonathan is an informer, a traitor. It's as though he's falling apart inside. To keep his head above water, he starts doing speed regularly. He buys it on Södermalm from a guy called Felix.

The summer flashes by in a haze. Iris contacts him from time to time, but she is never satisfied afterwards. He gives her whatever information he has, but it is of little value. That much he can work out himself.

It's the end of August. He is going to attend a boot camp in Västergötland, for offensive weapons training. He's out of amphetamine, and requests a large sum of money, in exchange for information about the training camp's structure and content. For the first time, Iris's eyes reveal something other than disappointment and indifference.

And it is there, during the training camp, that he is exposed. They practise martial arts, and their attack training revolves around paintball battles. In the afternoons, they compete in tug-o-war, play a version of rugby they call lightning-ball, drink beer, and light barbecues.

It happens on the last night: the phone falls into the wrong hands. Christian's hands.

'I don't want to do this,' Christian says. 'But I have to.'

He looks dejected, Jonathan thinks to himself. As though he really doesn't want to. Then Christian punches him in the gut. Jonathan recognises that feeling, and he accepts it, almost welcomes it. He deserves it. Part of him feels relieved. It's over, at last.

'Sorry,' Christian says. 'But what you have done …'

Jonathan thinks he can hear Christian sniffle, but he's not sure. It's dark, and in his stomach it's as though his guts are aching, cramping.

Christian hits him in the face. He's about to scream when his nose cracks, but he doesn't manage to do it in time, because everything turns black. When he comes round, he's lying on the floor in his tent. His face is sticky. It takes a second for him to work out that it's blood. His arms are tied behind his back, and a torch in his face blinds him, makes him close his eyes tight. His mouth is covered with gaffer tape.

'No,' he hears Christian say. 'Eyes open.'

Jonathan forces himself to obey. There's a sharp pain in his nose. Snot and blood combine in a brownish sludge that trickles down over the tape.

As his eyes get used to the stark, white light, he just can make out the mouth of a tube. Christian is holding a revolver, and his breathing is strained, his jaws clenched.

Jonathan tries to speak. Christian puts the gun down and rips the tape off.

'Where is he?' Jonathan hisses.

'I'm the only one here,' says Christian.

'I don't want to talk to you.'

'I'm the only one here,' he repeats. Then he crouches, bows his head down to Jonathan's, and whispers in his ear. 'He's waiting outside the tent. I want you to listen to me now. You have two options, and you are going to choose the first, because neither of us could cope with the second. Got that?'

Jonathan nods frenetically. Christian stands up again.

'One,' he says, louder. 'You tell your friend exactly what I tell you to say, and I intend to make sure you don't say anything other than that. Or you can choose option two.'

He puts the tape back on Jonathan's lips, and presses the barrel of the revolver to his temple. It is ice-cold.

Jonathan just wants to scream. He doesn't know what to choose. Christian cocks the hammer. Jonathan pisses himself. The warmth spreads across his groin and down along his thighs.

He doesn't want to die. He wants to be one of them. That's all he's got.

'Make the right choice now, for fuck's sake.' Christian spits.

When I wake up, I do so with Sam's hair in my face. She's lying with her back to me, with her bum against my stomach, and her shoulder blade to my chest. I'm sore, across my back, and naked. She's paler than I am, but while her skin is cool and smooth, mine feels hot and coarse, covered in dried sweat. I am completely devoid of energy; every movement is jerky and tremorous, and my mouth is dry.

The world is collapsing. It always starts with this: the walls tumbling inwards, towards and over me. And as the fear grows, the nausea follows. It's not withdrawal from the physical addiction to Serax that makes me turn the world inside out. It's the fear, the great swell of emotion, that my body simply cannot accommodate.

I force myself out of bed, hobble to the bathroom, and manage to open the tap. The water sloshes and splutters in the sink, and I bend myself over the rim of the toilet. I vomit as quietly as I can, but the convulsions are so powerful that it feels like my stomach is tearing, and I find it hard to breathe.

I black out. I'm hyperventilating. Tears force their way past my eyeballs.

I wonder how long I've been lying there on the bathroom

floor, sweating and wracked by cramps, with the smell of vomit all around me. I must have managed to flush, because the smell soon dissipates and there's nothing but water in the toilet bowl. Eventually, I manage to stand up. The world is tilted, wobbly. I open the bathroom cabinet and find a tube of Serax in the bottom of an old wash bag; I shake out two pills and take them, all without looking at myself in the mirror.

I was neither pissed nor high last night, yet the time after I left Salem feels like a dream sequence, a hazy twilight. Was it me that called her? Yes, yes it was.

I have no idea what we talked about.

I remember this. Sam, the way she dropped to her knees by the bed in front of me, and undid my fly. Locks of her hair tickled my hips. Even now, the next day, when all that remains is the memory of a sensation, I still gasp. I'd forgotten, or perhaps suppressed, how good she is.

In the bathroom mirror, I notice the claw marks on my shoulders — five on one side, but only four on the other. Seeing this fills me with regret, but maybe it's not as tangible as it should be. The Serax takes the edge off.

I squeeze a big blob of toothpaste onto my fingertip, and rub it on my teeth and gums. Then I go back to bed, and I'm relieved to find Sam still asleep there. She might not have heard me. When I put my arm across her tummy, which is softer than it used to be, it's the first time in a long time, yet it still feels as natural as anything I can think of. It's good to be home.

Her sleep seems dreamless, stock-still. When she does wake up, she keeps her eyes closed, puts her hand on my neck, and carefully strokes my hairline with her nails, which makes me shiver. She notices this and smiles, before she pushes one hand down to her thigh and breathes out loudly. Then she puts the finger to my lips and I take it into my mouth. The taste turns everything into a comfortable, white noise, and I forget everything, and the Serax buzzes by my temples, and soon she pushes my face down, giving me silent, determined instructions, and when I finally put my mouth against her, she's so hot it burns.

'What are you doing today?' she asks me afterwards.

'I'm going ... I have to see Grim.'

'Oh, right.' She's making an effort to avoid giving anything away, which gives everything away. 'Why?'

'I need to see him.'

Sam doesn't say anything. She stays in bed, and plays some sort of game on her phone while I get dressed. Her cheeks are rosy. I open my mouth, then close it again, and sit down on the edge of the bed.

'It's ... I need ...'

'I know,' she says.

She puts her phone down and runs her hand through her tangled hair. Then she laughs at something on her palm.

'I've got cum in my hair.'

'Sorry.'

'I kind of like it.' The smile disappears, and she's serious again. 'What do you talk about when you meet up?'

'Nothing in particular.'

'Do you talk about me?'

'Sometimes.'

I look away.

'Hey,' Sam says, and puts out her hand, stroking my forearm, 'it's okay.'

'Why do you say that?'

'Because you look like you're about to start blubbing.'

I give Sam a spare key and then I'm off, out onto Chapmansgatan, its pavements covered in slush and grit. I wonder where Goffman is. Since we parted company last, I haven't seen the black Volvo anywhere, and I'm sure Birck hasn't either. Goffman is probably sitting somewhere in Stockholm, waiting for something. I read the headlines as I pass the newsstand. No attack overnight. It might be empty words.

Sweetest sisters. Esther.

Ebi Hakimi's last words could have been the result of his brain sending impulses to his mouth to make noises that sounded like words — noises that might not mean anything. They might have been the answers to Birck's questions. Could have been a name. Who knows? Maybe Ebi Hakimi didn't even know himself.

'Have you missed me?' Grim asks as we sit opposite each other in the chilly visiting room.

'Yes.'

'Same here.' He leans across the table, and sniffs. 'You've had sex.'

I can't help blushing.

'Yes.'

'With Sam?'

'Yes.'

'Well done.' Grim smiles. 'Does she know you're here today as well?'

'Yes, she does.'

'Was that the first time you've had sex?'

'Since the break-up, yes.'

'How was it?'

'That's none of your business.'

'So, not great then?'

'I didn't say that.' I hesitate. I shouldn't be saying this, but something pulls it out of me, puts the words onto my tongue. 'She reminded me of something that I …'

'What did she remind you of?'

'That I used to say that I couldn't cope without her.'

Grim sniggers.

'Hollow fucking words.'

'It was true. That's how I felt.'

'Don't you feel that anymore?'

'I don't know.'

Grim doesn't seem to care all that much about this. He yawns — a loud, drawn-out gasp —before bringing his hand up to his face and smelling it. He grimaces.

'The drugs they give me. I'm sure I can smell them on my skin, in my pores. So fucking nasty.'

'You could just not take them.'

'How? They make sure I've swallowed them.' Grim has a spark of curiosity about him. 'Something is different this time.'

'What would that be?'

'Something about you.' He rests his arms against the edge of the table. 'Like you're full of remorse.'

'Yes.'

'Why?'

'I don't think I can stop. And I've only got two left.'

'You've only got two Serax left?'

'Yes.'

'Well, get some more then.'

'I can't. If I get another script, it'll be in my notes. I could get caught.'

'Have you had withdrawal symptoms?'

'I thought I was going to die.'

Grim looks at me, with a look that you could easily mistake for empathy if you weren't careful.

'I know the feeling,' he says. 'Keep trying. It's near enough impossible to come off them altogether without any help. The only way is to cut down gradually.'

'Do you really want me to get clean?'

'Yes, of course I do.'

'Why do you want that?'

'Why are you asking me that?'

'Ever since I started trying to quit, my life has been a fucking nightmare.'

'Fuck you, Leo. You're back at work, aren't you?'

'Yes, but …'

'But what?'

'I mean, it's like you enjoy this — seeing me in a state.'

'I don't. And that was a shitty thing to say.'

'I never know what you're up to. Is it any wonder I'm a bit suspicious?'

'As I said, if you don't believe me, fuck off. That's fine by me.'

Silence. I'm embarrassed, although I don't want to be, about having challenged him.

'What did you come for?' he asks.

The palms of my hands are clammy. I want to get up and walk away, but I avoid looking at the door, because that would give Grim the upper hand. It's not that easy to talk to someone when you have to tell the truth the whole bloody time.

'You know who Felix is, don't you? The dealer on Södermalm?'

'What the fuck is this? You collaborating with the drugs squad now?'

'This isn't about an investigation,' I say. 'I need his number.'

'How come?'

I don't answer.

'How come?' Grim insists.

'You know why,' I hiss.

'I thought you had his number.'

I shake my head.

'I got rid of all those numbers when I got back on duty. And I can't get it at HQ without arousing suspicion.'

I wonder what Grim is thinking. He might be trying to work out whether or not I'm telling the truth.

'I want a TV.'

'I can't arrange that,' I say. 'Too big. I can get you a better phone — anything bigger than that won't work.'

'One that I can watch telly and read the news on,' Grim says.

'I'll check with the robbery unit, see if they've got one lying around that they could donate.'

Grim shakes his head.

'A new one, with as pay-as-you-go SIM. Paid for with your own money. It's nearly fucking Christmas, after all.'

This makes me laugh. Pay-as-you-go is far harder to trace.

'No, 'fraid not. No pay-as-you-go.'

'Alright. One with a contract then.'

'Alright.'

'Do you promise?'

'I promise.'

Grim's eyes have the same quality as dolls' eyes: what they communicate depends on the beholder. You see what you want to see. He says Felix's number, one digit at a time.

'Will you remember it?' he asks.

'If you've given me the wrong number, if I don't get through to

244

Felix, I'll make sure they take away the phone you've got.'

'If you don't get through, it'll be because you've dialled the wrong number.'

The door opens, and Slog comes in. His big goatee is dense and red.

'Visiting time is over. It's time for John's morning session.'

'If you need more pills,' Grim says quietly, hopefully quietly enough for Slog not to hear, 'I've got other numbers you can call.'

'I thought you wanted me to get clean?'

Grim laughs.

'See you, Leo.'

'So.' I lean forwards. 'You mean you weren't hitting him, you were …' I flip through the notes. 'Dancing with him?'

'That's right.'

'He tells me this happened out on the street, and I've got two witnesses saying the same thing. Is that right?'

'What do you mean?'

'That you were dancing in the street.'

'Well, yes, that's right.'

'Isn't that a bit unusual? Especially when it's minus twenty?'

'I didn't think it was cold.'

'How come, if it's true that you were dancing, that ring on your finger looks a very good match for the mark on his cheek?'

'I don't fucking know.'

Her blood-alcohol level was 2mg/ml when they brought her in and put her in a cell to sober up. She ended up having to sit there quite a while before being dragged down here. It doesn't seem to have made any discernible difference. The woman still stinks of alcohol, and the stench fills the room. I feel sick.

Four hours ago, a man lost two teeth outside a pub on Vasagatan. He claimed that a woman had hit him. The woman claimed they were dancing. It could be a matter of how you define these things, but I doubt it.

'Thank you,' I say, and get up, because this has to end somehow. 'I don't have any further questions.'

Everything is back to normal.

I'm in my office, with the interview transcript in front of me and the door open. Phones ring in the other rooms, but not mine. A radio somewhere broadcasts a news bulletin and then plays The Beach Boys' version of 'Little Drummer Boy.' The voices and the chimes send me back in time, back to that journey through Stockholm in Goffman's car.

Later that day, on my way home, I spot Levin on the other side of Kungsholmsgatan. His coat is wrapped tightly around his bony frame, its collar turned up towards his cheeks to shield him from the snow and the gathering wind. It's so cold that any moisture in the air freezes, becoming tiny, glistening, fragments of pearl. Levin is walking along with his hands in the pockets of his long coat, determined but without appearing flustered or nervous. When a car rolls out onto the junction he raises one hand, getting it to stop. He jumps in the back seat, and I wait there, half a block away. The car disappears towards St Göran's. I didn't get a good look at the driver. It could have been Goffman.

I remember what Grim told me, about Levin visiting someone there. How he'd asked Grim to keep quiet about it. I wonder if it's true.

On a brick wall covered in advertising is a big poster of the Sweden Democrats party leader. He's smiling at the camera, under the banner THE PARTY FOR ALL SWEDES.

I take a Serax tablet from my pocket, and realise it's the only one I've got left. Fuck. I get Felix's number out. That was close.

If you think about it, you realise that it's too risky, so the only way is not to think about it at all, but just to do it.

I push the intercom buzzer and look around me. Maria Prästgårdsgata is nothing more than slush and parked cars, self-obsessed media types with mismatched outfits. No one's bothered, because there's nothing suspect going on here.

'Yes?' rasps a voice from the intercom.

'Hi.'

That's all that's needed. The lock clicks. I push the door and walk into the stairwell. Felix lives on the second floor, and I take the stairs, knock on the door, and wait. Behind the door I can hear music that sounds like it's come from an 8-bit Nintendo game being played loudly. The electronic din finds its way out into the stairwell, and bounces off the walls.

When the door eventually opens, Felix is beaming at me, bare-chested, but with a pair of jeans on. He is wiry and pale, like a dying man, which he might well be.

'Junker,' Felix says and licks his lips. 'It's been a while. Come in, come in, I'm just doing a stock-take.'

I close and lock the door behind me. Felix disappears into the little two-bed flat, and turns the music off. It smells stuffy and sour, a mixture of sweat and weed. On a table in the living room is a packet of heroin the size of a house-brick, zip-seal bags filled with powder or marijuana, and a variety of tubes in black, orange, and white, and blister-packs of tablets and capsules. Next to them is an open, half-full bottle of whisky, kept company by a heavy, low glass. Next to the table, on a wooden chair, Felix is sitting with a notebook and a pen.

'Covering costs?' I ask.

'If there's one thing that covers costs these days, this is it.'

Felix laughs. He grabs the bottle and carefully pours a couple of fingers into the glass, then sips.

'I just sold fifty grams of coke to a nightclub owner. She was going to treat her guest list. Before that, five grams of morphine to a fireman, and ten joints to a nursery nurse. He laughs again. 'I mean, a nursery nurse? This town is fucked up. I feel like Father Fucking Christmas.'

'They're called pre-school teachers nowadays.'

Felix takes another sip.

'And I'm a pharmaceutical distribution agent.'

I pull the roll of notes from the inside pocket of my coat and offer it to Felix.

'I'm in a hurry. Can you help me out?'

'Ah,' Felix says, putting the glass to one side. He takes the notes, and counts them. 'Serax on the wish-list.' He squints at me like a tailor sizing up his client. 'What sort of dose are you on now?'

'Twenty-five to fifty milligrams a day. I don't want to increase it, but I need to avoid the withdrawal symptoms.'

'Hmm,' Felix says, scratching his cheek. 'The thing is, I haven't got any Serax.'

I stare at him, and take two steps towards him.

'Give me the money.'

'Calm down, Junker. Chill. I thought I did when you rang, okay? Then I checked.'

Felix's eyes are darting between me and the sofa on the far side of the table — a worn-out, pale two-seater from IKEA, with two equally pale cushions on it. Behind one of them is bound to be a weapon.

'And?'

'I've got other benzos, okay? Believe me, you'll be thanking me for this.'

Felix starts rummaging around his table, and locates two tubes with white caps: one orange and one black.

'OxyContin,' he says, waving the orange one. 'Or Halcion. I'd go with Halcion. You can barely get hold of it anymore. And it's got a pretty flat effect curve, which should suit you if you're just trying to keep on top of the abstinence.'

'Halcion? You mean the sleeping pills from the Eighties? What the fuck would I want them for?'

'Listen. In the great fables, Halcyon was this bird that could calm storms and the waves in the sea. Trust me, there's something in it. Halcion is an extremely potent benzoid. You only need a tiny dose — never more than half a milligram, unless you want amnesia and to be wandering around like a zombie. Point 25 is enough for that wonderful chemical calm, but you're still lucid. Not only that,' he adds, with a wry smile, 'Halcion was part of the cocktail that did for Heath Ledger.'

Felix chucks me the tube. I catch it, and read the information on the side of the tube. It's in English. I pop off the lid, and my mouth starts watering. The pills are small, oval shaped.

'Those are point two-fives. I've got fifties, too, if you should need them. As long as you don't lie down, you'll be awake and really, really caned.'

'How much?' I ask. 'How much do you want for them?'

Felix waves the roll of notes.

'Should be more. But it's Christmas soon, isn't it? And it's not every day you get the honour of supplying an officer of the law. Well, actually, it is most days. But not such a corrupt copper as your good self.'

'Fuck you, Felix.'

'Merry Christmas.'

He was seventeen, and it hurt when he breathed.

From his bed in his room, Christian could see the pictures on the television, how his friends clashed with a load of Reds on Medborgarplatsen. The police were there. In the background, Christian could see Michael throwing the knuckleduster in a bin and then disappearing. Christian himself couldn't take part. Pneumonia had laid him low, and that really pissed him off. He would have really loved to be there, standing by their side. He tried to get on with his homework instead, but he couldn't concentrate.

A couple of months later, it was summer, and it was warm. He and Michael went to the Youth Movement parties. They did Nazi salutes. They laughed, but not at that gesture.

That evening, Christian got his first ever blowjob. Her name was Olivia, and she had the kind of breasts you dream about when you're seventeen. She was wearing a glossy, khaki-green latex vest with a neckline that revealed her deep cleavage.

'Wait,' she said, while they were standing there in the toilet.

She took a step backwards.

Olivia slowly undid the zip on the tight-fitting vest.

She smiled. She wasn't wearing a bra. As her cleavage opened, he saw it: the swastika that revealed itself on the skin between her breasts.

Christian and Michael kicked the fuck out of some nigger on the way home. His teeth smashed like glass.

That night, he lay on his bed in Hagsätra, and couldn't get to sleep. He was thinking, eyes closed. He felt a lump in his throat, and felt weird when he realised where this was going.

They went on torch-lit marches with shaved heads and heavy boots. They got spat at by red bastards and Swede-haters, who would shout that they didn't want Nazis on their streets. They really didn't get it, did they?

Christian and Michael were two of the youngest members of Sweden Democrat Youth. They were protected by the older ones, who were bigger and stronger. That's how brotherhood works.

He'd nearly died in Salem. His attackers were Turks. According to Michael, it was about more than the car. Michael said that those Turks had known that they were members of Sweden Democrat Youth. And, according to Michael, they hated Swedes.

Christian had started to change: he could feel it in his chest, in his hands, within himself, as though the essence of his being had altered.

In glossy shop windows, he could see his reflection and feel pride, belonging. As though he and his best friend had been allowed to join a group that had a secret in common, an insight. Who understood the problem and what the solution would have to be like.

And then, in a flash, came the disorientation and the fear.

'I don't get it,' Michael said one evening in late autumn that same year. He still had the phone in his hand. 'I don't get what the fuck just happened.'

'Who was that?'

'That was Nille.'

Nille, Niklas Persson, was a local hard man, leader of the group in south Stockholm.

'Okay?' said Christian.

'He's just been on the phone to the chairman.'

'What, he has?'

Michael nodded stiffly.

A couple of months earlier, they'd got a new chairman, a hawk-eyed man from Sölvesborg. Those eyes shimmered with his vision of what Sweden Democrat Youth stood for and should stand for.

'He's demanding that we fall into line,' Michael said now. 'Exactly the kind of shit we were afraid of.'

The rumour had been circulating for a long time, but nothing had happened. Apparently, the chairman and a small band of loyalists had been charting the members' backgrounds — above all, their use of violence. Sweden Democrat Youth was the future of the party, and if the party proper was ever going to become a significant player in the political arena, it was going to be necessary for its members to be able to keep themselves in check. No trouble. No Nazi references. No uniforms at meetings or demos. Having a few members who could be trusted was far preferable to having an army, greater in size, but unpredictable and with an unfortunate habit of ending up on the front pages of the papers. And now the purge had started, for real.

'What do you mean? Did you get kicked out?'

'Yes. Indefinitely. And I'm not the only one.'

Something inside Christian vibrated.

'Me too?'

'No, I don't think so. He didn't say anything about anyone else — he just said I wasn't the only one. Wait and see if your phone rings.'

'But I …' Christian tried to put his feelings into words. 'I don't want to stay, either way.'

Michael smiled, feebly.

'I admire your loyalty. But there's no fucking way you should leave just because I am.'

'But I want to.'

He looked at Christian.

'You sure?'

Christian looked away, down, at the phone his friend still had in his hand.

'Yes.'

Their calm conversation quickly became an enigmatic silence. Christian turned on his friend's PlayStation, gave him one of the controllers, and took the other one himself. They played ice hockey. Christian was Finland; Michael got to be Sweden. As they played, Michael got more and more agitated, even though Christian was letting him win. He gripped the controller so hard that the colour started to drain from his knuckles.

'I need to go for a fucking walk or something,' Michael said in the middle of the third period, and slung the controller to the floor. 'I can't just sit here. I'm too fucking angry for that.'

The streets were shiny from the rain, the sky was full of heavy clouds, blacker against the black sky, and they seemed to be pulsing above their heads. They walked side-by-side, hands in pockets, past Hagsätra precinct and away towards Lake Långsjön. They stopped by the tunnel and watched the commuter trains thundering past on the tracks above.

'It's such fucking ... hypocrisy.' Michael lit a cigarette. 'Everyone who's still there, they believe exactly the same things we do. The only difference is that they're too chicken to show it. And how the fuck are we going to change Sweden? Do you want one?'

Christian took a cigarette from the pack, lit it, and inhaled deeply.

'Yes,' he said after a while, having decided that he agreed. 'They're hypocrites, the lot of them.'

'The worst is that cunt from Sölvesborg. Who the fuck does he think he is anyway?'

Christian looked down at the ground, at shattered glass, crumpled cans, and a shredded carrier bag from ICA.

'I'm going to call Jens,' said Michael. 'He's going to be so fucking furious. You know he's been saying this all along, right? Ever since we got a new chairman, that this was going to happen?'

'Yes.'

'What's up with you?'

He looked up.

'What do you mean what's up with me?'

'You just seem … it's like this doesn't matter.'

Christian took a deep breath, watching the cigarette glow.

Then he said, 'I'm just so fucking disappointed.'

And Christian's phone never rang. He got to stay. He left anyway, out of loyalty. He called Nille and told him. Nille said he understood.

To demonstrate that what had happened was nothing short of treason, Christian and Michael put the windows through at the local party office.

The chairman reported them to the police. They were sentenced to heavy fines. The hate in Michael's eyes grew. It spread out, spread into Christian. They were about to turn eighteen.

As the cab pulls up outside HQ, the morning sky is restless, in constant motion. The thermometer on the taxi's dashboard shows the temperature outside at minus twenty-two degrees. The biting cold stabs at your cheeks, your fingers, everywhere. The storm is gathering.

The cogs in my brain are moving slowly and jerkily thanks, to sleep deprivation. I could do with something strong to get them moving, but all I've got is coffee. I don't want to take my first Halcion here. Halcion scares me.

The door to my room is pushed open by two thick chair legs. Behind them comes Birck, his rough hands gripping the chair's back. He pushes my wobbly extra chair out of the way with his foot, and dumps the new one in its place.

'There,' he says. 'Merry Christmas.'

'Thanks. But I'm getting quite fond of the old one.'

'What the hell is wrong with you?' Birck sits himself down on the new chair. 'Ah.'

Outside the window, a little way away, the dead trees are rustling.

'Jesus, it's blowing a gale,' he says.

'I know.'

Birck taps the armrest with the fingernail of his index finger.

'No news about Antonsson or RAF?'

'No,' I say. 'Such as?'

'I don't know. I can't get my head round it. Would they really kill him? Murder isn't covered by the statute of limitations. It just feels a bit clumsy.'

'The whole thing is clumsy. And you heard what Goffman said — Antonsson is a big player.'

'A little bird told me,' Birck says, distant, 'he's a real paranoid sort, and apparently he's locked himself in his house out in Stocksund, with police protection. A good way to spend taxpayers' money. Not only that, but the Security Police are constantly pulling in members of RAF's inner circle, interrogating them as if they were terrorists.'

'They might be.'

'Yes.' Birck gets up from the chair. 'Or they might be kids from tough estates who've listened to too much Rage Against the Machine. What are you up to?'

'I'm working on the assault on Vasagatan.'

'Ooh, how exciting.'

'What about you?'

'An eighty-five-year-old man threatened a seventy-nine-year-old woman with a breadknife. The man is bedridden, has been for three years, and the woman is deaf. But he did threaten her — she's very specific about that, if you believe what the interpreter says. And you should, shouldn't you. Interpreters are good people.' He grasps the back of the chair. 'Are you around for a while?'

'I don't know.'

'Are you going to St Göran's?'

'No, I went the day before yesterday.'

'Was it alright?'

'Yes.'

Birck looks at me, unsure.

'Be careful.'

'You know I am.'

257

This makes Birck laugh. He lifts the chair off the ground, manages to open the door, and backs out of the room.

'Right, I'm off, and I'm taking my comfortable chair with me. See you.'

After a while, I put the old chair back, and once it's in its place on the other side of the table, I have a sense that things are as they should be.

'Have you heard?' Michael said down the phone.

'Heard what?' said Christian.

He wasn't quite with it, having been dragged from his sleep by the ringtone.

He looked over at his alarm clock: seven minutes past eleven in the morning.

'Daniel Wretström has been murdered down in Salem.'

'Who is Daniel Wretström?'

'One of ours.' Michael sounded devastated. 'The drummer in *Vit Legion* (White Legion). Murdered by a bunch of niggers.'

Christian sat up in bed.

'But he's not from Stockholm, is he? What the hell was he doing there? Were they doing a gig there?'

'He was just visiting. I think he's got cousins here, or something.'

The drummer from Vit Legion, murdered. Impossible to take in.

It was the tenth of December. They had been members of Swedish Resistance for less than two weeks. Jens Malm was in charge of their initiation, and he'd introduced Christian and Michael to a handpicked group of their members.

It took a while to get it straight — who Jens Malm actually was. At a party, Christian had seen a photo of two men holding a wreath. The masked men were wearing black bomber jackets, black jeans, and tall boots. The statue: Gustav II Adolf in Gothenburg. The two men stood with their heads bowed, as if in mourning.

'The seventh of November 1992,' Malm said as he appeared alongside Christian with a glass of beer in his hand. 'The first time we were able to join the commemorations. I'm on the left there. I went down with my friend.'

He said it with pride. In the centre of the wreath was a symbol that Christian recognised: the Wolfsangel. It symbolises defence, and resistance.

'Who's that?' Christian asked. 'Your friend?'

'His name was Linus,' Malm said. 'He was murdered on the way home from the station three months later by a gang of niggers.'

Malm didn't say so, but Christian already knew. He'd been told: a week after that, Malm had put a knife in one of the attacker's throats. It had been in the papers — Christian had seen the clippings.

When Malm raised his glass to drink, Christian spotted the tattoo on the underside of his right arm: there it was again, The Wolfsangel. Discreet, but elegant.

'Fancy getting one?' Malm said with a smile.

'I can't get a WAR tattoo, but I might get a Swedish Resistance one.'

'If you do, make sure that it's visible when you want it to be, but that you can hide it with a long-sleeved shirt or a high collar.'

Visible tattoos raised your status: you get stigmatised by the rest of society, but within the movement it's seen as concrete proof of your ideological conviction. It took three months until he and Michael had both done it: the slogan and symbol of the Swedish Resistance on their chests.

Malm nodded approvingly.

He was from Nyköping, but, beyond that, information about his background was hard to come by. He'd been a member of the Nordic Reich party, but left for WAR, the White Aryan Resistance. He led a large number of their attacks on refugee hostels, and advanced the movement's positions. After being convicted of manslaughter he was sentenced to jail, and when he was released a few years later he no longer had ties to WAR. No one knew why. From a distance, he observed the Sweden Democrats and their youth wing, watching as the party atrophied while he laid the foundations for what would become Swedish Resistance. Jens Malm's life story included plenty of the sort of anecdotes that were ideal for recounting while drinking beer and holding your right arm aloft. People said he'd once been attacked by two police dogs who mauled his legs while he stood, emotionless, with a pennant in one hand and his other, the right, raised in a sharp salute. That he had single-handedly chased five AFA activists away from a demo in Kungsträdgården. That he'd stolen weapons from the Hell's Angels to finance the struggle.

He showed Christian and Michael an SS dagger that had once belonged to Reinhard Heydrich, the SS officer who founded the Sicherheitsdienst intelligence agency and who the Führer himself had described as a man of steel.

My God.

Christian got to touch it, even got to feel the weight of it in his hand. It was heavy. He felt filled with history, and with his own engagement: as though a part of him had always been hollow and the struggle they were fighting for had taken root inside him, and had made him whole.

Joining Swedish Resistance was a decision for life, not something that could be undone. Christian and Michael swore the oath:

I, as a free Aryan, do solemnly swear an irrevocable oath: to be joined in common cause with my brothers in the movement and I proclaim that from this point on I will have no fear of death, nor my enemy. The struggle requires more than words alone and I am duty-bound to do what is necessary to save our people, our borders and our culture, from the foreign threat. Duty-bound to bring absolute victory to the white race. We are in the midst of an all-out war, and we will not lay down our arms until the enemy is reduced to the last man. Through our struggle, we shape our children's future.

The words felt dangerous, malignant. Important.

Christian and Michael were given reading lists and *The Swedish Resistance Handbook*, and they learnt to follow the rules laid down by the organisation. Keep tabs on your alcohol intake. Avoid drugs during demonstrations and other actions. Never attack from a position of numerical weakness, only from a position of strength. If we are demonstrating and you have been given the honour of carrying the banner, concentrate solely on not dropping the banner, no matter what; it must always stand upright, as a symbol for the struggle.

They were instructed to conduct themselves calmly and carefully: the struggle would take time. According to Jens Malm, there were over a hundred of them altogether. Malm called the man from Sölvesborg a race-traitor and a hypocrite, telling them that the purging of Sweden Democrat Youth was part of a worrying broader trend in the nationalist movement, which was being beaten back by forces that hated Swedes, hated the white race.

Less than a week after Daniel Wretström's murder, they made a pilgrimage down to Salem. Everyone was there. They raised toasts to Daniel, and talked about how they'd meet again, in Valhalla. There was something vaguely comical about the whole thing, with all these pub-racists who happened to be there changing their tune to suit their audience, claiming to listen to Ultima Thule and to be part of the struggle, yet who moved politely to one side when they met mongrels on the underground. There were people who would stand alongside nationalists when it suited them, but who didn't dare stand up and be counted when it really mattered.

The solidarity struck a chord all the same. There were so many of them. When you hear the noise from a crowd like that, it's hard to remain unmoved.

They saw members of the Sweden Democrats. They saw Nille and others from Sweden Democrat Youth.

'I hope they behave themselves,' Michael muttered. 'Otherwise they'll get thrown out next.'

They listened to speeches, about sorrow and struggle and freedom. They raised toasts. Several were in tears, but not Christian. He was still caught up in the belonging, in the common cause, and he clenched his fists in simmering rage at the thought of what one of their number had been put through.

It was weird being back in Salem. It was the first time since the assault. Time doubled back on itself, and in an instant he was back in the car park, being chased by the dark shadows. But this time he didn't run away. This time he stood his ground, and showed resistance.

Afterwards they headed back to Bandhagen with Jens Malm, sitting in the very car that might have been the reason for everything that followed. It made a pleasant sound, and Jens was playing White Legion for Daniel. He was moved, and told them about the gigs he'd been to, what an accomplished drummer Daniel had been. They got to Bandhagen but kept going, on into the city centre. Malm just couldn't stop talking, reminiscing. Eventually, they turned back. Michael needed to get home.

Christian was in the back seat. Through the window, he looked out on the estates lining the route of the Metro's Green Line, as the small houses in Stureby gave way to the heavy, grey apartment blocks of Högdalen and Rågsved.

To the sound of White Legion, they rolled down Glanshammarsgatan, listening to a drummer who was the same age as them when his life was taken from him.

One year later, when Jens Malm appointed Michael as leader of the Stockholm chapter of Swedish Resistance, Christian stood by his side.

Big ideas need little people.

This was their time.

It's the end of August, and Jonathan's stint at the training camp is over. His nose is broken after Christian's blows, and on the inside his divided loyalties are tearing him apart.

At first he fears for his life, convinced that other members are going to attack him. The fear follows him at night, into his dreams. But he eventually realises that only he, Christian, and one other person know. No one else has any idea of his treacherous behaviour.

He gets the chance to explain things to Christian. How they tricked him. How they gave him money, which kept him on the speed, and got him stuck in its grasp. Christian reassures Jonathan that he'll get the chance to make them pay.

October. Autumn sweeps in over Stockholm. The leaves on the trees outside Jonathan's flat turn yellow, go stiff, get picked off by the wind, and then fall to the ground.

Iris contacts him one evening. She rings the safe phone, and when the call comes through he counts the rings: one, two, three … If he doesn't answer by the fifth, he doesn't answer at all — that was their arrangement. This time, though, he answers after three. They arrange to meet in the usual place, in Iris's car, on a little street close to Stora Skuggan's old bandstand. It's cold, and as he approaches the car she starts the engine, as she always does. He curls up in the passenger seat, and Iris drives off.

'No one following you?' she asks.

'I wouldn't have come if there had been.'

'It's important that you're sure.'

'No one followed me.'

'Good.'

She asks for an update on Swedish Resistance, what's going on, and what they're planning, when and how. He gives her those parts of the truth that he's been instructed to tell her, things that are pretty irrelevant, but enough for her not to suspect that he's pulling the wool over her eyes. He tells her about their faction's most recent meeting, and how they're planning to synchronise with Gothenburg and Malmö to increase their strength. How Jens Malm came up with the idea, and developed a strategy for its implementation.

That's how they're organised, in factions. Jens Malm is the national, supreme leader. Underneath him are the leaders of the four city-based factions.

'Okay, Jonathan. Good.'

Iris isn't making notes. She never does, but Jonathan's pretty sure she records their conversations. He just doesn't know how.

They roll past the roundabout by Sveaplan, towards Odengatan. Jonathan is sitting low down in the passenger seat, and feels strangely protected from the world outside. Iris's car makes him feel safe. They stop at a red light, and Iris reads something on her phone.

'Shit,' she says before realising her mistake, Jonathan can tell.

'What is it?'

'Nothing. Not anything to do with us.'

'Tell me.'

She shakes her head. She seems to be weighing it up, and she glances over at him.

'Do you know who Martin Antonsson is?'

'Yes. Of course I do. He's one of the people who finances ...'

She bites her lip.

'RAF are contemplating an attack on him.'

'Eh?'

'I don't know any more than that.'

The lights change to green.

'Not yet. But I've had it confirmed by two different sources — there's even some technical evidence that points to it.'

'What kind of evidence?'

'Amongst other things, we found a plan of Antonsson's house at the home of one of the suspects. I can't say any more than that. But you need to keep this quiet. I'm only telling you because one of you needs to know, if you're in his presence.'

Jonathan avoids looking at her, staring instead at the road and the tarmac disappearing underneath them.

'I need money,' he says.

This is sufficient for her to understand. Silence and information, in exchange for compensation. That's how it works now. At least, that's what Iris thinks.

'You can drop me by T-Centralen underground station,' he says.

They always split up in different places, and never at the same time of day. Irregularity is the key to keeping their connection invisible and unknown, to keeping it intact.

When he gets out of Iris's car on Vasagatan, he heads straight underground, through the turnstiles down to the platforms, where he takes the Red Line southbound. Then he changes at Slussen, and gets a train towards Hagsätra instead. He avoids looking around, because no one else is. If he's being followed by Iris's colleagues, unusual behaviour would be risky. Only a handful of passengers get on through the same door as him, and he changes carriages at every station. By Gullmarsplan he's sure: no one's following him, and only then does he get his phone out and call Christian.

'We need to meet up,' says Jonathan. 'I'm on my way to yours.'

Jonathan spends that night lying awake in bed, and that's when the thought first occurs to him. He's been so preoccupied by the information he's received that he hasn't had time to stop and think about what it might mean. After telling Christian, he was commended and asked to keep a low profile. He was told that Christian would tell his superiors, so that the people who needed to know would be told.

'Good, Jonathan,' said Christian. 'That's good. Now go home and get some sleep.'

And it is now, lying there in the dark, listening to the sound of his own breathing, that the thought strikes him: Ebi.

He's in Radical Anti-Fascism, in the small black group. If Jonathan can get them to abandon their plan, Antonsson will continue supporting the nationalist struggle. And Ebi — his old friend, the one who used to protect him — will be okay. Jonathan shuts his eyes. They've seen each other at demos, at a distance, but have kept out of each other's way.

The next morning, Iris's money has reached his account. He calls Felix. For the next week, he is constantly high, partying non-stop. It's the only way to keep the thoughts at bay.

By the evening of the nineteenth of October, the drugs have run out. He should leave it, take Christian's advice and lie low, do what's asked of him, but in the end it's no longer an option. He's started hallucinating, and sometimes sees Ebi in front of him, appearing on underground platforms and in the crowds on Drottninggatan, even standing at the foot of the bed when Jonathan wakes up sweating and not knowing where he is. The drugs make him disoriented. Then they run out, and give way to the anxiety.

It falls around him, and it takes him over.

JA: it's jonathan, can we meet?
EH: why?
JA: need to talk

EH: about what?

JA: can't say here.

EH: yes you can, say here. what's it about?

JA: heard a rumour you're about to lose it altogether.

EH: what do you mean? what was the rumour?

JA: can we meet up?

EH: no. what's the rumour?

JA: attack on martin antonsson

JA: hello?

No answer. Fucking stupid immigrant cockroach. How the hell can Ebi not realise what a big deal it is for him to be contacting him — practically high treason?

Jonathan deletes the messages as soon as he's read them. What the fuck is he going to do? It's like he's living between the lines, a pseudo-life full of doubt.

He asks Christian whether there's any news on Antonsson. Nothing. Iris contacts him, asking for information, asking him to confirm or deny a rumoured attack on a Jewish school. Members of Swedish Resistance have been seen in the vicinity, as if they are doing reconnaissance. Jonathan denies it. Three days later, they carry out the attack, daubing JEWISH PIGS and 1488 on the front of the school.

Jonathan protests his innocence when Iris calls, upset and angry, and he says he has been misinformed.

A few weeks later:

JA: have you even checked it out?

EH: yes.

JA: and?

EH: how did you find out?

JA: doesn't matter. can you stop it happening?

EH: no.

JA: why not?

EH: because it's the right thing to do.

JA: have you told anyone? that I know about it?

EH: are you mental? if people find out that I've even had contact with you I'll get kicked out, and branded a traitor.

Jonathan reads the last sentence of Ebi's message over and over again. He doesn't know how to answer. Jonathan doesn't hate Ebi. He hates what Ebi is fighting for. He calls Iris, asking for more money. She demands new information in return, and he has nothing to give her. Despair creeps up on him, gets inside him, and brings with it a new thought: maybe he should let it happen. He has at least tried. *It's the right thing to do.* It's hard to stop someone who believes in something.

Jonathan doesn't make up his mind until the night before the demo in Rålambshovs Park, and when he does, it's down to a very strange coincidence.

During the strategy meeting and the party that follows out in Enskede, Jonathan takes Christian to one side. Christian is drunk, but he looks down.

'What's wrong?' says Jonathan.

'Nothing. It's … no, it's nothing.'

'Have you heard anything new?' he says.

'About what?'

Whenever they discuss things like this, things that somehow relate to Jonathan's treachery, he feels shame.

'Antonsson.'

Christian nods slowly, and puts his beer can on the worktop.

'He's got protection. Nothing's going to happen.'

Jonathan is in the bathroom, looking in the mirror. His nose has healed nicely. He can hear the music, the laughter, the rallying cries, and the slogans through the door. They're geeing each other up ahead of the counter-demo.

He hates loneliness, more than anything, but he stays calm.

Christian's instructions and orders are almost therapeutic. They bring order to the chaos in Jonathan's heart.

It gets late, far too late, that night. If he goes back to Hallunda, he's hardly going to get any sleep at all. He asks if he can stay over.

'Yeah, course.' The leader puts his arm around Jonathan. 'You're one of us. You've shown us that you're getting more trustworthy all the time. Take the sofa in the kitchen. You're not the only one staying the night.'

And there it is, lying on the table by the sofa, the little dark-blue player. He finds it in the dark, listens to it, hears the man's voice, and the woman's. He hears Ebi's name, and goes rigid.

He lies there, staring at the Dictaphone. Once he's made up his mind, he doesn't hesitate, which he later finds surprising.

JA: by the swings tomorrow at 8. I've got something you need.
EH: what?
JA: you'll find out when you get there. you have to come. alone.

The swings were the only place he could think of where he wouldn't need to give Ebi more details, which he wanted to avoid in case someone were to see their messages. Something's not right, Jonathan thinks to himself. Something is very, very wrong. He waits for Ebi's reply. Nothing arrives. What does Ebi's silence mean? Should he trust it?

Then he leaves the flat in Enskede, with the Dictaphone in his pocket. He holds his breath as he makes his way out.

That morning, the news is showing parts of yesterday's televised debate. In the debate, the chief of the National Police Agency is doing his best to fend off a lefty criminologist, who sees Ebi Hakimi's death as the result of an abuse of power rather than incompetence on the part of the police. Amateur footage from the demo in Rålambshov Park shows a passing glimpse of a masked Ebi Hakimi, holding one corner of a large banner. In the edge of the frame you can make out blue and yellow flags. This is before the chaos, when it was still nothing more than a demonstration and counter-demonstration between RAF and Swedish Resistance. At that point, Birck and I were sitting opposite Lisa Swedberg, seeing her alive for the last time.

I wonder how her parents reacted when they found out about her death. Unlike Ebi Hakimi's, Lisa Swedberg's death has gone pretty much unnoticed by the media, possibly because the security police have done their utmost to hush it all up.

Sooner or later, cracks will appear. They always do.

Birck and I are both standing watching the television, each holding a cup of coffee. It's Saturday, and I wish I was off. Outside the walls of HQ, the weather was so awful that it was impossible for me to walk here from Chapmansgatan; I had to order myself a taxi, again. The wind isn't that strong yet; but since it's minus twenty-

272

five degrees out there, it's still scarcely bearable. Windswept, tired policemen pass each other in the corridor with their rucksacks and bags, thick coats, and jackets.

'Don't shed a tear for Ebi Hakimi,' Birck says, watching as the chief of the National Police Authority's slightly smug smile fills the screen, and the criminologist's voice patters away from out of shot. 'Is that what he's getting at?'

'I think so.'

'Fucking ponce,' Birck says — it's not clear who he's referring to — and sips his coffee.

The TV is now showing archive footage of the violent clashes in Umeå in September. This is followed by more archive film, this time from a march in central Stockholm a week or so later. The marchers belong to The Party of Swedes, and they are accompanied by a rolling wall of police vans separating them from their opponents.

Birck turns the telly off.

'Are you going to take one, or what?'

The tube of Halcion is in my hand, clearly visible. I must have taken it out of my pocket. Instinctively, I push it back where it came from.

'Be careful with those,' he says. 'They don't look like they came from the chemist's.'

'I don't take them. I just like to know I've got them.'

Birck doesn't say anything. He heads off towards his room instead. I read the transcript of the victim's interview — the man with the ring print on his cheek after the assault in Vasagatan — and then send it off for registration and entry into the ledger.

Outside HQ, ambulance sirens screech past. The phone rings. I don't bother answering. And soon Edith will be here. To mark the occasion, the radio announces that they'll be playing music with a storm theme: 'You're the Storm' by The Cardigans, 'Call it Stormy Monday' by T-Bone Walker, Massive Attack's 'Weather Storm', and, of course, 'Hurricane' and 'Blowin' in the Wind', by Bob Dylan. I sit there listening to T-Bone Walker and the lyric *the eagle flies on Friday, and Saturday I go out and play* over and over again when the door swings open, and there's Birck in the doorway.

'Why don't you answer the phone?'

'Oh, was that you?'

'Come to my room.'

Birck's room is the same size as mine, but it feels bigger. He's got a smaller desk, and the walls are covered in binders on tightly packed shelves. It's light, and smells faintly of his aftershave. A large dark-blue rug covers part of the floor, despite this being against Health and Safety directives. In one corner, two thriving plants thrust vigorously from their pots; in the other, a little flat-screen telly is tuned to one of the news channels.

'I didn't know you had a TV,' I say.

On the desk there's a computer and a telephone. The receiver is lying to one side, and a little red lamp is flashing.

'Are you on the phone?'

'It's Oscar Svedenhag.' Birck closes the door behind him, sits down on the chair, and picks up the receiver and puts it to his ear. 'He's here now. I'll put you on speaker.'

I flop into Birck's spare chair, an older version of the one he tried to give me. It's even more comfortable than it looks. The speaker on the phone crackles. Otherwise there's silence, apart from the clinking noise from the plumbing and someone singing *he knows if you've been good, so be good for goodness' sake.*

'Right,' Birck says. 'Say hello, Leo.'

'Er, what's this about?'

'I think …' Oscar sounds composed, but underneath the veneer of calm there's a tremble in his voice, as though he's just been shouting at someone. 'It's just the two of you there that can hear me, right?'

'Just me and Leo.'

'Aren't all calls recorded, automatically?'

'No,' says Birck.

'Leo,' says Oscar, 'when you were here, at Cairo, I was taking something out of the oven. What was it?'

'What?'

'I want to make sure it's you.'

'Don't you recognise my voice?'

'If you don't answer, I'll put the phone down.'

I let the answer wait until Birck tuts at me.

'Brownies.'

'Okay,' Oscar says, noticeably calmer. 'Thank you.'

'What's this about?'

'I think something's about to happen.'

'What?'

'I don't know for sure. It might ... there's some really weird shit going on. Everyone ... I don't know, it could just be me getting paranoid. I'm going to have to go to three funerals next month. Thomas, Ebi, and Lisa. It might be that.

'I'm really sorry about that,' Birck says, 'but we're not counsellors.'

'I know that, it's just ... I think something's going to happen. That it's going to kick off soon.'

'What?' I insist. 'What's going to happen?'

The speaker crackles again. A fridge opens and closes, and a bottle-top is removed with a sharp hiss. *You better be good for goodness' sake!*

'I've got a few things here, from Ebi. I think it's best if you come here.'

'This isn't our case,' I say. 'You need to talk to the Security Pol—'

'No chance. Never. Not after the fucking witch-hunt they've put us through, with their fucking terrorism paranoia. If I show them this, they're going to hit the roof.'

'It's gratifying to hear that you'd rather come to us, but we ca—'

'I'd rather not talk to anyone. But I feel I have to.'

Birck quickly scribbles something on a Post-it:

lie

'It's going to take us a while to get there,' I say. 'What with this weather and everything.'

It's the morning before the demo, and Jonathan has slept far too little; in fact, he hasn't really slept at all, and the effects of the alcohol are still evident. There's a stinging sensation behind his eyes, and an ache round his temples. And right till the last minute he doesn't know: is Ebi coming?'

When he does show, as he's walking towards the swings in Hallunda that morning, it's like a weird dream. The last time they saw each other was at the end of one summer, a long time ago. It's a stark contrast to the way things are now, in the middle of December, when Hallunda is grey and cold, and the snow crunches underfoot. And yet the feeling is familiar, and striking. Something inside him remembers.

'What have you got?' Ebi asks, avoiding looking at Jonathan's shaved head.

'This.' He holds out the Dictaphone. 'There's a load of sound files on it, conversations between two people. You get named. Someone called Lisa says your name.'

Ebi is surprised by this, and doesn't even want to touch the Dictaphone.

'I'm guessing you know what this is about?' says Jonathan.

'No. No, I don't.'

'Don't lie to me. Listen to it. And whatever it is you're up to, you must stop.'

'We do what the fuck we want.'

Ebi sits down on one of the swings. Jonathan stuffs the Dictaphone in his pocket, and sits on the other one. Where he always used to sit.

'Why him?' says Jonathan, quietly. 'Why Antonsson?'

'You know why.'

'No. There are loads of other potential targets.'

'The recording studio. His warehouse. His money. And so on.' Ebi has had his head bowed, but lifts it now, his eyes meeting Jonathan's. 'Not to mention the fact that he's a committed fucking Nazi.'

National Socialist, Jonathan thinks to himself, and gets the urge to throw himself on Ebi and hit him as hard as he can. Their breath appears like white puffs of light smoke that mix together.

He holds out the Dictaphone again.

'Take it,' he says. 'I don't want it. I don't want … I don't want you getting in shit.'

Ebi seems to hesitate. Then he takes the Dictaphone from Jonathan's hand. Their fingers touch. Ebi's skin is warm. Jonathan holds his breath.

'You don't want Antonsson getting in shit. That's what this is about.'

'I don't want anyone getting killed.' Jonathan breathes out. 'That's all.'

Ebi's body stiffens, and his eyebrows shoot up.

'Eh?'

'I don't want you to kill him, it wo—'

'Is that what you think we're about to do?'

'What the hell else is it going to be?'

Ebi's reaction is laughter, but it's neither mocking nor happy. Jonathan can tell — he can see it in his eyes.

'What the fuck … we'd never do that. Who the hell's been saying that?'

Iris's name rests on his tongue. He can't say it.

'He's got a recording studio, and a warehouse full of music and merchandise. That's all we're after. We're not trying to get at him personally. Well,' Ebi corrects himself, 'not like that, anyway.'

'That's not what it sounds like if you listen to the Dictaphone. She, what's her name ... Lisa thinks you're going to physically hurt him.'

'There are voices advocating that,' Ebi says. 'But they're always shouted down. It's way too dangerous. And wrong.'

A sense of relief spreads through Jonathan's body. In Ebi's hand: the Dictaphone. He turns it round, upside down, and swipes his thumb across the blank screen.

'You know ... do you know what this is?' Ebi says, seemingly a bit gentler now. 'I mean, who it belonged to?'

'No.'

'The sociologist who was murdered.'

'What?'

'Did you miss that?'

'No. I've heard about that, but I didn't know it belonged to him.'

'They think we did it. That RAF was responsible.'

'Who thinks that? The cops?'

'Yes.'

'Well, did you?'

'No fucking way. Definitely not.' He laughs to himself. 'I'm even pretty sure that one of our members had a thing going on with him.'

'So what makes the police think it was you?'

'There are certain ... there's evidence that points to us. But I'm pretty certain that someone's trying to frame us, to fuck things up for us. This demo today, I think it'll be the last one we'll be able to do for a while. As long as we've got the cops tailing us, we're not going to be able to do anything. I don't suppose you happen to know anything about this?'

'What do you mean, about what?'

'Why the cops are constantly on our backs.'

Jonathan gets off the swing.

'What the fuck's that supposed to mean?'

Ebi stares at him, without flinching. Then he sighs and shakes his head.

'Nothing. I don't know. I'm so bloody confused. I shouldn't be talking to you, I wish I'd never come. I can't … I can't trust you.'

Jonathan's sudden jump off the swing has left it rocking back and forth.

'Sit back down,' Ebi insists.

Jonathan stops the swing, and sits down. He's cold.

'The sociologist was called Heber,' Ebi says. 'You haven't spoken to him?'

'Why would I have spoken to him? I don't even know who he is.'

Ebi scrapes the snow with the toe of his shoe.

'He was researching us. Interviewing people from your side and my side.' Ebi fiddles with the little device. 'How do you get it going?'

'You press it,' Jonathan says, and gets off the swing, and leans over Ebi's shoulder. He can smell Ebi's hair. It's newly washed, healthy. 'Here. Press here.'

'Thanks.' Ebi turns the little machine on, and a list of files fills the screen. 'I think these are the interviews he did.'

'What I heard sounded like an interview, too,' says Jonathan. 'Are you on it, too? Did you get interviewed as well?'

'No,' says Ebi. 'He never interviewed me. I think he wanted to, though. He tried. He'd heard about Antonsson, and wanted to talk to me about it. And …'

'What?'

Ebi turns off the Dictaphone. Jonathan wonders what he's thinking.

'How did you get hold of this?' he asks slowly.

'Someone I know had it.'

'Who?'

Jonathan says the name.

'And how did it get to him?' Ebi asks.

'I don't know.'

Ebi stands up.

'He must have taken it from Heber, that night. How else could he have got hold of it? And that means it must have been ... It has to be ...'

'What do you mean?'

'I can't talk about it now. We'll have to talk about it another time, if we meet again. But you should be looking closer to home.'

'What does that mean?'

'I haven't got time.' He stops. 'See you at the demo, I suppose.'

'Yes. Be careful.'

That's all. And that's the last thing he says to Ebi.

Café Cairo opens at ten. That gives us half an hour till Oscar Svedenhag has to open the doors for the day. Birck parks his Citröen just as the radio informs us that the Met Office have raised their state of alert ahead of Edith's arrival, and have now issued a Class 3 warning for the greater Stockholm area.

'This is going to be a hell of a night,' says Birck.

'I know.'

We move quickly through the cold. The little street is shielded by buildings, making the wind less evident, but it still manages to grab the door and whip it open, almost slamming it into the wall.

The eczema on Oscar's chin is larger, redder, and even shinier that it was when I last saw him.

'We didn't really say hello last time,' Birck says, and stretches his hand out once we've managed to shut the door behind us. 'Gabriel.'

'Oscar,' he says, taken aback by Birck's politeness.

Cairo seems smaller without the customers. The tables have been cleaned, and are surrounded by neatly arranged chairs. The smell is a mixture of detergent and coffee. There's a freshly brewed pot behind the counter, and Oscar grabs three cups — two black and one red. There's a white box on the counter top, about the size of a shoebox.

Oscar gives Birck and me a cup each, and opens the box.

'This is Ebi's,' he says. 'His roommate put it to one side when he got injured, because he was scared that he wasn't going ... well, that he wasn't going to come back. Some of it is from the flat; the rest is stuff Ebi had on him when he got injured.'

Oscar clears his throat, as though the sound might chase the thought away.

'I thought he lived alone,' says Birck. 'He was the only one registered as living at that address.'

'The Electoral Register is one thing,' Oscar says. 'Reality is another.'

The box contains small keepsakes like leaflets, badges, and stickers, old photos from festivals and demos, a key that might be for a bike lock or some kind of box, and a mobile phone. I pick it up.

'It's on,' I say.

'Yes,' says Oscar, his voice thick. 'Apparently, his roommate kept it on. They had the same phone, so her charger worked.' He picks up one of the photos. 'This is what I thought was strange. It's taken with a digital camera and then printed.'

The picture shows four serious, young men, standing in a line but without touching each other. They have shaved heads, each one is wearing heavy boots and tight jeans, and the sun is behind them. They're holding a banner in front of them that's dirty yellow with what looks like blue lettering. The colours are hard to discern because of the backlight, but the words are clearly visible: IMMIGRANTS OUT! SWEDEN FOR THE SWEDES!

'This is before a NSF-demo about three years back,' Oscar says. 'These guys are now members of Swedish Resistance. It was founded by Patrik Höjer, a guy from Strängnäs who was involved in the White Power music scene in the mid-Nineties. He was friends with the people who shot Björn Söderberg, the journalist. They were very big in the aftermath of the murder in Salem, in terms of membership numbers, or whatever you want to call them. Then they gradually fell away, but were resurrected just after the Sweden Democrats made it into parliament.'

'Is there a connection?' Birck asks. 'Between them being elected, and this lot coming back?'

'I'm sure there is. There were people who felt let down by the Sweden Democrats when they started toning down their racist image. Today, Swedish Resistance is bigger than ever — there are at least a hundred of them, maybe more, in Stockholm alone. Anyway, it was this picture that made Ebi get involved in politics, and join RAF.'

'How do you know that?'

'Because we asked him. We always do. Everyone has to go through a fairly long process before they're let in, considering the risk that they … well. We want to make sure that people are genuinely passionate about what we're passionate about, and that they're not just pretending, for whatever reason.'

'How old are they in this picture?' I say.

'They must be about nineteen there. They're the same age. And this guy,' Oscar says, pointing at the young man second from right in the picture, 'I know he was nineteen when the picture was taken. His name is Jonathan Asplund, and he was a childhood friend of Ebi's. They both grew up in Hallunda. Apparently, Jonathan was a kind person, incredibly warm and generous towards everyone he met, but very amenable. Receptive to other people's opinions and ideas. A lot of his friends weren't Swedish, like Ebi. Jonathan and Ebi drifted apart during high school. That's where it started.

'Where what started?' Birck says.

'He was seventeen or so, I suppose, and was drifting further and further to the right. Well, in fact, it was like this; there was a little group of right-wing extremists in Hallunda. It wasn't even an organisation — just a group of snide racists who liked drinking beer and listening to white-power music like Totenkopf and White Aggression. He started hanging out with them, and it went from there, until, well …' He taps the picture. 'Sometimes that's enough. They get brainwashed by older guys. One of Ebi's friends showed him the picture, and Ebi was completely distraught. When he told the story, he almost had tears in his eyes. But for Ebi it wasn't just the fact that he'd lost a friend. He realised that if even someone like Jonathan could get dragged into this kind of shit, then anyone could. Ebi wanted to actively combat that, and he felt like RAF was a good tool for doing so.

'What is it about this stuff then?' Birck looks from the picture down at the rest of the stuff in the box. 'This doesn't tell us anything.'

'I thought they didn't talk anymore,' Oscar says, scratching at his eczema, his nails scraping on the raw skin. He picks up the mobile phone. 'But they did. At least occasionally, and certainly just before Ebi's death.' He opens the text messages on the phone. 'Here. It starts in October ... well, you can read it yourselves.'

I lean over Birck's shoulder and read the text conversation:

JA: it's jonathan, can we meet?
EH: why?
JA: need to talk
EH: about what?
JA: can't say here.
EH: yes you can, say here. what's it about?
JA: heard a rumour you're about to lose it altogether.
EH: what do you mean? what was the rumour?
JA: can we meet up?
EH: no. what's the rumour?
JA: attack on martin antonsson
JA: hello?

'Does Ebi Hakimi not answer this?' asks Birck.
'No,' says Oscar. 'He doesn't.'
'Do you recognise this?'
'You mean the attack?'
'Yes.'

'Yes, I recognise it. But it sounds a lot worse than it actually was. We were planning to sabotage his recording studio.'

'Recording studio,' Birck repeats. 'Am I supposed to believe that?'

'You believe whatever the hell you like. Do you want to see the rest of the messages, or what?'

'Yes.'

'Look. Those earlier ones were sent on the nineteenth of October, I think it was. This is early November.'

JA: have you even checked it out?
EH: yes.
JA: and?
EH: how did you find out?
JA: doesn't matter. can you stop it happening?
EH: no.
JA: why not?
EH: because it's the right thing to do.
JA: have you told anyone? that I know about it?
EH: are you mental? if people find out that I've even had contact with you I'll get branded a traitor, and kicked out.

'Is that right?' I ask. 'That he would've been kicked out if anyone had found out he'd been talking to Asplund?'

'That depends,' says Oscar. 'We don't like spies.'

'This isn't the KGB and MI6 we're talking about,' says Birck.

'No, but the principle is the same.'

'But he's not even spying,' I say. 'He was trying to help you.'

'True,' says Oscar. 'But that's not how it would've looked. I mean, they were childhood friends after all.'

My gaze lands on the knife-block behind the counter. The knife that was missing last time I was here is still missing.

I feel a heavy lump in my chest as I read the texts. At first I can't explain it, but then I realise what it is. It's the coldness in the words the childhood friends exchange, how the gulf between them is so huge, and how every word is met with suspicion. I can imagine them now, in their beds, on opposite sides of town, lying there late at night reading the messages over and over again, trying to decipher what they mean. I recognise that alienation all too well.

'Then it goes quiet between Ebi and Jonathan for a while, at least as far as I can see. He might have deleted the messages, though — erased the history. But if he had, surely he would have got rid of these, too. Jonathan writes to Ebi the evening before the demo in Rålambshov Park, late, and it was just this:'

JA: by the swings tomorrow at 8. I've got something you need.
EH: what?
JA: you'll find out when you get there. you have to come. alone.

'So they meet up at eight, the morning before the demo?' I say.
'Well, that's what we have to assume,' says Birck.
'Do you know what Hakimi does next?'
'Yes,' says Oscar. 'He comes here. We had a meeting here before the demo, starting at eleven. He'd just talked to Lisa Swedberg. He told us that she was ill and wasn't going to make the demo.'

I inspect the photo of the four young men again. You can make out heavy scars on Asplund's face, one of which cuts right across his eyebrow, running like a parenthesis over his left cheek.

'He's got some serious scars,' I say.
'They nearly all do,' says Oscar.
'He mentions the attack on Antonsson,' Birck says cautiously. 'Your attack on Antonsson.'

You can feel how this puts Oscar on the defensive.
'Which is why I hesitated about showing you this.'
'You'd planned it?'
'Not me. But I knew that there was a plan.'

'So who knew about the plan?'

'I'm not about to tell you that. And you've got no right to demand an answer either.'

Birck looks over at me, and shakes his head. There's no point. Besides, I suspect we'll find out as soon as we get in the car.

'What was he going to get?' Oscar says. 'Hakimi, I mean. What was he going to get from Asplund, do you know?'

I glance at Birck. He blinks twice.

'No,' I say. 'No idea.'

Only when Birck has got into the driver's seat, and I've slumped into the passenger seat beside him, do I pull out my phone and end the call. I turn my head, towards Goffman's weathered face in the back seat. Next to Goffman is his colleague, Iris.

'Did it work?' I ask, with the phone in my hand. 'Could you hear?'

'Very well indeed,' Goffman replies, before putting away his own phone.

The heavy doors slam shut behind Christian. He was let in and had to show his ID. He was searched, and had to put his coat and shoes in plastic trays, which then went through a security check as he walked through a metal detector. The detector beeped. The security guard, a grumpy man with a fat neck and chubby hands, nodded wearily at the chain just visible by his collar.

'It's that thing,' he said. 'Take it off.'

'Do I have to?'

'No. But you're not coming in if you don't.'

The little swastika, handmade from real silver, was placed in a tray that was far too big for the purpose, making the necklace look like a miniature.

The place: Mariefred Young Offenders. They'd sent Michael here, because of his young age. The area was enclosed by a high, beige wall and an equally high chain-fence. The top portion of the fence was angled inwards, towards the institution, to impede escape. It was terrifying.

'Thank you,' said the guard. 'There won't be anyone else in the visiting room, but there's a camera in there. So if anything happens, we'll see it.

Christian put his chain back on and hid it under his shirt. It felt cool against his chest.

The visiting room they showed him into was smaller than he'd expected. Michael was already sitting there. The first thing Christian noticed was that one of his cheeks was slightly swollen and purple-red. He suspected he knew why, but didn't ask, because he couldn't face having his fears confirmed.

In front of Michael was a table with a light-wooden tabletop and, on the opposite side, a chair meant for Christian.

It had been three weeks — no longer — since the last time they'd seen each other. But it certainly felt like more. Michael was wearing clothes that weren't his: grey tracksuit bottoms and an equally grey long-sleeved top. They made him look pale.

'Hi,' Christian said, as he sat down.

'You've got the chain,' Michael said, looking at his shirt collar.

'Course I have.' Christian pulled it out. 'I had to take it off at security.' He paused. 'How's it going?'

Michael blinked once, slowly, as though the question had made him tired.

'Alright. I guess.'

He seemed to be trying to smile, and when he did, Christian spotted two gaps in his upper jaw — missing teeth.

He looked up at the clock above the door. Less than half an hour ago he'd been sitting on the train on his way here. It seemed unreal, that more time hadn't passed.

'You're getting respect,' said Christian. 'Everyone's bigging you up.'

'I know.'

On a patch of grass on the outskirts of Skarpnäck's shopping precinct, they'd clashed — Swedish Resistance and a bunch of reds. It had been a peaceful demonstration against racism, with young families and students gathered to demonstrate their disgust at xenophobia. At least that's how it was described in the media, afterwards. That's how it always turned out in the media.

They were there in an organised counter-demonstration to show their distaste, show their hatred and their strength.

They had turned twenty. Christian was working at a builders' merchant's near Älvsjö, and Michael at a plumbing company based down by Globen Arena. They'd both booked the day off.

There were loads of them, nearly fifty. A group calling itself Radical Anti-Fascism had got wind of the event, and saw a chance to attack the object of their hatred. There were fewer of them; they hadn't managed to round up enough supporters to pose a physical threat.

Christian, Michael, and the others were armed with shields, flares, and pokers. They sang marches as they made their way to the field.

The crowd stood there with banners and placards, in the middle of the field. Pushchairs jostled for position with pensioners and students who linked arms, forming a chain. A fat, black woman was speaking on the stage. Her voice was nasal and whiny. Only a handful of police were on hand to observe the whole thing.

Michael threw a flare straight into the crowd. Christian threw a second. Smoke rose along with fear, thick and vermillion.

Radical Anti-Fascism came rushing over from the other side of the field. They stopped just a little way short of Swedish Resistance. Radical Anti-Fascism took two steps forward. Swedish Resistance took three. The distance between them was shrinking, becoming claustrophobic.

Everything turned into a tangle of fighting talk and fighting. The police, broad-shouldered men with truncheons and shields, ran towards them. Christian spotted them out of the corner of his eye, and when they got close enough he could see the panic in their eyes: they weren't expecting this.

Not far from Christian stood Michael, and one of the reds hit him across the throat with a wooden pole.

Michael squealed and groaned, bent double, while Christian

jumped on the bastard. It was a man about his age, maybe a year or so younger. He had a scarf wrapped around his face, and his hood pulled up.

Christian hit him in the chest with his elbow, and they fell to the floor, with Christian landing on top. He pulled the scarf away, punching the exposed face with his clenched fist, and the sensation as his knuckles connected with the cheekbone tore him up inside.

Now he could see Michael in his peripheral vision: he had got to his feet and was massaging his throat.

'That fucker could've killed me,' Christian heard him hiss, through all the screams and brawling.

Michael took a step forward, and kicked the scum in the face. His lip split, and a thick stream of blood gushed out, splattering onto his cheek and the ground by his head.

Christian got up, dropping the scarf, which he had been grasping the whole time. His hands were shaking.

Michael kicked the face again, harder this time. There was a crack as the jawbone broke, and a hoarse scream from the activist's throat.

It almost sounded like a word, Christian thought, but he couldn't make out what.

Michael was winding up for another kick, and Christian put his arm around his shoulders, trying to lead him away.

'That's enough,' he hissed. 'Look at me — that's enough, that's enough.'

Michael batted Christian's arms away without making eye contact.

He kicked again, this time in the temple. The young man's eyes opened wide as if in surprise and his mouth was open. Christian could see down his throat as he lay there, but no sound emerged. Instead, his legs started shaking.

Michael took one step forward, and lifted his boot above the man's face, like the instant before you kill an insect. Then he stamped.

The man's eye popped out of its socket.

Christian moved away and threw up.

Michael was praised within the group for his conviction and his capacity to put ideology into action; but for the Swedish judicial system, such qualities are of no value. He was sentenced to six years in prison. Christian got off, after his careerist lawyer managed to sell his plea of self-defence. When the verdict arrived, he was overwhelmed by relief at having avoided punishment, but then came the shame. He should have shared this with his friend. The guilt at having got away with it, that all the blame was put on Michael, was hard to bear.

'Have the others been here?' Christian asked now.

'No. No one apart from you and Jens. They haven't been approved by the institution yet. But they'll come.'

'I sent in seven or eight applications yesterday.' He attempted a smile. 'You're sorely missed.'

Michael nodded.

'Good. That's good.' He leant forward, over the table. 'It's your turn now. You're taking over until I get out.'

'But I'm not sure if I'm the right man.'

'Why wouldn't you be?'

'I'm not like you.'

'What the fuck is that supposed to mean?'

'I don't have your leadership qualities. You know that.'

It had never even been an issue between them. Michael was the obvious front man. Christian was his sidekick.

'You'll have to do little jobs for me. That's all you need to worry about. We can keep in touch by phone and stuff. It'll be fine.'

Christian stared at his hands.

'I don't know if I can.'

Michael smiled.

'You need to believe in yourself, just like you believe in our struggle. You deserve to believe in yourself, your own abilities.'

Next time he visited, Christian was worried that Michael would look much worse than he did the first time. Bruises and grazes were one thing. Christian had heard the rumours: there were people inside who hated Michael and what he stood for, who were going to hurt him. But when Christian arrived, Michael was sitting in the chair, looking relaxed and healthy. The bruises from last time had gone.

'Don't you worry,' he said, smiling. 'I've sorted it.'

'You've sorted it? How did you manage that?'

'That doesn't matter.'

The time that followed was a period of decline. Swedish Resistance became weaker, people left, and way too few people joined. It wasn't Christian's fault, but it felt like it.

The man from Sölvesborg was elected leader of the Sweden Democrats. They talked about it on the phone, how that tendency, which had been present during their time in Sweden Democrat Youth, had started to take hold in the party proper: falling into line. Purging and streamlining.

'His problem is that he thinks washing out peoples' mouths cleanses their thoughts as well,' Michael said. 'But that's just not how it works.'

'But he's attracting supporters,' Christian said. 'A lot of supporters.'

Michael sniggered down the phone.

'A bunch of hypocrites, the lot of them. If it carries on like this, they'll drop the immigration issue and then want to open the doors to everyone. They're attracting people who really should be on our side, with us. This is a bigger obstacle for us than anything else.'

But which is our side? Christian thought to himself. Who are we? At the latest group meeting, ten people had shown up.

'Don't you think they're still on our side?' said Christian. 'They're toning it down to try to move forwards, and upwards in the polls.'

'It doesn't matter. They're populists, they're not after anything other than power. As soon as they get close to the arenas of mainstream politics, their own politics are going to be affected. The party has no heart, no true ideology.'

A man standing nearby shouted his name sharply.

'I have to go. Speak soon.'

'Yes,' Christian said, and felt a pang of sadness at how he missed him. 'Speak soon.'

He visited his friend whenever he could, watching him being broken down by the institution. It hurt, and everything felt shaky. Eventually, the anguish he felt before the visits outgrew the relief that he felt when he'd been.

He started feeling desensitised, numbed. He saw a girl getting hassled by three guys on the underground. They got off, leaving her in peace, just as Christian had decided to intervene.

He tried to recruit her to Swedish Resistance, but failed. She called him a Nazi swine.

'You do realise that this is probably the slowest car journey in history?' says Iris.

Iris Berger is my age, with dark, shoulder-length hair, locks of which fall straight over her cheeks. She's wearing a dark-brown mac. It makes her seem twenty years older. She's sitting with her hands in her pockets and her face turned away from Goffman as we move through the streets of Kungsholmen back towards HQ. Her eyes are large and brown, so dark that I can see the shop-fronts of Hantverkargatan reflected in them.

'I can't drive any faster in this weather,' Birck says, with a sharp intake of breath, as he slams on the brakes so as to avoid ruining Christmas for the old dear with the walking frame, who is beating a determined path across the road, just a little way from the pedestrian crossing.

I've got a feeling this year's for me and you, so happy Christmas ...

Goffman sticks his head out between me and Birck.

'Could you turn that off?'

I can see a better time, where all our dreams come tr—

'Thanks.' Goffman joins his hands, folding the long fingers across one another. 'What did the messages say?'

'You should have read them aloud,' Iris's voice says from behind me.

'Wouldn't that have been a bit weird, in the circumstances?'

Birck says. 'Who the hell reads things out loud?'

I pull Ebi Hakimi's phone from my pocket and give it to Iris.

'Jonathan Asplund makes contact with Ebi Hakimi in October,' says Birck. 'He says there's a rumour going round that RAF are about to lose it altogether, as he puts it. He's referring to the planned attack on Antonsson. I'm guessing he was worried about his childhood friend. It's a pretty fucked-up situation, so it's understandable that Hakimi is confused, and intrigued.'

We move slowly along the road. Iris gives Goffman the phone, and he puts it in his pocket without even looking at it.

'In their last conversation,' Birck says, 'the night before the demo, Asplund says that he's got something that Hakimi needs, and asks to meet by the swings at eight. I'm guessing that they used to meet up there.'

'My attention span is dreadful. I drift off.' Goffman blinks once, twice, three times, and studies his fingernails. They're clean, as though he'd just had a manicure. 'This is a very strange puzzle.' He sighs. 'And I hate puzzles.'

Birck rolls up towards Bergsgatan. Iris is restless and bored in the rear-view mirror. On a corner, the wind gets hold of an advertising billboard, which flies off and somersaults in mid-air, before crashing to the ground and scraping noisily along the road. It's not snowing, but the persistent wind whips up the snow that has already fallen, forming drifts which cling resolutely to the walls of the buildings.

'Asplund and Hakimi meet up on the morning of the demo in Rålambshov Park,' Goffman says. 'The night before, Asplund has told Hakimi that he has something which Hakimi needs. Might that be the Dictaphone?'

'Yes,' says Iris, 'But it's a tenuous link.'

'That,' says Goffman, 'is precisely the problem.'

'I don't see why it's tenuous,' says Birck. 'Asplund gives it to

Hakimi, who gives it to Swedberg, and that's how it ends up with us.'

'Yes,' says Goffman. 'Perhaps. In that case, how did Asplund come to have it?'

'He might be the attacker,' I say.

'Exactly,' Birck says. 'You see, contrary to what SEPO would have you believe, it's not just Muslims and communists who are capable of committing serious crimes.'

'No,' says Iris, who apparently hasn't heard Birck. 'It's not Asplund.'

'How do you know that?' I ask.

'He's got alibis for both murders.'

'So you've had him in?' asks Birck. 'Why?'

No one says anything. Birck sighs.

'Swedish Resistance,' I say. 'Who are their leaders?'

'Nationally, it's a guy called Jens Malm,' says Iris. 'A nasty bastard. They're divided into geographical groups, the largest being the Stockholm one. That's the one Asplund belongs to. Jonathan's immediate superior, or whatever you want to call it, is a guy named Christian Västerberg.'

'Isn't it possible that it was them?'

'That's unlikely,' says Iris. 'The main threat comes from the left, not the right.'

'One thing I don't get,' I say. 'Is how Asplund came to know that RAF were planning an attack on Antonsson?'

'Asplund is Iri—' Goffman begins, before he smiles and shakes his head.

'For fuck's sake,' says Iris, staring daggers at him.

'What?' I say.

'I'm getting old. Sorry. Sometimes my mouth gets there before my brain.'

'I don't get it,' I say.

'Well, I do,' Birck says, coldly. 'He knew the same way you knew he had alibis for both murders. You told him. Lisa Swedberg was

298

your informer,' he says to Goffman. He moves his stare over to Iris. 'Jonathan Asplund is yours.'

Iris reacts as though it were an accusation. It might be.

'Well, we can rule out Asplund, then,' I say.

'Yes. Although, of course,' Goffman says hesitantly, as the phone rings and he moves his hand towards his pocket. 'That would explain why …' He puts the phone to his ear. 'Hello? What? When was this? And the attacker … I understand. Okay. We're on our way.'

He leans back in his seat. Everyone's waiting. Those seconds of silence are so awkward that I want to put the radio on again.

'He's been stabbed,' he says, as though he were telling us the time of day. 'About ten minutes ago, during a speech at Central Station.'

'Who?' says Birck. 'Antonsson?'

'No.'

The dying man's last words were recorded on the Dictaphone, slurred by his accent, the medication, and his brain injuries. They are being deciphered in my head.

'Who killed Thomas Heber?'

'Sweetest sisters.'

Swedish Resistance.

'Who's next?'

'Esther.'

SD. He's saying Sweden Democrats. It's *him*.

Fuck.

'Is he still alive?' Iris asks.

Goffman doesn't reply.

IV

SOME DAY SOON
WE WILL ALL
BE TOGETHER

The hands were perfectly still on the tabletop. A wedding ring shone on the ring finger, discreet yet elegant. The woman it belonged to looked urgently at Christian sitting in the seat in front of her.

'Tell me,' she says, 'how things have been recently. Shall we start there?'

She didn't have any paper, no folder or file. Not even a pen. He wondered if this was part of her job, keeping everything in her head, or whether she just didn't care.

'Good. Like normal.' He hesitated, checked that the chain around his neck was hidden by his T-shirt. 'What do you want me to say?'

'What you're feeling. What you've been doing recently, how you're getting on.' She smiled. 'It's up to you.'

Time passed relentlessly, yet stood still. Nothing was as normal, yet things were still the same.

'I feel sort of unsure … somehow. And I don't really have anyone to turn to. I guess that's why I came here.'

He'd seen an ad on the bus the week before: DO YOU NEED SUPPORT IN YOUR LIFE? TALK TO ONE OF OUR CBT-CERTIFIED COUNSELLORS — FREE OF CHARGE! He'd made a mental note of the address but hadn't planned to go, until he ended up going past the place on his way to the gym. He'd made an appointment, and then, standing on the pavement outside, wondered what he was playing at. Now there he was, still wondering.

'You feel unsure,' she repeated. 'In what way?'

'Well, I don't know about unsure. Lonely. My best friend's been inside a few years. That might be it.'

'Inside?' The counsellor said. 'You mean he's in pris—'

'Yes.'

She nodded.

'I understand.'

He looked around. The room was light and airy, looking like an estate agent's ad. He looked down at his hands, and saw that they were tightly clenched. He tried to relax.

Swedish Resistance was falling apart. It was, he thought, that defeat which disturbed him the most. He couldn't lead them — he didn't have his friend's abilities. Their activities had become more sporadic than systematic, and the numbers turning up when something did actually happen were getting smaller and smaller. It was obvious to anyone that they were in deep trouble.

'Are you still in touch?'

'A bit, by phone and stuff. I do visit him, but I get rejected every other time I apply for a permit. It … he's in a right fucking state in there. I know that, and I can't do anything about it. That is fucking hard to take.'

'But this being unsure, or loneliness, how does that show itself?'

'I don't get out much. I stick to the people I know.'

Erik, Klas, Daniel, Frank, Jack. He could turn to them, but they were all members of Swedish Resistance. There was no one else. He felt isolated, enclosed within himself. He hadn't spoken to his mum since Christmas. Nearly six months. His relationship with Anton was even worse. They lived such different lives. Sometimes blood-ties don't mean a thing, Christian thought, and the insight came as something of a surprise. Anton had a family, kids with blonde hair and symmetrical faces. His wife was beautiful. They looked like Green Party types, which was disgusting.

A memory came to him: Christian was fifteen. He got a band hoodie from Anton, who looked pleased. The top would soon bring him and Michael together.

'Can you talk to them?' she asked. 'Your friends?'

'Not really. Well, I could, but I don't want to.'

'I understand.'

He wondered if she did. Wondered if she was Swedish, how long she'd been married, whether her husband was Swedish, who she voted for. He looked down, because her eyes were bright blue, and it was as though she would see through him in an instant.

'I ...' he began. 'Sometimes I see people in town, my age. They're holding hands, pushing the pram in front of them. I imagine that they're on the way home, that they've just bought something for their kid. They've got jobs in service industries or whatever, and they live in a little house, or maybe they own a flat just south of Södermalm. We get the same underground train and get off at the same station, and walk home. And I'm struck by what different lives we live, everything that they've achieved while I haven't ...'

'What?'

His gaze turned to the large window. The sky outside was the same colour as the walls inside.

'They've followed a straight line, while mine's been stuttering along the whole time.'

'What's made yours so stop-start then?'

'I ... what I believe in, what I'm fighting for. Or believed in and fought for.'

He regretted it straightaway, could hear the follow-up question word for word in his head, before it came.

'What did you believe in?'

He looked down at his hands. They were clenched again.

'Nothing. Never mind.'

Swedish Resistance had taken up all his time: leafleting, putting up posters, planning parties, planning actions and demos — in spite of a dwindling membership — and the calls and the visits to Mariefred Young Offenders. Jens Malm was at him every week. He had the same job as he'd had five years ago, and lived in the same flat. When he tried to work out how many women he'd slept with over the past year, he got to twelve before he stopped counting. He could remember the names of slightly more than half of them. He met them at parties and in town. Most of them were younger; they looked up to him and Michael. He exploited that and he knew it was wrong, but he just didn't care anymore.

It was this that scared him the most, he now realised. That he didn't care anymore.

'It feels like this is important to you,' she said. 'What you believe in, and fight for.'

'It has … it's taken up so much of my time. I'm almost standing still in all the other spheres of my life.'

'But you're having doubts, is that what you mean? It sounds a bit like it.'

Christian didn't answer. He wondered how long he'd been sitting there, whether the hour was nearly up. He regretted it now. He should never have come here, shouldn't have walked in when she opened the door to him.

He looked at the clock above the door. Quarter past one. He'd been there for fifteen minutes.

'I don't know,' he said eventually, and realised that was the truth.

He remembered the assault down in Salem all those years ago, and could still feel the pain, the vulnerability. Along with the memory came the hate, mixed with all the other times he'd met them on the street, on football pitches, down dark alleys. It was a plague, a disease, even spreading to their own side: he was thinking about the Sweden Democrats. One of their most recent recruits was a Polish woman, a self-proclaimed feminist. Fucking hell. The country needed cleaning up, from the inside out.

'We all need something to give our lives meaning,' the counsellor said. 'Sometimes it can take up a lot of our time, at the expense of other things. That's just the way it is. There are twenty-four hours in a day and seven days in a week. You can't fit it all in.'

It wasn't as though Christian was expected to do everything. From inside the institution, Michael, with Jens' blessing, tried to reform parts of Swedish Resistance into a prison group for convicted comrades. It didn't work. The prison service staff and the existing prison groups made sure they never got the chance to establish themselves.

'Apart, we're no stronger than anyone else,' Michael used to say. 'But together we're something much, much bigger.'

Which was true. At least, that's what Christian had always convinced himself of.

'This friend of yours, who's inside now,' said the counsellor.

'Yes?'

'Tell me about him.'

Christian chewed his bottom lip till he was afraid he was going to bite through it, and stared out the window again. The sun seemed to be about to fight its way through the clouds.

He felt nervous, for some reason he couldn't quite put into words. Then he told her: they'd grown up a couple of streets apart. They met at a party. They had interests in common. They liked the same music, had similar taste in clothes. They found each other, and where others came apart during the transition to adulthood, he and Christian had, if anything, become closer. That was all. He looked at the counsellor, hoping that would be enough.

'What's he in for?'

'Assault.'

'And you're worried that prison life is getting him down?'

'I know it is. I can even hear it in his voice when we talk on the phone.'

He'd now been inside for over five years, and had only ever been given short spells on parole. As if that, watching the incarceration take its toll, wasn't enough, Christian had heard things. During his visits, the screws would make ominous, knowing comments. They never said anything directly, but between the lines it was perfectly clear: when they met, Michael was sometimes bruised across his cheeks, around the eyes, and occasionally his lip would be busted. He made noises as he sat down or stood up, clutching at his stomach or his ribs. This wasn't supposed to happen, but it did, and Christian knew why: because of what he believed in, and his decision to stand up for it.

'You told me you'd sorted it,' Christian said to him. 'That you'd sorted it.'

'It's not that simple, Christian,' he replied. 'But it's nothing to worry about.'

He wondered what Michael meant, but despite his questions he never got an answer.

After an hour, he stood up from the chair, shook the counsellor's hand, and left her room. He thanked her, but he wasn't coming back.

When he got back out onto the pavement, a warm gust blew between the houses, and he looked up towards the sky, and felt the sun warming his face.

At first you can't make out any more than a hoarse sound cutting through the murmur of the crowd, but as the frames are shown again and again, the word that someone is shouting emerges.

Traitor.

It's a weird scene. He was going to make the speech outdoors, by the Christmas market on Sergel's Square, but, because of the storm, the party had applied to hold the meeting at Central Station, in the main hall. For some reason, the request was approved, and that's where it happens. Maybe it's because there are so few protesters, and they're so harmless. They're at the back, holding a banner. They didn't have permission to enter the station, so those that are there have managed to evade police checks on the way in. Once they've made their way in, the police have apparently decided to concentrate their surveillance on them. This is unfortunate, because it's a distraction.

There are lots of people in the hall, many of them listening, but many pass through, oblivious, laden with luggage and shopping bags, hurrying towards the train that is almost certainly going to be cancelled because of the weather. Kids are wandering around with balloons, like the ones you'd get at a fun fair — shiny, festive red, with the train company's initials printed in white capitals. A Father Christmas shuffles back and forth in one corner, handing them out. Christmas songs fill the hall, and for those who witness it via mobile-phone footage, the start of the speech is drowned out by *a beautiful sight, we're happy tonight, walkin' in a winter wonderland.*

He gives his speech from a round stage, as wide and as round as a garden trampoline. On either side, two speakers amplify his deep voice; the backdrop is the party's name and the blue liverwort flower that is their emblem. Three bodyguards wearing dark suits stand in front of the stage, while the audience is encircled by a couple of dozen uniformed police officers as well as countless others who are not visible, since those in charge at the personal-protection unit within SEPO have planned an exemplary surveillance operation.

He's fairly still, occasionally taking a step forwards, or to one side, but most of the time he doesn't move from his spot in front of the colourful backdrop. He alternates between a serious tone and a more light-hearted approach, getting a laugh for a joke about the state of Sweden's railways. He also warns passengers to be careful in the storm, since Edith isn't the kind of lady you want to argue with.

'This is, by all accounts, not one of those genteel little storms. Please do take care.'

He starts his speech by asking why he is here today, and refers to the latest report from The Institute for Social Research, which shows how kids in minority families are deliberately spied on and controlled by their own families, to ensure they are not exposed to a Western upbringing. From there he goes on to talk about Swedish traditions, Swedish values — so no change there. He then goes on, however, to talk about multiculturalism's impact on social change. He talks about the positive side, but is careful to point out its more complex consequences.

In the background chimes the robotic voice announcing delays, platform alterations, and, less frequently, departures. The weather is causing chaos. The duration of the speech is extended by the interruptions of his supporters, who applaud enthusiastically each time he raises his voice to deliver a political sucker punch.

'Being Swedish has to mean openness, generosity of spirit,' he says, 'welcoming people who do come, enabling them to become part of this great nation. The responsibility does not rest with them. We cannot demand it of them. What we can ask of the refugee arriving here is that he or she is prepared to adopt Swedish values and Swedish culture. But for that to even be possible, the idea of being Swedish needs to be open and inclusive. That responsibility lies squarely with us.'

Applause. He smiles.

One of the many balloons bursts. The bang is so loud that it makes people jump. Maybe that's what set it off. Who knows?

'Here he comes,' Birck says, freezing the image. 'See him?'

'Yes.'

A shadow moves behind the stage. You can't tell how tall he is, but he's dressed in black, with his hood pulled up over his head.

On the face of it, this is like being in the lion's den. It's never going to work. Whoever it is is going to get shot, or, perhaps even worse, beaten to death, within seconds of raising his hand. But then everything goes black. No one knows why — whether it's part of the plan, or if it's down to the weather.

A power cut.

What we do know is that it lasted for precisely seventeen seconds.

We're standing next to each other in a broom cupboard in the police station at Central Station, going through the mute images from CCTV, but this particular clip comes from a recording on a mobile phone.

'You've got twenty-three cameras to choose from,' I say, 'and you go for the piddly little mobile phone?'

'I wanted to hear the sound,' Birck says, and glances up at the bank of screens in front of us.

'You see this?' the constable says, standing there in front of the screens showing the footage, visibly in shock. 'Here he is. He's hidden by the pillar, so you don't get a good look. Do you think he did that on purpose?'

'What, hid from the CCTV?' I say.

'Yes.'

'No, I don't think so.'

We watch the images captured by the surveillance camera. The man is standing still; he appears to be watching the stage. His chest is just visible, and his breathing looks heavy.

All the screens go black during the power cut. When the power comes back on, the party leader has collapsed to the floor and the microphone is rolling away from his hand. He looks surprised, and something approaching sadness spreads across his face. Someone screams, and then lots of people scream. You can tell from their faces. The knife is lying on the floor in front of the stage, and the assailant is gone. The black-and-white images make the blood appear dark grey against the white shirt.

'Wouldn't you say that the technique is pretty similar to the one Heber's attacker used?' says Birck. 'Like the knife wound is in about the same place as Heber's.'

'Yes.'

And Heber died from that injury. At any second, this could become a political assassination, not merely an attempt at one.

'One more time,' I say, and nod to the constable.

'The whole thing?'

'No, just the last few seconds before the power cut.'

We study those last seconds again. The recording comes from a camera showing the area immediately to the right of the stage, from so far away that the assailant is no more than an inch tall on the screen.

All around us, in the neighbouring rooms, the phones are ringing. The office at Central Station isn't very big, and the muted sounds seep through the dividing walls.

The knife that was lying next to the stricken party leader was recovered by a uniformed officer, who did everything right, by the book. She handled the weapon with great care and sent it immediately to HQ, who then sent it off for analysis. Before she did so, I peered at the footage over Birck's shoulder, trying to get a look at the knife lying on the floor of the hall.

'That's the one, isn't it?' he said.

It certainly looked like it would fit right into the knife-block at Café Cairo.

'Yes. Same knife, same method as used against Heber. I'm pretty damn sure it's the same attacker.'

The party leader is taken to hospital, and the floor is flooded with police officers, struggling to evacuate the station and secure the crime scene. It's pointless; any forensic evidence that might be there is going to get destroyed regardless.

The same attacker. It should be straightforward, but we've got nothing, and its just mayhem. Apart from Central Station, the chaos is probably worst around Västerbron Bridge. The police radio crackles into life with a voice informing us that the high winds have caused a driver to lose control and collide with a traffic light. The driver got away with concussion, but the traffic light wasn't so lucky. Weakened by the impact, it was unable to withstand Edith's force, slowly laying itself across the carriageway and causing a pile-up.

'How the hell did he get away?' I say. 'How the fuck did he make it out of there?'

Birck leans against the wall, closes his eyes, and then pushes them, hard, with his fingertips. He grimaces. I drum on my thigh with my fingers. *Can't think of anything to think.*

'I don't know,' says Birck, without opening his eyes. 'It didn't look like there were many officers in that direction.'

'They should have had the whole building secured.'

'Yes. But right behind the stage? And how far can you get in, what was it, seventeen seconds?'

He turns towards the constable, his eyes still closed.

'Yes,' the constable says nervously, looking at Birck. 'Seventeen.'

'The bodyguards know what they're doing, you can tell. But they only need to be distracted for two, three seconds. He gets seventeen here. Not only that, but it's dark.'

My body registers the first wave of chaos ebbing away. I'm feeling light-headed, as though I need to eat or drink something to avoid blacking out, but it isn't that. I clutch the tube of Halcion in my pocket.

We didn't have a hope. We weren't even close. We were heading in the wrong direction right to the very end.

'Fuck!' Birck screams, and slams his hand against the wall. 'Shit, shit, shit, shit.'

The constable looks scared. Birck's face is red; he's just standing there, breathing heavily. I should say something, but I don't know what.

'Let's do without the hysteria,' he eventually says, calmer, 'and do what we're supposed to, look at what's actually happened and what we know.' He opens his eyes. 'You okay?'

'Why do you ask?'

'Your forehead's all shiny. Are you hot?'

'Oh, right. Yes. No. I'm alright.'

I'm not really alright. I need some water.

'Okay,' he says. 'Let's look at what happened. What do you say to that? And where the hell are Iris and Goffman, by the way?'

'Iris went off to make a call to see how they were getting on with the evacuation. As for Goffman, I've got no idea.'

'Here,' says the constable. He reels the various recordings back and forth on the screens. 'Here he is. It's ... a couple of seconds after the power came back on.'

The camera has captured part of the area surrounding Central Station's food court. Many people are using the torch function on their mobile phones. Those who aren't sitting eating junk food,

314

waiting for things to improve, are dragging heavy bags and cases back and forth. When the lights come back on and Central Station is once again bathed in cold light, people quickly return to whatever it is they've been doing. A masked man zigzags his way past them, the bottom part of his face covered by a scarf, and the top of his head hidden by his thick hood. He disappears out of shot.

According to the first witness statements, the man rushed out to a waiting car. Others said he boarded one of the commuter trains. According to a third account, he disappeared down into the underground.

'Where does he go from here?' Birck says.

'He heads towards the trains,' I say. 'Check the cameras near the platforms.'

A glossy film of sweat lines the officer's upper lip. He takes a handkerchief from his pocket and wipes it across his mouth.

'Who has a hanky nowadays?' says Birck.

'It was a present,' the officer mumbles, staring at the screens.

It's fifty-seven minutes since the attack. Birck puts his phone to his ear, and as soon as they answer he asks for a list of all the mainline, commuter, and bus services that have left the station in the past hour.

'Have they?' he says, taken aback. 'Okay. Who was that? Well, thanks.' He hangs up. 'Somebody beat me to it — someone from HQ.'

I stare at one of the screens, which the constable has paused on an image of the attacker.

'Who the hell is that?' I say.

'I can't find him,' the constable informs us. 'I can't pick him up anywhere after that.' He's dejected, as though he's just failed an important test. 'I'm sorry. For the time being, that's our last picture of him.'

He's a big man, broad-shouldered, and wearing dark clothes. That's all we can discern from the footage.

'We're too far behind,' Birck says, more to himself than to anyone else. 'Everyone's too far behind. To just go out looking for him is hardly going to help. He's not going to be moving around for the hell of it.'

'Ebi Hakimi finds out from Asplund about the rumours of an attack,' I say. 'Asplund is a member of Swedish Resistance. His immediate superior is Christian Västerberg.' I look up from the floor. I need some water. 'Where do we find him?'

Autumn. The release date had been set: three months to go. He'd got the text late last night, from a number he didn't recognise. Christian didn't dare respond.

A date, that was all the text consisted of. If Michael had had the chance to send him a message, wouldn't he have written a bit more? Maybe he was scared.

It was coming up to eleven in the morning. He wasn't due in till twelve today, having taken the morning off to sort out the dwindling stock of flyers. Jens Malm called him almost every day. Most of the time, it was hard to know what he actually wanted. It was as though he was blaming Christian for their lack of progress.

'Those of you who make up the Stockholm division are our front line,' he'd often say. 'If you don't make any progress, nor can we.'

They were severely depleted. Those who still stood with them were the ones who always would, come what may — the faithful, the most committed. And that was good, Malm said. Money, on the other hand, was in short supply.

Christian watched children chasing each other across the playground outside his block. If he'd gone back to the counsellor he would probably have told her about this, about how he found himself wanting to stand there and watch them, without being able to explain why.

The phone rang. He pulled it out and put it to his ear, answering without taking his eyes off the playground. One of the kids was being chased around by the others. At this distance, their voices seemed unnaturally small.

'Yes, hello,' Christian said.

'It's me.'

Michael. He went stiff, then took a step away from the window and sat himself down on one of the kitchen chairs.

'Hey, what's up?'

'I … this is bad, Christian. Really fucking bad.'

'But what's up? I got your message, three months left, that's fucking great.'

'I don't think I'll make it that far. I've … I need money.'

He'd tried to put a brave face on things, Christian knew that. He also knew about the rumours that flourished: that during his time inside, Michael had been a target for other groups, criminal Islamists and left-wing extremists convicted of serious assaults and attempted manslaughter. As if that wasn't enough, the director of the institution was known to be Jewish.

Now it came out: the words streamed out of the handset, and Christian struggled not to miss anything.

Michael had tried to survive by paying his way out of trouble. It had worked, until the money ran out.

'How much do you need?' said Christian.

'More than you've got.'

'How much?'

'Fifty thousand.'

'Shit.'

The word escaped from his mouth before he had the chance to stop it. That was considerably more money than he had.

'Jens has helped me up to now, but I don't think he's got much left.' His voice got quieter. 'I'm not going to make it, Christian. I'm serious now — this isn't a joke. If I don't sort this out, I won't be able to walk out of here.'

Christian felt the panic spreading across his chest.

'What should I do?'

'Talk to Jens. I've promised to do some legwork for him when I get out, in return for his support. And now he doesn't have any money himself, but he does have a direct line into the Sweden Democrats. And they've got money.' There's a short silence, crackling on the line, and then, 'I've got to go now.'

It was perfectly logical, really. In exchange for their help once Michael was released, Malm was to try to arrange some backhanded transfer. It was pretty straightforward, as long as it stayed under the radar: there was a year to go till the election. Right now, money was pouring into the Sweden Democrats from every conceivable source, as well as from a few inconceivable ones. Besides, there were still forces within the Sweden Democrats who supported Swedish Resistance — forces that tried to look after their own.

This was how Jens Malm explained it to Christian when they met up later that afternoon, after Christian had rung in sick. They sat in Malm's car, a cool, silver BMW, and Christian wondered how he could afford it. The place: a layby by the southbound E4 motorway, a no man's land on the edge of the southern suburbs.

'All we need to do,' Malm said, 'is make sure we hold it together. And this must not, under any circumstances, get to the party leadership. That cunt from Sölvesborg would shit himself with fear at the thought of losing votes over this. I'll talk to my contact, and see how much he can get his hands on. How much was it he needed?'

'Fifty.'

'Fifty. We should be able to sort that.'

He looked at Malm, realising that this was the first time they'd met up, just the two of them. The leadership met once a week, but there were always another two or three people present.

Malm took out his phone and sent a text. He was over forty now,

319

but his features were still sharp: defined cheekbones, his hair as thick and as well groomed as ever. He was wearing a light autumn coat and a discreet scarf, looking more like a lawyer or an estate agent. When Malm lifted his hand to adjust the rear-view mirror, the arm of his coat slid down, and Christian could see the three words tattooed under his forearm, in discreet capitals: LOYALTY — DUTY — DESIRE. The motto and mantra of Swedish Resistance. And beside them, an older Wolfsangel.

The layby contained a little truck-stop café and a car park, and two public toilets. A handful of cars were parked a little way away. The E4 rumbled beneath them, a chain of cars shooting past.

'Right,' he said as he put the phone away. 'We'll have to see what he says. Shouldn't take too long.' He looked at Christian. 'How are things with you?'

'Yeah, okay. I suppose.'

'You were a bit quiet at the last meeting.'

'I was knackered — I came straight from work.'

Malm nodded thoughtfully.

'Only a radical, uncompromising organisation is capable of overturning the current system. That's what I've always said, and that's what I'm saying now, even though we're fighting against the tide.' His eyes met Christian's, and he smiled. 'And knackered soldiers are better than no soldiers.'

Christian smiled, too. They sat in silence for a while. The door to the café swung open, and a lone, overweight woman emerged. She made her way to her car, and as she sat down in the driver's seat, the little Opel rocked violently.

'I really hope we can help him out,' said Malm. 'He deserves it, after all he's done for us.'

The Opel drove off. Beyond the Opel was a Mazda. Christian saw something moving in the back seat. It took a minute for him to realise that it was a woman, straddling a man. She had one hand in her hair and the other round one of the headrests.

Malm's phone beeped and buzzed. He opened the text. 'Fifty thousand,' he said, nodding. 'Green light. I'll call him to sort out the details.'

Relief washed over Christian.

'Who's your contact?'

'Niklas Persson, or Nille. He's got himself all the way up to party headquarters.'

Christian remembered him. He was the one who had informed Michael of his expulsion from Sweden Democrat Youth. That was a long time ago, but Christian still remembered it clearly, the sadness in his eyes. How furious he had been himself.

'I know who he is.'

'I know you know.' Malm laughed. 'I think he still feels bad about chucking you two out.'

'He never chucked me out,' Christian said. 'I left of my own free will, out of loyalty.'

'Oh yes. That's right.' Malm nodded. 'That's your biggest asset, Christian, your loyalty.'

In the car a little way away, the woman's hips moved frantically, almost in spasm, before she collapsed into the back seat. Christian thought he could hear her moans.

That same evening, the phone rang. It was Malm.

'Not happening,' he said. 'We're fucked.'

'What are you on about?'

'Don't talk to me like that.' Malm's voice was cold. 'Calm yourself down.'

'Sorry. I apologise. What's happened?'

Malm had spoken to Nille and explained why they needed the money, and they had agreed the details between them. They'd arranged to meet in an old factory in Solna for the handover. After waiting for half an hour, Malm had sensed something was wrong. He'd called Nille, who hadn't answered. After fifteen minutes, Nille had called back, stressed and anxious.

Someone had heard their conversation. Had heard *Swedish Resistance*, had heard *prison*, heard the prisoner's name.

The news had reached the party leader within five minutes. The leader had immediately put a stop to the transaction. Apparently, he had lost his temper, which was very unusual: they were at the start of an election campaign. They needed to focus on themselves and the voters. They had obligations to their donors. The money wasn't meant to save convicted Nazi inmates. And then: Let the Nazi get beaten to death, for all he cared.

Once he'd stopped shouting, he'd sacked Nille.

'You need to contact him,' Malm said. 'So he knows.'

'But he ... if he doesn't have the money ... they're going to ...'

'I know, but what the hell are we going to do?'

'There must be another way.'

'He needs the money right now,' said Malm. 'There's no way to get hold of it legally.'

'Well, illegally then?'

'Never, Christian.' Malm's voice darkened. 'It would never serve the interests of the nationalist struggle, and that must always come first. Don't forget that. Everything has to be done with that in mind. And on this occasion ...'

'What?'

'I forbid you to do it. That's an order. Contact him and explain.'

Malm didn't give orders very often. He managed to get what he wanted anyway. So when he did, it felt almost like a threat.

Christian checked the time.

'He was going to get in touch at ten. That's when he's allowed to make a call.'

'That's in twelve minutes.' Malm cleared his throat. 'That means you have twelve minutes to work out what you're going to say to him.'

The line went dead. Christian looked at the phone, and it was all he could do not to sling it against the wall.

Thirteen minutes later, it rang. Christian sat on his living-room floor and tried to decide what to do. When he pressed green and put the phone to his ear, he realised he still didn't have a clue what to say.

Michael sounded hopeful, alert, despite it being late.

'Is it all sorted?' he asked.

Christian closed his eyes.

'No.'

Then he explained, and when he'd finished he went quiet. There were no more words.

'Okay.' Michael sounded calm. 'I see. So it was the leadership, then?'

'The leader himself,' Christian said.

'I see,' he repeated.

Christian wondered how serious the threats against him were, but he didn't ask, didn't want to risk sounding like he doubted him.

'What happens now?' said Christian.

'I don't know.'

He survived, as it turned out, thanks to simple good fortune: he was moved to another institution, closer to Stockholm, to prepare him for life on the outside. The decision came from the prison authorities three days after their conversation.

Back in Mariefred, they hadn't managed to get him on his own, and the threat to him at the new place was smaller. Instead of being beaten to death, he was punched a few times and took a few kicks in the gut.

He pissed blood for a couple of weeks, but that, outwardly, was all.

Outside Jonathan's flat in Hallunda, the storm is raging. He's standing by the window with his back to the telly, where updates about the attack on the party leader alternate with information about Edith's relentless progress.

In daylight, Hallunda is no more than great concrete hulks of buildings and graffiti-covered walls — lawless country. It's been like that for a long time, but much more so since the May riots, when cars were torched and the niggers battled the police, who called them monkeys and made everything worse. Now, in this weather, Hallunda rises in the darkness like a great, grey ruin.

Jonathan has been ripped off. Again. They've tricked him. Why do I have to be such an idiot, he thinks to himself.

And, at the same time, he's ashamed.

He looks at himself in the reflection in the glass: the short hair, the pronounced eyebrows, one of which is bisected by a big scar, the bulbous nose, low cheekbones, narrow, stretched eyes. He's wearing black, baggy jeans and a white T-shirt. Poking out from the sleeve is a tattoo — the word SWEDEN and a swastika. His arms are pale and spindly. He avoids looking at the tattoo.

He picks up the phone and calls Christian. The ring tone is choppy and scratchy, but there's no answer.

He peers over at the door to the flat, and then at the knuckleduster on the windowsill in front of him. That's all he's got, if anything happens.

Jonathan moves away from the window. He doesn't want to see himself. Standing there, close to the wall, he can feel the storm; he can feel the draught by the skirting boards. The windowpane shakes, as if it were about to give way.

He rings Christian again. He doesn't answer.

The flat has a little hallway, a door leading to the bathroom, a kitchenette where the day's washing up is still waiting. He's lived here since he left home three years ago. One wall is covered with a huge Swedish flag. Jonathan has written SWEDISH RESISTANCE by hand, in the yellow cross. On the desk is a wrapped parcel, with a dressing gown inside. *To Mum from Jonathan*, he's written on the tag, which is shaped like Santa's hat and tied to the ribbon.

It just rings and rings, but no one answers.

The windscreen wipers in Iris's car attempt to provide some visibility through the windscreen, but their motion is in vain. Christian Västerberg is registered as resident at 19 Olshammarsgatan in Hagsätra, a journey that would normally take just over fifteen minutes. In this weather, it's a different story.

Around us, Stockholm is on the verge of collapse. The airports at Arlanda and Bromma have cancelled all flights. In the Baltic, the sea level is rising, and Edith has pushed the waters of Lake Mälaren to more than a metre over normal levels, and the great turmoil in the water is smashing huge sheets of ice onto the shore.

Emergency Service vehicles are blocking the road. Iris lowers the window and holds up her badge towards the unmoved constable.

'Where are you going?' the officer shouts.

'Hagsätra,' says Iris.

'Eh?'

'Hagsätra.'

He laughs.

'Good luck.'

Iris closes the window again. The radio plays a festive tune, *It's worth the wait the whole year through, just to make someone happy like you.*

'Christian Västerberg,' Birck says thoughtfully. 'Who is that?'

'Something of a low-profile member of Swedish Resistance. We

327

know he acts as a go-between for the members and the leader of the Stockholm division, Keyser. Västerberg and Keyser have been friends since childhood.'

'Keyser,' I say. 'Where have I heard that before?

'About ten years back, he kicked a left-wing activist in the face, so hard that his eye popped out of its socket. He got a very harsh prison term.'

'No,' I say. 'It wasn't that.'

'Considering their notoriety, we actually know very little about them. Their operation is completely closed. As I was saying, Asplund was our contact inside the movement.'

'Shouldn't you have been keeping an eye on them?' says Birck.

'You can always think that,' Iris says, cuttingly. 'At least you can always think that afterwards.'

'This isn't the boy scouts we're dealing with. This is a militant neo-Nazi organisation. Damn right that you, with all your resources, should hav—'

'Our department relies on two things: what happens out there, and intelligence that informs us of it. We don't put people under constant surveillance, especially people who are not suspected of any criminal activity. And we, too, have limited resources. We have focused heavily on RAF. We have our mole within Swedish Resistance, as I said, and he was previously able to give us precise information about their plans. We have not had any indications about this.'

'Asplund might not have known about it,' I say.

'No,' Iris says stiffly. 'Maybe he didn't. We don't even know if it was them. We don't even know who the assailant was.'

No one says anything. Behind us, a tree is blown down, crashing into the fence that lines the road. The fence gives way, bulging out across the carriageway.

That's when it comes to me: Christian Västerberg. I think he had a friend with an unusual surname — could have been Keyser.

There was an assault in Salem, years ago, and I think they were involved. I was still living at home, but I spent almost no time there. I wonder if Grim knows about it. Maybe. I can't remember whether Västerberg was the victim or the perpetrator. Maybe those kinds of details don't really matter.

Christian Västerberg lives in one of the tower blocks, near a pizzeria. We climb out of the car, and the snow finds its way inside my coat, under the collar, in my eyes and mouth, everywhere.

A harder, sharper wind arrives, like a wave.

One minute, Birck and Iris are standing next to each other. He's looking something up on his phone, she's putting the car keys in her pocket. Then a shadow falls, fast and heavy, and the next minute, Iris has flung herself at Birck, and a deafening crash — like a skip hitting the ground — makes the earth shake, and my ears pop. A ten-centimetre-thick roof panel, several metres across, has fallen from one of the buildings.

'Thanks,' Birck says, shocked.

'You're welcome.'

I look up towards the sky, which is being torn apart. The clouds are dark and heavy. When the next gust arrives, the noise escalates to a roar and we duck, instinctively. There's a creaking sound nearby, but I don't know where, because the noise is too weak when it reaches us, and can't be identified. On the other side of the road, part of the façade is being ripped off. Roof tiles drop, crash to the ground, and shatter.

Iris looks at Birck.

'Are you okay?'

'I think so.'

She turns around. The roof panel fell so close to the car that it took out one of the wing-mirrors.

'Car's fine, too,' she says, 'more or less.'

Christian turns his gaze away from the television, where pictures of the attack roll on a constant, never-ending loop. Where's Michael? He wants to contact him, but he doesn't dare.

The phone keeps ringing, over and over again. It's Jonathan. He doesn't answer.

A torrent of regret flushes through him, so strong that he almost gets carried away on it, and he realises he won't be able to hold out for very much longer.

The time inside had left Michael with a few new scars and a new iciness to his stare. It had also strengthened his resolve: he'd made it. He'd survived. The worst scars were not visible. Later, Christian would think, Michael could get very down, introverted and absent in a completely different way than before. He got a job as a caretaker in a warehouse. He hated it, and did the bare minimum required so as to keep hold of the job.

The first meeting after Michael's return was attended by three more people than the one before. This brought the total to seven.

'You mustn't blame yourself,' Michael said, 'that we got so small while I was inside. I know you did your best.'

Christian didn't know what to say. Had he done all he could? He didn't know the answer to that question. Michael had never blamed him for the failure, their dramatic decline. Michael had nodded and looked sad. He said he understood. But, he'd added, it wasn't over yet.

'It's a different climate now,' Michael went on. 'Not just here, but across Scandinavia, too. We've got the whole of Scandinavia with us.' He laughed. 'Do you see? And soon enough, the whole of Europe.'

It was just after the general election. TV pictures showed the Man from Sölvesborg, beaming. The Sweden Democrats had passed the famous 4 per cent threshold, and had possibly succeeded in holding the balance of power in Swedish politics. That was what the election had really been about, not which of the two electoral blocs would come out on top. Sweden was split, divided. The Sweden Democrats got all the attention, both before and after election night itself.

'It's just a matter of time now,' Michael said as he watched the images.

'A matter of time till what?'

'Till someone kills him.'

Christian glanced over, wondering what he meant. That the party leader had enemies was universally known, and in the near future that fact would become all too obvious: the far left hated him. Before long, parts of the far right would feel the same way.

Michael threw all his energy into Swedish Resistance. The membership grew to over fifty, all of whom paid subs. They were able to move to larger premises. Their warehouse moved to another area. Some of them had been involved in the past, but most of them were new recruits, who they'd enlisted via high schools and the internet, via contacts' contacts. The media ran stories about them in what was presumably supposed to be an alarming tone. The effect was the opposite: they started becoming visible again. People joined up.

Christian and Michael were inspired by history: during the course of the year, they read Arthur Kemp's seven hundred-page

March of the Titans: the complete history of the white race, as well as the new edition of *The Racial Elements of European History,* first published in 1927, by the author Hans F K Günther. They made for outstanding, uncompromising reading.

Everything fell into place, and the Stockholm division grew. People signed up — not just in working-class suburbs, but in the city's wealthiest neighbourhoods, too. They walked through central Stockholm handing out flyers, accompanied by a police escort. Christian stood at Michael's side, shocked and overwhelmed. Before long, the membership had reached one hundred.

'This is mental,' said Christian.

'And this is just the beginning,' said Michael, smiling.

Some people end up on the sidelines of history — as spectators — just watching as it unfolds before them. Others find themselves at the epicentre, shaping events, making a mark that changes everything.

Sitting in front of the telly, Christian returns to the past, and submerges himself in memories. They blur and overlap, merge into a haze. Too much has happened. People can't turn the chaos of reality into a neat order.

Michael had said this sort of thing before. At first it had been a joke, always followed by a laugh more than anything else: how they should throw Molotov-cocktails through the Migration Service's windows. Burn down refugee centres — swat a load of flies in one go. It had always been like that. Even in October and November, when the plan was sketched out and the details began to take shape, Christian still didn't believe it was actually going to happen. When Jonathan informed him that the SEPO had got wind of an imminent threat against Martin Antonsson, Christian passed it on to Michael. Michael's eyes lit up.

It wasn't the first time this had happened, nor the first time they'd deployed a similar strategy.

They attacked RAF and all the others, and they were attacked just as often. Sometimes it felt like a game to Christian — a serious game, where both sides played by the same rules with violent consequences.

Their plans were always uncovered — sometimes within an hour or so, sometimes within a couple of days. Despite this, their plans had the desired effect: to irritate and to undermine their opponents.

This time there were more details, and they gradually fell into place: they could use Jonathan, his connection to SEPO, and exploit the fact that RAF were planning an attack on Martin Antonsson. A missing knife at Café Cairo would ensure that the police focused their enquiries on them, and would exacerbate the reds' internal conflicts at the same time. All bureaucracies have finite resources, and the police's close surveillance of RAF would temporarily give Swedish Resistance free reign.

No one apart from Michael and Christian was to find out the truth. Not even Jens Malm.

That's not how it turned out.

They didn't tell anyone else, but there were certain details and issues that had to be dealt with on the hoof, with others nearby. Christian thought he could see their eyes widen and their ears prick up.

'I think people suspect what's going on,' he said one evening in November. 'I think it's about to go tits up.'

'What makes you think that?'

'It's more of a feeling.' He looked at Michael. 'Don't you think?'

They stood in a secluded corner of a bar on Folkungagatan. A dark, heavy rain was falling outside. The neon signs glowed.

'Yes,' Michael said eventually.

'Well, then, we'll call it off.'

Michael shook his head.

'We keep going. No one knows yet — there might be a few who suspect something, but they're on our side. That's what's important.' He lowered his voice. 'I've talked to Jens about it.'

'And what did he think?'

Michael didn't say anything, but the look of excitement on his face was enough of an answer.

They caught the underground home that night. Michael looked calm and collected, with his hands in his jeans pockets and a slight smile on his face. Christian tried to smile, too. The resulting grimace was tight, like a muzzle.

The fifth of December, a few weeks earlier: the tabloid *Expressen* published a few articles about racist abuse carried out by several active Sweden Democrats on various internet forums. All those exposed were expelled from the party. The leader threw out anyone who dared to tell the truth.

The Traitor. The Spineless Bastard. The Populist.

The hatred grew and grew, you could almost feel it.

On internet forums and in blogs written by his friends and comrades, known and unknown, the reactions erupted. Christian was sitting at his computer when the phone rang. It was only as he pulled the phone from his pocket that he noticed how slippery it was, and realised he was sweating. He stared at the forum topic he had just read, from the first post to the most recent. Michael might be right, he thought to himself. *It really looks like people support what we're planning. If he succeeds now, he could end up becoming a hero.*

They really had the wind in their sails now. The dice fell in their favour, time and time again.

Christian didn't recognise the number illuminating his phone's display. He pressed to accept the call, and put the phone to his ear, without saying anything.

It was a male voice, deep and calm: 'Hello? Anyone there?'

Christian snapped the lid down on his laptop.

'Yes.'

'Who am I talking to?'

'Who are you calling?'

'I was looking for Christian Västerberg. Have I called the right number?'

'Who is this?'

'My name is Thomas Heber, and I'm a researcher at Stockholm University.'

'Okay?' Christian thought about hanging up. 'And what do you want?'

Then he explained.

Christian said yes, but couldn't say why. They met in a windowless seminar room at the library in Skärholmen. He refused to have the interviews recorded. Heber took notes.

He'd already interviewed lots of people before Christian, in movements like Swedish Resistance, as well as their opponents, like RAF. That was all he could say about his interviewees, and he would never reveal anything more to anyone, not even under police interrogation.

He could say whatever he liked, Heber promised. Christian was anonymous to the extent that he could reveal a crime in progress, and Heber wouldn't do anything about it, wouldn't do anything other than listen.

Heber explained that that was just an example, but Christian felt a strange giggle bubbling in his chest. The laugh in his throat became a silent retching. Christian's vision became blurred.

He was close to falling apart. He was sweating. Heber didn't seem to notice, or maybe it was just that he didn't care.

Much of the conversation was about Christian's own life. At first, he regretted having agreed to this. Talking about himself was unusual, uncomfortable, but Heber was skilful, Christian had to admit. He was a man who inspired trust, and the conversation

soon started to make Christian feel temporarily safe, giving him a
sense of security that seemed to grow. Heber always let him finish
whatever he was saying before asking another question. There
were a couple of times when he didn't want to answer, and when he
shook his head, Heber said that it was fine, no problem, and moved
on to the next question.

Talking about himself was liberating. It was as though the angst
disappeared.

The betrayal, the treachery, when it came, a few hours later,
went almost unnoticed.

'Have you heard the rumour?' he asked.

'No,' Heber said, eyebrows raised.

Christian was carrying a heavy burden in his chest. It was
suffocating him. And then he told Heber, in two sentences. Heber
took it in with a surprised expression.

'You mean someone's going to have a go at the leader?'

'Yes.'

Christian wondered what he was thinking.

'Can you stop it happening?' said Heber.

'I wouldn't dare. I can't say any more about it, because no one
knows where or when. I've already said too much. I've already … if
anybody finds out …'

'No one is going to find out,' said Heber.

Christian was sweating. He couldn't keep it in any longer. It had
been so long, and during that time he'd done a lot of things he
shouldn't have done, hurt so many people. He felt lost.

The room tilted. He blinked.

'I know someone who will,' he said eventually.

He told Thomas Heber, who couldn't pass it on, who should have
kept it to himself, but who might have felt exactly the same way as
Christian: this just cannot happen.

Later, Michael called him on the night of the twelfth with

instructions to steal a knife. He couldn't say no, couldn't put up any resistance. It was only when he was told where to go after breaking into Café Cairo — the university — that he realised what was going on.

Someone is banging on his door. He walks over to open it.

Images of the attack are still rolling on the telly. He can feel his own pulse in his temples. He can feel just how close he is to history, how this story will be told, how close he is to its epicentre. It's huge. And he feels guilt, a guilt so heavy that now, when the flat is filled with nothing but darkness, it seems impossible to bear, yet he can do nothing about it.

So he bears it, the man who is just a number, just 1601 in a dead researcher's field notes.

Jonathan calls again. He's keeping away from the window now. Any minute now, it's going to get cracked by the wind, he's sure of that. He's rolled down the blinds, but he doesn't know why. Perhaps to avoid shards of glass, but the blind is made from fabric. It might not help.

He starts thinking about the Dictaphone, wondering where it is now. He gave it to Ebi, but what happened after that isn't clear. Did he keep hold of it? Did the police find it on him when he died?

Maybe it fell out of Ebi's pocket during the demonstration. It might still be lying there, on the ground in Rålambshov Park.

They've duped him. That's the only explanation. And he was taken in by it. They're always cleverer than him, always one step ahead. Jonathan has been a pawn in Christian's hands. He feels so predictable. So stupid.

And at the same time: so scared.

The party leader. Christ. A genuine opportunity to get rid of him for good. Jonathan has seen and heard that being discussed, in internet forums as well as amongst his friends.

But now it's happened — Jesus, what if he dies?

It keeps ringing, until eventually there's a click and the ringing stops.

'Hello?' Jonathan says. 'Hello? Christian?'

It's a bad line. The storm makes everything rasp and crackle. Then, through the noise, that voice: 'Yes.'

'Why didn't you answer?'

'I ...'

He doesn't finish the sentence.

'Hello?' says Jonathan.

'Yes, I'm here.'

'You knew about this.'

'Yes.'

'This is ... you, both of you, have tricked me. You've played me like a fucking, what's it fucking called ...'

'I know,' says Christian. 'It was necessary.'

'Swedish Resistance have had it now. You do realise that, don't you?'

Christian doesn't reply.

'Do you support them doing this?'

He hears the storm, and nothing else.

'Hello? Are you still there?'

'Yes.'

Jonathan slumps on to the bed.

'Do you support them doing this?'

'I can't answer that, Jonathan.'

'Is he there?'

'Who?'

'*Him.*'

'No.'

'You're lying.'

Christian doesn't respond.

'How are things with him?'

'I don't know,' Christian says. 'I have to go now.'

The call ends. Jonathan sits there on the edge of his bed, phone in hand.

Behind the blind, the force of the storm smashes the windowpane. The flying shards slash gaping holes in the fabric.

340

Christian puts his phone away and turns to Michael.

'He knows.'

Michael's eyes are blank.

'Who?'

'Jonathan.'

'Oh, right. Good.'

'How are you feeling?'

Michael takes the towel from his forehead.

'I'm bleeding quite a lot. Feel a bit dizzy. But I'm glad that bastard is dead.'

'You don't know whether he is or not.' Christian glances at the telly. 'They've haven't said so yet.'

'It's a matter of time. The knife hit its target.'

'How can you be so sure? It was so dark in there.'

'What do you take me for? Have you told the others that it was us?'

'No, not yet.'

'Get a message out to all the members. They need to know.'

Christian doesn't say anything. He doesn't send a message either. He heads to the bathroom, takes a clean towel from the cupboard, wets it, and then gives it to Michael. His face is spattered with dried blood from the wound on his forehead. He wipes himself off with the towel.

'Did you get that message sent?'

'Eh?'

'The group message.'

'Oh, right.' Christian hesitates for a second, then pulls his phone from his pocket.

'No, sending failed. I suppose that'll be the storm.'

'Try again.'

'I will.' He sits down opposite his friend. 'What happened?'

'The power went. That was my only chance, so I took it.'

'I meant your forehead.'

'A bit of a roof-tile hit me. It was only the size of a coin, so it didn't knock me out, but it was fucking sharp.' He smiles. 'Do you realise what we've done? This changes everything. Whatever happens to us, things will never be the same again.'

'Why did you come here?'

'I didn't know where to go. I had to get inside, but I wasn't about to go home. If they know it was me ... I'm pretty sure they don't, but if they do, then that'll be the first place they look. But I didn't want to be outdoors — fuck that. This storm is killing people. Once my head stops bleeding, I thought I'd go down to your basement. Is that okay? If they come, you can just say you don't know where I am.'

Christian stands up, goes and gets the key to the basement, and puts it on the table in front of him.

He takes a deep breath.

'Do you remember,' he says, 'at the beginning of December, when Heber called you? From a payphone?'

'Yes.' The towel has already turned a deep red. 'Why won't it fucking stop bleeding?'

'That was me,' he says.

'Eh?'

'I was the one who told him. He got in touch with me to ask whether I might be prepared to do an interview. I told him during that interview.'

Michael looks up from the towel. The look he gives Christian feels like a dagger. He never suspected it, Christian now realises: Michael trusted him, right to the end.

'Eh?'

'It was me,' he repeats. 'I told him your name during an interview. I told him what you were planning to do.'

'You?'

'Yes.'

'You're having a laugh.'

Christian feels a burning sensation behind the eyes, feels the tears pushing their way out.

'No.'

Michael stands up, but does so too quickly and sways wildly, putting his arm out to hold himself up against the wall.

'Why? What did you do that for?'

'I had to.'

'But ... how ... why ...?'

Winded, he collapses back onto the sofa.

'You are dead,' Michael says. 'You got that? You are dead to me.'

'Yes.'

'And Heber is dead, because of you.'

'I know,' Christian says.

'You were the one who stole the fucking knife, for fuck's sake.'

'I didn't know what you wanted it f—'

'Don't lie!' he roars. 'Don't lie to me again. You knew fucking full well what I wanted it for. You even asked me if I'd chucked his phone in the water. You were the one who got Jonathan to make SEPO concentrate on RAF instead. You're as much a part of this as I am. How the hell can you ... have you called the cops as well? Are they on the way?'

'No.'

'Have you?' he screams.

'No.'

343

'If you're lying now,' he says, his breathing shallow and laboured. 'I'm going to shoot the first person who comes through that door. Got that? I'll shoot everyone. Is that what you want?'

'I haven't called them, Michael,' Christian says, staring at his hands.

'Look at me, for fuck's sake.'

He braces himself to obey. It hurts. It hurts way too much for him to be able to stand it.

'I haven't called them.'

This wasn't what was supposed to happen. Michael shouldn't even be here now; he should be lying low. That's what he said. Christian wasn't to contact him.

'How the hell could you be so stupid?' Michael's voice is quiet, suddenly collected. As usual, Michael sees the big picture, knows what has to be done. 'Why the hell didn't you say anything?'

'I tried. But you wouldn't listen.'

'Is that all you've got to say? That you tried?'

And it is. He realises that now. There's nothing more to say.

'Yes.' He stands up again, picks up his phone. 'I'll try and send that message again.'

This time he doesn't bottle it. He goes to the kitchen and opens the pantry. The strip light in the kitchen blinks once, twice, three times. He feels along the top shelf with his hand. There. There it is.

He returns, phone in one hand, revolver in the other. It's loaded. The same revolver that took Lisa Swedberg's life. Was that Christian's fault, too? He doesn't know anymore. He doesn't know anything.

A phrase pops into his head, something someone said, or wrote to him once, a long time ago, *They can laugh if they want, sneer at us — we're moving forward, they're standing still.* He can't picture her face. It's gone, like everything else.

Michael notices the weapon in Christian's hand. Now he's on his feet, quickly, and this time the adrenalin keeps him steady. He raises his hands, his palms facing outwards.

'Christian …'

'Sorry,' he says, and takes the safety off.

Christian then puts the revolver in his mouth, the barrel against his palate.

Outside, roof-tiles whipped off by the wind swirl past, falling downwards. The sound of them crashing to the ground is masked by the thud inside the apartment.

The stairwell is in darkness when Iris forces the door. I push the glowing red switch. The lights on the landings flicker and then come on. Christian Västerberg lives on the fifth floor, one of six in the block on Olshammarsgatan 19.

Iris and Birck get out their weapons.

'Where's yours?' she asks.

'I haven't got one,' I say.

Her phone receives a text message. She reads it with a neutral expression.

'It's from Paul,' she says, 'His condition is unclear. They are operating now. This was fifteen minutes ago.'

'Where is Goffman?' says Birck.

'He's been going through Västerberg's file. He's on his way now.' She turns to me again. 'You don't have your fire—'

She's interrupted by a noise that gives all of us a start, and makes my heart race. Despite the constant rumble of the storm, the shot rings in our ears, loud and sharp.

'One shot, no more,' Iris says, when the only thing that follows the sound is silence and the whining of the storm outside. 'That could mean anything.'

'Reinforcements,' Birck says. 'We nee—'

'There's no time for that. Go first.' She looks at me. 'And you stay right here.'

'No.'

'You're unarmed, Leo,' Birck says. 'Wait.'

'I'll follow you up.'

Neither of them protest, maybe because there's no time for that. I follow them up the stairs, one flight at a time. Their arms are outstretched, gripping their black weapons with the barrels pointing diagonally downwards. We stick close to the walls.

On the third floor, a click from behind makes me jump, and for a split-second I wish I had stayed down there by the entrance.

Someone has opened a door directly behind me — a young man. I pull out my badge, and push it to the opening.

'Shhh,' I say. 'Police.'

'What …'

'Call the police. Tell them shots have been fired at Olshammarsgatan 19. Ask them to send ambulances. And stay inside.'

Birck and Iris are a couple of steps ahead of me. I hurry to catch up with them. For the first time in ages, I'm scared. Behind me, the young man closes the door. Hopefully, he's calling the police. Or else his first call is to the press.

We're soon at the foot of the stairs that lead up to the first floor. From here, we can see the doors of the three apartments— one to the left at the top of the stairs, one straight ahead, and one on the right.

'I think his is the one straight ahead,' I say. 'Doesn't that say Västerberg?'

'I don't know,' Birck says, squinting. 'Maybe. In that case, we're going to have to get closer.'

'It says Västerberg,' says Iris.

We cling to the wall up the last few stairs, our winter coats rustling against its uneven surface. I'm studying the floor, and there it is. I tap Birck on the shoulder, and point.

A little drop — no bigger than a coin — of blood.

Iris sweeps past the door and positions herself on one side, me and Birck on the other. The lights flicker, which makes everyone stiffen and breathe in sharply. I can smell Birck's aftershave again. There's no sound coming from inside the flat, but it might be being drowned out by Edith's hissing and rumbling.

Birck points at the door handle, and nods at Iris. She carefully places her hand on it and then pushes downwards. It's locked. She quickly withdraws her hand.

Shit.

'Christian,' Iris says out loud. 'My name is Iris, and I'm a police officer. I have two colleagues with me. Their names are Leo and Gabriel. We really need to talk to you. Could you open the door?'

I'm surprised by how neutral, almost warm, she sounds, like a determined but considerate big sister.

'Christian,' Iris says again.

'Christian is dead,' says a male voice from the other side. It sounds thick and muffled, as though its owner has a cold. And is very close to the door. 'But it wasn't me. He did it himself.'

'I understand,' Iris says, looking at Birck. Her knuckles whiten around the weapon. 'Don't worry. What's your name?'

No reply.

'Can you tell us your name?' she says. 'Are you sure he's dead? He might ...'

The man's laugh comes through the door. It's empty laughter, carrying no meaning.

'I'm sure. He shot himself in the head.'

'Can you open the door?'

The only sound is heavy breathing, for a long time. Then: 'Yes.'

'We want to talk to you and see how Christian is. Nothing else. Okay?'

'I told you, he's dead.'

'We want to talk to you.' Iris repeats.

'Can you stand in front of the peephole? I want to see you.'

'I'm afraid we can't do that,' Iris says. 'You'll see us when you open the door.'

'Are you armed?'

'Yes. But we're not going to use our weapons. We have to carry them. Do you understand?'

'Yes.'

'Are you going to open up?'

'I'm opening the door now.'

Iris looks down at the door handle. A lock clicks. The door opens slowly outwards. I don't know what's happening. I'm behind Birck, who takes a step forward as the door swings open.

'Shit,' Iris hisses.

She moves to one side so fast that her speed surprises me. But she's still too slow.

A shot rings out from inside the flat, and Iris screams as the wall behind her is splattered red.

Iris grabs her arm. The black firearm falls from her grasp onto the shiny floor of the landing. Then she gets pulled into the flat.

I twist around the door and end up on the other side, where Iris was standing a moment earlier. As I pass the doorway, an arm is around Iris's throat, and she's being dragged further into the apartment. The arm belongs to a man who is hidden by Iris, so I can't see his features. He's wearing dark clothes, seems to be bleeding from the head, and his forearm is thick. Beyond the little hall is a living room, and there, on the floor, is a lifeless body. Christian Västerberg? Or is he the one holding Iris?

Now I realise.

I don't even know what Västerberg looks like.

Where I'm standing, pressed against the wall, Iris's blood is smeared, and it's getting on my clothes.

'Pick it up,' Birck hisses, and makes a cocking gesture

Iris's gun is lying on the floor, just in front of my shoe. I swallow and bend down, pick it up, feel the weight in my hand. My heart beats so hard that I get dizzy. It's a P226, 357. Fuck me. I could kill a car with this.

'Are you alright?' he asks. 'Cock the gun, for Christ's sake.'

I hold my breath while I pull back the bolt, putting a round in the chamber. I hear a click as it locks in place. My back has suddenly got very, very hot.

'Goffman's on his way,' I say. 'Should we wait? We need to notify them of the hostage situation.'

'Wait? Not a chance.' Birck peers round the door and into the flat. 'I don't see him. Do you?'

I grip the weapon, and my temples are pounding. A black vignette is encroaching on my field of vision. Tunnel vision. I blink again and again; I need to control my breathing.

The lights are off in the hall. The body is lying there, lifeless, on the living-room floor. A pool of blood has formed by his head. He's not breathing.

'No,' I manage. 'I don't know where he is.'

After the hallway, the flat divides off in a T, with the living room straight on, one room to the left and one to the right. The living-room window reflects no shadows, other than my own, just visible in the doorway. I wonder whether the room has other doors, and how many rounds he's got left in his weapon, and whether Sam would cope, if something did happen to me now.

'You go first,' Birck says.

I've got one foot in the hall. Above me, I can just make out the shadow of a lampshade. Birck's left hand comes into view, feeling for the switch. He finds it, and there's a click.

The light is strong and clear. There are coats on hooks, and a neatly folded Swedish flag on the shelf. The rug on the floor is a bit crooked — perhaps after he forced Iris in with him.

I keep looking straight ahead, avoiding looking down and seeing the gun in my hand.

I follow the wall on the right-hand side, and Birck takes the left. He's rooting through the pockets of the coats, looking for something. He eventually finds the ID-card. Christian Västerberg is staring sternly into the lens. The face is sharp and well-defined, symmetrical, and it belongs to the body lying on the floor in front of us. I find time to wonder what he was thinking about as the picture was taken.

The TV in the corner is on. It's showing *Meet Me in St. Louis*.

'Did he come yet?' asks the little girl. 'I've been waiting such a long time, and I haven't seen a thing.'

'Did who come?' Judy Garland asks.

'Santa Claus,' says the wide-eyed girl.

The lines from the film melt into the buzz of the storm, forming a background tapestry of noise. The living-room window is creaking as though it might give way at any second. I turn to the right, around the corner, weapon first. My cheeks feel flushed and hot. The barrel of the P226 is getting slippery in my grip. I can't put my finger on the trigger — I don't dare.

The door to the kitchen is open. An electric advent wreath lights the windowsill. The fridge door is decorated with a few Christmas cards and photos, and that's it.

'Leo,' Birck says quietly, behind me.

I turn my head. Birck is standing in the same position as me, but facing the other way, towards another open door. I can make out the end of a bed, a bedspread. The light's not on in there.

Birck scans the floor, where the bloodstain is smeared across it. It leads into the bedroom. There's a sound of panting and grunting.

The light flickers — once, twice, three times. I struggle to focus.

'We're here now,' Birck says. 'We're by the bedroom door. We don't want to take you by surprise. We're coming in.'

Behind us, the living-room window gives way with a heavy crash, like a porcelain dinner service hitting the floor.

'Can you hear me?' Birck says, louder.

No reply. Birck looks at me. His expression is cool, collected. The barrel of the P226 is now shaking in my hands. I can't relax my arms. My shoulders ache. It's as though the weapon is releasing a poison, a toxin, that's spreading through my body.

When I blink, I see Waltersson, lying there in Visby harbour, holding his throat after I'd shot him. It wasn't supposed to happen, I think to myself. I wasn't supposed to be there, then, and I shouldn't be here now. I'm not supposed to make it out of here.

In the bedroom, my hand trembles along the wall, searching for the light switch.

'I'm going to turn the light on, okay?'

No response. It's like he can't hear me.

'I'm going to turn the light on,' I repeat. 'But I want to know that you understand what I'm saying first. I don't want you getting any surprises. Okay?'

I turn on the light, and finally I can see him.

It could be him, the masked man from the CCTV cameras at Central Station — the man who might have succeeded in taking the life of a party leader. I'm not sure.

One of the bedroom's walls is covered with paintings, wardrobes, and a bookcase. In a corner are a desk and chair. The single bed, in the middle of the room, is made up and smooth. He's waiting on the far side, holding Iris in front of him as a shield. He has his left arm around her throat, his hand level with her shoulder. His grip is so tight that she's struggling to breathe. His right hand is holding a revolver, its barrel switching back and forth between me and Birck. A trickle of blood from a wound on his forehead has run down to his eyebrow, around his eye, and is following his cheekbone.

'Take it easy now,' says Birck. It's not clear who he's talking to.

Iris's right arm is hanging, limply. I can see the bullet's little entry hole in her mac; it looks almost black. She's breathing in short, heavy breaths. As is the man holding her. She's shorter than him, and his grip is pressing her head towards his shoulder. She is constantly writhing, desperately trying to work herself free. She makes a fist with her left hand and jerks her elbow into his ribs, which makes him lurch forward with a groan.

'Sit still,' he hisses. 'Keep still, you stupid cunt.' And he puts the gun to her temple. 'You too. Stand still.'

'Okay,' Birck says. 'We're going to keep still. Can you tell us what's happened?'

He makes a stiff shake of his head, right then left. The revolver is now steady in his hand, no longer oscillating between Birck and me. It is now pointed at an invisible target somewhere halfway between the two of us.

'Could y—'

'Shut up. Stop talking.'

He tightens his grip on Iris. She lifts her good arm, places her hand around his wrist, and grasps at it, trying to get some air.

'Tell us what happened,' Birck repeats. 'With Christian. Why's he lying out there like that?'

'He was a fucking traitor.'

'Is that why you did it?' I ask.

He suddenly goes stiff, raises his eyebrows, and yet keeps his frown intact. Then he points the gun at me. I hold my breath.

'It wasn't me. He did it himself. He shot himself.'

'Why did he do that?' says Birck.

'Stop talking,' he screams, pointing the revolver at Birck.

'Well, what are we going to do then? How do you want this to end?'

'Get out of here.'

'I'm sorry, but we can't do that,' I say, slowly. 'We would have to take Iris with us in that case.'

He shakes his head violently.

'Yes,' Birck says. 'Let go of Iris, and let her come over here. Then we'll retreat. I promise.'

'Then you'll shoot.'

'No, we won't shoot.'

He looks at us carefully, as though he's trying to work out who is weakest, who would struggle to shoot him — who he ought to shoot first to give himself the best chance of getting out of here.

'We're not going …' is as far as I get.

Iris tilts her head up, backwards, pressing against his shoulder. Her mouth is level with his throat. I can see her teeth. I blink, and then they're clenched onto his earlobe.

He whines, and his determined stare is resolutely fixed on us, as is the revolver. His face goes from wintry white to deep red, and he strains to breathe through the pain.

A stream of blood runs across Iris's mouth, over her chin and down her throat.

He seems to be composing himself, and he looks down, adjusting his grip on her. Then he clenches his left hand and punches the little hole in Iris's mac. He hits her once, lets the hand rest there, and then pushes it against the wound. Iris's body convulses as though she's being hit by a huge electric current, and a hiss escapes through her teeth. He hits her again. Iris groans again, louder.

Third time around, she loses control. Her teeth let go of his ear. She spits. A little clump of blood and skin drops onto the floor.

Then she screams.

'Get back,' he snarls. 'Get back.'

'What are you going to do?' says Birck.

'Get back.'

'We'll get back if you tell us what you're going to do. We don't want anything unexpected to happen here.'

'I'm getting out.'

'Out of the flat?'

'Yes.'

'In this weather?' says Birck, but his voice is shaky. 'Come on, think about this.'

'Get back!' he screams, and the spit sprays from his mouth.

Iris is still hanging in his grip, limper than before. She's stopped screaming, and seems to be getting weaker, her head resting on his shoulder. The blood from his earlobe is smeared through her hair.

We take one step backwards; he takes three steps forwards. He comes past the bed. Soon we're so close that we can see the colour of his eyes. Birck and I back off one step at a time, until we're out in the living room, by Christian Västerberg's lifeless body. Splinters of glass from the blown-in window lie across his chest, and embellish the scarlet halo around his head.

I can almost feel it, how the man in front of us has to force himself to avoid it, doing all he can not to look at the body one last time.

'Backs to the TV,' he snarls. 'Backs against the TV.'

357

I back off, and stand in the shards of splintered glass. The wind making its way inside is so cold that it burns. I've got cramp in my arms. He's moving slowly forward, step by step, shunting Iris ahead of him. The revolver is alternating between me and Birck again.

'How did you get here?' he asks. 'How did you get here,' he repeats, louder, when none of us answer.

The reason for the silence is that we really shouldn't lie, but we'd really prefer not to tell the truth, either. The fact that we came by car, Iris's car, gives him a genuine escape route. It is a cause for hope, and hope can be fatal. It makes people more desperate, more drastic in their actions. That said, it is extremely risky to lie to a man with a gun in his hand, particularly when he is using a hostage as a shield.

'By car,' Birck says.

'What car?'

'A Volvo. Registration number WHO 327.'

'Give me the keys. Chuck them over.'

'We can't do that,' I say.

The barrel of the gun returns to Iris's temple.

'I'll shoot her if you don't.'

I try to make eye contact with Iris.

'Give them to him.'

Her forehead is shiny, and her eyes are bloodshot. She shakes her head.

He adjusts his grip and puts his hand against the hole in her mac again. His thumb feels for the bullet-hole in the fabric. It disappears into the hole.

Iris gasps for breath, hoarse and rasping, her mouth open, her eyes wide as if in surprise and her left hand tugging at his forearm. When she does get hold of it, it won't budge, and all she can do is try to control her breathing, as though she were dealing with an asthma attack.

'Give them to me,' he screams.

She lets go of him, rummages in her pocket, and pulls out the keys. He grabs them, and carries on shunting her in front of him.

He stops, apparently listening out for something. The only sound is the hum of the storm and the quiet sound of the television behind me, with Judy Garland singing *Have yourself a merry little Christmas, and let your heart be light.*

Out in the hall, the front door is open.

'Is there somebody out there?' he asks. He puts the gun to her temple. 'Answer me! Is there?'

'No,' I say.

... next year, all our troubles will be out of sight.

He makes his way into the hall, facing towards us, backing out. He takes one, two, three steps. Iris is dragged along with him, unable to offer any resistance. He's just inside the door.

There's no one there, and then, in the blink of an eye, he appears. He's behind them in the doorway. The long, bony fingers are lightly wrapped around a black firearm, identical to the one in my hand.

'Michael,' Goffman says, pushing the barrel against his neck. 'We meet at last.'

You can see how his sharp, focused stare makes way for a cloudy, vacant expression, and his body slackens as the last of the adrenalin leaves his system. It's over. At first he seems despondent as Goffman carefully takes the weapon from his hand, but I think he's almost relieved to be rid of it.

He lets go of Iris. Her legs go from underneath her, and she falls to the floor in the hall. Birck rushes in and crouches over her. I'm left just standing there amongst the crushed glass, and I drop my weapon. Christian Västerberg's head is lying close to my left shoe. His lips are coated with gunpowder. Blood is streaming from a hole in the back of his head.

Goffman has got him onto his front on the floor of the landing. He's completely still. He's blinking and breathing, but that's it.

Way, way ahead of us, we can just about see the blue lights of the ambulance taking Iris to Södermalm Hospital. From the passenger seat of Goffman's car, my eyes follow it into the distance until the flashing lights disappear.

The man is sitting in the back seat between Birck and Durelius, a sturdy constable from the Southern District. Durelius was first on the scene, despite having come from Rågsved on foot — no small feat in this weather, and well worth a place in the back seat. He's surprisingly calm, considering it's probably the first time he's sat in a car with someone guilty of anything more serious than shoplifting.

We're surrounded by squad cars, two in front and two behind, as if we were escorting a minister. Our passenger is sitting with his chin against his chest, and Birck's pistol in his ribs.

'How are you doing, Michael?' Goffman asks.

'My ear,' he says.

'I'm sure that'll heal nicely. It's only the earlobe.'

'It hurts,' he snarls back.

He's pale, no doubt in need of a drip and a hospital bed — the kind of perks that are hard to come by if you've just tried to kill a politician.

'Did she really bite it off?'

'Yep,' says Birck.

Goffman is wearing a dark-grey suit under his coat, a white shirt, and black tie. His normally neat, well-combed hair is all over the place. The storm tugs relentlessly away at the car, reminding me of a plane making its final approach for landing. It makes me nauseous.

'Do we know anything about his condition?' I say. 'Is he going to survive?'

'He's still in theatre,' Goffman says, and lifts his gaze up to the rear-view mirror. 'If he does end up surviving, how's that going to make you feel, Michael? Like you failed?'

He doesn't seem to have heard the question.

He isn't obliged to say anything more than his name and his ID-number. And if he were to say anything beyond that, it needn't be true. He doesn't have to say a word. We might never know any more than that it was him.

'Keyser,' Goffman changes tack. 'Unusual name. Is it Turk—'

'Dutch. It means emperor.'

That's all he says.

Late that evening, I'm sitting in Birck's office, following the television news. Everyone's waiting for news from the hospital, but none comes. I wonder what that means.

when are you coming home? Sam asks.

soon

i'll be asleep

i'll try not to wake you up

Online, on far-right blogs and forums, Keyser's actions are being endorsed by many. Screenshots from these sites are being published on the major newspapers' websites and on social media, and discussed on the television news.

'What?' says Birck. 'Why are you looking at me like that?'

'That was close,' I say. 'You could've carked it. Outside Västerberg's place, when that roof panel came down.'

'Oh, that, yeah. Yes, I had a bit of luck there.'

'You had Iris.'

Birck says nothing, and carries on staring at the screen. I stay there. Ten o'clock comes, and then a quarter past. Then the news comes in from Karolinska Hospital: the leader has undergone surgery for the injuries he sustained during the attack. He was awake when he arrived at Karolinska, but lost consciousness shortly before he was anaesthetised. He lost a substantial amount of blood, but not as much as might have been expected. His condition remains critical, but the team of doctors operating on him consider the operation to have been a success.

I realise that I've been holding my breath, and that I'm holding the tube of Halcion in my hand. I go out into the corridor to tell Birck, but can't find him.

'Birck? He left,' one of the constables in the lunchroom tells me, distracted by the television.

'Where was he going?'

'He said he was going to Södermalm Hospital,' the constable laughed, 'in this weather. What a plank.'

22/12

The wind is still blowing outside the window on Chapmansgatan, but it's nothing compared to when I got home last night.

Edith's full impact is now plain to see. The streets are lined with smashed roof-tiles. A bin is lying a little way away, a full fifty or sixty metres from the slab it was standing on. It's now that I notice the car parked on the street, halfway between the slab and the bin. The windscreen is smashed. The bin must've crashed into it before being swept along by the wind. Parts of the cladding on the building opposite have been ripped off, revealing the insulation underneath.

I return to the bed, where Sam is still in a deep sleep. A little thread of saliva runs from her mouth to a little wet patch on the sheet. She was asleep when I got home, and I didn't want to wake her.

'I've got to go,' I whisper.

'It's Sunday,' Sam mumbles and rolls over. 'Or is it still Saturday?'

'No, it's Sunday.' I push my lips against her forehead. 'But there's not a policeman in Stockholm who's off-duty today.'

'Did you get him?'

'Yes.' I stroke her hair. 'We did.'

'Are you okay?'

'Not a scratch. For once.'

'Have you spoken to your family?'

'What do you mean?'

'Checked they're okay, after the storm?'

'Oh, right. No. But I will.'

She yawns and stretches her hand up to my face, scratching my stubble with her nails.

'You need a shave.'

'I know.'

I give her a long kiss before I stand up. It seems so obvious, and it might be just that, the familiarity of it all, that makes me ask.

'Will you be here when I get back?'

She props herself up on her elbows.

'Do you want me to be?'

'Yes.'

She smiles faintly. I don't think she noticed my hesitation. I wonder if we can get through this, again.

'You'll have to wait and see,' she says.

23/12

I'm sitting in my office, having dragged an old radio in from the neighbouring room. They're playing a Christmas song, a lone voice singing mournfully *Some day soon, we all we be together, if the fates allow.*

Only a few minutes have passed since Jens Malm of Swedish Resistance declined to make any comment about Michael Keyser's actions, and just a matter of hours since the Sweden Democrats released a statement, confirming that the party leader is doing well under the circumstances, and that he hopes the Swedish judicial system will be allowed to run its course and that no blood will be spilled in his, or anyone else's, name. The message concludes with the Sweden Democrats wishing Sweden a quiet and restful Christmas.

The office Christmas party starts in an hour, but I'm not going. The pre-party has already started, out in the lunchroom. My colleagues are drinking beer and playing 'guess the crook': a projector shows images of contemporary and historical criminals. Some faces are more familiar than others. First one to shout the right name — and you do have to shout to be heard — wins a hundred kronor.

I hear voices near my door. It's Olausson and someone else.

'That someone actually dared,' says Olausson. 'I didn't expect that for a minute. We're very lucky he survived.'

The other one agrees.

'Now, I don't fucking vote for the Sweden Democrats,' Olausson continues, 'but a lot of the time they've got a point, you have to give them that. Did you hear the speech, before he got knifed?'

The other one says that yes, he's heard bits of it since the attack.

I think about Thomas Heber, the lone researcher who may have fallen for Lisa Swedberg. Everyone is missed by someone, and I wonder what Heber's parents are doing right now. I wonder whether the little boy, John Thyrell, has been following the news and knows what's going on; whether he and his family were in their flat on Döbelnsgatan when Edith hit, or on their way somewhere. For a minute, I'm about to call them and check that the boy is still alive, but then I stop myself.

I think about all the questions instead — the ones that remain unanswered, the ones that always will. Most of them are insignificant, but they're unanswered, and that bothers me. Like why Lisa Swedberg slept on the sofa instead of the bed, when her host was away travelling. Maybe Birck was right. Maybe she just preferred the sofa.

There are several black holes, gaps, as there always are in a police investigation. You can never reconstruct the whole story. That's the nature of the past. It's always a fleeting thing, always incomplete.

I wonder how the annual Christmas serial ends, what the story is actually about. I might try and see the last episode tomorrow, with Sam.

There's a knock on the door. It's Charles Levin. 'Mentor' isn't really the right word for him, but it's the best I can think of.

He's lost weight, which makes him seem taller, sort of stretched. His normally smooth, shaved head is now displaying two or three days' stubble, and his round, black-rimmed glasses are sitting halfway down his great hawk's beak of a nose. He has a hat in his hand, and ends up standing in the doorway with his thick winter coat open and an eye on my spare chair.

'Is that alright to sit on?'

'Yes.'

He closes the door behind him.

'Jees, only just,' he says, once he's sat down. 'This chair has aged worse than I have.'

I turn the radio down. Our contact during the autumn has been sporadic and terse. I've tried to call him countless times, and on those few occasions when he did answer, I think it was down to the fact that he hadn't checked who was calling first.

We've bumped into each other a few times since I got back on duty — chance meetings in the corridor, quick 'hello's in the canteen after Levin had left the National Police Authority and had business at our place.

It's always like this: unanswered questions, no contact, strange coincidences, and odd details. Like finding out that Levin was the one who had me placed with Internal Affairs, that he'd done so under duress, that someone above him was turning the screw — someone who knew about his past, a past that nobody else seems to know about. Or Grim saying that Levin was visiting someone at St Göran's; that may be true, and it may be significant — or maybe not.

And now this, as though nothing had happened, and all of this was just a web constructed inside my head — Levin knocking on my door, the day before Christmas.

'Have you come to try my spare chair?'

'No,' Levin says. 'No, I haven't.' A short silence. 'I understand you've had a quiet first month back?'

'Oh, yeah, dead quiet,' I reply. 'Nothing to report.'

He laughs, but it seems forced. He adjusts his position on the chair, carefully. The backrest creaks loudly.

'It's frightening,' he goes on. 'Isn't it?'

'Keyser?'

'Yes. It makes the Sweden Democrats look like an innocent party, in the eyes of the public. As if they've gone, well, mainstream.'

'But they have. I just heard Olausson outside, and even he — a prosecutor, for God's sake — reckons they've got some valid arguments.'

'Is that what he said?'

'Yes.'

'Him too, eh?' Levin says thoughtfully.

We fall silent.

'I hear Goffman arrived in the nick of time,' he says eventually. 'He has a habit of doing that.'

'Do you know each other?'

'Too well. Some day I'll tell you all about it.'

We sit there in silence. It's tense — far too tense.

'Is it right that you visited St Göran's a while ago?' I say quietly.

Levin seems unmoved by the question. I attempt to read his hands, looking for a sign. They lie motionless in his lap, his fingers intertwined.

'Yes, that's right,' he says. 'As you know, I'm retiring after Easter. You're supposed to write your memoirs when you retire. I've got six months left, so this is a bit of a head start, I suppose. I haven't got very far. I do a bit whenever I get the time. My visit to St Göran's concerns an investigation from a while back — a case I never managed to solve, and which I'll be writing about in the book. My head is getting cloudier, and I needed to double-check a few facts, so I went to see one of the people involved. She's a resident of St Göran's.'

I study the skin around Levin's eyes — the tiny, tiny muscles that tense when someone is lying. Levin smiles slightly, as though he knows what I am after. That might be why he's here, I think to myself. Levin suspected that Grim wouldn't keep it to himself. He wanted to find out what I know, and make sure I wasn't planning to do anything about it. Whatever *it* is.

'If that's the case,' I say, 'why was it so important to keep your visit under wraps?'

'The investigation concerns a murder, or possibly manslaughter. It was never cleared up, but it was deemed to be a murder investigation, and of course the statute of limitations has recently been removed for such crimes. If word got out that I was visiting this person, it might give the victim's family false hope, and I want to avoid that. And these things always get out, as you well know, one way or another.'

It could be true. I clear my throat.

'Where are you spending Christmas, Leo?'

'With Sam, and then I'm going to Salem. Why do you ask?'

'I was just wondering.' Levin opens his hands. 'I do care.'

'Do you really?'

'What kind of question is that? Of course I do.'

Levin looks at me as though he wants to touch me. I cross my arms. I feel like a child, and I suspect I might look like one too.

'But then,' Levin goes on, 'it's as though some kind of gulf has opened up between us, since right back in May. As though we can't talk to each other. But I do care about you.'

'But that's down to you,' I say, surprised. 'You're the one avoiding me, even more so since you admitted to being involved in the Gotland affair. Which, by the way, you got off with very lightly. A fucking note? How respectful is that, really? You could have fucking said it to my face.'

'I understand that you're upset Leo, and I—'

'I'm not upset. I'm furious.'

'I'm sorry that it turned out the way it did, but I had no choice. And I can't tell you what you want to know, that stuff you've been asking about when you've called.'

'Who made you do it? What have they got on you?'

Levin smiles — a pale smile, devoid of happiness.

'I cannot answer that question.'

'Why not?'

'It's not possible.'

That little note, written in Levin's handwriting, a style so elegant and neat that the reader could almost miss the foreboding, dark content of the words — I have read it so many times that I know it off by heart:

> I'm glad I can sit at your bedside and hear your breathing. Hear that you're alive, just as I did after the events on Gotland. Events that, no matter how you look at it, can be traced back to me, not you.
>
> I was given a memo. It instructed me to put you on our unit: someone who could be held to account if necessary. They'd done a search, and considered you an eligible candidate. Everything was hypothetical, 'if', 'in the worst case', and 'in the event of one of our operations being compromised'.
>
> It came from above, from the paranoid people, and I had no choice. They were threatening to leak details from my past. They still are. I can't say any more. Not now.
>
> Forgive me, Leo.
>
> Charles

'The memo,' I say. 'Can I see that, at least?'

'Don't play the fool with me, Leo. As with any important memo, it was destroyed a long time ago.'

'Who destroyed it?'

'Me, of course.'

I open my mouth, but nothing happens. Air and silence are all that come out. It's hopeless, and I know it.

Levin rises slowly from the chair and pulls out a thin, brown envelope from his breast pocket, and places it on the table.

'I just wanted to come and wish you Merry Christmas and give you a little present. I do hope you like it. I found it rather insightful — I read it myself first.'

I pick up the envelope and feel its contents.

'What is it?'

'It's the only copy in existence, as far as I know.' He puts his hat on. 'I'm sorry, but I'm afraid I have to go. I'm having dinner with a good friend at Operakällaren.'

'Okay.'

'Have you asked for anything for Christmas?' he asks, adjusting his hat.

'A coffee machine. What about you?'

Should I have got him something? Was he expecting me to? What might that have been, in that case? If there had been some kind of truth serum available, I'm pretty sure I would have grabbed the bull by the horns and tried to pour some into him.

'I don't ask for things anymore.' He says it without a trace of sadness or relief, and puts his hand on the door handle. 'I hope you get your coffee machine. A person is only as good as their coffee.' He hesitates for a second. 'And you and Sam, you mentioned her name. Are you … is everything okay between you two?'

'Yes,' I say.

Levin smiles weakly.

'I can tell. It's like you've come home.'

I think he might be right, but I don't say anything.

'Merry Christmas, Leo.'

'Merry Christmas.'

My mentor opens the door, and proceeds to disappear through it. I wonder when we'll meet again. The noise from the party rises briefly and then falls.

I open the little envelope. It contains a thin, old book, no more than thirty pages long, a novella written by someone called L.P. Carlsson and published in 1901. The cover is beige and worn, with

371

the title printed in black: *The Falling Detective*. Sitting there, in my room, I read it from cover to cover.

Then I put the book away, lock the door to my office, and take the tube of Halcion from my pocket.

Despite the country being in hibernation, my footsteps are restless. It's Christmas Eve, and it's half-past six in the evening. I leave Salem, heading for Rönninge railway station. During the day, I've experienced only snippets of the feeling of being part of something bigger, something that everyone in all the other houses and all the other living rooms share. The rest of the time, I've felt remarkably lonely.

staying at mum's tonight, Sam writes in a text.

see you tomorrow? I send back, waiting for the train.

yes, she replies and then, a few seconds later, *I love you*

Those words take my breath away, as I stand there, alone on the platform.

Everything is so quiet.

I travel from Salem to the place where I might actually belong. I don't know what I'm supposed to be doing here, but I know that I'm doing it for my own sake, more than for anyone else's.

I'm met with a smile as I open the door.

'Merry Christmas, Leo.'

I undo my coat, and sit down on the chair I always sit on, and I don't know what I feel. It might be anger, at the fact that I can't stay away. Perhaps it's relief, at finally being here, not having to pretend to be something that I'm not. I put the mobile phone, his Christmas present, on the table between us.

'Merry Christmas, Grim.'

Acknowledgements

Thanks to my Swedish publishers, Piratförlaget, for your support, your encouragement, and for believing in me and Leo. If it weren't for you, this story would have remained just an idea. An extra thank you to Sofia, my outstanding publisher, and Anna, my fantastic editor. You always take the story's side, right to the end.

Thank you Marina, Anna, Marc, and all the others at Pontas Agency, who helped my stories reach more readers than I ever dared hope or imagine.

Thank you, Leif, for good company, wise words, and, not least, for taking the time to read *The Falling Detective* when I needed it most, and saying what you thought was good and what needed improving. I (almost) always agreed with you.

My thanks also go to Gösta, Astri, and Christine.

Thanks Mum, Dad, and my little brother, and thanks to Karl, Martin, and Tobias. And thank you, Mela, for being so wise and perceptive about the big things, the small things, and everything in between, for your humour, understanding, warmth, and love. Without you, I would be not only a significantly worse writer, I would be a worse person, too. I love you.